The Fall and Rise of Reginald Perrin

'Would it surprise you, Reggie, to learn that overall sales, across the whole spectrum, were down 0.1 per cent in April?'

'Not altogether, C.J.'

The Francis Bacon stared down as if it knew that C.J. had bought it for tax purposes.

'I don't say to myself: 'Oh well, C.J., it's a bad time all round.' I say: "C.J., this is intolerable." But I don't say to you: "Pull your socks up, Reggie," I say to you: "Overall sales, across the whole spectrum, were down 0.1 per cent in April." I leave you to draw your own conclusions – and pull your socks up.'

'Yes, C.J.'

'I didn't get where I am today without learning how to handle people.'

'No, C.J.'

I give them a warning shot across the bows, but I don't let them realize that I'm giving them a warning shot across the bows.'

'Yes, C.J.'

'Not that I want to be entirely surrounded by yes-men.'

'No, C.J.'

So there it is, Reggie. Go full steam ahead on the exotic ices project, no holds barred, this is the big one, but don't forget the whole spectrum.'

'I won't, C.J.'

David Nobbs

The Fall and Rise of Reginald Perrin

Mandarin

A Mandarin Paperback

THE FALL AND RISE OF REGINALD PERRIN

First published as *The Death of Reginald Perrin*
by Victor Gollancz 1975
First paperback edition published 1976
Reprinted 1976, 1978 (twice), 1979, 1985
by Penguin Books
This edition published 1990
Reprinted 1990
by Mandarin Paperbacks
Michelin House, 81 Fulham Road, London SW1 6RB

Mandarin is an imprint of the Octopus Publishing Group

Copyright © David Nobbs 1975

A CIP catalogue record for this book
is available from the British Library
ISBN 0 7493 0379 4

Printed in Great Britain by
BPCC Hazell Books
Aylesbury, Bucks, England
Member of BPCG Ltd.

Thursday

When Reginald Iolanthe Perrin set out for work on the Thursday morning, he had no intention of calling his mother-in-law a hippopotamus. Nothing could have been further from his thoughts.

He stood on the porch of his white neo-Georgian house and kissed his wife Elizabeth. She removed a piece of white cotton that had adhered to his jacket and handed him his black leather briefcase. It was engraved with his initials, 'R.I.P.', in gold.

'Your zip's coming undone,' she hissed, although there was nobody around to overhear her.

'No point in it coming undone these days,' he said, as he made the necessary adjustment.

'Stop worrying about it,' said Elizabeth. 'It's this heatwave, that's all.'

She watched him as he set off down the garden path. He was a big man, almost six foot, with round shoulders and splay feet. He had a very hairy body and at school they had called him 'Coconut Matting'. He walked with a lope, body sloping forward in its anxiety not to miss the eight-sixteen. He was forty-six years old.

Swifts were chasing each other high up in the blue June sky. Rover 2000s were sliding smoothly down the drives of mock Tudor and mock Georgian houses, and there were white gates across the roads on all the entrances to the estate.

Reggie walked down Coleridge Close, turned right into Tennyson Avenue, then left into Wordsworth Drive, and down the snicket into Station Road. He had a thundery headache coming on, and his legs felt unusually heavy.

He stood at his usual place on the platform, in front of the door marked 'Isolation Telephone'. Peter Cartwright joined him. A West Indian porter was tidying the borders of the station garden.

The pollen count was high, and Peter Cartwright had a violent fit of sneezing. He couldn't find a handkerchief, so he went round the corner of the 'gents', by the fire buckets, and blew his nose on the *Guardian*'s special Rhodesian supplement. He crumpled it up and put it in a green waste-paper basket.

'Sorry,' he said, rejoining Reggie. 'Ursula forgot my tissues.'

Reggie lent him his handkerchief. The eight-sixteen drew in five minutes late. Reggie stepped back as it approached for fear that he'd throw himself under the train. They managed to get seats. The rolling stock was nearing the end of its active life and Reggie was sitting over a wheel. The shaking caused his socks to fall down over his ankles, and it was hard to fill in the crossword legibly.

Shortly before Surbiton Peter Cartwright had another sneezing fit. He blew his nose on Reggie's handkerchief. It had 'R.I.P.' initialled on it.

'Finished,' said Peter Cartwright, pencilling in the last clue as they rattled through Raynes Park.

'I'm stuck on the top left-hand corner,' said Reggie. 'I just don't know any Bolivian poets.'

The train arrived at Waterloo eleven minutes late. The loudspeaker announcement said that this was due to 'staff difficulties at Hampton Wick'.

The head office of Sunshine Desserts was a shapeless, five-storey block on the South Bank, between the railway line and the river. The concrete was badly stained by grime and rain. The clock above the main entrance had been stuck at three forty-six since 1967, and every thirty seconds throughout the night a neon sign flashed its red message 'Sunshin Des erts' across the river.

As Reggie walked towards the glass doors, a cold shiver ran through him. In the foyer there were drooping rubber plants and frayed black leather seats. He gave the bored receptionist a smile.

The lift was out of order again, and he walked up three flights of stairs to his office. He slipped and almost fell on the second floor landing. He always had been clumsy. At school they had called him 'Goofy' when they weren't calling him 'Coconut Matting'.

He walked across the threadbare green carpet of the open-plan third floor office, past the secretaries seated at their desks.

His office had windows on two sides, affording a wide vista over blackened warehouses and railway arches. Along the other two walls were green filing cabinets. A board had been pegged to the partition beside the door, and it was covered with notices, holiday postcards, and a calendar supplied gratis by a Chinese Restaurant in Weybridge.

He summoned Joan Greengross, his loyal secretary. She had a slender body and a big bust, and the knobbles of her knees went white when she crossed her legs. She had worked for him for eight years – and he had never kissed her. Each summer she sent him a postcard from Shanklin (IOW). Each summer he sent her a postcard from Pembrokeshire.

'How are we this morning, Joan?' he said.

'Fine.'

'Good. That's a nice dress. Is it new?'

'I've had it three years.'

'Oh.'

He rearranged some papers on his desk nervously.

'Right,' he said. Joan's pencil was poised over her pad. 'Right.'

He looked out over the grimy sun-drenched street. He couldn't bring himself to begin. He hadn't the energy to launch himself into it.

'To G.F. Maynard, Randalls Farm, Nether Somerby,' he began at last, thinking of another farm, of golden harvests, of his youth.

Thank you for your letter of the 7th inst. I am very sorry that you are finding it inconvenient to change over to the Metzinger scale. Let me assure you that many of our suppliers are already finding that the new scale is the most realistic method of grading plums and greengages. With the coming . . . no, with the *advent* of metrication I feel confident that you will have no regrets in the long run . . .

He finished the letter, dictated several other letters of even greater boredom, and still gave no thought to the possibility of calling his mother-in-law a hippopotamus.

Another shiver ran through him. It was an intimation, but he didn't recognize it as such. He thought that perhaps he was sickening for summer 'flu.

'You're seeing C.J. at eleven,' said Joan. 'And your zip's undone.'

Promptly at eleven he entered C.J.'s outer office on the second floor. You didn't keep C.J. waiting.

'He's expecting you,' said Marion.

He went through into C.J.'s inner sanctum. It was a large room. It had a thick yellow carpet and two circular red rugs, yellow and red being the colours that symbolized Sunshine Desserts and all they stood for. In the far distance, in front of the huge plate window, a few pieces of furniture huddled together. There sat C.J. in his swivel chair, behind his rose-wood desk. In front of the desk were three embarrassingly pneumatic chairs, and on the yellow walls there hung three pictures – a Francis Bacon, a John Bratby, and a photograph of C.J. holding the lemon mousse which had won second prize in the convenience foods category at the 1963 Paris Concours Des Desserts. The window commanded a fine view over the Thames, with the Houses of Parliament away to the east.

Young Tony Webster was there already, seated in one of the pneumatic chairs. Reggie sat beside him. His chair sighed. It reclined backwards and had no arms. It was very uncomfortable.

David Harris-Jones entered breathlessly. He was a tall man and he walked as if expecting low beams to leap out at him from all sides.

'Sorry I'm — well, not exactly late but — er — not exactly early,' he said.

'Sit down,' barked C.J.

He sat down. His chair blew a faint raspberry.

'Right,' said C.J. 'Well, gentlemen, it's all stations go on the exotic ices project. The Pigeon woman has put in a pretty favourable report.'

'Great,' said young Tony Webster in his classless voice.

'Super,' said David Harris-Jones, who had been to a minor public school.

Esther Pigeon had conducted a market research survey into the feasibility of selling exotic ices based on oriental fruits. She had soft downy hair on her legs and upper lip.

Reggie shook his head suddenly, trying to forget Miss Pigeon's soft downy hairs and concentrate on the job in hand.

'What?' said C.J., noticing the head-shake.

'Nothing C.J.,' said Reggie.

C.J. gave him a piercing look.

'This one's going to be a real winner,' said C.J. 'I didn't get where I am today without knowing a real winner when I see one.'

'Great,' said young Tony Webster.

'The next thing to do is to make a final decision about our flavours,' said C.J.

'Maurice Harcourt's laying on a tasting at two-thirty this afternoon,' said Reggie. 'I've got about thirty people going.'

C.J. asked Reggie to stay behind after Tony Webster and David Harris-Jones had left.

'Cigar?'

Reggie took a cigar.

9

C.J. leant back ominously in his chair.

'Young Tony's a good lad,' he said.

'Yes, C.J.'

'I'm grooming him.'

'Yes, C.J.'

'This exotic ices project is very exciting.'

'Yes, C.J.'

'Do you mind if I ask you a personal question?' said C.J.

'It depends on the question,' said Reggie.

'This one's very personal indeed.' C.J. directed the aluminium spotlight on his desk towards Reggie's face, as if it could dazzle even when it wasn't switched on. 'Are you losing your drive?' he asked.

'No, C.J.,' said Reggie. 'I'm not losing my drive.'

'I'm glad to hear it,' said C.J. 'We aren't one of those dreadful firms that believe a chap's no good after he's forty-six.'

Before lunch Reggie went to see Doc Morrissey in the little surgery on the ground floor, next to the amenities room.

C.J. had given Sunshine Desserts everything that he thought a first-rate firm ought to have. He'd given it an amenities room, with a darts board and a three-quarter size table tennis table. He'd given it a sports ground in Chigwell, shared with the National Bank of Japan, and it wasn't his fault that the cricket pitch had been ruined by moles. He'd given it an amateur dramatic society, which had performed works by authors as diverse in spirit as Shaw, Ibsen, Rattigan, Coward and Briggs from the Dispatch Department. And he had given it Doc Morrissey.

Doc Morrissey was a small wizened man with folds of empty skin on his face and, whatever illness you had, he had it worse.

'My legs feel very heavy,' said Reggie. 'And every now and then a shiver passes right through me. I think I may be sickening for summer 'flu.'

The walls were decorated with diagrams of the human

10

body. Doc Morrissey stuck a thermometer into Reggie's mouth.

'Elizabeth all right?' said Doc Morrissey.

'She's very well,' said Reggie through the thermometer.

'Don't talk,' said Doc Morrissey. 'Bowel movements up to scratch?'

Reggie nodded.

'How's that boy of yours doing?' said Doc Morrissey.

Reggie gave a thumbs down.

'Difficult profession, acting. He should stick to the amateur stuff like his father,' said Doc Morrissey.

Reggie was a pillar of the Sunshine Dramatic Society. He had once played Othello to Edna Meadowes from Packing's Desdemona.

'Any chest pains?' said Doc Morrissey.

Reggie shook his head.

'Where are you going for your holidays this year?' said Doc Morrissey.

Reggie tried to represent Pembrokeshire in mime.

Doc Morrissey removed the thermometer.

'Pembrokeshire,' said Reggie.

'Your temperature's normal anyway,' said Doc Morrissey.

He examined Reggie's eyes, tongue, chest and reflexes.

'Have you been feeling listless and lazy?' said Doc Morrissey. 'Unable to concentrate? Lost your zest for living? Lots of headaches? Falling asleep during *Play for Today*? Can't finish the crossword like you used to? Nasty taste in the mornings? Keep thinking about naked sportswomen?'

Reggie felt excited. These were the exact symptoms of his malaise. People said Doc Morrissey was no good, all he ever did was give you two aspirins. It wasn't true. The little man was a miracle worker.

'Yes, I have. That's exactly how I've been feeling,' he said.

'It's funny. So have I. I wonder what it is,' said Doc Morrissey.

He gave Reggie two aspirins.

*

11

Maurice Harcourt laid on a very good ice cream tasting. Nobody from head office liked visiting Acton. They hated the factory, with its peeling cream and green frontage, halfway between an Odeon cinema and an East German bus station. It reminded them that the firm didn't only make plans and decisions, but also jellies and creamed rice. It reminded them that it owned a small fleet of bright red lorries with 'Try Sunshine Flans – they're flan-tastic' painted in yellow letters on both sides. It reminded them that C.J. had bought two lorries with moulded backs in the shape of jellies. Acton was dusty and commonplace, but everyone agreed that Maurice Harcourt laid on a very good ice cream tasting.

Reggie had invited a good cross-section of palates. On a long table at one end of the first floor conference room there were eighteen large containers, each one holding ice cream of a different flavour. Everyone had a card with the eighteen flavours printed on it, and there were six columns marked: 'Taste', 'Originality', 'Texture', 'Consumer Appeal', 'Appearance' and 'Remarks'. The sun shone in on them as they went about their work.

'This pineapple one is too sickly, darling,' said Davina Letts-Wilkinson, who was forty-eight, with greying hair dyed silver, lines on her face, and the best legs in the convenience foodstuffs industry.

'Mark it down,' said Reggie.

'I like the mango,' said Tim Parker from Flans.

Tony Webster was filling in his card most assiduously. So was David Harris-Jones.

'This lime's bloody diabolical,' said Ron Napier, representing the taste buds of the Transport Department.

'Write it all down,' said Reggie.

Davina kept following him round the room, and he knew that Joan Greengross was watching them. The ice creams made him feel sick, his brain was beating against his forehead, and his legs were like lead.

'Isn't this terrific?' said David Harris-Jones.

'Yes,' said Reggie.

12

'A sophisticated little lychee,' said Colin Edmundes from Admin., whose reputation for wit depended entirely on his adaptation of existing witticisms. 'But I think you'll be distressed by its cynicism.'

Reggie went up to Joan, wanting to make contact, not wanting her to think that he was interested in Davina Letts-Wilkinson's legs.

'Enjoying it?' he said.

'It makes a change,' she said.

'That's a nice dress. Is it new?' he said.

'You asked me that this morning,' she said.

Tim Parker took Jenny Costain to Paris. Owen Lewis from Crumbles got Sandra Gostelow drunk at the office party and made her wear yellow oilskins before they did it. But Reggie had never even kissed Joan. She had a husband and three children. And Reggie had a marvellous wife. Elizabeth was a treasure. Everybody said what a treasure Elizabeth was.

Reggie smiled at Maurice Harcourt, and licked his cumquat surprise without enthusiasm.

'Excuse me,' he said.

He rushed out and was horribly sick in the 'ladies'. There wasn't time to reach the 'gents'.

They were driven back to head office in the firm's bright red fourteen-seater bus. The clutch was going. Davina sat next to Reggie. Joan sat behind them. Davina held Reggie's hand and said, 'That was a lovely afternoon. Clever old you.' Her hand was sticky and Reggie was sweating.

At five-thirty they repaired to the Feathers. Faded tartan paper decorated the walls and a faded tartan carpet performed a similar function with regard to the floor. Reggie still felt slightly sick.

The Sunshine crowd were in high spirits. David Harris-Jones had three sherries. Davina stood very close to Reggie. They smoked cigarettes and discussed lung cancer and alcoholism. Tony Webster's dolly bird arrived. She had slim legs and drank bacardi and coke. Owen Lewis told two dirty

13

stories. Davina said, 'Sorry, darlings. I must leave you for a minute. Women's problems.'

While she was away Owen Lewis winked at Reggie and said, 'You're on to a good thing there.'

'Reggie,' said Colin Edmundes, 'you have left undone those things that you ought to have done up.'

Reggie did up his zip and left in time to catch the six thirty-eight from Waterloo.

The train was eleven minutes late, due to signal failure at Vauxhall. Reggie dragged his reluctant legs along Station Road, up the snicket, up Wordsworth Drive, turned right into Tennyson Avenue, then left into Coleridge Close. It was quiet on the Poets' Estate. The white gates barred all vulgar and irrelevant traffic. The air smelt of hot roads. Reggie marched his battle-weary body up the garden path, roses to left of him, roses to right of him, shining white house in front of him. House martins were feeding their first brood under the eaves. The front door opened and there was Elizabeth, tall and blonde, with mauve slacks over her wide thighs and a flowered blue blouse over her shallow breasts.

They ate their liver and bacon in the back garden, on the 'patio'. Beyond the garden there were silver birch and pine. The liver was done to a turn.

They didn't speak much. Each knew the other's opinion on everything from fascism to emulsion paint.

He knew how quiet Elizabeth found it since Mark and Linda had gone. He always intended to make conversation, always felt that in a minute or two he would begin to sparkle, but he never did.

Tonight he felt as if there was a plate of glass between them.

The heat hung stickily. It would grow dark before it grew cool.

Reggie stirred his coffee.

'Are we going to see the hippopotamus on Sunday?' he said.

'What do you mean?' said Elizabeth.

'I meant your mother. I thought I'd call her a hippopotamus for a change.'

Elizabeth stared at him, her wide mouth open in astonishment.

'That's not a very nice thing to say,' she said.

'It's not very nice having a mother-in-law who looks like a hippopotamus,' he said.

That night Elizabeth read her book for more than half an hour before switching the light off. Reggie didn't try to make love. It wasn't the night for it.

He lay awake for several hours. Perhaps he knew that it was only the beginning.

Friday

He got up early, put on a suit with a less suspect zip, and went out into the garden. The sky was a hazy blue, thick with the threat of heat. There were lawns on two different levels. An arch covered in red ramblers led down to the lower level.

An albino blackbird was singing in the Worcester Pearmain tree.

'Are you aware that you're different from all the other blackbirds?' said Reggie. 'Do you know that you're a freak?'

Ponsonby, the black and white cat, slunk guiltily into the garden. The albino blackbird flew off with a squawk of alarm.

Reggie's limbs felt heavy again, but not quite as heavy as on the previous evening.

'Breakfast's ready,' sang out Elizabeth. She wasn't one to hold a grudge just because you had called her mother a hippopotamus.

He went into the kitchen and ate his bacon and eggs at the blue formica-topped table. Elizabeth watched him with an anxiety that she couldn't quite conceal, but she made no allusion to his remarks of the previous evening.

'Who were you talking to in the garden?' she asked.

'The blackbird,' he said. 'That albino.'

'It's going to be another scorcher,' she said as she handed him his briefcase. She removed a piece of yellow fluff from the seat of his trousers, and kissed him good-bye.

He turned left along Coleridge Close, past the comfortably prosperous houses, but then he had an impulse to make a detour. He turned left into Tennyson Avenue, right into Masefield Grove, and down the little snicket into the park.

He decided to catch the eight forty-six instead of the eight-sixteen.

He crossed the park slowly. One of the keepers gave him a pleasant, contented smile. He went through the park gate into Western Avenue, known locally as 'the arterial road'. Here the houses were small and semi-detached, and there was an endless roar of traffic.

There was a parade of small shops set back from the main road and called, imaginatively, Western Parade. Reggie went into the corner shop called, imaginatively, The Corner Shop. It sold Mars bars, newspapers, Tizer, cream soda and haircuts.

'*Mirror* please, guv,' said Reggie.

'Three new pence,' said the newsagent.

'Bar of Fry's chocolate cream please, mate,' said Reggie.

'Going to be another scorcher,' said the newsagent.

'Too right, squire,' said Reggie.

Next door to The Corner Shop was the Blue Parrot Café. Reggie had lived in the area for twenty years and had never been through its portals before.

The café was drab and empty, except for one bus crew eating bacon sandwiches. The eponymous bird had been dead for years.

'Tea please,' said Reggie.

'With?'

'With.'

He took a gulp of his sweet tea, although normally he didn't take sugar.

He remembered going to a café just like this, with Steve Watson, when he was a boy. It was on a railway bridge, and when they heard the steamers coming they would rush out to get the numbers.

He opened the *Daily Mirror*. 'WVS girl ran Hendon witches' coven' he read.

They used to stand on the bridge directly over the trains, getting all their clothes covered in smoke. Steve Watson still owed him one and three. He smiled. The bus crew were watching him. He stopped smiling and buried himself in his paper.

'Peer's daughter to wed abattoir worker'; 'Council house armadillo ban protest march row'.

Steve Watson had gone to the council school and without Reggie's realizing it his parents had knocked the relationship on the head.

He went up to the counter.

'Cup of char and a wad,' he said.

'Come again,' said the proprietor.

'Another cup of tea and a slice of that cake,' said Reggie.

Once Steve's elder brother had come along and tossed himself off, for sixpence, just before the passing of a double-headed munitions train on the down slow track. Later Reggie's parents had always sent him down to the country for his holidays, to Chilhampton Ambo, he and his brother Nigel, to his uncle's farm, to help with the harvest, and get bitten by bugs, and hide in haystacks, and get a fetish about Angela Borrowdale's riding breeches.

Reggie smiled. Again he caught the bus crew looking at him. Didn't they have a bus of their own to go to?

He finished his tea, wrote his piece of cake off to experience, and set off for the station.

The eight forty-six was five minutes late. There was a girl aged about twenty in the compartment. She wore a mini-skirt and had slightly fat thighs. No-one looked at her thighs yet all the men saw them out of the corner of their eyes. They shared the guilty secret of the girl's thighs, and Reggie knew that at Waterloo Station they would let her leave the compartment first, they would look furtively at the depression left in the upholstery by her recently-departed bottom, and then they would follow her down the platform.

He folded his paper into quarters to give his pencil some support, puckered his brow in a passable imitation of thought, and filled in the whole crossword in three and a half minutes.

He didn't actually solve the clues in that time, of course. In the spaces of the crossword he wrote: 'My name is Reginald Iolanthe Perrin. My mother couldn't appear in our local Gilbert and Sullivan Society production of *Iolanthe*, because I was on the way, so they named me after it instead. I'm glad it wasn't *The Pirates of Penzance.*'

He put the paper away in his briefcase, and said to the compartment, 'Very easy today.'

They arrived at Waterloo Station eleven minutes late. The loudspeaker announcement blamed 'reaction to rolling stock shortages at Nine Elms'. The slightly fat girl left the compartment first. The upholstery had made little red lines on the back of her thighs.

The computer decided that the three most popular ice cream flavours were book-ends, West Germany and pumice stone. This was found to be due to an electrical fault, the cards were rapidly checked by hand, and this time the three most popular flavours were found to be mango delight, cumquat surprise, and strawberry and lychee ripple.

Reggie held a meeting of the exotic ices team in his office at ten-thirty. Tony Webster wore a double-breasted grey suit with a discreetly floral shirt and matching tie. His clothes were modern without being too modern. Esther Pigeon wore an orange sleeveless blouse and a green maxi-skirt with long side vents. Morris Coates from the advertising agency wore flared green corduroy trousers, a purple shirt, a huge white tie, a brown suede jacket and black boots.

'What is this?' said Reggie. 'A fashion show?'

David Harris-Jones telephoned at ten thirty-five to say that he was ill in bed with stomach trouble, the result of eating forty-three ice creams.

Joan provided coffee. Reggie explained that there would be trial sales campaigns of the three flavours in two areas – Hertfordshire and East Lancashire. David Harris-Jones would be in control of Hertfordshire and Tony Webster of East Lancashire, with Reggie controlling the whole operation.

'Great,' said Tony Webster.

Esther Pigeon gave them the results of her survey. 73% of housewives in East Lancashire and 81% in Hertfordshire had expressed interest in the concept of exotic ice creams. Only 8% in Hertfordshire and 14% in East Lancashire had expressed positive hostility, while 5% had expressed latent hostility. In Hertfordshire 96.3% of the 20% who formed 50% of consumer spending potential were in favour. Among the unemployed only 0.1% were in favour. 0.6% had told her where they could put the exotic ice creams.

'What does all this mean in laymen's terms?' said Reggie.

'This would be regarded as a reasonably satisfactory basis for introducing the product in the canvassed areas,' said Esther Pigeon.

The sun was streaming in on to the dark green filing cabinets, and Reggie watched the bits of dust that were floating around in its rays. He could feel his shivering again, like a subdued shuddering from his engine room. Suddenly he realized that Esther Pigeon was talking.

'Sorry,' he said. 'I missed that. I was looking at the rays of dust in the sun. They're rather pretty.'

There was a pause. Morris Coates flicked cigarette ash on to the floor.

'I was saying that there were interesting variations from town to town,' said Esther Pigeon, who had huggable knees but an indeterminate face, and was usually ignored by 92.7% of the men on the Bakerloo Line. 'There was a lot of interest in Hitchin and Hertford, but Welwyn Garden City was positively lukewarm.'

'Hitchin has a very nice church,' said Reggie. It slipped out before he could stop it. Everyone stared at him. He was sweating profusely.

'It's very hot in here,' he said. 'Take your jackets off if you want to.'

The men took their jackets off and rolled up their sleeves. Reggie had the hairiest forearms, followed by Esther Pigeon.

He was very conscious of his grubby white shirt. The sartorial revolution had passed him by. He resented these well-dressed young men. He resented Esther Pigeon, whose vital statistics were 36–32–38. He resented Tony Webster who sat quietly, confident yet not too confident, content to wait for his inevitable promotion. He resented the film of skin which was spreading across their forgotten coffees.

They turned to the question of advertising.

'I was just thinking, off the top of the head, beautiful girl,' said Morris Coates. 'Yoga position, which let's face it can be a pretty sexy position, something like, I'm not a writer, I find it much easier to meditate – with a cumquat surprise ice cream – one of the new range of exotic ice creams from Sunshine.'

'Ludicrous,' said Reggie.

Morris Coates flushed.

'I'm just exploring angles,' he said. 'We'll have a whole team on this. I'm just sounding things out.'

It wasn't any use being angry with Morris Coates. It wasn't his fault. Somebody had to man the third-rate advertising agencies. If it wasn't him, it would be somebody else.

'What about sex?' said Morris Coates.

'What about something like, off the top of the head, I like to stroke my nipple with a strawberry and lychee ripple,' said Reggie.

Morris Coates turned red. Esther Pigeon examined her finger nails. Tony Webster smiled faintly.

'All right, fair enough, sex is a bum steer,' said Morris Coates. 'Perhaps we just go for something plain and factual, with a good up-beat picture. But then you're up against the fact that an ice cream carton *per se* doesn't look up-beat. Just thinking aloud. Sorry.'

'Well I'll be interested to see what you come up with,' said Reggie.

'Incidentally,' said Morris Coates, 'is the concept of a ripple, in the ice cream sense of the word, fully understood by the public?'

'In the Forest of Dean, in 1967, 97.3% of housewives understood the concept of a ripple in the ice cream sense of the word,' said Esther Pigeon.

'Does that answer your question?' said Reggie.

'Yes. Fine,' said Morris Coates.

Reggie stood up. The sweat was pouring off him. His pants had stuck to his trousers. He must get rid of them before he said something terrible.

To his relief they all stood up.

'Well anyway we'll expect something from you soon, Morris,' he said. They shook hands. He avoided Morris's eyes. 'Fine. We'll be in touch,' he said.

He shook hands with Esther Pigeon.

'Well, thank you again, Miss Pigeon,' he said, avoiding her eye. 'That was a very comprehensive and helpful report.'

'This is a potential break-through in the field of quality desserts,' said Esther Pigeon.

When Morris Coates and Esther Pigeon had gone, Tony Webster said, 'I must say how much I admired the way you handled Morris and his third-rate ideas.'

Reggie looked into Tony's eyes, searching for hints of sarcasm or sincerity. Tony's eyes looked back, blue, bright, cold, with no hint of anything whatsoever.

Reggie couldn't bear the thought of going to the Feathers for lunch. He must get away. He must be able to breathe.

It was very hot and sticky. He walked across Waterloo Bridge. It was low tide. A barge was chugging slowly up-stream. In the Strand he saw a collision between two cars driven by driving instructors. Both men had sunburnt left arms.

Reggie realized that he was hungry. He went into an Italian restaurant and sat down at a table near the door. On the wall opposite him there was a huge photograph of Florence.

The waiter slid up to his table as if on castors and smiled with all the vivacity of sunny Italy. He was wearing a blue-striped jersey. Everything irritated Reggie, the long menu with its English translations, the chianti flasks hanging from the ceiling, the smiling waiter, sautéed in smug servility.

'Ravioli,' he said.

'Yes sir. And to follow? We have excellent sole today.'

'Ravioli.'

'No main course, sir?'

'Yes. Ravioli. I want ravioli followed by ravioli. I like ravioli.'

The waiter slid off towards the kitchens. The restaurant was filling up rapidly. Soon Reggie's ravioli arrived. It was excellent.

A couple in their mid-thirties joined him at his table. He finished his ravioli. The waiter took it away and brought his ravioli. The couple looked at it with well-bred surprise.

The second plate of ravioli didn't taste as good as the first, but Reggie ploughed on gamely. He felt that their table was much too small, and all the tables were too close together. He came out in a prickly sweat. The couple must be staring straight into his revolting, champing jaws.

They were clearly in love, and they talked animatedly about their many interesting friends. Reggie wanted to tell them that he too had an attractive wife, and two fully grown children, one of whom had herself given birth, in her turn, to two more children. He wanted to tell them that he had friends too, even though he rarely saw them these days. He wanted to tell them that his own life had not been without its moments of tenderness, that he was not always a solitary muncher at the world's crowded tables.

Their heads dipped towards the River Arno as they ate their minestrone. Reggie finished his second plate of ravioli. The waiter slid complacently up to the table with the sweet trolley.

'Ravioli, please,' said Reggie.

The waiter goggled at him.

'More ravioli, sir?'

'It's very good. Quite superb.'

'Ravioli, sir, is not a sweet. Try zabaglione, sir. Is a sweet.'

'Look, I want ravioli. Is that clear?'

'Yes, sir.'

Reggie glared defiantly at the happy couple. He caressed one of their feet under the table with his shoe. The man put his arm round the woman's waist and squeezed it. Reggie drew his shoe tenderly up a leg. The woman held the man's hand and squeezed it.

Their main course arrived. Reggie watched them eating, their jaws moving rhythmically, and he felt that he never wanted to eat anything again.

His third plate of ravioli arrived. He ate it slowly, grimly, forcing it down.

Every now and then he touched the happy couple's legs with his feet. This made them increasingly tender towards each other, and their increasing tenderness made Reggie increasingly miserable.

He shovelled two more envelopes of ravioli into his mouth and chewed desperately. Then he kicked out viciously with his foot. The happy man gave an exclamation of pain, and a mouthful of half-chewed stuffed marrow fell onto the table.

During the afternoon the merciless sun crept round the windows of Reggie's office. It shone on Joan Greengross's thin arms, which were sunburnt except for the vaccination mark. It mocked the dark green filing cabinets, the sales graphs, the eight postcards from Shanklin (IOW), the picture of the Hong Kong waterfront which illustrated May and June on the Chinese calendar.

Everything was normal, yet nothing was normal. There he was, dictating away, apparently in full command of himself, and yet everything was different. There was no longer anything to prevent his doing the most outrageous things. There was nothing to stop him holding a ceilidh in the Dispatch Department. Yet he didn't. Very much the reverse.

He felt an impulse to go down to C.J.'s office, walk up to C.J.'s desk, and expose himself. One pull on his zip, and, hey presto, a life's work undone. That was power.

'Are you all right?' said Joan.

'Of course I am. Why?'

'We're in the middle of a letter, and you haven't spoken for ten minutes.'

24

He felt he owed her an explanation.

'Sorry. I'm rather full of ravioli,' he said.

He finished the letter. Joan was looking a little alarmed.

'One more letter,' he said. 'To the Traffic Manager, British Rail, Southern Region. Dear Sir, Every morning my train, which is due at Waterloo at eight fifty-eight, is exactly eleven minutes late. This is infuriating. This morning, for reasons which I need not go into here, I caught a later train, which was due in at nine twenty-eight. This train was also exactly eleven minutes late. Why don't you re-time your trains to arrive eleven minutes later? They would then be on time every morning. Yours faithfully, Reginald I. Perrin.'

Reggie had four whiskies at the Feathers. Davina stood very close to him. Owen Lewis from Crumbles told three dirty stories. Reggie went to the 'gents' and before he had started Tony Webster came in and stood at the next urinal. There was a slot machine on which was written: 'The chocolate in this machine tastes of rubber.' Reggie couldn't go. He never could when Tony Webster was standing beside him. He pretended that he'd been, shook himself as if to get the last drips off, did up his zip, and left the 'gents'.

When Tony Webster came out of the 'gents' Reggie tried not to look embarrassed. He bought a bacardi and coke for Tony's dolly bird. She was wearing a mini-skirt that was short but not too short, and a thin lace blouse that you could almost see through. She had a flat chest and artificial blonde hair. Reggie didn't imagine that Tony Webster had any problems in bed.

He walked home the long way, across the park. There were cricketers practising in the nets, and he watched some children clambering over a brightly coloured tubular dragon erected for them by the Parks Department.

He plunged into the quiet jungle of the Poets' Estate. He sauntered along Masefield Grove. How was it that his legs kept going forward like this, even though he wasn't telling them to? He looked down at his legs, and they seemed to be separate beings, strolling along down there. It was lucky they weren't keen on mountaineering, dragging him up Annapurna on their holidays.

The pollen count was high, and he could hear Peter Cartwright sneezing inside Number 11, Tennyson Avenue.

He walked slowly up Coleridge Close. His neighbours at Number 18, the Milfords, were watering those parts of their front garden which were already in shadow. Later they would go for a snifter at the golf club.

His neighbours at Number 22, the Wisemans, had been told that the golf club had no vacancies.

'You're late,' said Elizabeth.

'I missed the train,' he lied.

'I don't mind, but it's all dried up,' she said.

He hadn't the energy to explain that man had only existed for a minimal proportion of this earth's history, Britain was only a small island, he was just one insignificant speck which would be gone for ever in another thirty years, and it really didn't matter if two small lamb chops were all dried up.

He ate his dried-up lamb chops in the back garden, on the 'patio', underneath the laburnums. A magpie fluttered hesitantly over the garden, and small birds whose names he didn't know were flitting from bush to bush.

'I thought we might go for a run tomorrow,' he said.

'That would be nice,' said Elizabeth.

'I thought we might take Tom and Linda and the kids, seeing that they haven't got their car.'

'That would be nice,' she said.

Their daughter Linda had married an estate agent, who had just driven his car into the wall of one of his firm's properties, a house valued, until the accident, at £26,995. They had two small children.

'I thought we might run over to Hartcliffe House and see what that new game reserve's like,' he said.

'That would be nice,' she said.

He rang Linda and Tom. The plan was accepted with enthusiasm.

Over his coffee he studied his maps, working out a route that would avoid the traffic.

'You remind me of your father, sitting there like that with your maps,' said Elizabeth.

Reggie's father was always poring over maps and saying: 'Right, then, what's the plan of action?' and then telling you what the plan of action was.

'You're getting more like him every day,' said Elizabeth.

She meant it kindly, so Reggie didn't show that he was hurt.

'Right, then, what's the plan of action for Sunday?' he said. 'We drive down to see your mother in the morning, right?'

Elizabeth smiled with relief, because he hadn't called her mother a hippopotamus.

Saturday

A long line of steaming cars growled sinuously into the Hartcliffe Game Reserve. They were queuing to get in, and soon they would be queuing to get out. It seemed as if the whole world was on safari in Surrey.

Behind them, hidden by a discreet ridge, was the stately home itself. On their left were the toilets and a souvenir stall. On their right was the Tasteebite Cafeteria.

They paid their £1.50, and got their souvenir programme. Ahead of them the newly-built road wound over the grassy slopes in a gentle switchback. Above them the sun glinted on Vauxhalls and Fords. Below them the sun glinted on Fords and Vauxhalls. Here and there, among the cars, a few confused animals could be seen.

'Look, Adam, giraffe,' said Reggie's daughter Linda.

'Gifarfe,' said Adam, her three-year-old son.

'Look, Jocasta, zebra,' said Linda's husband Tom.

'Szluba,' said Jocasta, their two-year-old daughter.

Reggie and Elizabeth sat in the front, and Tom and Linda sat with their children in the back. A merciless pseudo-African sun beat down on the pleasant English parkland.

Reggie pulled up on the hard shoulder, the better to observe a yak.

'Look. Yak,' said Elizabeth.

They stared at the yak. The yak stared at them. Nobody spoke. There isn't much to say about a yak.

Reggie gazed at the scene malevolently. The lower branches of fine old oak trees had been denuded by giraffes. The trees looked like huge one-legged women wearing green skirts. On the right, on the tired over-worked grass of Picnic Area 'A', a few young zebra were lost among the picnickers. On the left, beyond the yak, some llamas were neatly parked in rows, sated with safety and food. Beyond the parked llamas the great herds of Fords and Vauxhalls roamed, their hungry cameras ready to pounce.

Reggie drove slowly on, past the yak, past the llamas.

'What's that?' said Adam, pointing excitedly.

'A waste-paper basket,' said his father Tom.

Reggie had been in a good mood all morning, but it was hot in the car, it smelt of children and garlic, and his good mood had gone.

'What did you have for supper last night?' he asked.

'Squid, provençale style,' said Linda. 'Why?'

'I just wondered.'

Tom was highly regarded in the Thames Valley. He put witty house adverts in the local papers, brewed nettle and parsnip wine, smoked a briar pipe, made the children eat garlic bread, had a beard which stank of tobacco, home-made wine and garlic, and had built a stone folly in his back garden.

They crawled slowly past the new Ministry of Transport sign for 'Caution: Elephants crossing'. A herd of okapi came into view, and they stopped to watch those charming central-African ruminants. Hartcliffe has the largest herd of okapi in the Northern Hemisphere.

'Look. Okapi,' said Elizabeth.

'They come from central Africa,' said Tom.

'What's that?' said Adam, pointing to a small bird.

'A starling,' said Reggie grimly. You brought them all this way to see the largest herd of okapi in the Northern Hemisphere, and all they were interested in were bloody starlings. That was what came of being progressive parents, and having bright red open-plan Finnish playpens, and not insisting on fixed bedtimes.

Reggie moved on again. Ahead was lion country.

'You are approaching lion country,' said a notice. 'Close all windows. If in trouble, blow your horn and wait for the white hunter.'

A high wire fence separated the lions from the more reliable beasts. They drove into the lion enclosure under a raised gate. Above them in his watch tower the white hunter scanned the horizon with watchful eyes.

'Lions soon,' said Linda, who was running to fat and often walked around her home stark naked, so that the children wouldn't grow up with inhibitions.

'Lines,' said Adam. 'Lines. Lines. Lines.'

'That's right. Lions,' said Tom.

Jocasta was picking listlessly at the 'We've been to Hart-cliffe' sticker on the back window.

'Are the windows all shut?' said Elizabeth.

'Windows all shut,' said Tom.

The cars ahead had reached the lions, and traffic came to a standstill. It was sweltering. The damp patches under Linda's armpits were spreading steadily.

'Why are lines?' said Adam.

'Why are lions what, dear?' said Linda.

'Why are lines lines?'

'Well they just are, dear.'

'Why?'

'Because they come from other lions.'

'Why aren't lines ants?'

'Because they don't come from ants' eggs.'

'Why?'

'Why lines lines?' said Jocasta.

'Why am I me?' said Adam.

'Why I me?' said Jocasta.

'Shut up,' said Reggie.

'Reggie!' said Elizabeth.

'Father, please. I must ask you not to speak to them like that,' said Linda.

The children shut up.

The line of cars moved forward another ten yards, then stopped.

'Are you sure the children can't get at those windows?' said Elizabeth.

'Don't nag, mother,' said Linda.

It was growing hotter all the time. Rivulets of sweat were running down inside Reggie's vest and pants, and the non-stick wheel-glove Adam had given him for Christmas was getting horribly sticky. The car smelt of sweat, garlic, children and hot engine. Jocasta began to cry.

They passed a fat lazy jaguar. The jaguar animal stared at a Jaguar car without recognition of brotherhood.

'I done biggies,' said Adam proudly. 'I done biggies.'

'I've done biggies,' corrected Elizabeth.

'Let them talk as they want to, mother,' said Linda.

'They should be helped to speak correctly. They may want jobs with the BBC one day,' said Elizabeth.

'Please, mother, it is up to us,' said Linda.

'Yes. We don't count these days,' said Reggie.

'It's just that we have our own ways of bringing up the children,' said Tom. 'We try as far as possible to treat them not as children, but as tiny adults.'

'Oh shut up, you bearded prig,' said Reggie.

'Reggie!' said Elizabeth.

'No,' said Linda grimly. 'If father feels like that, it's best that he should get it out of his system.'

'I done poopy-plops in my panties,' said Adam.

'Yes,' said Tom. 'And I wonder if you really think that was a good idea, Adam. It's going to get a bit uncomfortable for you later on, you know.'

'For God's sake!' said Reggie. 'This is supposed to be an outing.'

'I think on reflection the game reserve wasn't a very good idea,' said Tom.

'Oh, thank you. That's very helpful,' said Reggie.

The cars in front moved on a few yards.

'Move on, darling,' said Elizabeth.

'I'll move on when people start enjoying themselves,' said Reggie. 'All right. I shouldn't have brought you here. I'm a failure. Everything I plan's a failure. But we're here now – and I'm not moving on until you bloody well start enjoying yourselves.'

The car behind started hooting. Reggie wound down the window.

'Shut up!' he shouted.

'Stop making a spectacle of us,' said Elizabeth.

'Yes, you hate that, don't you?' Reggie turned round and gave two fingers to the driver in the car behind.

'Father, not in front of the children,' said Linda.

'They aren't children. They're tiny adults,' said Reggie.

'Well not in front of the tiny adults then,' said Linda.

'Please, darling, move on,' said Elizabeth.

'Not till you enjoy yourselves.'

'We are,' said Linda. 'We're enjoying ourselves very much.'

'It's interesting,' said Tom. 'It's sociologically fascinating.'

'It's a marvellous outing,' said Elizabeth.

'Oh all right,' said Reggie angrily.

He took the clutch off too quickly and the car stalled.

'Oh blast the bloody thing. I hate cars. I hate bloody machines,' said Reggie.

He started up again, drove off very fast and came to a halt violently a few inches from the car in front. Jocasta began to cry again. Nobody spoke.

'Look. There are the lions,' said Elizabeth at last.

'Look. Lions,' said Linda.

Two mangy lions were lying listlessly on the grass. They looked sheepish, as though they knew they were out of place. More a shame of lions than a pride.

'Look at the nice lions,' said Elizabeth.

'Please don't anthropomorphize,' said Tom. 'Lions aren't nice. We want the children to grow up to see reality as it is.'

'Ah, but is it?' said Reggie, turning to look Tom in the face.

'Is what?'

'Is reality as it is?'

'Well of course it is,' said Tom.

'Don't be absurd, father,' said Linda.

The car shuddered several times and stalled. Steam was pouring from the bonnet.

'It's over-heated,' said Tom helpfully.

'Thank you, Stirling Moss,' said Reggie.

A cloud passed all too rapidly over the sun. Beyond the trees, to the west, were the villages of Nether Hartcliffe, Upper Hartcliffe, and Hartcliffe St Waldron.

'Those lions are pathetic,' said Reggie. 'I've seen livelier lions in Trafalgar Square.'

'Trafalgar Square,' said Adam.

'Faggar square,' said Jocasta.

'I'm not basically a lion person,' said Tom. 'And neither is Lindypoos.'

'If I was a lion I don't think I'd entertain this mob,' said Reggie. 'I mean it's pathetic. The lengths we have to go to to stop people dying of boredom.'

'It stops the lions dying too,' said Linda.

The car in front moved on.

'Have we seen enough?' said Reggie.

It seemed that they had seen enough.

He pressed the starter. Nothing happened. He tried again and again.

'Damn. Damn. Damn,' he said.

'Don't go on,' said Elizabeth. 'You'll only flat the battery.'

The car behind started hooting again.

'Ignore him,' said Elizabeth.

'Cars that won't start, lions that won't move, bloody hell,' said Reggie.

Inside the car it grew hotter – and hotter – and hotter.

'I don't see why we shouldn't open a window a little,' said Linda.

They opened a window a little. Jocasta began to cry in earnest.

'Wet botty,' said Adam, and he too began to cry.

'You see, Adam,' said Linda. 'Perhaps daddy was right. Perhaps it wasn't such a good idea after all.'

Reggie tried the engine again. It wouldn't start.

'It's no use,' said Elizabeth. 'You have to sound the horn and wait for the white hunter.'

'Rubbish,' said Reggie. 'I'm getting out to have a look.'

'Is that altogether wise?' said Tom, in estate agents' language for 'you bloody fool'.

'The damned animals are probably doped,' said Reggie. 'And if you don't like it you can put it in your briar pipe, stick a cork in your mouth, stuff a bulb of garlic up your arse and drown yourself in your own nettle wine,' and he opened the door and stepped out into a world blessedly innocent of sweat and poopy-plops.

'Come back, you fool!' said Tom.

Reggie walked towards the lions. A few yards from the car there was a hollow tree trunk. He stood on it and glared defiantly at the two lions. They watched him with bored, slightly puzzled eyes.

He heard a car horn hooting, and Elizabeth called out 'Come back!'

One of the lions stirred slightly.

He was Goofy Perrin, butt of Ruttingstagg College. He was younger brother Perrin, always a bit of a disappointment compared to Nigel. He was family man, father, man of a thousand compromises. He was company man. He was a man who had given his best years to puddings.

He walked slowly up the hill, over the spongy grass, towards the lions. One of the Hartcliffe estate cars was rushing towards him, but he didn't hear it.

One of the lions stood up. The other lion growled. Suddenly everything was confusion. The lions were moving towards him, he turned and fled, there was a frantic chorus of car horns, Elizabeth was running towards him. He looked over his shoulder. One of the lions crumpled up and collapsed lifeless on the ground.

Reggie tripped over the hollow tree trunk. Screams. Horns. Elizabeth's white face and imploring hands reaching down towards him. Behind him the other lion, gathering speed. Reggie was no longer family man. No longer company man.

No longer educated Western man. He was lunch, red meat ripe for the ripping.

He was half on his feet again, scrambling away from the lion. The lion was only a few feet away. Elizabeth was pulling him away, he didn't want to die. The lion seemed to hang for a moment, motionless, waiting to pounce. And then it just crumpled up, and lay on the ground, twitching gently. And Reggie was standing up, alive. And Elizabeth was beside him. And the estate car had pulled up and a man was shouting, 'You fool! You bloody fool! What are you trying to do – kill yourself?' And it couldn't have happened, but it had, and there were the dead lions to prove it. Later he found out that they weren't dead, merely stunned with poisoned darts, fired by the white hunters, vigilant in the Surrey heat.

Reggie's legs and whole body were shaking. It was humiliating to find out how afraid you were of dying.

'Reggie?' said Elizabeth, after they had been silent for several minutes. 'Why did you do it?'

He couldn't explain it, even to himself.

'I didn't think they'd charge at me,' he said lamely.

'Those men were furious,' said Elizabeth. 'I thought they were never going to let us get away.'

They were sitting in the garden. It was ten o'clock, almost dark, the pink in the western sky slowly fading, the orange glow of London growing stronger in the east. They'd got the sprinklers going.

The Wisemans' downstairs lavatory flushed.

'You weren't – you weren't trying to kill yourself, were you?'

'No, of course not.'

'Well, why then? What were you trying to prove?'

What, indeed? That he was not just a product of Freudian slips and traumatic experiences and bad education and capitalist pointlessness? That he was more than just the product of every second of every minute of every day of his forty-six years? That he was capable of behaving in a way that was not

35

utterly predictable? That his past was not his future's gaoler? That he would not die at a certain minute of a certain day that had already been determined? That he was free?

'Must we talk about it? It's past history,' he said.

'We never talk about anything.'

The winking green light of an aeroplane was sliding in front of the stars.

'What do you mean?' he said.

'Oh, words occasionally pass our lips. But we never talk. We never discuss our problems.'

'We've been into all that. I'm past it. You should have married Henry Possett.'

'Not that.'

He could see Ponsonby's grey-green eyes shining from underneath the roses.

'We're growing apart,' said Elizabeth.

'You may be growing apart. I'm not,' said Reggie.

'Why don't we bring our holidays forward, seeing the weather's so good?' said Elizabeth.

'I like autumn holidays.'

'I know, but . . .'

Elizabeth's 'but' hung on the warm night air. A gentle breeze stirred the leaves of the apple trees. Elizabeth's 'but' drifted away towards the stars, a moment of hesitation moving further and further away. In millions of years' time strange creatures on distant planets would record Elizabeth's 'but' on their instruments and would think: 'There must have been a strange, evasive people in some weird land, millions of years ago.'

He realized that Elizabeth was speaking.

'Sorry,' he said. 'I was thinking.'

'What about?'

'Nothing. What were you saying?'

'The last two days. You've been a bit odd, Reggie.'

'You have to be odd every now and then.'

'Other people don't. The Milfords don't.'

'That's because they're odd all the time.'

He wished that he could enfold her in his loving, manly, hairy arms and make love to her, under the stars and aeroplanes on their fresh-mown, newly-sprinkled lawn. Unfortunately that wasn't possible.

Suddenly Elizabeth began to cry. He stood behind her canvas chair and put his arm round her. He hadn't seen her cry for a long time, and he pressed his body against hers through the canvas.

'I'm sorry,' he said. 'I'm sorry, darling.'

He handed her his handkerchief, initialled: 'R.I.P.'. She blew her nose on it.

'Do you think you ought to see a doctor, Reggie?' she said.

'What on earth for? There's nothing wrong with me.'

'Isn't there?'

He had decided not to go with her to her mother's. He had other plans. It was essential to allay her fears, or she wouldn't leave him on his own.

'Actually I saw Doc Morrissey this week,' he said. 'I've been feeling tired and irritable. He said it was nothing. Just over-work. I'll be taking things a little easier from now on.'

'Oh, darling, I'm glad!'

He kissed her hair. It smelt of twenty-five years ago.

'I've been under a lot of pressure,' he said.

'I know you have.'

He took the teapot and emptied it over a flower bed.

'I'm tired. I think I'll hit the hay,' he said.

'Better move the chairs in,' said Elizabeth.

'It's not going to rain.'

'You never know.'

He moved the chairs in. Elizabeth switched off the sprinklers.

Reggie stretched out his body till his toes were touching the foot of the bed.

'Reggie?'

'Yes.'

'Everything is going to be all right, isn't it?'

'Of course it is.'

Elizabeth looked at him over the top of her book.

'Darling?'

'Yes.'

'Look at me.'

He looked.

'You do still love me, don't you?' she asked.

'Yes, of course I do.'

'I nag, don't I?'

'No.'

'I do.'

'We all nag sometimes.'

'I vowed I'd never nag. I couldn't stand the way mother nagged. I'm not getting to be like mother, am I?'

'No.'

'We're getting old, Reggie.'

'Yes.'

He kissed her on the lips. Her tongue entered his mouth. He remembered, as he always remembered, their first long liquid exploring kiss, oblivious to the world, on a seat at Waterloo Station, waiting for the last train to Aldershot.

'I do love you,' he said. 'I really do. It's just that I'm tired, that's all.'

'I'm not surprised, tonight,' she said.

'We'll try again tomorrow.'

'You'll be tired tomorrow. You're always tired after we've visited mother.'

'I'll make you glad you didn't marry Henry Possett.'

'Don't keep going on about Henry Possett.'

They heard the Milfords returning home after their snifter at the golf club. The engine was switched off. Then, a few seconds later, two car doors were slammed in quick succession. Then the garage door shut with a bang. Then the front door opened, and then that too was slammed.

'Noisy buggers,' he said. 'I'm going to speak to them in the morning.'

Elizabeth closed her book and switched off the light.

'Darling?' said Reggie. 'Do you mind if I don't come and see your mother tomorrow?'

'Why? We've arranged it all.'

'I know, but ...' He hesitated. Don't, Reggie, he told himself. You'll destroy everything. Is that what you really want? 'I've got some work to do.'

'You didn't mention it before.'

'I forgot.'

'You said you weren't going to work so hard.'

'I won't have to after I've finished this little bit.'

'I really ought to go,' she said. 'She isn't at all well.'

'Well, you go.'

'I don't like to leave you.'

'You've left me before.'

'Yes, but ...'

'You're worried about me. There's no need to. I'm not going off my head, you know. Really I'm not.'

'Mother'll be disappointed.'

'She'll be thrilled.'

He put his hand in hers.

'Everything's going to be all right, my darling. You'll see,' he said.

'I hope so,' she said.

He squeezed her hand, and she gave him an answering squeeze.

'You'll see,' he said.

Sunday

Sunday morning, heavy with apathy. Breakfast in the garden, boiled eggs in the hazy sunshine. Barely enough wind to stir the laburnum leaves and rustle the colour supplements.

Elizabeth was slow. She read about Maria Callas, whom she would never meet, and Bolivia, where she would never go, and cold carp, Rumanian style, which she would never eat. She took an age up in the bedroom, titivating. Reggie took great pains to be absolutely normal, for fear she'd change her mind and stay. And all the time his hands itched to help her on her way. They wanted to fit her bra, smooth her hair, zip her dress, open the garage door. It was a full-time job controlling them. Now come on, hands, he had to say. Show a stiff upper lip. You're British, you know.

Men cleaned their cars in rivers of detergent. Mr Milford set off to play nine holes, prior to having a snifter at the nineteenth. Pub carpets were hoovered, on underground stations West Indian porters spread sand over white men's spew, a pantechnicon overturned outside High Wycombe, and still Elizabeth wasn't ready.

He went up to their bedroom. She was doing her eyes.

'Shouldn't you be getting off?' he said.

'Anyone would think you wanted me out of the way.'

'It's just that there'll be a lot of traffic on the Worthing road, if you don't beat the rush.'

At last she was ready. He escorted her to the front door.

'Have a good day, darling,' he said.

'There's cold meat on the bottom shelf of the fridge, covered in foil,' she said.

'Cold meat. Good.'

'There's some of that pork. And some Danish salami.'

'Lovely.'

'And there are some salady bits in the salad drawer.'

'Fine. Good. Salady bits.'

'I don't want to come home and find it hasn't been eaten.'

'It'll be eaten.'

'If you want something for tea, there's a cake in the cake tin.'

'Cake. Fine,' he said.

They had got as far as the garage door.

'Are you sure you'll be all right?' she said.

'I'll be all right.'

'Don't work too hard.'

'I won't.'

She drove slowly out of the garage. Hurry up, he thought, please hurry, before the suspension collapses.

She stopped.

'The aspirins are in the medicine cupboard, if you get one of your thundery headaches,' she said.

'Good. Fine. Lovely. Well, have a good day.'

'Yes. Don't work too hard.'

'Give my love to your mother.'

'Yes. Don't do anything I wouldn't do.'

'No.'

He watched her drive down Coleridge Close and turn into Herrick Rise. She changed into second gear too soon. Suddenly he realized how much he would miss her if she was killed in a crash. He wanted to cry: 'Come back! It's all a mistake.' But she had gone.

He went back into the living room. The house was filled with her absence. The only noise was the faint wheezing of Ponsonby, asleep on the sofa.

He made himself a long glass of orange squash, with three cubes of ice. The haze was thickening. It was only just possible to see that the sky was blue.

He had never been unfaithful to Elizabeth – and he hadn't

been ashamed to admit it. But she would never look at that Reggie Perrin, the faithful husband, again.

Would it show?

He took off his shirt and vest, smelled them with mild fascinated distaste, and threw them into a corner.

He sat in one of the fluffy white armchairs, facing the french windows. The fitted carpet was dove-grey, there was a faint yellow-green tinge in the patterned wallpaper.

There was a brown Parker Knoll armchair, and a piano which nobody played now Linda had married. Colour was provided by a standard lamp with a bright orange shade. There were orange cushions and an orange rug. On the walls hung pictures of Algarve scenes, painted by Mr Snurd, their dentist. He hadn't liked to refuse them, for fear Mr Snurd would stop giving him injections.

He picked up the telephone. There was still no need to go through with it.

He dialled. He could hear his heart beating in the emptiness of the house.

'Three-two-three-six.'

'Joan?'

'Yes?'

'It's Reggie here, Joan. Reggie Perrin.'

He cursed himself for his admission that there might be other Reggies.

'Hullo,' she said, surprised.

'Look, I'm sorry to bother you on a Sunday but something pretty important's cropped up.' He hoped his voice wasn't trembling. 'I wondered if you could pop over.'

'What – now?'

'Well, if it's not a nuisance. It'll only take an hour or so.'

'I'm in the middle of doing the Sunday dinner.'

'Well couldn't you finish doing the dinner and take a taxi over? I'll reimburse you.'

He sat naked from the waist up, on the settee. He tried to picture Joan, standing in the hall perhaps, near an umbrella stand, even her apron immaculate, and certainly not naked from the waist up.

'Couldn't you come over here?' she said.

'Not really.' He lowered his voice. 'I can't explain over the phone. I'm not alone.'

'Oh.'

'Suffice it to say that the whole future of Sunshine Desserts is at stake – not to mention Reginald Iolanthe Perrin.'

'All right,' she said. 'I'll come.'

He put his hand over the mouthpiece and let out a huge sigh of relief.

Then he went into the bathroom and had a shower.

He imagined taking a shower with Joan, running a piece of Yorkshire pudding gently across her glistening stomach, and then eating it together, nibbling till their lips met. Perhaps my imagination's diseased, he thought.

When he'd put on some clean clothes, he got out a bottle of medium dry sherry and two glasses. He decided to have a glass while waiting.

He sipped his sherry, trying not to drink too fast. The sun moved slowly across the sky, creature of habit, suburban orb. Pink hats bobbed home from church, joints of beef began to splutter in pre-set ovens and somewhere, inevitably, there would be the hottest June temperature since records began.

Mrs Milford left in the smaller car, to join Mr Milford for a snifter. A coven of puffy clouds with thick dark edges gathered round the sun. Reggie became afraid that he would sweat again, and this fear made him sweat.

He had another shower and changed into light grey trousers and a blue open-neck shirt. It made him feel young. Surely today even Joan would sweat?

The one o'clock news spoke of thunderstorms in the west, with flooding at Tiverton and freak hailstones at Yeovil. The hottest June temperature since records began had been recorded at Mildenhall, Suffolk. He had a second glass of sherry.

The phone rang, and his heart almost stopped. But it was

only Elizabeth, safely arrived in Worthing. No, he wasn't working too hard. No, he wouldn't forget the cold meats. No, he probably wouldn't bother to have apple sauce with his cold pork, but if he did he'd certainly remember that there were Bramleys in the fruit rack. Goodbye, darling. Kiss kiss.

The living room ran the full depth of the house, and a small window looked out over the front garden. Reggie stood by the window, to see Joan before she saw him.

At last the taxi came. She looked immaculate in a blue and white summer dress. She walked calmly up the garden path, between flocks of somnolent greenfly. She peered uncertainly at the house, as if waiting for the porch to nod and say, 'Yes, this is it.' She was relaxed, unsuspecting, a secretary arriving to do some work in Surrey.

She rang the bell. It sounded cool and clear, in the thick heat.

He opened the door.

'Hullo, Joan,' he said. 'Come in.'

'Sorry I was so long.'

'Rubbish. It's good of you to come.'

'So this is your house,' she said. 'It's nice.'

'Have a sherry.'

She looked at him in surprise.

'Just a little one, before we go upstairs.'

'Well, all right. Thank you.'

He handed her the sherry. She still suspected nothing. Presumably she pictured a group of men in conference, in a study, upstairs.

'Cheers.'

'Cheers.'

He sat down. She followed suit, pulling her dress down as far as it would go towards her bony knees.

'What's all this about?' she asked.

'Later.'

'I thought it was urgent. Look, Reggie, I've come twenty-five miles. Can't we get straight down to it?'

'We'll get down to it in a minute, Joan.' He was holding his arm across his lap so that she wouldn't see the bulge of excitement in his trousers. 'Have some more sherry?'

'No thank you.'

The world was full of her bony knees, thin arms, magnificent bust. She would repulse him, smack his face, ask for a transfer to another department.

'Where are these other people?' she asked.

He took her in his arms and kissed her pert lips, her snub nose. He had expected resistance, not a hard little tongue feeling its way into his mouth, and hands groping for his thighs.

His hands grasped her legs and felt their way up her thighs. Ponsonby decided that he had seen enough and left the room.

Suddenly Joan went tense. Reggie took his hands away.

'What about your wife?' she said.

'She's gone away for the day. She's at the hippopotamus's.'

'The what?'

'Oh – er – I mean her mother's. She resembles a hippopotamus. Her mother, I mean. Elizabeth doesn't resemble a hippopotamus at all.'

He poured her another sherry. They drank. He kissed her glistening, medium dry lips.

'What about the neighbours?' she asked.

'They can't see in.'

He ran his lips along her thin right arm.

'Why now?' she said. 'Why today, after all these years?'

'Suddenly it all seemed such a waste,' he said.

For forty-six years he had been miserly, miserly with compliments, miserly with insults, miserly with other people and miserly with himself.

She kissed his right ear. He was pleased that she was so amenable, yet he felt cheated of the pleasures of seduction.

The phone rang. He tried to ignore it, but the habit was too strong for him.

It was Elizabeth. He stiffened, motioned to Joan to keep quiet.

'Yes, I'm all right . . . No, I haven't had lunch yet . . . No,

I'm not working too hard.' Joan leant forward to run her tongue gently over his ear. She was irresponsible, exultant, not a bit the way he'd imagined. He tried to look stern and frightened. 'Do I? I don't think I sound funny . . . It's probably just the line . . . No, I'll be having it soon . . . Pickle . . . Well of course it's on the shelf where you keep the pickle, in the jar marked "pickle" . . . No, I'm not angry . . . I'm perfectly all right. How's your mother? . . . Oh dear . . . Oh dear . . . Yes . . . No, I'm all right . . . Of course I'm sure . . . Bye bye, darling.'

He put the phone down.

'Anything wrong?' said Joan.

'Her mother's got to go into hospital.'

'Oh, I'm sorry.'

She kissed him gently on the lips. He stood up, held out his arms to her, and pulled her up off the settee. She raised her eyebrows.

'Is it safe?' she said.

'Of course it is,' he said.

They left the room. The orange cushions which his wife had embroidered herself were crumpled evidence of his betrayal.

'I don't like to go into our room,' he said. 'We'll use Mark's.'

'Your son?'

'It's all right. He left home two years ago. It won't be aired, but it shouldn't matter in this heat.'

'No.'

They went into Mark's room. Mark had decorated it himself – green and purple paint – posters of Che Guevara and Mick Jagger. It had the sad air of an abandoned bedroom. Nothing had been altered – but it was tidy – and without Mark's dirty socks and pants strewn all over the floor it looked cold and lifeless. But it would make a suitably unsuitable setting for their love.

'All right?' he asked.

'Fine.'

46

'I – er – I haven't got any – anything – we don't use them – Elizabeth's got a thingummybob,' he said, embarrassed.

'It's all right.' She was embarrassed too. 'I've got something in my bag.'

'You mean . . .?'

She blushed.

'I always carry it, just in case.'

He showed her the bathroom.

'Joan?'

'Yes?'

'Don't . . . er . . .'

'What?'

'Don't come back undressed at all. I want to . . . you know . . . undress you.'

He sat on Mark's bed. Well, Mark old thing, your old dad's not a has-been yet.

Che Guevara looked at him sternly.

'Come off it, Che,' he said. 'You liked a bit yourself. It wasn't revolution all the time.'

Mick Jagger gazed down on him mercilessly.

'The permissive society comes to Coleridge Close,' said Reggie.

It's going to be all right. I'll prove I'm not past it at forty-six.

I'm sorry, Elizabeth, but I do love you just as much as ever.

What's she doing in there? Hurry up.

Don't tell me you never had any sexual troubles, Che.

Already he couldn't really remember what Joan looked like.

He hoped she hadn't taken off her tights. He needed to do that himself.

Oh hell, he thought, I do believe I'm going to be shy.

Truth is, Che, I'm a bit of a coward. Wouldn't have been much shakes in a revolution. Senior sales executive, yes. Picking off the filthy Fascist pigs one by one, no.

She came in, shyly. She hadn't taken off her tights. They sat on the bed.

47

Turn your head to the wall, Che, there's a good chap.

'Well,' he said, awkward, unused to this sort of thing, 'better get undressed.'

He started to pull the tights off her. He bent down and kissed her thigh, rolled the tights off her knees, kissed her bony knees, her legs smelt of bracken, he caught Che's eye, then unbuttoned his shirt, he was sweating, damn it, he was sweating again.

They were naked. They stood together. He was five inches taller than her. Her breasts were magnificent. He wanted to praise them but didn't know how to do it. 'What beautiful breasts' would sound stilted and 'Christ, you've got a marvellous pair of Bristols on you' would sound crude. So he just held them in his hands, and smiled foolishly.

It was the hour for washing up the Sunday dinner things, as Reggie Perrin said awkwardly, 'May as well get into bed.'

The sheets were cold even on this hot day. They lay side by side and turned to look at each other very seriously.

'To think it took me eight years,' he said. 'Hardly in the Owen Lewis class.'

'Yes, but they all have to wear yellow oilskins with him.'

The sun went behind a cloud. He pressed his body against Joan's, and a series of fierce shudders ran through him. He could feel his forty-six years of existence streaming through his fingers and toes into the clammy summer air.

In the dark cosy cave of Mark's bed he put the knobble of her knee in his mouth and bit it, very gently, so as not to leave embarrassing toothmarks. Suddenly his fear of impotence started up, the joy began to ebb away.

It was at this moment that the front door opened. Reggie thought, It can't be the front door. It's a projection of a subconscious fear. I fear Elizabeth will return, and I make myself hear her return. And then he heard the door slam shut very solidly, very physically, only one person slammed the door like that: Mark, his son, struggling actor and erstwhile admirer of Che Guevara. They should have insisted on taking Mark's front door key when he left home.

'It's Mark,' he whispered.

'Oh God.'

'Quick. Into the wardrobe.'

'Hullo. Anyone at home?' called out Mark.

'He'll come in here. Quick.' Reggie practically pushed Joan into the wardrobe. He flung her clothes in after her and slammed the door. He began to dress, hurriedly, both legs in the same leg of his pants, hopping frantically, Che witnessing his humiliation, Mick Jagger laughing secretly.

'Hullo,' Mark called out again.

Reggie went to the door.

'Just coming. I was having forty winks,' he shouted. 'Get yourself a drink.'

He hurriedly made the bed, opened the window wide, blew a kiss and an apology through the wardrobe door, and went downstairs.

Mark was lounging in an armchair, drinking whisky. He was wearing suede shoes with huge buckles, Levis, and a 'Wedgwood-Benn for King' T-shirt.

'Hullo, Pater, me old darling,' he said.

'Hullo old son.' He was always liable to use awkward phrases when dealing with Mark. Mark unnerved him. Mark was shorter and slimmer. He looked like a smaller edition of Reggie, portrait of the father as a young man, and Reggie found it curiously disconcerting. 'What brings you to this neck of the woods?'

'Just thought I'd pop down and see the old folks.'

Off-stage – and he was off-stage more than on – Mark didn't look like an actor. He had adopted a cockney accent at the age of fourteen, dressed with a maximum of informality, and only came home when he wanted money.

'Your mother's out. She's gone down to Worthing to see Granny.'

'Oh.'

'What are the two sherry glasses for?' said Mark.

'What? Oh, for drinking sherry.'

'Twit.'

'We had a sherry, your mother and I. Before she went.'

'Oh.'

Reggie dumped himself down on the settee. He looked around for handbags or other incriminating evidence, but couldn't find any.

Mark kicked off his shoes and smiled genially. He had holes in his socks again. Elizabeth had once said: 'Peter Hall won't want you in the Royal Shakespeare Company if you've got holes in your socks,' but despite remarks of that kind Mark still got on better with her than with Reggie.

Mark saw Reggie's involuntary glance and put his shoes on again. So he did want money.

'Why didn't you go with the old lady, then?' said Mark.

'I've got some work to do.'

'I thought you said you were taking a nap.'

'Just for half an hour. I was tired. I've been working all morning. Have you had lunch?'

'I'm not hungry.'

He never was. No wonder he was only five foot seven. You didn't get tall without working for it.

'It's hot,' said Reggie.

'Yeah.'

Reggie couldn't think of anything except Joan, stuck in the wardrobe. Upstairs there was a new life, a life in which your son didn't think you a poor sort of fish.

'Why didn't you tell us you were coming?'

'Why bother? If you'd been out I'd have made myself at home.'

Mark made a habit of arriving unannounced so that they couldn't stiffen their resolution not to lend him any money. He lit a cigarette and began a coughing fit.

'You smoke too much,' said Reggie.

'Rubbitch.'

'Well I'd better get upstairs and get on with my work, if you don't mind,' said Reggie.

'Upstairs?'

'Yes, I've one or two things to finish off upstairs. Look, old

50

stick, go into the kitchen and have something to eat. Get me something too. There's cold meat in the fridge, and some salady bits.'

'In a minute. I just want to go up to my room and look for something.'

'You can't. I mean, it's always in a minute with you, isn't it? Delay, delay, delay. I'll have to do it in the end.'

'Oh all right, then. I'll go and do the bloody food first. God, I wish I hadn't come home. Nag, nag, nag. You're like an old woman.'

'Don't slam the door.'

Mark slammed the door. Reggie hurried up to Mark's bedroom and opened the wardrobe. Joan came out stiffly, clutching her clothes.

'Sorry about this,' he whispered. 'He's coming up here any minute. Go into Linda's room, get into bed. I'll get rid of him as soon as I can.'

They tip-toed along the corridor, he clothed, she naked, carrying her clothes.

Linda's room had been redecorated now that she was married. It had pale pink flowery wallpaper and the wan neutrality of a guest room.

Joan hopped into bed. Reggie kissed her, blew her another kiss from the door, and hurried downstairs. Mark had laid out pork, salami, a piece of lettuce and a tomato each. Reggie got out a bottle of hock.

They took their plates and glasses into the living room.

'Sorry I got cross,' said Mark.

'That's all right, old prune.'

Silence. The sun went in behind a thicker, darker cloud.

'That's a new picture over the mantelpiece, isn't it?'

'Yes. Albufeira.'

Reggie knew that Mark looked down on him for buying Mr Snurd's pictures.

'I need me Edwards seen to.'

'Edwards?'

'Me Edward Heath. Teeth.'

Reggie never understood Mark's rhyming slang.

'How's big fat sis?' said Mark.

'Linda? She's fine.'

He poured a second glass of wine.

'How's work?' he asked.

'So so.'

'Auntie Meg wrote and said how good she thought you were in that ad for fish fingers.'

'Jesus Christ, I can do without praise for bloody adverts!'

'I know, but you were good. I mean you can be good or bad in an advert just as much as in a play.'

'Sorry. Can't eat any more,' said Mark. 'Dad?'

'Yes?'

'Could you be a darling and lend us a few bob – just a quid or two – just to tide me over. Just a fiver. I'm seeing this man on Tuesday, he thinks there's a real chance of me getting a job with his rep.'

'Which rep is that?'

Mark looked embarrassed.

'Wick. It's a bit off the beaten track but it's got a fantastic reputation. It's a fantastic jumping-off ground.'

'Into the sea?' said Reggie.

'I just need a tenner to see me through.'

Reggie hesitated.

'Please, dad. You couldn't refuse your own dustbin, could you?'

'Dustbin?'

'Dustbin lid. Kid.'

'Oh. Well how much do you really need?'

'Well – they'd like me to go up there and suss the joint – say – er – thirty quid. I'll pay you back.'

'You haven't paid the last lot back yet.'

'No, but I will.'

'All right. I'll give you forty. But this really is the last time.'

Ponsonby came in through the French windows and waited for Mark to make a fuss of him. It had gone dull and gloomy outside, and the heat hung even more heavily without the sun.

Reggie wrote out the cheque and Mark stroked Ponsonby.

'Well, Ponsonby, me old fruit cake,' he said. 'What's my dad been getting up to, then? Keeping a fancy woman upstairs, is he?'

Reggie gulped and Ponsonby miaowed.

'Look, Mark, here's the cheque,' said Reggie. 'Now the thing is, I have got a bit of work to do, I don't want you to think I'm turning you out, but . . .'

The doorbell rang. He couldn't let anyone else in, not with Joan upstairs.

'Aren't you going to answer it?'

'I suppose so.'

He went reluctantly to the door. It was Elizabeth's brother Jimmy, otherwise known as Major James Anderson, of the Queen's Own Berkshire Light Infantry, stationed at Aldershot. He had a ginger moustache and was wearing mufti.

'Sorry to barge in like this. Fact is, something I want to . . . er . . . oh hullo, Mark,' said Jimmy, marching into the living room.

'Hullo, Uncle Jimmy,' said Mark.

'Where's Elizabeth?' said Jimmy.

'She's gone to see your mother,' said Reggie.

'Must get down there myself.'

'Drink, Jimmy?'

'It's ten past three. Almost tea time. Whisky, please,' said Jimmy.

Jimmy parked himself in one of the fluffy white armchairs. He sat stiffly, regimentally. Even Mark sat up a bit in the presence of the military.

'Cheers,' said Jimmy, sipping his whisky. 'Well, Mark, how's things on the drama front?'

'Not too bad, Uncle Jimmy.'

'All the world's a stage, eh?'

'Pretty well.'

'Jolly good.'

'How's the army?'

'Oh, mustn't grumble. Saw you on the idiot box last week. Just caught the end of it. You were all sitting round eating fish fingers and smiling. Nice to see a play with a happy ending for a change.'

'Yes, it was a good play,' said Mark. 'A bit short, but interesting.' He winked at Reggie, and Reggie felt pleased to be able to enjoy a private joke with Mark.

The sun, which had made another effort to penetrate the cloud, disappeared once again. The room seemed very gloomy now.

'Look,' said Jimmy. 'No beating about the bush. Bit of a cock-up on the catering front. Muddle over shopping. Fact is, right out of food. Just wondered if you'd got anything. Just bread or something. Pay of course.'

'No, no, Jimmy. I wouldn't hear of it.'

'Oh, thanks. Decent of you. Wouldn't have asked, only kiddies yelling, general hoo-ha. Feel bad about it. Third time it's happened.'

'Not to worry, Jimmy.'

'Your dustbins all right, are they?' said Mark.

Jimmy looked at him in astonishment.

'Think so, yes. Bit bashed about. Dustmen don't take much care,' he said.

There was a ring at the bell. Reggie went to the door. It was Linda and Tom, accompanied by Adam and Jocasta.

'Hullo,' he said. 'Come on in.'

'You don't look very pleased to see us,' said Linda.

'Nonsense. I'm delighted.'

'Our little man brought the car back, so we thought we'd pop round to – you know – see if you're all right,' said Tom.

'I'm fine. Why shouldn't I be?'

'No reason. None at all.'

'Come in, all of you. Jimmy's here, and Mark.'

'Oh. Only we rang Worthing, and heard you were alone,' said Linda.

'I was. I'm not now,' said Reggie.

He escorted them into the living room. There was much standing up and sitting down. Mark said, 'Hullo, droopy-drawers,' to Linda, and Tom frowned, and when Tom frowned Mark smiled, and when Mark smiled Linda gave him a look, and when Tom saw her giving him a look he gave Linda a look.

'Yes, we thought we'd pop along and make sure you weren't depressed or anything,' said Linda.

'Pressed or anyfing,' said Adam.

'Preffed or fing,' said Jocasta.

'No, I'm not depressed or anything,' said Reggie. 'What would you all like to drink? Tea? Whisky? Sherry?'

'Tea time,' said Jimmy. 'Usually drink tea this time. Whisky for me, please.'

Tom drank sherry, Linda gin. Mark stuck to whisky, Adam and Jocasta spilt orange juice.

'I did poopy-plops in my panties,' reminisced Adam.

'Would you two like to go and play in the garden?' said Reggie.

'Do you mind if Tom and I pop up to my old room for a moment?' said Linda.

'What on earth for?' said Reggie.

'We've been having an argument. Tom says the spire of St Peter's Church is visible from it. I'm sure it isn't.'

'No, you can't go upstairs,' said Reggie hastily. 'We're bringing out some new products and I'm working on them up there and it's all a bit hush-hush.'

Linda looked at him in astonishment.

'What do you think we are? Industrial spies?' she said.

'Of course not. It's the rules, that's all. I'll just go and move them. Won't be long.'

He hurried upstairs. Joan had hidden herself completely under the bedclothes.

'It's all right,' he whispered. 'It's me.'

Her face emerged cautiously.

'Linda's turned up now – and she wants to come in here,' he whispered.

'It's like Piccadilly Circus in this house,' she said.

'Sorry. It's one of those days. There's six of them down there. I honestly think you'd better go.'

'Oh God.'

'I know, but it's not my fault. Have you got enough for a taxi?'

'Yes.'

'I'll reimburse you later. Slip out as soon as you're dressed. I'll keep everyone in the living room.'

'I feel like a criminal.'

'I'm sorry.'

'You seem nervous, father,' said Linda, on his return.

'What, me? Am I? Perhaps it's the heat,' said Reggie.

'Awkward customer, the heat,' said Jimmy. 'Known sane men go mad in the tropics because of the heat. Makes you think.'

Reggie saw Linda frown at Jimmy. Something in the attitude of Mark and Jimmy made it clear to him that Tom and Linda had told them about his episode with the lions.

'Well,' he said. 'I see you've told them about my little episode with the lions.'

'Tricky blighters, lions,' said Jimmy.

'I thought you'd got more garden,' said Mark.

'Garden?'

'Garden fence. Sense.'

'That isn't an authentic example of cockney slang, is it?' said Tom.

'Oh. She's sharp today, isn't she?' said Mark. 'She's been sleeping in the knife box.'

'I did biggies in my panties,' said Adam, coming in through the french windows, dragging the best part of a hollyhock behind him.

'I'll bet you did, you dirty little bugger,' said Mark.

Jocasta followed Adam, dragging in the worst part of the hollyhock.

Tom and Linda beamed. 'We're great believers in letting them learn to use the toilet at their own pace,' said Tom.

'May be something in it,' said Jimmy, standing at the french windows and surveying the back garden. 'Garden's in good nick.'

Mark moved towards the door.

'Where are you going?' said Reggie.

'For a bangers.'

'Bangers?'

'Bangers and mash. Slash.'

'Ah. Yes. Well would you mind waiting a minute, old thing. The – er – the lavatory is blocked.'

Reggie thought he heard steps on the stairs.

'What's wrong, father?' said Linda.

'Nothing's wrong, except that everybody keeps asking me what's wrong,' said Reggie.

'Yes, you've got a fine garden,' said Jimmy. 'I say, come here, Reggie. Look. Woman crawling through bushes.' Reggie went reluctantly to the window. The others followed. 'See the cone-shaped bush, two o'clock, middle foreground? Behind that. There's a woman crawling through your shrubbery.' He opened the window. 'You – you there,' he shouted, and Joan Greengross scampered off as fast as she could. 'Quick. After her.'

'No,' said Reggie, grabbing hold of Jimmy's arm. 'It's – it's only Mrs Redgross. Poor woman – she crawls around in shrubberies. She's not quite right.'

'You're as white as a sheet, dad,' said Mark.

'We had a nasty incident with her. I'd rather not talk about it,' said Reggie.

There was a distant peal of thunder.

'Better get off before Jupiter plooves,' said Jimmy. 'Well, thanks for the drinks. Make me own way out. Crawls through shrubberies, eh? Rum. Makes you think. So long, all.'

'That's odd,' said Reggie, when Jimmy had driven off. 'He left without any food. He came to borrow some food.'

'That's odd too,' said Linda. 'He came to borrow some food from us on Wednesday. He said there'd been a cock-up on the catering front.'

'I find the words people use fascinating,' said Tom. 'I'm very much a word person. We both are.'

In the dark recesses behind the settee Adam was pummelling Jocasta.

'Shouldn't you stop them?' said Reggie.

'It doesn't do them any harm,' said Linda.

'Adam's working out his aggressions, and Jocasta's learning to be self-reliant,' explained Tom.

'Oh, I see,' said Mark. 'I thought he was bashing the living daylights out of her. Can I go for me hit and miss now?'

'Hit and miss?' said Reggie.

'Piss.'

'Oh. Yes, I think I just heard the lavatory unblock itself.'

It grew steadily darker. Another peal of thunder broke over them.

'Well if you're sure you're all right we may as well try and beat the storm,' said Linda.

'I've told you I'm all right,' said Reggie.

'Too dark now to see that spire anyway,' said Tom.

As Tom and Linda drove off down Coleridge Close the first drops of rain began to fall.

Reggie and Mark went back into the living room.

'Great hairy twit,' said Mark. 'What did she want to marry him for?'

'I don't see how you can talk about him being hairy,' said Reggie.

'What do you mean?'

'Well your hair isn't exactly short, is it?'

'Oh God. Not that.'

'I don't mind long hair as such, old prune. Good lord no! I hope I'm more reasonable than that. What difference does the length of your hair make? None, to me. I'm just thinking of your work.'

'If I play long-haired parts I have to have long hair.'

'Yes, but what about short-haired parts?'

'So if I get a short-haired part I'll have a bloody hair cut.'

'There's no need to swear at me, Mark. I've just given you forty quid.'

Oh God, Reggie. Shut up.

'I hope you don't go for auditions wearing a "Wedgwood-Benn for King" T-shirt.'

'What's wrong with it?'

'It's not exactly the height of elegance. I'd like to think we brought you up to have rather better taste than that.'

A flash of lightning illuminated Mr Snurd's pictures of the Algarve.

'Have the money back if you want,' said Mark.

'I didn't say that.'

'You have to bring up every bloody little thing, don't you?'

'There are lots of things I don't bring up. You don't wash your feet but I draw a veil over it. I just happen to mention your hair and you go berserk. Your generation are too damned sensitive by half.' Stop it, Reggie. But I can't. It's got to come out. 'In my day we expected a bit of criticism. We took it for granted. We weren't so damned sensitive in my day.'

Mark made a gesture imitating the winding up of a gramophone.

'All right. I'll leave you. I've got work to do anyway,' said Reggie angrily.

'Don't slam the door, Dad.'

Reggie slammed the door.

He went upstairs and stood at the landing window watching the great drops of rain fall on the parched earth. A high wind was battering the roses and hollyhocks, and creating havoc among the lupins and delphiniums. He was shaking with humiliation and anger and frustration.

If only Mark respected him. If only he could behave to Mark in a manner worthy of respect. If only Mark hadn't come today. It was all so pointless. Did they all have to play these pathetic roles – infant, son, father, grandfather, dotard – generation after generation?

59

He climbed up into the loft. There were piles of mementos up there, relics of his past. He must get rid of them.

Mark watched the rain gloomily. He wanted to get away. His father always made him acutely conscious of being a failure, of disappointing his father's hopes, of not being taller. Jimmy made him ashamed of being an actor. Who did they call in when there was a dock strike? The national theatre? No, the army.

Reggie sat on a cross-beam, listening to the rain pattering on the roof. He had rigged up an electric light in the loft, but beyond its reach there were pools of mysterious darkness. Here there were old set squares, a copper warming pan turned green, six tiny fir trees that had been part of the scenery on a model railway axed in a nursery economy drive. There were thirty-seven electric plugs, twelve bent stair rods, the battered remains of a blow football game, his old school tuck box full of faded curtains. All these ghosts would have to go.

He found a pile of old wedding photos that hadn't been good enough to be included in the album. Could that gawky, close-cropped young idiot really be Lance Corporal Perrin? Could the naive girl in the shapeless utility wedding dress really be Elizabeth? He could hardly bear it now, the strained smile of his mother, war-widowed in 1942. Elizabeth's father, on forty-eight hours' leave, smiled stiffly. Her mother smiled over-brightly, a budding resemblance to a hippopotamus already faintly discernible beneath the gallant home-made hat. The embarrassments of yesterday might be bearable, but these reminders of the embarrassments of long ago were infinitely more painful. They too must go.

He could smell a dead bird in the loft, but he felt a revulsion at the thought of touching it, maggots and all, or even at feeling its shape through a newspaper as he cleared it up.

He came across a handsome mounted photo of the Ruttingstagg College Small-Bore Rifle Team – Spring 1942. Five close-cropped idiots. Standing (l. to r.): Reynolds, L.F.R.;

Perrin, R.I.; Seated: Campbell-Lewiston, D.J.; Machin, A.M. (Capt.); Campbell-Lewiston, E.L.

There was a list of all the engine numbers seen on a magical journey from King's Cross to Edinburgh, in the carefree days of 1936. A cricket scorebook full of matches played with dice, in the steamy jungle of his bedroom, in the sticky days, the painful idyllic days of adolescence. England v. R.I. Perrin's XI. Australia v. Golden Lodge Preparatory School. England against a team of all the girls Reggie had secret crushes on. Now he would burn all memories of those long hours of self-absorption, which had so worried his parents. Cricket and masturbation had been his only interests, sometimes separately, sometimes together.

At Ruttingstagg College, in Nansen House, in Lower Middle Dorm, during the Clogger Term, the other boys had listened to him talking in his sleep.

'He bowls to Perrin. Perrin drives. Six. England 186 for 8. Perrin 161 not out,' and then someone would throw a dead thrush at him, and he would wake up.

Moonlight streaming in through the curtainless windows of the bare wooden dormitory. Convoys on the main road. Owls hooting. Beds creaking. Wakeful hours. Now, thousands of dead thrushes later, Reggie collected together other items from the secret archives of the loft. Some of them he would show to Mark. All of them he would burn.

He climbed cautiously down the ladder, clutching his mementos. His spell in the loft had calmed him. The rain, beating ineffectually on the roof, had soothed him. He felt ashamed of his anger with Mark.

They sat deep in their armchairs, sipping tea and eating buttered toast. The thunder was moving away to the north.

Reggie wanted to say, 'Mark, I love you. If I have resented you, it's because I saw in you too much that reminded me of myself. We are angry with our children for making the same mistakes as we did, partly because we have an illogical feeling that they ought to have learnt from our mistakes, and partly because they remind us of our own enormous capacity for folly. Forgive me, my son.'

What he actually said was, 'The rain's almost stopped.'

'Yeah,' said Mark.

'I've never told you this — eat some more toast, there's a good chap — but you know how angry I was when you were expelled from Ruttingstagg? The fact is, I was expelled too.'

'I know,' said Mark.

'What?'

Reggie stood up, a little annoyed to find that his revelation was not a revelation.

'One of the cruds told me,' said Mark.

'Which one?'

'Slimy Penfold.'

'I hated Slimy Penfold. Now I don't hate anyone.'

Reggie stood with his back to the brick fireplace, warming his backside on the memory of winter fires. Behind him were the white cottages of an Algarve village. In front of him was his son.

'Why didn't you tell me you knew?' he said.

'I was ashamed,' said Mark. 'I was more ashamed of you being expelled than me.'

'I hated Ruttingstagg,' said Reggie.

'Then why the bloody hell did you send me there, you great soft berk?'

Reggie smiled indulgently at his son's choice of words, and since he couldn't answer the question he sat beside Mark on the settee, and patted his knee twice.

'I've been sorting out some old souvenirs and things,' he said. He put the mementos on the Danish coffee table, half of which he had given Elizabeth for Christmas, she having given him the other half. He could smell Mark's feet.

'Here are some pictures of our wedding,' he said.

'Let's have a gander then.'

'That's old Uncle Charlie Willoughby, standing next to Grandpa Tonbridge.'

'Who's the loonie standing beside Granny Exeter?'

'That's the best man. Acting Lance Corporal Sprockett.'

'And who's the geyser with the boozer's conk?'

'That's Uncle Percy Spillinger. Grandpa Tonbridge's brother. You met him when you were a boy. We don't see him these days.'

'Why not?'

'He's frowned upon. He made a lot of money without doing a day's work, he enjoys spending it, he drinks and he says what he thinks. I like him. He must be nearly eighty now. Why the hell haven't I seen him for twenty years? It's ridiculous.'

Reggie poured another cup of tea. The rain had stopped.

'It doesn't look a very happy wedding,' said Mark.

'It wasn't,' said Reggie. 'The in-laws didn't approve of me, because I wasn't an officer or a war-hero. I was terrified they'd find out that I'd been expelled from Ruttingstagg. It was very difficult to get to Tonbridge, because all the cars had been laid up for the duration and the station was marked "Inverness" to confuse the Germans. It confused the guests all right. Acting Lance Corporal Sprockett had to stand on the platform with a loud-hailer and a carnation in his buttonhole shouting "Change here for Paddock Wood, Headcorn, Ashford, Folkestone and the Perrin-Anderson wedding." We ferried everyone to the church in a ten ton truck.'

'Poor dad.'

'The reception was in an incredibly draughty hotel. There were dried egg sandwiches, snoek canapes and whalemeat bridge rolls. The Andersons had pooled their ration books to get the ingredients for the cake. Grandpa Tonbridge had a face about eight miles long. Auntie Katie Willoughby made rude remarks about Uncle Percy Spillinger's war effort, Acting Lance Corporal Sprockett made a terrible speech, I had a nose bleed, and then suddenly we heard a doodlebug. Its engine cut out.'

'Christ!'

'We all lay on the floor. I held your mother's hand. The doodlebug fell on the British Restaurant two hundred yards away. All the hotel's windows were blown out and the cake collapsed.'

'God.'

'Well actually that seemed to break the ice.'

'And the icing.'

'Very good. After that it was all quite fun. They picked up Uncle Percy Spillinger two days later in Tenterden, playing bagpipes at the top of the church tower and singing "Scotland the Brave".'

There was a long silence. Neither of them liked to say anything, for fear it would break the mood.

'Would you like a beer, old carthorse?' Reggie said at length.

'I'd love one.'

Reggie poured a couple of beers, while the gloom of the storm began to lift. It was the hour of religious programmes on television.

There were pictures of Reggie with his parents. His father, the bank inspector, pointing at something in every picture. His mother, the bank inspector's wife, always looking in the direction in which his father was pointing. His father died of a bullet through the head and his mother died of not having any interests in life except his father.

There was a picture of a very young and handsome Jimmy, on Littlehampton beach, and a snapshot of Reggie and Nigel at Chilhampton Ambo, grinning fit to bust, no doubt dreaming of Angela Borrowdale's riding breeches.

Reggie wanted to say, 'This is nice, old parsnip, sitting here together, just the two of us,' but he was afraid that if he said it it would cease to be nice.

He picked up his next memento. It was an empty box. Then the doorbell rang. Damn. Damn. Damn.

It was Major James Anderson, of the Queen's Own Berkshire Light Infantry, no longer so young and handsome.

'Sorry to bother you,' said Jimmy. 'Fact is, bit of a cock-up. Forgot the blasted food.'

'Yes. I know.'

'Got home. Hungry family. No chow. In the doghouse. Came back quick as I could.'

'Mark and I have been having a beer. Will you join us?'

'Fact is, Reggie, ought to get straight back. Well, just a quick one, if you insist.'

Reggie led Jimmy back into the living room, and poured out another beer.

'Well, Mark,' said Jimmy. 'How are things on the drama front?'

'Not too bad, Uncle Jimmy.'

'All the world's a stage, eh?'

'Something like that.'

'Jolly good.'

Jimmy lolled to attention in the brown Parker Knoll chair, and took a long draught of his beer.

'I was just showing Mark some of the things I found in the box room,' said Reggie.

'Carry on. Don't mind me. Going in two shakes of a lamb's tail,' said Jimmy.

Reggie handed round the empty box.

'This is an empty box of Nurse Mildew's Instant Wart Eradicator,' he said.

'You've got to be joking,' said Mark.

'I once had twenty-five warts. Nothing cured them. All remedies failed,' said Reggie.

'Awkward wallahs, warts,' said Jimmy. 'Get one, before you can say "Jack Robinson", covered in the blighters.'

'Then someone recommended this stuff,' said Reggie. 'Within a week, no warts. I haven't had a wart since.'

'There was a ring at the door. It was Tom.

'Hullo, Tom, what can I do you for?'

'I just called round to – to call round,' said Tom.

'I'm perfectly all right.'

'Of course you are. Linda just thought we rushed off rather, so one of us would look after the children and the other one would pop over and see if you wanted company. We tossed for it.'

'And you lost?'

'Yes. No, I won. So here I am.'

'Well, come on in. Jimmy's here, and Mark.'

'Oh well, if you're . . .'

'No, come and have a drink now you're here.'

Tom sat on the settee, beside Mark, much to Reggie's annoyance.

'Beer, Tom?'

'No, thanks. I only drink draught. Bottled stuff's all gas and gaiters.'

'Does blow you up, bottled beer,' said Jimmy.

'Another one, Jimmy?'

'Please.'

Reggie gave Tom a glass of wine and Jimmy a beer.

'Kids in bed?' said Mark.

'No. Jocasta rather likes *Late-Night Line-Up*.'

'I was just showing Jimmy and Mark some of my souvenirs,' said Reggie.

He handed round a small stuffed trout in a glass case.

'This is the only fish I've ever caught. It's a trout. I caught it at my boss's place on the River Test.'

The stuffed trout was passed from hand to hand.

'Interesting,' said Jimmy politely.

'I eat a lot of fish,' said Tom. 'I'm a fish person.'

A shaft of uncertain sunlight lit up the room. Reggie handed round a notebook full of figures.

'This is a list of all the engine numbers I saw during August 1936,' he said.

'Interesting,' said Jimmy.

'M'm,' said Tom.

Mark gave his father a puzzled look.

'You certainly saw a lot of engines,' said Jimmy.

'I saw every one of the streamlined engines designed by Sir Nigel Gresley,' said Reggie.

'I pity these train spotters today,' said Jimmy. 'All these diesels. Nothing to it.'

'This is an old cricket scorebook,' said Reggie. 'I used to

play cricket matches with dice. Listen to this one. It's England v. My Girls.'

'Your Girls? Who were they?' said Jimmy.

'They were all the girls I'd got a crush on. I must have been about fourteen. England batted first and made 188 all out. Leyland got 67. Danielle Darrieux took 4 for 29. Here's the girls' reply:

The fat receptionist at Margate	b Voce	28
Jill Ogleby	c Leyland, b Larwood	2
The tall girl on the 8.21	not out	92
Greta Garbo	l.b.w. Voce	30
Mrs Slimy Penfold	run out	1
Jennifer Ogleby	c Hutton, b Verity	9
The blonde waitress at the Kardomah	b Verity	0
Angela Borrowdale	c and b Verity	0
Violet Bonham Carter	not out	16
Extras		11
Total (for 7 wickets)		189

The scorebook was passed from hand to hand. Reggie felt calm, at peace. His legs were no longer exceptionally heavy. His body no longer ached.

'I hated cricket,' said Tom. 'I didn't get the point of it.'

'Pity the tall girl on the 8.21 didn't get her ton,' said Jimmy. 'Might have done, if Violet Bonham Carter hadn't hit two sixes off successive balls.'

Mark handed the scorebook back to his father without comment.

'Very interesting souvenirs,' said Jimmy politely. 'Nice to keep a few mementos.'

'I'm going to burn them all,' said Reggie.

Jimmy stood up smartly.

'Well, better be off,' he said. 'Tempus is fooging away.'

'Don't you want that food?' said Reggie.

'By jove, yes! Nearly forgot,' said Jimmy.

Reggie and Jimmy went into the kitchen.

'There are some eggs, a little cold pork, some Danish salami,

67

a lemon mousse, some rhubarb tart, half a loaf, bacon, butter and some odd salady bits. What would you like?' said Reggie.

'That'll do fine,' said Jimmy.

Reggie packed the food into two carrier bags and handed them to Jimmy.

'That'll keep the wolf from the door,' said Jimmy.

Jimmy offered Mark a lift to the station, and this was accepted.

'Cheerio Tom,' said Mark. 'Look after me water.'

'Water?'

'Water blister, sister.'

Reggie slipped Mark an extra fiver and said, 'Take care, old thing.'

'Toodle-oo, Reggie,' said Jimmy. 'Thanks for the nosh. Don't work too hard. Don't want you suddenly kicking the bucket on us.'

There were great pools of water lying in the gutter, but the pavements had dried. Jimmy drove rapidly.

'Think your father's overdoing it a bit,' he said. 'Mentioned it, tactfully as I could. Fancy the thrust got home.'

As he pulled up in a large puddle in the station forecourt, Jimmy sent a spurt of water over three schoolgirls and a quantity surveyor.

The joyous evening sunlight streamed into the living room. Reggie poured another drink.

'It's cooler tonight,' he said.

'Yes,' said Tom. 'I'm glad. I sweat very freely. I have very open pores.'

'Really?'

'Linda sweats quite a bit too. She's got very open pores.'

'I wonder if you'd mind leaving now, Tom. I've got a lot of work to do.'

'No, if you're sure you'll be . . .'

'I'll be all right.'

Reggie escorted Tom into the hall.

'Goodbye, Tom. Don't forget you're both coming to dinner on Tuesday night.'

'No. Now you're sure . . .'

'Yes. Goodbye.'

Tom drove off. Reggie went out into the garden and lit a bonfire. The whole western sky was aflame. He threw the wedding photos on the fire. Hats curled and blackened. He threw the small-bore rifle team on the fire. Campbell-Lewiston, E.L., curled and blackened. His past went up in smoke, heat and little bits of ash. A bat fluttered weakly round the eaves. There was a screech as Ponsonby caught a mouse.

Reggie rang Joan, then rang off hurriedly. Her husband might answer, and in any case there was nothing to say.

The bonfire went out. The flame of the sky grew more and more subtle. The bat screamed, so high that only other bats could hear it. Reggie heard the Milfords going off to the golf club for a snifter, and in the Wisemans' house someone was learning the piano.

He rushed upstairs to see if there were any tell-tale traces of Joan. But there weren't.

The telephone rang. He answered it in the bedroom. It was Elizabeth.

'Hullo, dear. Are you all right?'

'I'm fine.'

'Mother's going into hospital tomorrow morning. I'll have to stay.'

'Well, all right, you stay then.'

'Are you sure you don't mind?'

'Not in the least.'

'Oh.'

'Well, I mean I mind. But I don't mind because I know you've got to.'

'You'll be all right?'

'Yes.'

'The C.J.'s and things are coming on Tuesday.'

'Yes.'

'Perhaps you ought to put them off?'

'Yes.'

'Did you find the food all right?'

'Yes. Mark came.'

'You didn't lend him anything?'

'Of course not.'

'Only it's bad for him, in the long run.'

'Yes. And Jimmy called. He'd run out of food again.'

'Again? It's getting beyond a joke.'

'Have you had the rain?'

'Yes, have you?'

'Yes.'

'If you want cocoa there's some on the shelf where I keep the hot drinks.'

'Fine.'

'Now you're sure you'll be all right?'

'Yes.'

'Don't leave any windows open when you go to work.'

'No.'

'You've fed Ponsonby, have you?'

'Yes.'

'Well – I'll see you when I see you.'

'Yes.'

'Good-bye, darling.'

'Good-bye, darling.'

Reggie went downstairs and fed Ponsonby. It was almost dark and blessedly cool.

He made himself a mug of cocoa and stretched out in an armchair. Ponsonby sat on the settee and watched him.

'Hullo, Ponsonby,' he said.

Ponsonby purred.

'You know, Ponsonby,' he said, 'when I was young I looked with envy at grown-ups. People in their forties were solid, authoritative figures. Not for them the pangs of adolescence, the flushing cheeks, the pimples – "shag spots" we used to call them at Ruttingstagg, Ponsonby. I had terrible shag spots in 1942. They were masters of the universe.'

Ponsonby purred.

70

'Well now I'm forty-six, Ponsonby. But I don't feel solid and authoritative. I see the young strutting around like turkey cocks – self-assured, solid, terrifying.'

Ponsonby watched him closely, purring all the time, trying to follow his drift.

'Now, Ponsonby, the question's this, isn't it? Do the young today see me as something solid and authoritative, were the people whom I thought so solid really feeling just like I am now? Or have I and my generation missed out? Have the tables been turned at exactly the wrong moment for us? What do you think, Ponsonby?'

Ponsonby purred contentedly.

'You don't think anything, do you? Good job, too. Or perhaps it's just me that's missed out. Old Goofy. Yes, the nasty boys used to call your master Goofy. Goofy Perrin. Coconut Matting Perrin. Weren't the nasty boys nasty?'

Ponsonby's purring grew slower and deeper.

'We never know other people's secret thoughts, Ponsonby. Does Harold Wilson dream about being a ping-pong champion? Did General Smuts have a thing about ear wax? The history books are silent. So, you see, we never know quite how abnormal we are. Perhaps we're all terrified we're abnormal and really we're all quite normal. Or perhaps we're terrified we're normal and really we're abnormal. It's all very complicated. Perhaps it's best to be born a cat, but you don't get the choice.

'It's not very nice getting steadily older all the time, Ponsonby. It's a bit of a dirty trick. One day I'll die. All alone. I'll pay for my funeral in advance, and I'll get a free wildlife shroud, plus plastic models of twenty-six famous dead people.

'I don't altogether like the way the world's going, if you want the honest truth. But I'm going to fight, Ponsonby. I'm going to give them a run for their money.' He stood up. 'I'll show them, the bastards,' he shouted.

Scared by Reggie's shouting and standing up so suddenly, Ponsonby rushed out into the kitchen. Reggie heard the cat door clang behind him as he went out into the garden.

He couldn't get comfortable that night. There was someone else in bed with him. He switched on the light.

He knew what it was now. It was his right arm. For a moment it had seemed like a separate being, with a mind of its own.

He shivered.

Monday

In his usual compartment, on the eight-sixteen, Reggie turned to the crossword page. He furrowed his brows, then he wrote: 'I am not a mere tool of the capitalist society.'

Peter Cartwright was surprised by his fast progress. Peter Cartwright was stuck.

Reggie looked up at the grey canopy of the sky. It was cooler and fresher after the storm, with an easterly breeze and a hint of more rain to come.

The door handle seemed very large, out of all proportion. It would be so easy to turn it. All he'd have to do then would be to open the door and step out. So easy. There would hardly be time to feel anything.

It wasn't that he wanted to die. It wasn't as simple as that. It was just that there was he, and there was the handle, and there were the rails speeding past, and he could feel their pull.

He smiled at Peter Cartwright. Peter Cartwright smiled at him. Had he noticed anything? Could a man go through such an internal struggle and reveal nothing of it in his face?

Reggie wrote again in the spaces of his crossword. 'Today I am seeing Mr Campbell-Lewiston,' he wrote. 'Mr Campbell-Lewiston is our new man in Germany. Mr Campbell-Lewiston is going to get a little surprise.'

He folded the paper up and put it in his briefcase.

'Rather easy today,' he said.

'Damned if I think so,' said Peter Cartwright.

The pollen count was high, and Peter Cartwright had a

violent sneezing fit near Earlsfield. The train reached Waterloo eleven minutes late. The loudspeaker announcement attributed this to 'the derailment of a container truck at Hook'.

Reggie caught sight of an old woman among the crowds on the station forecourt, and he tried to avoid her, but it was too late. She was bearing down on him. She looked about seventy-five, but could equally well have been sixty-five or eighty-five, or even ninety-five. She was gaunt, an old scarecrow, and her legs were covered in thick black hair.

She always asked the same question. It was embarrassing to be caught by her. It made you look a fool in front of the other commuters, so many of whom took pains to avoid her.

'I wonder if you can help me?' she said, in a deep, cracked voice like an old rook. 'I'm looking for a Mr James Purdock, from Somerset.'

'I'm awfully sorry,' he said. 'I'm afraid I don't know him.'

He arrived at 9.05. The third floor was still deserted. There were grey-green covers on all the typewriters.

He sat at Joan's desk for a moment, wondering what it must be like to be her. He looked at his eight postcards of Pembrokeshire – cliffs, golden sands, impossibly blue skies and turquoise seas – and they made him feel sad.

He felt his thighs, imagining that he was feeling her thighs, imagining that he was her feeling his thighs, imagining that he was her feeling her own thighs.

She arrived with Sandra Gostelow and caught him there. He felt embarrassed, although he knew that they couldn't see into his thoughts.

'I was just testing the chairs,' he said, and his blushes gave the lie to his words. 'We must have our secretaries comfortable.'

He went into his office. Joan followed. She was wearing a dark green dress which he hadn't noticed before.

'You're seeing Mr Campbell-Lewiston at ten,' she said.

'Yes,' he said. 'I'm seeing Mr Campbell-Lewiston at ten.'

It was as if the events of the previous day hadn't happened. He couldn't refer to them. He hoped she would.

'Don't forget Colin Edmundes wants to see you about the new filing cabinets,' she said.

Joan ushered Mr Campbell-Lewiston in. He was wearing a lightweight grey suit and carried a fawn German raincoat. When he smiled Reggie noticed that his teeth were yellow.

'How are things going in Germany?' said Reggie.

'It's tough,' said Mr Campbell-Lewiston. 'Jerry's very conservative. He doesn't go in for convenience foods as much as we do.'

'Good for him.'

'Yes, I suppose so, but I mean it makes our job more difficult.'

'More of a challenge,' said Reggie.

Joan entered with a pot of coffee on a tray. There were three biscuits each – a bourbon, a rich tea and a custard cream.

'There are some isolated regional breakthroughs,' said Mr Campbell-Lewiston. 'Some of the mousses are holding their own in the Rhenish Palatinate, and the flans are cleaning up in Schleswig-Holstein.'

'Oh good, that's very comforting to know,' said Reggie. 'And what about the powdered Bakewell Tart mix, is it going like hot cakes?'

'Not too well, I'm afraid.'

Reggie poured out two cups of coffee and handed one to his visitor. Mr Campbell-Lewiston took four lumps of sugar.

'And how about the tinned treacle pudding – is that proving sticky?'

'Oh very good. Treacle tart, sticky. You're a bit of a wag,' said Mr Campbell-Lewiston, and he laughed yellowly.

Suddenly the penny dropped.

'Good God,' said Reggie. 'Campbell-Lewiston. I thought the name was familiar. Campbell-Lewiston, E. L., Ruttingstagg. The small-bore rifle team.'

'Of course. Goofy Per . . . R. I. Perrin.'

They shook hands.

'You're doing pretty well for yourself,' said Reggie.

'You too,' said E. L. Campbell-Lewiston.

'You were a nauseous little squirt in those days,' said Reggie.

E. L. Campbell-Lewiston drew in his breath sharply.

'Thank heaven for small bores, for small bores grow bigger every day,' said Reggie.

'What?'

'I really must congratulate you on the work you're doing in Germany,' said Reggie. 'Do you remember the time you bit me in the changing room?'

'I don't remember that.'

'I think you've done amazingly well with those flans in Schleswig-Holstein,' said Reggie. 'And now what I'd like you to do is pave the way for our new range of exotic ice creams. There are three flavours — mango delight, cumquat surprise and strawberry and lychee ripple.'

'I can't believe it. I've never bitten anyone.'

Reggie stood up and spoke dynamically.

'Aren't you listening?' he said. 'I'm talking about our new range of ice creams.'

'Oh, yes. Sorry,' said E. L. Campbell-Lewiston.

'I'd like you to try it out in a typical German town,' said Reggie. 'Are there any typical German towns?'

'All German towns are typical,' said E. L. Campbell-Lewiston.

Reggie sipped his coffee thoughtfully, and said nothing. E. L. Campbell-Lewiston waited uneasily.

'Is there any particular way you want me to handle the new ice creams?' he asked at length.

'Wanking much these days, are you?' asked Reggie.

'I beg your pardon?'

'We used to call you the phantom wanker. No wonder you could never hit the bloody target.'

E. L. Campbell-Lewiston stood up. His face was flushed.

'I didn't come here to be insulted like that,' he said.

'Sorry,' said Reggie. 'I'll insult you like this, then. You don't clean your teeth properly, you slovenly sod.'

'Just who do you think you are?' said E. L. Campbell-Lewiston.

'I think I'm the man in charge of the new exotic ices project,' said Reggie. 'I'm the man who's expecting you to take Germany by storm, and I have every confidence you will. I was tremendously impressed by your article on the strengths and limitations of market research in the *International Deep Freeze News*.'

'Oh thank you.'

They stood up and Reggie handed Mr Campbell-Lewiston his raincoat.

'Yes, I found your analysis of the chance element inherent in any random sample very persuasive.'

'I hoped it was all right.'

At the door E. L. Campbell-Lewiston turned and offered Reggie his hand.

'Er . . . all this . . . I mean, is it some kind of new middle management technique?' he asked.

'That's right,' said Reggie. 'It's the new thing. Try it out on the Germans.'

Joan came in, pad in hand.

'C.J. wants to see you at eleven,' she said.

'Stuff C.J.,' he said. 'I'm sorry about yesterday, darling.'

'It was one of those things,' she said.

'It did happen, didn't it? You did come to my home yesterday?'

'Well of course I did, silly.'

He held his hand out towards her across his desk and she stroked it briefly. Her skirt was working its way up her leg, but today she didn't pull it down.

It had begun to rain. A train clattered along the embankment.

'We'd better start work,' he said.

'I suppose so.'

He was shy of dictating to her. It seemed so foolish, when you wanted to make love, sending letters about mangoes.

'What about tonight?' he said.

'I suppose I could get a baby-sitter.'

'What about your husband?'

'He's away – on business.'

'Tonight, then.'

'Tonight.'

'I suppose we'd better start, then.'

'I suppose so.'

'Your breasts are wonderful.'

She blushed.

'To the Secretary, Artificial Sweetening Additives Research Council. Dear Sir . . .'

Reggie strode purposefully across the thick carpet, trying to look unconcerned, as befitted a man starting a new life.

'You wanted to see me, C.J.?' he said.

'Yes. Sit down.'

The pneumatic chair welcomed him to its bosom with a sympathetic sigh.

'Don't forget you're coming to dinner tomorrow evening, C.J.,' he said.

'No. Mrs C.J. and I are looking forward to it immensely.'

'Good.'

'By the way, Reggie, Mrs C.J. doesn't see eye to eye with our piscine friends. I hope that doesn't upset any apple carts.'

'No, C.J.'

'People and their fads, eh?'

'Not at all.'

'Still, if you don't like something, you don't like it.'

'Too true.'

'No use kicking against the pricks.'

'Certainly not, C.J.'

'Neither Mrs C.J. nor myself has ever kicked against a prick.'

'I imagine not, C.J.'

'Now, to business,' said C.J. 'I didn't get where I am today by waffling.'

'No.'

'Never use two words where one will do, that's my motto, that's my axiom, that's the way I look at it.'

'Absolutely, C.J.'

The treble glazing in C.J.'s windows kept out all noise. There was a thick, carpeted silence in the room.

'Would it surprise you, Reggie, to learn that overall sales, across the whole spectrum, were down 0.1 per cent in April?'

'Not altogether, C.J.'

The Francis Bacon stared down as if it knew that C.J. had bought it for tax purposes.

'I don't say to myself: "Oh well, C.J., it's a bad time all round." I say: "C.J., this is intolerable." But I don't say to you: "Pull your socks up, Reggie." I say to you: "Overall sales, across the whole spectrum, were down 0.1 per cent in April." I leave you to draw your own conclusions – and pull your socks up.'

'Yes, C.J.'

'I didn't get where I am today without learning how to handle people.'

'No, C.J.'

'I give them a warning shot across the bows, but I don't let them realize that I'm giving them a warning shot across the bows.'

'Yes, C.J.'

'Not that I want to be entirely surrounded by yes-men.'

'No, C.J.'

'So there it is, Reggie. Go full steam ahead on the exotic ices project, no holds barred, this is the big one, but don't forget the whole spectrum.'

'I won't, C.J.'

'How did it go with Campbell-Lewiston?'

'Very well indeed, C.J.'

C.J. gave Reggie a cool, hard look.

'Middle age can be a difficult time,' he said. 'Not that we're one of those firms that squeeze chaps dry and then abandon them. We value experience too highly.'

Joan's eyebrows said, 'How did it go with C.J.?'

His hunched shoulders said, 'So-so.'

That was how people talked about C.J.

'Tea trolley!' shouted the tea lady over by the lift.

'Coffee?' said Reggie.

'You know my rules. I pay my way.'

Stupid woman. I'm worshipping your body, and you talk to me of rules.

'I'm buying you a coffee,' he said sharply.

'Well all right then. Just this once. Just a coffee, though.'

He bought her three jam doughnuts and a cream horn.

'Tonight,' he said.

'Tonight,' said Joan.

The phone rang. It was Elizabeth.

'Mother's having an operation tomorrow,' she said. 'She's convinced she's going to die. She wants you to come down tonight. She thinks it'll be her last chance of seeing you.'

He bought some chrysanthemums in London but they wilted on the train.

In his briefcase there were grapes, oranges and a paperback by Georgette Heyer.

He sat in the crowded buffet car. On the menu there were 'eggs styled to choice with hot buttered toast, poached or fried'. The style of his egg was fried and broken.

'They're all breaking today. I can't do nothing with them,' explained the steward. 'It's making my bleeding life a misery, I can tell you.'

'We all have our problems,' said Reggie.

They passed Gatwick. A big squat jet was taking off in the grey murk. The train slowed down. Reggie willed it to go faster, to get him to Worthing while the flowers still had some life in them.

Workmen in luminous orange jackets stood and watched the train as it passed. It began to gather speed. Reggie ordered another coffee. He would have preferred a Carlsberg and a miniature bottle of whisky, but he didn't want his mother-in-law to smell weakness on his breath.

There were brief snatches of rich, wooded countryside between the trim, boxy towns, and along the south coast there were glimpses of an oily uninviting sea.

He took a bus to the hospital. The air was heavy – hostile to chrysanthemums. The town smelt of rotting seaweed and chips. At the entrance to the hospital there was a stall selling fresh flowers.

The corridors of the hospital smelt of decline and antiseptic, and they reminded Reggie of his future. He found Blenheim Ward without difficulty. A coloured nurse wheeling a trolley of syringes and swabs smiled at him as he entered.

There were ten beds on the left and ten on the right. All were occupied. On the trestle table in the middle of the ward there were cut-glass vases full of roses and chrysanthemums.

Elizabeth's mother was in the sixth bed on the right, propped up on two pillows, surrounded by chrysanthemums, grapes, oranges and paperbacks by Georgette Heyer. Elizabeth sat at her bedside.

Elizabeth smiled nervously at Reggie, and as she kissed him her eyes were imploring him to behave.

'I brought you these,' he said, embarrassed, holding out the flowers. Elizabeth's mother looked pale.

'Oh, Reginald, you shouldn't have,' she said.

'They wilted on the train.'

'Never mind,' said Elizabeth. 'It's the thought that counts.'

'Get a chair, Reginald,' commanded her mother.

There were two tubular chairs wedged together at the far side of the bed. They had got jammed together. Reggie pulled and pushed and twisted, but he couldn't disentangle them. In the end he took both chairs.

'Sorry,' he said to the woman in the next bed.

'That's all right,' said the woman.

81

'She can't hear you,' boomed Elizabeth's mother. 'She's as deaf as a post.'

The 'deaf' woman gave her a venomous look.

Reggie sat on the chairs. They wobbled. He grinned sheepishly at Elizabeth.

'You'll stay the night, won't you?' said Elizabeth.

'Yes. I'll stay,' said Reggie.

He opened his briefcase, took out the oranges and grapes and a paperback by Georgette Heyer.

'I brought you these,' he said.

'Now that's very naughty of you, Reginald,' said his mother-in-law.

Reggie was stung. She didn't even say thank you.

'I won't be able to take them where I'm going,' she said.

Reggie's eyes met Elizabeth's.

'You aren't going anywhere,' said Elizabeth. 'You're going home.'

'Of course you are,' said Reggie.

'You'll find you've not been forgotten,' said his mother-in-law.

'Mother, please.'

'You can do what you like with the silver but I want you to keep the grandfather clock. And I'd like you to look after Edward's gold hunter. He was attached to that watch.'

'It's very kind of you. Thank you very much,' said Reggie. 'But you're going to be all right.'

'We'll see. Mind you, the doctors are all English, I'll say that for them.'

Reggie looked round the ward. Most of the women were elderly. A few had elderly husbands at their bedsides, hushed and helpless. Some had nobody. They had retired to Sussex, to bungalows by the sea. Now their husbands had died, they knew nobody, their bungalows were two miles from the sea, their sons were in New Zealand, they couldn't manage the hill up from the shops, they were ill.

'You'd better put the chrysanths in a vase,' said Elizabeth's mother. 'We don't want them dying. They must have cost enough.'

'I can afford them,' said Reggie.

'I hope so,' said Elizabeth's mother.

No, thought Reggie, you still don't think I can support your Elizabeth in the manner to which you think she should expect to be accustomed.

He went along to the nurses' room and filled a vase with water. He walked back, braving the stares of the old ladies. He was Goofy Perrin and he clutched the vase firmly.

He sat down on his chairs and handed the vase to Elizabeth. She arranged the flowers.

'Very nice,' said her mother.

'He assured me they'd last the journey,' said Reggie.

'You were done,' said Elizabeth's mother.

Elizabeth's hand touched Reggie's, squeezed it, as much as to say: 'You're always done – and I love you for it, huggable old bear.' But Reggie was not in the mood. He removed his hand. Then he felt awful, and felt for Elizabeth's hand and squeezed it.

It was seven forty-four. There were still forty-six minutes to go.

'What did you have for supper?' he asked.

'Sausages and mash, and tapioca. Revolting,' said his mother-in-law.

An old woman three beds away stirred in her sleep and shouted: 'Henry! Stop it! Stop it, Henry!'

'She's been going on all day,' boomed Elizabeth's mother. '"Henry," she goes, "stop it. Stop it, Henry." She's mental, poor soul.'

Reggie was convinced that the whole ward could hear, and his skin crawled with embarrassment.

The coloured nurse came round with a trolley on which there were tins of Ovaltine, Milo and Horlicks.

'I'm afraid you don't get one, Mrs Anderson. Operation tomorrow,' said the coloured nurse.

'I don't want any,' said Elizabeth's mother.

The coloured nurse went on to the deaf woman, who plumped for Milo.

'I feel sorry for her,' hissed Elizabeth's mother at the top of her whisper. 'She's got such thick lips. But then I believe their men like thick lips.'

Seven fifty-one. Thirty-nine minutes to go.

'Tell us to go if we're tiring you,' said Reggie.

'Want to go, do you?'

'No, no. But we don't want to tire you.'

Seven fifty-two. Thirty-eight minutes to go.

'The people in the ward seem quite nice,' said Elizabeth.

'I don't talk to them,' boomed her mother. 'That one's as deaf as a post and the one on the other side isn't quite the thing at all.'

Stinging ants of embarrassment marched up Reggie's back.

'I'm sure they can hear you,' he whispered.

'I can't hear you. Speak up,' bawled his mother-in-law.

'I'm sure they can hear you,' he said.

'Nonsense!'

Seven fifty-three. Thirty-seven minutes to go.

'What did you have for tea?' said Reggie.

'Just a cup of tea, and a biscuit. The biscuit was soggy.'

Seven fifty-three and a quarter. Thirty-six and three-quarter minutes to go.

The clock struggled up the hill to eight o'clock.

'Do you like hippos?' said Reggie, and he heard Elizabeth's sharp intake of breath.

'What extraordinary things you do come out with sometimes, Reginald. Yes, as a matter of fact I've got rather a soft spot for them. They're so ugly, poor things. Do you like them?'

'No,' said Reggie.

The nurses drew the curtains around one of the beds. After a few moments there were animal screams from behind the curtains. Nobody took any notice. They talked, listened to their earphones or just stared vacantly into space.

Reggie disliked the sight of blood, gobs of spittle on pavements, the backsides of cats, injections, and animal screams from old women behind curtains. He had made himself face, inch by painful inch, some of these realities, but he had never conquered them.

There came another cry: 'Henry! Stop it! Stop it!'

'There she goes again. Have some grapes, Reginald.'

'I don't like to eat all the grapes I brought. It makes it look as if I bought them for myself,' said Reggie.

'Don't be absurd. Nobody's remotely interested in you,' said his mother-in-law.

Reggie reached out, tore off a handful of grapes and leant back in his chairs.

The grapes were sour. The fruiterer had done him.

The minute hand of the clock slipped slowly towards eight-thirty. The curtains round the old woman's bed were drawn back, and she was calm again. Elizabeth was talking to her mother about a mutual friend, and Reggie had a few minutes off. He spent them in Chilhampton Ambo. Nigel was lying beside him on the grain piled high in the truck as they went slowly up the winding track that led from Twelve Acre to the Dutch Barn. He was dreaming of Angela Borrowdale's riding breeches.

'. . . don't you agree, Reginald?' said his mother-in-law.

'What? Yes. Absolutely!'

Elizabeth smiled.

'I've always had a private ward before,' boomed her mother. 'But I can't afford it with all this terrible inflation. It's coming to something. I blame the Labour government. And you wouldn't see *them* in the public wards. You wouldn't see Harold Wilson and Roy Jenkins in the public wards. They'd have a private ward in the London Clinic just to have a carbuncle lanced. Your father would have turned in his grave rather than go in a public ward. I'm only glad he's been spared all this. Every time you open your paper! Hooligans and vandals and that dreadful Willie Hamilton, how would he like to be a queen? I blame television. Your father once saw David Frost in a restaurant, and didn't think much of his table manners. Though he is very kind to his mother.'

Reggie thought: 'This is me in twenty-five years' time, and Mark and Linda coming to visit me, and watching the clock, but it isn't going to be like that.'

It was almost time to leave.

'Look after her, Reginald,' said Elizabeth's mother. 'She's delicate, Reginald. Don't forget that.'

'She's never been ill since I've known her,' said Reggie.

'I dare say, but she's not strong. I know. I'm her mother.'

Reggie sighed.

'I'll look after her,' he said.

They stood up. Reggie took his chairs back. He put them in their place by the radiator.

'Thank you,' he said to the 'deaf' woman, although she had done nothing. 'Sorry,' he said to her, although he had no reason to apologize.

'That's all right,' she said.

'You're wasting your breath. She can't hear you,' said Elizabeth's mother.

Reggie went to say good-bye to his mother-in-law.

'Kiss her,' mouthed Elizabeth.

He kissed her mother on the cheek. She sniffed his breath to see if he'd been drinking.

'Be good, Reginald,' she said.

'And you. I'll see you soon,' he said.

'We'll see,' she said.

'Nonsense,' he said.

Reggie took Elizabeth's arm as they left the ward.

'Turn round and wave,' hissed Elizabeth out of the side of her mouth.

They broke step together, like two tennis players bowing to the royal box at Wimbledon. They turned and waved. Elizabeth's mother waved back vigorously.

As they walked down the corridor there was the clink of cups being washed up. A nurse was whistling, and they could hear the old woman crying: 'Stop it! Stop it, Henry! Stop it!'

*

The flat plain between the coast and the downs was covered in bungaloid growth. The lower slopes of the downs were scarred with estates of weird geometric shapes, cold, inorganic, loveless.

Elizabeth drove past bay windows, gnomes, crazy paving, rockeries, hydrangeas, terrazo tiling, timber facing and stone finishings, past bungalows called 'Ambleside' and 'Ivanhoe' and 'The Nook' and 'Villa Blanca' and 'Capri' and 'Babbacombe'. The road turned to the left and ran along the downs like a geological fault.

Her mother's bungalow was called 'East Looe', and it faced south. It was set between two ranch-style bungalows but it favoured a more English style of whimsy. It was L-shaped, with a huge rustic chimney piece in the corner of the L.

Reggie sat in front of the electric fire, while Elizabeth did the cooking. The ingle-nook was panelled with polystyrene, giving a Cotswold stone effect. He switched the fire on, as the evening was slightly cool, and the magical coals twinkled into life.

He sighed, sipped his mother-in-law's sherry, went out to take a turn round the garden. The evening was cold and clammy like dried sweat. Lights began to twinkle all over the coastal plain.

The garden was kept in regimental trim by an old soldier who came in twice a week, gave the lawns a short back and sides, planted things in rows, squared off the flower beds, and cut the rose bushes to identical shapes and sizes.

He went back into the kitchen to help Elizabeth.

'You're in the way,' she said.

'I'll go,' he said.

'No, stay, but stand somewhere else.'

He stood by the window. His legs ached with the tension of visiting the hospital.

Elizabeth dropped a spoon and cursed violently.

'Relax,' he said.

'"Relax!" he says. You've been prowling round like a caged lion ever since we got back.'

He kissed her on the back of the neck and put his arms round her waist.

'I'll ruin the gravy,' she said.

He pressed his body against her back.

'What's got into you tonight?' she said.

There was home-made vegetable soup and roast beef. After the soup Reggie drew the curtains.

Elizabeth sighed.

'She'll be all right,' said Reggie.

'I hope so.'

The beef was red and juicy.

'How old is she?' said Reggie.

'Seventy-three.'

'She'll be all right.'

There was fresh fruit salad to follow.

He wanted to leave the washing up but she insisted.

'I can't bear to come down to it in the morning,' she said.

'You can't go down in a bungalow,' he said.

'You know what I mean,' she said.

He pushed his hand up her skirt as she washed the dishes. It would be all right tonight.

He pressed too hard as he dried one of her mother's best sherry glasses, and it broke in his hands.

After that they went to bed. The visitors' bedroom was pink and white. Pink carpets, white walls. Pink blankets, white sheet. Pink lips, white skin.

'It doesn't matter,' said Elizabeth.

'It does to me,' said Reggie.

'I don't mind,' she said.

'I bloody well do,' he said.

She kissed him sympathetically.

'It's not all that important,' she said. 'You mustn't make too much of it. It happens to everyone.'

'Rubbish,' he said.

'It'll probably be all right tomorrow,' she said.

'It'll never be all right again,' he said.

A motorcycle roared past, shattering the night with its tactless virility.

'Go to sleep,' said Elizabeth.

'I'm not giving up that easily,' said Reggie.

He writhed and tossed. Elizabeth's fingers stimulated him tactfully. He felt an incipient response. He thought about factory chimneys and the Post Office Tower. But it was no good. He thought about Joan Greengross, Angela Borrowdale's riding breeches, huge breasts, the Wightman Cup played in the nude. All to no avail.

The sweat was pouring off him and his head ached. He admitted defeat and lay back exhausted.

Elizabeth kissed him gently on the lips.

'You've had a long day,' she said.

'Everyone has a long day, for God's sake, but they aren't all bloody well impotent,' he said.

'Visiting hospital is exhausting,' she said.

'For God's sake don't be so understanding all the bloody time. It makes me feel a complete fool,' he said.

'I understand just how you feel,' she said.

His mouth felt extremely dry. He longed for a glass of water.

'It's the bungalow,' she said. 'It put you off.'

'I must say it doesn't help,' he said. 'I was out in the garden earlier. Her gardener must be the only man in England who prunes salvias.'

Elizabeth kissed him on the right ear.

'I do love you,' she said.

He turned towards her and kissed her on the lips.

'I'm sorry,' he said.

'There's nothing to apologize for,' she said.

'You should have married Henry Possett,' he said.

'I didn't want to marry Henry Possett,' she said.

He tugged at the cord which dangled over their heads. Darkness descended on 'East Looe'.

Tuesday

'Excuse me,' said the tall thin man on Worthing Station. 'Aren't you Reggie Perrin?'

'Good Lord! It's Henry Possett!'

Henry Possett had a long, sharp nose and a receding chin. His lips were practically non-existent. He looked like the outline of a man in a cartoon.

It was a grey, misty morning. The train pulled in three minutes late. It was quite full already, and they had to sit with their backs to the engine. Reggie felt vulnerable, as if there was more likelihood of a crash because he couldn't see where they were going.

'Do you live in Worthing?' said Henry Possett.

'No,' said Reggie. 'We're visiting Elizabeth's mother in hospital.'

'How odd. Vera's in there too,' said Henry Possett.

'Your wife?' said Reggie.

'My sister. I haven't married. How is Elizabeth?'

'She's fine,' said Reggie.

'I'm glad to hear that,' said Henry Possett.

A light aeroplane was taking off from Shoreham airport.

'Are you still in the – er – ' said Reggie.

'Still in the same business,' said Henry Possett.

'Good,' said Reggie. Henry Possett worked for the government.

'You?' said Henry Possett.

'Still in the same old racket,' said Reggie.

It was high tide, and a German coaster was entering Shoreham harbour.

'Two children, wasn't it?' said Henry Possett.

'Yes,' said Reggie. 'Linda's married. Mark's on the stage.'

'Vera and I have shared a flat in Worthing for twelve years now. It's better than living alone,' said Henry Possett.

'I suppose so,' said Reggie.

'Ah well,' said Henry Possett. 'It's no use crying over spilt milk.'

'I suppose not,' said Reggie.

By Haywards Heath the train was really full. Conversation had dried to a trickle. Henry Possett got the crossword out. Reggie did the same.

'I shan't cancel tonight's dinner party,' wrote Reggie. 'Ha ha ha. Ha ha ha ha ha ha ha ha.'

'Finished,' said Henry Possett. 'Very easy today.'

He folded up his paper very neatly, smoothing the pages down with his long, thin fingers.

'Bloody hell,' wrote Reggie.

Doc Morrissey stared at Reggie gloomily. Owen Lewis from Crumbles had just told him, 'I've hurt my back. I think I must have strained it on the nest.' Owen Lewis hadn't believed him when he'd said that he'd got back trouble too. People never did believe that doctors could be ill.

Reggie was nervous. That meant it was going to be personal problems, and Doc Morrissey's heart sank.

'You've been to C.J.'s blasted fishing weekend, haven't you, Reggie?' he said, getting Reggie's medical card out of his filing cabinet.

'Yes,' said Reggie. 'I caught a trout.'

'I'm going this weekend. I've never caught a blasted fish in my life. Tell me, what's it like?'

Reggie told him what C.J.'s fishing contests were like. They were to convenience food circles what Royal garden parties are to the nation. Doc Morrissey scratched his ear gloomily with a thermometer and fixed his eyes on a diagram of the female chest.

'C.J. has delusions of grandeur,' he said, when Reggie had finished. He sighed. 'Now, what can I do for you?' he said.

'I've got this friend,' said Reggie. His eyes avoided Doc Morrissey's. 'He's too shy to speak to a doctor about it himself. He's – er – he's afraid he's going impotent.'

'How old is he?' Doc Morrissey consulted Reggie's card. 'Forty-six, is he, like you?'

'Forty-six-ish.'

'How long since he last – since he first thought he might be going impotent?'

'Two months and three days.'

Doc Morrissey tapped nervously on the desk with his thermometer.

'Has he had spells of apparent impotence before?' he asked.

'He's had short spells when he hasn't fancied it. But he hasn't had a spell quite like this when he's fancied it but hasn't managed it.'

'I see.'

'Is it sort of normal – I don't know much about these things – is it normal for someone of about forty-six to have this problem?'

'Something like fifty people out of a thousand are impotent at forty-six. Temporary spells of impotence are much more common.'

'I see.' Reggie stared at the surgery's frosted glass windows. 'What should I advise my friend to do?'

'Relax and stop worrying. Impotence can be caused by fear of impotence. Fear is a very potent thing.'

Reggie shifted awkwardly on his chair.

'My friend gets the impression from books that he may be slightly under-sexed,' he said.

'Characters in books are always over-sexed. Authors hope it'll be taken as autobiographical,' explained Doc Morrissey.

'I see. Well you've eased my friend's mind a bit,' said Reggie, standing up.

'Good,' said Doc Morrissey.

At the door Reggie turned to look Doc Morrissey in the face.

'So difficulties of this kind aren't unheard of?' he said.

Doc Morrissey returned his gaze mournfully. 'I've got a friend who hasn't managed it for five months,' he said.

In his lunch break Reggie bought large scale maps of Hertfordshire and Lancashire. He spread the map of Hertfordshire on his desk, plonked his pending tray down on the map and traced a line with his pen round the outside of the tray.

Then he did the same with the map of East Lancashire, using his waste paper basket instead of his pending tray.

Joan summoned David Harris-Jones and Tony Webster. Reggie handed them the maps and explained that the oblong wedge on the map of Hertfordshire and the circle on the map of Lancashire were the areas chosen by the computer for the sales campaign.

'Are you ready to go into action?' said Reggie.

'I'm just tying up one or two loose ends,' said David Harris-Jones.

'I'm just clearing the decks,' said Tony Webster.

'I'd like you both to go up to your areas and go around for a day or two with the area salesmen,' said Reggie.

'Great,' said Tony Webster.

'Super,' said David Harris-Jones.

Reggie felt an impulse to invite some more people to his dinner party. But not Tony Webster.

He got rid of Tony Webster but asked David Harris-Jones to stay.

'I wonder if you could come to a little do I'm giving tonight,' he said.

'Erm . . . I think so. In fact, I know so. In fact, thank you very much,' said David Harris-Jones.

Reggie asked Joan to come into his office. The sun was glinting in off the windscreen of C.J.'s green Bentley, parked in its special place beside the sooty embankment.

Joan sat with her skirt well up above the knee, pad poised for dictation.

'No letters now,' said Reggie. 'It's just that I'm giving a little do tonight.'

'Oh how nice.'

'Yes, well, it's a bit awkward really. About us, I mean.'

'I understand.'

Joan pulled her skirt down over her knees.

'I wonder if you'd get me Miss Letts-Wilkinson,' he said.

Joan left his office without a word. A few moments later his buzzer buzzed.

'Miss Letts-Wilkinson on green,' she said crisply.

'Hullo, Davina,' he said.

'Reggie, darling! This is a surprise to brighten my dreary little afternoon.'

'I know it's short notice, Davina, but would you like to come to the Perrinery tonight? If you're not dining out or anything.'

'I'd love to, Reggie. A quelle heure?'

'What?'

'At what time?'

'Oh. Seven-thirty.'

'Super!'

'I'll see you this evening, then, Davina.'

'Lovely!'

'Yes.'

'Bye, Reggie.'

'Bye, Davina.'

'And thanks.'

'Don't mention it.'

'No, honestly, thanks. Super.'

'Good.'

'Bye, Reggie.'

'Good-bye, Davina.'

'Lovely!'

'Good.'

He put the phone down and went into the outer office.

'Ring Directory Enquiries for me,' he said. 'Get the number of a Mr Percy Spillinger, of Abinger Hammer, and give him a ring.'

It would be fun to set Uncle Percy Spillinger alongside the C.J.s.

A few minutes later he heard her saying: 'Mr Spillinger? I've got a call for you. No, a call. C-A-L-L. Charlie-Able-Love-Love. Hold on.'

Reggie's buzzer buzzed.

'Hullo, Percy,' he said.

'Percy who?' shouted Uncle Percy Spillinger.

'No, you're Percy,' shouted Reggie.

'I know that, you fool,' shouted Uncle Percy Spillinger. 'Who're you? Charlie?'

'I'm Reggie Perrin.'

'What, that arse who married my niece and we got bombed and the booze ran out?'

'Yes.'

'How are you my boy?'

'Very well, thank you. Long time no see.'

'Long what?'

'Time no see.'

'Not with you, old boy. Line's bad. Damned telephone men, they're all idiots. What was that about the sea?' bawled Uncle Percy Spillinger.

'It doesn't matter,' said Reggie as quietly as he possibly could.

'Can't quite catch your voice. Not used to it. Long time no see,' said Uncle Percy Spillinger.

'Yes.'

'If you're Reggie Perrin, who's this Charlie?'

'Sorry. I didn't catch that. You're shouting.'

'I can't hear you. You're shouting,' shouted Uncle Percy Spillinger.

'What was it you said?' shouted Reggie.

'I can't remember. Last time I saw you your children were so high,' bawled Uncle Percy Spillinger. 'Oh, you can't see my hand over the phone, can you? Well, they were about as high as my telephone table. But then I suppose you've never seen my telephone table, have you?'

'No.'

'Anyway it was a long time ago, that's the point I'm trying to make.'

'Yes. Percy, the thing is, would you like to come to my house at dinner time tonight?'

'Will there be any booze?'

'Yes. Lots.'

'I'll come.'

'I'll send a car for – six-thirty.'

'Will Charlie be there?'

'There is no Charlie,' said Reggie. 'My secretary was spelling "call".'

'Not with you.'

'Call is spelt Charlie-Able-Love-Love.'

'Sorry. This line's terrible. Charlie Able what?'

'Love-Love. Love-Oboe-Victor-Easy.'

'Charlie loves Victor? Disgusting! I like a good time but I don't hold with perversion. It isn't natural.'

'There's nothing disgusting about it.'

'If Charlie's able, and Victor's easy, it sounds pretty disgusting to me,' said Uncle Percy Spillinger.

Reggie walked through the open-plan office to the loo. He was embarrassed in case people had heard his stupid conversation. He knew he was embarrassed because he could hear himself whistling.

There were two cubicles in the loo. And Tony Webster was standing in the other one.

Reggie couldn't go. Not till Tony Webster had left. And Tony Webster stood there, washing his hands and brushing his hair and saying what a stimulating experience the exotic ices project was going to be.

Damn Tony Webster, whose whole body functioned to perfection.

*

Elizabeth rang while he was dictating his evening letters to Joan.

'Well, she's had her operation,' she said. 'She's as comfortable as can be expected.'

'Oh, good.'

'There's no point in your coming down tonight. She won't recognize anyone.'

'No.'

'I'll have to stay down here for a bit.'

'Of course.'

He didn't want her to stay too long in Worthing. Not with Henry Possett there.

'Come back as soon as you can, won't you?' he said.

'Of course, darling,' she said.

Joan gave Reggie a quizzical look.

'Did they mind your cancelling the dinner party?' said Elizabeth.

'No,' said Reggie. 'Nobody minded.'

Joan pulled her skirt even further down over her knees.

At Waterloo Station he allowed the cracked old woman with the hairy legs to accost him.

'Excuse me,' she croaked. 'I wonder if you can help me? I'm looking for a Mr James Purdock, from Somerset.'

'I'm awfully sorry,' said Reggie. 'I'm afraid I can't.'

Uncle Percy Spillinger sat in the back of the hired Cortina. The evening sun shone on the back of his neck as they drove northwards through Leatherhead. He was wearing full evening dress with tails. He was smoking a pipe. He had a fine collection of coloured spills, and had brought four of them, in various hues, with green predominating, in the sense that two of the four spills were green. As they turned a corner the sun lit up his big red boozer's conk. He smelt of mothballs.

C.J. sat at the wheel of his dark green Bentley. Beside him sat Mrs C.J. C.J.'s speed never exceeded fifty miles an hour, in deference to the wishes of Mrs C.J.

'I wish we didn't have to go to this dinner,' said Mrs C.J.

'We all have to make sacrifices,' said C.J. 'I didn't get where I am today without making sacrifices.'

Davina Letts-Wilkinson sat with her beautiful legs hidden beneath one of the buffet tables of a semi-fast electric train. She was wearing a short glittering silky dress. It was cut low, revealing a pair of firm, unmilked breasts beneath the turkey-mottled skin of her middle-aged neck. As luck would have it, she had shaved her armpits that morning.

She added a little more gin to her tonic, and smiled at the young man sitting opposite her. He smiled back, then stared fixedly at the scenery.

Linda stood at the open bedroom window, stark-naked, letting her pores breathe.

'Must you stand at the window like that, darling?' said Tom, pulling on a clean vest.

'You're the one who told me how important it is to let your pores breathe.'

'Yes, but not in full view of the whole Thames Valley.'

Linda gave him a teasing, slightly malicious glance.

'I'm only just beginning to realize how bourgeois you are,' she said.

Tom felt a surge of irritation. He tied his yellow tie savagely so that the knot pulled at his throat. You didn't have to be bourgeois to object to your wife standing starkers in full view of the whole Thames Valley. Just because they were progressive-minded and had a folly in their garden and cooked with garlic, it didn't mean they were Bohemian. He was a reputable estate agent, noted for his witty adverts in the Thames Valley press. He had a position to keep up. If he didn't keep it up, their enlightened, non-bourgeois, rustic-urban life would collapse around their ears.

Linda fitted a bra over her sagging breasts. There were folds of flesh on her stomach, just as there were on his.

It was impossible to maintain any passion for a woman

who wandered around the house naked, but he couldn't tell Linda that.

'Come on, Lindysquerps. We'll be late,' he said.

Linda sighed. She wanted to be late. She dreaded dinner with her parents. And she had recently begun to discover an extraordinary fact. Tom, her lovely comfortable bearded Tom, bored other people stiff. It was their silly fault, of course, but it didn't make it any less embarrassing for her.

She couldn't understand why he didn't make love to her so often these days. Goodness knew, she gave him enough encouragement, wandering around in the nude half the time.

She dressed slowly. With luck they'd miss most of their pre-dinner drinks. That was always the stickiest time.

The drinks and glasses were on the sideboard. At suitable points all round the room there were Oxfam ashtrays, and coasters which Elizabeth had bought from the Royal Society for the Protection of Birds. They had charming pictures of British birds on them. A series of bowls, decorated with pictures of dying country crafts, had been filled with olives, crisps, peanuts, cocktail onions and twigs. The french windows were open, and the rich evening sunshine was streaming in.

Davina was the first to arrive. She kissed him on the cheek, and handed him a huge bunch of roses.

He offered her a drink and she chose a dry martini.

'Where's Elizabeth?' she asked.

'She's at her mother's. Her mother had an operation this morning. It was successful, I'm glad to say.'

Davina sat on the settee and crossed her beautiful legs.

'So we're alone,' she said.

'Till the others come.'

'Oh. Oh, I see.'

She blushed and uncrossed her legs. There was an awkward pause.

'God, I needed this drink,' she said. 'C.J. was a pig this

99

afternoon.' She flashed a smile at Reggie. 'Who else is coming?'

'C.J.'

'What? Why didn't you tell me? I wouldn't have worn this. This isn't C.J. at all. Fancy not warning me. Just like a man.'

Next to arrive was Uncle Percy Spillinger.

'Good lord! You're in tails,' said Reggie.

'Don't you dress? Oh! Don't know the form these days,' said Uncle Percy Spillinger.

He kissed Davina gallantly on the hand. 'You're more beautiful than ever, my dear,' he said.

'I didn't know you two knew each other,' said Reggie.

Uncle Percy Spillinger stared at him in astonishment.

'I'm her blasted uncle, man,' he said.

'This isn't Elizabeth, Percy. This is Davina Letts-Wilkinson.'

'You're more beautiful than ever, whoever you are,' said Uncle Percy Spillinger.

Next to arrive were the C.J.s. Mrs C.J. carried a medium-sized bunch of roses, and when she saw Davina's larger bunch she developed a pink spot on both cheeks.

They stood in a little circle in the middle of the room, while Reggie poured drinks.

'I presume your wife's in the kitchen,' said C.J.

'No. She's dead,' said Uncle Percy Spillinger.

'What?' said C.J.

'He's talking about his wife,' explained Reggie.

'She died in 1959. I buried her in Ponders End. Why on earth would I keep her in the kitchen? Man's a dolt,' said Uncle Percy Spillinger.

Reggie explained why Elizabeth couldn't be there. C.J. proposed a toast to her mother's speedy recovery. They sat down. Reggie pressed snacks upon them, but they ate only sparingly.

'I like your pictures,' said Mrs C.J. 'Are they Scotland?'

C.J. gave her a look.

'The Algarve,' said Reggie. 'Our dentist paints them.'

'What's his name?' said C.J.

'Snurd.'

'I don't think I've heard of him. Has he much of a reputation in the art world?' said C.J.

'No, but he's a good dentist,' said Reggie.

'It doesn't sound as if they're a very good investment,' said C.J.

'I didn't buy them as an investment,' said Reggie.

'I once bought six sets of false teeth in a bazaar in Tangiers,' said Uncle Percy Spillinger. 'You never know, a thing like that might turn out to be worth its weight in gold. I thought I might find some chap, lost his teeth, be glad of a spare set.'

'Gorgeous,' said Davina.

C.J. frowned at her dress.

'I never could resist a bargain,' said Uncle Percy Spillinger.

'I think the weather's picking up again,' said Mrs C.J.

Reggie gave C.J. and Uncle Percy Spillinger large whiskies, managed to prevail upon Mrs C.J. to have some more medium sherry, and insisted on Davina having another dry martini.

David Harris-Jones arrived, looked dismayed at seeing C.J., said, 'I say, I didn't know you were going to be here sir,' to which C.J. said, 'Now then, David, no formalities,' to which David said, 'No, sir. Of course not.'

At last Tom and Linda arrived. Further introductions were effected. Tom apologized for being late, giving Linda a sharp glance. Reggie explained Elizabeth's absence.

'I do think mother might have told us,' said Linda.

'I don't expect she wanted to worry you,' said Reggie.

Reggie poured drinks all round. Only Mrs C.J. refused. She said, 'Don't forget you're driving,' to C.J. out of the corner of her mouth, and he flashed her a furious look.

'Is this a – maybe I'm wrong – some sort of a woodpecker on my mat?' said David Harris-Jones hurriedly.

'Yes. Great spotted,' said Davina.

'I once bought a stuffed woodpecker in Chipping Norton,' said Uncle Percy Spillinger. 'I bought it for a rainy day.'

'What's this on my mat?' said Mrs C.J., and C.J., who

hadn't got where he was today by looking at birds on mats, gave her a look which said: 'Shut your trap.'

'Corn bunting,' said Davina.

Trust Mrs C.J. to get the drabbest mat, thought C.J. What was wrong with the woman?

'It was reduced,' said Uncle Percy Spillinger. 'It was faulty you see. I don't suppose there's much call for faulty woodpeckers.'

'How come you know so much about birds, Davina?' said Reggie.

'I used to go out with an ornithologist,' said Davina.

'Lucky fellow,' said Uncle Percy Spillinger. 'You haven't half got a nice pair of pins on you.'

'We get a terrific lot of birds in our garden,' said Linda, and immediately wished she hadn't. It would set Tom off.

'I put up several nest boxes last year, and they've been very successful,' said Tom. 'I love birds. When I was courting Linda we used to go on long bird-watching rambles, didn't we, squiffyboots?'

Reggie smiled. They needn't have worried when Linda came home looking as if she'd been pulled through a hedge backwards. She had been pulled through a hedge backwards.

'We always ended up in some lovely country restaurant,' said Tom. 'Remember the day we saw the marsh harrier and had that marvellous woodcock bourguignonne?'

There was a pause.

'Mrs Spillinger had pins like yours,' said Uncle Percy Spillinger. 'She was short-sighted. She ate my stuffed woodpecker, and died.'

'You have my deepest sympathy,' said C.J.

'It happened in 1921,' said Uncle Percy Spillinger. 'I'm speaking of the first Mrs Spillinger.'

'Have another olive,' said Reggie.

'No, thanks. I must leave room for what's to come,' said Mrs C.J.

'If there is anything to come,' muttered C.J. into her ear.

'Oh,' she said.

102

'What's that?' said Reggie.

The pink spots reappeared on her cheeks.

'I thought I saw a mouse,' she said lamely.

'These bowls are lovely,' said David Harris-Jones hastily. 'There's a thatching scene on this one.'

'These old country crafts are dying out,' said Tom.

'Not before time,' said C.J.

'We can't agree with you there, can we, Lindyplops?' said Tom.

'All this nostalgia for the past. What this country needs is a bit of nostalgia for the future,' said C.J.

'I buried her in Ponders End,' said Uncle Percy Spillinger.

'I thought as it's a nice evening it might be warm enough in the garden,' said Reggie.

Their hearts leapt. Food!

Reggie led them out into the garden. There was no sign of any preparations for a meal.

Gallantly they admired his garden. The absence of damp mould, dry scourge, leaf rash, red blight and horny growth was warmly praised. Uncle Percy Spillinger walked with the assistance of Davina's slender left arm.

'You've got green fingers, Reggie,' said C.J.

'I once bought a finger off a chap I met in a pub in Basingstoke,' said Uncle Percy Spillinger.

An aeroplane was leaving a white trail right across the sky.

'I thought in the event of accident a spare finger might come in handy,' said Uncle Percy Spillinger.

'Do you have a nice garden?' said David Harris-Jones.

'We think so,' said Linda. 'We've gone in for shrubs rather than flowers.'

'We're shrub people,' said Tom.

The albino blackbird flew into the garden, saw the crowd, pinked with alarm, and flew back into the Milfords' garden.

'I mean some chap might have said to me: "It's a blasted nuisance. I seem to have lost a finger,"' said Uncle Percy Spillinger. 'And I'd be able to say: "Say no more. I've got just the thing for you back at the hotel. I could let you have it for a couple of quid."'

'Gorgeous,' said Davina.

Tom took Linda to one side by the compost heap and whispered, 'You said it was dinner.'

'I thought it was,' said Linda.

'It doesn't look like it.'

'Well we can't go until we're sure it isn't.'

'I'm starving.'

'So am I.'

By the potting shed Mrs C.J. whispered, 'Is it dinner?'

'I don't know,' said C.J.

'You said it was.'

'I thought it was.'

'What do we do?'

'Try not to put your foot in it, if it's possible. Leave it to me. I'll find out.'

'I think we may as well go in now,' said Reggie.

Mrs C.J. offered Uncle Percy Spillinger the assistance of her plump arm.

'Perfectly capable of walking,' he said gruffly.

Reggie offered them more drinks. C.J. and Mrs C.J. declined.

'Bit awkward for you, your wife being away when you've got everything to get ready for us,' said C.J.

'Not really,' said Reggie.

There was a pause. In the distance a passing goods train mocked them with its eloquence.

'Well, this is nice,' said Mrs C.J.

'Mind if I take my coat off?' said Uncle Percy Spillinger.

'Not at all,' said Reggie.

Reggie handed round twigs and crisps. Everyone took as large a handful as decency permitted.

'What was your line of country, Spillinger?' said C.J.

'Oh, this and that,' said Uncle Percy Spillinger, who was wearing purple braces. 'Sometimes more this than that, sometimes more that than this. I dug tombs in Egypt. I dived for pearls in the China Seas. I worked in an off-licence in Basingstoke. I got in a rut, you see. It was change, change, change all the time. It got very monotonous.' He smiled at C.J., then turned to David Harris-Jones. 'Are you in this stupid pudding caper too?' he said.

'Yes,' said David Harris-Jones. 'I mean, no. I mean, I am – but it isn't stupid – it's a very challenging and exciting and rapidly expanding field.'

'Well,' said Mrs C.J. helplessly, 'this is all very nice.'

'Super,' said Davina.

'Well it certainly isn't supper,' said Uncle Percy Spillinger. 'Joke,' he explained.

Reggie smiled.

'Let's have another drink and take it into the dining room,' he said.

They all accepted another drink, in their relief.

Reggie led the way into the dining room. It was a dark, dignified room, with an oval walnut table and dark green striped wallpaper. It smelt of disuse. The table wasn't laid, and there was no food to be seen.

'I thought you'd like to have a look at it,' said Reggie.

'Oh – er – it's – er – very nice,' said Mrs C.J.

'Are these pictures by Snurd as well?' said C.J.

'Yes,' said Reggie.

'I don't think there's going to be any food at all,' said Uncle Percy Spillinger.

'Oh, are you hungry? You'd better eat all these things up,' said Reggie.

He led them back into the living room, piled a bowl high with onions, twigs, olives and crisps, and gave it to Uncle Percy Spillinger.

Reggie insisted on giving them all one for the road.

'Your tits remind me of the third Mrs Spillinger,' said Uncle Percy Spillinger to Davina.

Davina blushed. C.J. frowned, and Mrs C.J. said hurriedly, 'What a lovely vase,' and then realized that there wasn't a single vase in the room. C.J. glared at her.

'She died in 1938. A road safety poster fell off the back of a lorry and killed her,' said Uncle Percy Spillinger. 'She was spared the outbreak of war, so it was a blessing in disguise.'

David Harris-Jones hiccupped.

'Sossy,' he said. 'Sorry. I mean sorry.'

Everyone watched Uncle Percy Spillinger as he wolfed down his bowl of cocktail delicacies.

'Been fishing much this year, C.J. old bean?' said David Harris-Jones suddenly.

'Not much. I've got my annual fishing contest this week-end, though,' said C.J.

'Who's going from the firm this year?' said Reggie.

'That idiot Doc Morrissey,' said C.J. 'I forget who else.'

'I'm not going,' said David Harris-Jones. 'Am I, C.J., old bean? The face doesn't fit, that's why.'

C.J. looked at David Harris-Jones with eyes that went straight through him.

'If the face doesn't fit, don't wear it,' said David Harris-Jones. 'And I'll tell you something else, C.J., old bean. What's grist to the mill is nose to the grindstone.'

C.J. sat still for a moment, trying to work out whether David Harris-Jones's proverb made sense or not. Reggie poured gin into everyone's glasses, regardless of what they had been drinking before.

Uncle Percy Spillinger moved closer towards Davina on the sofa.

'Am I a wicked old man?' he said.

'You're a darling,' said Davina. 'You're lovely. Everything's lovely. This is a lovely house. Isn't it a lovely house, C.J.? But then I suppose you've got an even lovelier house. But Reggie's house is very lovely.' She leant across towards the Parker Knoll chair and said in a loud whisper to Mrs C.J., 'C.J. doesn't like women in industry. He thinks they talk too much.'

'Do you like old beans, old bean?' said David Harris-Jones, and he roared with laughter.

'Your lips remind me of the sixth Mrs Spillinger,' said Uncle Percy Spillinger.

'How many wives have you had?' said Davina.

'Five,' said Uncle Percy Spillinger.

Davina kissed Uncle Percy Spillinger on the forehead.

'You're a darling,' she said.

'Hey, don't I get a kiss?' said David Harris-Jones.

Davina kissed David Harris-Jones, who was sitting on the piano stool.

'You needn't kiss C.J.,' said Mrs C.J. 'No doubt you've done that often enough already.'

'Kate!' said C.J. 'My wife finds company difficult,' he explained.

'We must be off,' said Linda.

'Me too,' said Davina. 'I could eat a horse.'

'I had horse once,' said Tom. 'It was surprisingly good. Marinade it in wine and coriander seeds, then . . .'

'Shut up, Tom,' said Linda.

David Harris-Jones fell off the piano stool and lay motionless on the carpet.

'Your kiss upset him, my dear,' said Uncle Percy Spillinger.

'My kiss? Why?'

'Wrong sex. He's a nancy-boy. A/c-D/c. He reminds me of a purser I knew on the Portsmouth-Gosport ferry. Wore coloured pants.'

'They don't have pursers on the Portsmouth-Gosport ferry,' said C.J.

'I wouldn't know about that, but he wore coloured pants. I bet you £50 *he's* wearing coloured pants,' said Uncle Percy Spillinger.

'You're on,' said C.J. 'Ladies, avert your eyes.'

He laid David Harris-Jones down on the settee. C.J. undid David Harris-Jones's zip and opened his trousers. The male members of the party watched as C.J. pulled David Harris-Jones's trousers down.

'They're not exactly coloured,' said C.J.

107

'They're not exactly plain, though, are they?' said Uncle Percy Spillinger.

David Harris-Jones's underpants were plain white, but they were embroidered with the face, in blue cotton, of Ludwig van Beethoven.

'The bet is null and void,' said C.J.

'I agree,' said Uncle Percy Spillinger.

'Take me home, Tom,' said Linda.

'Just a moment,' said Reggie. 'I think I'd better tell you why there was no food. It's because we're all greedy. There's not enough food in the world yet we all have dinner parties, Tom talks of nothing but food, it's about time something was done about it. You would have had paté, red mullet, fillet steak, lemon meringue pie and cheese. Instead I'm sending the money to Oxfam. Here's my cheque for £20. You would all have to invite us back, so instead you can all write out cheques for Oxfam as well.'

C.J. drove slowly, because he knew he had had too much to drink.

'I'm starving,' he said. 'What use is that to Oxfam? We could have had a damned good dinner and sent twice as much to Oxfam.'

'But you wouldn't have done,' said Mrs C.J.

'Your remark about the Letts-Wilkinson was inexcusable,' said C.J. 'There's absolutely no excuse for saying something as inexcusable as that.'

His engine hummed expensively. His headlights emphasized the mystery of woods and hedgerows. But C.J. had no eyes for mystery.

'I don't know what's come over you these days,' he said.

'Don't you?' said Mrs C.J.

'No, I do not,' said C.J.

'Then it's about time you did,' said Mrs C.J.

C.J. pulled up with a squeal of brakes.

'Get this straight,' he said. 'Make a public exhibition of yourself at home if you must, but not in public. I cannot afford to have you letting the side down. I didn't get where I am today by having you let the side down.'

'Where are you today?' said Mrs C.J. scornfully.

Tom drove slowly, because he knew he had had too much to drink.

'I'm worried about your father,' he said.

'Well don't you think I am?' said Linda.

A tawny owl flew across the road.

'Tawny owl,' said Tom. 'Did you see the tawny owl?'

'Bugger the tawny owl,' said Linda.

Tom drove on in silence. A stoat ran in front of the car, but he refrained from comment.

'Why did you tell me to shut up?' said Tom.

'You were being a bore.'

'What?'

'You're a boredom person, Tom.'

Tom ground his teeth and drove slower still to annoy Linda, but he said nothing. He had an ideal marriage, and he wasn't going to let his own wife spoil it.

Davina Letts-Wilkinson shared Uncle Percy Spillinger's hired car, at Uncle Percy Spillinger's insistence.

'To Abinger Hammer, by way of Putney Heath,' he said.

'Cost you, guv,' said the driver.

'Expense is no object,' said Uncle Percy Spillinger. He put his right hand on Davina's left knee, in the dark privacy of the back seat. They were going fast, along a dual carriageway.

'When I said you had lips like the sixth Mrs Spillinger, I was proposing marriage,' he said, and the driver swerved suddenly into the middle lane, causing an outburst of hooting from behind.

'I know,' said Davina.

'I know I'm not an ideal catch,' said Uncle Percy Spillinger. 'I'm eighty-one. For all I know I may not be capable.'

The driver swerved again and almost hit the central reservation.

'We have to face these things,' said Uncle Percy Spillinger. 'The spirit is willing but the flesh is an unknown quantity.'

The driver had moved over to the slow lane. Now he turned left and pulled up in a side road.

'Do us a favour,' he said. 'Finish your conversation before I drive on. I can't concentrate.'

'These are intimate matters, not for your ears,' said Uncle Percy Spillinger.

'I can't help hearing if you shout.'

'I'm slightly deaf,' said Uncle Percy Spillinger. 'It comes to us all.'

'Cor blimey, all right, I'll go for a flaming walk,' said the driver, and he got out of the car and began walking up and down the pavement.

Davina kissed Uncle Percy Spillinger on the lips.

'I'll give you my answer in the morning,' she said. 'I've had too much to drink tonight.'

'There is one thing,' said Uncle Percy Spillinger. 'It's only fair to mention it.'

'What is it?'

'Not every woman wants to be buried at Ponders End.'

'Ponders End?'

'All my wives are buried at Ponders End.'

'Oh.'

'But I won't insist on that, if you insist I don't. There's got to be give and take in marriage.'

'Yes.'

'Tomorrow, then.'

'Tomorrow.'

'You do like me a little bit, don't you?'

'You're a darling.'

'We'd better get that driver chappie in before he gets pneumonia.' He wound down the window and shouted out, 'Driver!'

The driver got in the car and slammed the door.

'Lead on, Macduff,' said Uncle Percy Spillinger.

'I'm not Macduff. I'm Carter,' said the driver.

'I spoke figuratively,' said Uncle Percy Spillinger.

'Macduff's got 'flu,' said the driver.

David Harris-Jones was lying on the settee. Reggie had pronounced him unfit to drive home.

'What did I say?' he asked.

'You kept calling C.J. "old bean".'

'What?'

'You said: "What's grist to the grindstone is nose to the mill."'

'What?'

'You said: "Do you like old beans, old bean?"'

'What? And then I apologized, did I?'

'No, you roared with laughter.'

'Oh my God! I said: "Do you like old beans, old bean?"'

'Yes.'

'Oh my God!'

'They had a bet about whether your underpants were coloured or not.'

'What?'

'They took down your trousers to see.'

'But I've got my Beethoven pants on.'

'Yes.'

'Oh my God! Did I really say: "What's grist to the nose is mill to the grindstone?"'

'Yes.'

'There's only one good thing about it,' he said. 'At least I wasn't wearing my Mahler jockstrap.'

After he'd put David Harris-Jones to bed in the spare room, Reggie rang Elizabeth.

'Hullo,' she said sleepily.

'Hullo. How's your mother?'

'She's all right. Do you know what time it is? It's nearly twelve. I was asleep.'

'Is it? Sorry.'

'Are you all right?'

'Of course I am. It all went off very well.'

'What went off very well?'

'Nothing. My quiet evening at home. My quiet evening at home went off very well.'

'Are you sure you're all right?'

'I'm all right, I tell you.'

An owl hooted, and a dog barked. Banal noises of a summer's night.

'You'll never guess who I met at the hospital,' said Elizabeth.

'Henry Possett.'

'Yes. He told me he met you on the train.'

'Yes. He never married, then.'

'No.'

'What, you just had a few words with him, did you, and then went home?'

'No, he took me out to dinner.'

'Oh.'

'You're not annoyed, are you?'

'No.'

'You are.'

'I am not annoyed. Why should I be annoyed? I couldn't care bloody less about Henry Possett.'

After he'd slammed the phone down Reggie became worried that he'd upset Elizabeth. He imagined her lying there, miserable, alone, unable to sleep. He rang her to apologize.

'Hullo,' she said sleepily.

'It's me again,' he said. 'I just wanted to say I'm sorry I woke you up.'

'You've just woken me up again,' she said.

'Sorry,' he said.

Wednesday

Reggie lay in bed, staring at the ceiling, trying not to think of Henry Possett. How could she want to kiss a man with such thin lips?

The clock struck two. It was warm, and he lay naked beneath a thin sheet. Sleep wouldn't come. His mind was a-whirl with plans.

First there was his speech on Friday. Then C.J.'s fishing contest on Saturday. After that his work would be finished. He'd go down to the south coast somewhere, leave his clothes in a neat pile on the beach. He'd need money. He began to work out a way of getting enough money for his needs, without arousing suspicion.

An owl struck three. He put his pyjamas on and went downstairs. He made himself a mug of cocoa, poured himself a large whisky, and sat at the kitchen table.

Ponsonby rushed in through the cat door and jumped onto his lap with a stifled yelp.

'Hullo, Ponsonby,' said Reggie. 'Your silly master couldn't sleep. No. He couldn't. He's got plans, you see. He's got to make a speech on Friday, to a conference to celebrate international fruit year. "Are we getting our just desserts?" by R. I. Perrin. What a silly title the silly men thought up. Well, it's not going to be quite what people expect. Then there's C.J.'s fishing contest. There'll be a surprise there as well.'

Ponsonby purred lazily.

'Cheers, Ponsonby. Here's to the success of my plans.'

He raised his glass of whisky. Ponsonby's puzzled eyes followed it. He looked at Reggie questioningly.

Reggie fetched a saucer of milk and put it by the table.

'Bottoms up, Ponsonby,' he said.

Ponsonby lapped up the milk, then returned to Reggie's lap.

'Well, we've got to do something unpredictable occasionally, haven't we?' said Reggie. 'Nobody thinks much of me. Past it. On the slippery slope. Sad, really. Not a bad chap. Always buys his round.

'I'll show them, though. I think I surprised them tonight. Well, you've got to. There comes a time in your life, Ponsonby, when you think: "My God, I'm two-thirds of the way to the grave, and what have I done?"

'Well I'm going to do a few things. I am. Things I should have done years ago. I'm going to put a few cats among the pigeons, if you'll excuse the expression.'

Ponsonby purred.

'I admire cats. You think you've got their number and suddenly off they go. You don't see them for a fortnight, you give them up for dead, and back they come.'

David Harris-Jones tottered into the kitchen, unable to stand up straight, his eyes bloodshot, his face a pale greyish-green. He staggered towards the sink.

'Cocoa?' said Reggie.

'Aspirin,' he gasped.

Reggie poured him a glass of water and gave him three aspirins. He was wearing a pair of Reggie's pyjamas, which were very much too broad for him.

Reggie soaked a dishcloth and handed it to him.

'Press it against your forehead.'

'Thanks.'

Ponsonby popped out for a bit of mousing. The two men sat in silence, in the kitchen, in the temperate night, David holding a damp dishcloth to his forehead, Reggie sipping cocoa and whisky. By the time they went to bed dawn was breaking.

Reggie was lulled to sleep by the dawn chorus. Birds sang on the farm, in his dream. He was riding on the cart that carried the grain to the barn, playing in the haystacks at threshing time, applying calamine lotion to his bites, in that chalky, grainy season. Half-awake, he lived again his incipient manhood, drank his first pints in the village pubs, and on the way home he peed on the glow-worms to put them out. Half-asleep, he saw Tony Webster riding naked through the streets of Chilhampton Ambo with Angela Borrowdale on a huge chestnut horse and he saw himself with white hair and a cracked, leathery old face, watching through a telescope. He looked through the telescope and saw himself watching through another telescope, and he was completely bald.

He left David Harris-Jones sitting on the bed in the guest room, in his vest, holding his pants and trying to summon up the will power to stand up and put them on. At his side was the damp dishcloth.

He didn't do the crossword on the train. All that seemed childish now.

The train reached Waterloo eleven minutes late. The announcer said, 'We apologize for the delay to the train on platform seven. This was for connectional purposes.' Again he allowed the cracked old woman with the hairy legs to accost him.

'Excuse me,' she croaked. 'I wonder if you can help me? I'm looking for a Mr James Purdock, from Somerset.'

'I'm awfully sorry,' said Reggie. 'I'm afraid I can't.' He wanted to say more, much more. 'I would help you if I could,' he said, but she had gone, and was even now accosting a loss adjuster.

Joan was wearing a midi that hid her knees. Reggie went briefly through his mail. It was necessary to perform all the normal functions. He must allay all suspicion between now and Friday, otherwise he would never get a chance to put his plans into action.

'How did your dinner party go?' she asked coolly.

'Quite well, thank you,' he said.

At ten o'clock Roger Smythe from public relations rang. Reggie arranged to meet him for lunch next day to discuss his speech for Friday.

Leslie Woodcock from Jellies looked in shortly afterwards.

'Hullo,' he said. 'I hope I don't intrude.'

'No, come in,' said Reggie. 'Sit down.'

Leslie Woodcock had a strange walk, with his legs held well apart due to a secret fear that his knees were swelling to an enormous size. He sat down and produced a grey folder which he handed to Reggie.

'I hope you're holding your Thespian talents available for our drama effort this year, Reginald,' he said in his dry, whining voice.

'Yes,' said Reggie. There wasn't much point in telling him that he wouldn't be there.

'Oh good. A lot of people found the Brecht rather heavy going last year, so we're doing a sort of musical spoof about the fruit industry. We're calling it "The Dessert Song". Book by Tony Briggs, lyrics by yours truly.'

'Oh, that sounds interesting,' said Reggie.

'I have the synopsis here. I rather fancy you for the part of Farmer Piles — a slightly risqué reference, perhaps, but all in good clean fun.'

'I'll have a look at it,' said Reggie.

'Well, I must get back. My jellies are calling me.'

'Thank you, Leslie.'

He dictated some letters rapidly, giving an impression of keenness.

The phone rang. Could Reggie see C.J. at eleven-thirty? Reggie could. C.J. wanted to see David Harris-Jones as well, and they couldn't trace him. Could Reggie oblige?

Reggie obliged. He rang his home. David answered weakly.

'How are you, David?' he said.

'I've just put my left sock on.'

'C.J. wants to see you at eleven-thirty.'

'Oh my God!'

Ditto, thought Reggie. 'Oh my God' for me too. It was all

116

very well no longer being afraid of C.J., but today's interview could be distinctly awkward. Supposing C.J. decided he was unfit to deliver his talk on Friday?

As soon as Joan had left his office he began his work. He had to learn how to forge his own signature, to sign his name in a way that was sufficiently like his own signature to pass muster in a bank, but sufficiently unlike it to pass as a forgery to a hand-writing expert.

He was concentrating so hard that he didn't hear the tea lady's shout of 'Tea trolley'.

Joan came in with a coffee and a jam doughnut. He hid his sheet of signatures hastily.

'My turn today,' she said, not coldly, but without any special warmth. 'You've done it three times running.'

'Thank you, Joan,' he said.

It needs as much generosity to receive charity as to give it. Are we so screwed up, he thought, that we can accept nothing without paying it back?

He entered the silent, padded world of C.J.

'Sit down, Reggie,' said C.J.

The carpet was so soft that he could hardly lift his feet. He trudged on, seeming to reach C.J.'s end of the room incredibly slowly. He sat down. The pneumatic chair sighed in sympathy.

'I suppose I should apologize for last night,' he said.

'It was an odd way of getting your point across, but it was worth making,' said C.J. 'As somebody once said, "I like what you say, but I don't defend your right to say it".'

'I think it was the other way round, C.J.'

'Oh. He got it wrong. Well anyway you see my point.'

Reggie stared at the Bratby, the Francis Bacon, the picture of C.J. holding the champion lemon mousse, the blue sky beyond the treble-glazed windows.

'Speech coming on all right?' said C.J.

'Very well, C.J.'

'Good. Big fillip for the firm, getting a speaker at the

conference. I didn't manage it without pulling one or two strings. I know you won't let us down.'

Marion brought in two black coffees. Perhaps C.J. was feeling a little frail this morning too.

'Mr Harris-Jones is here, sir,' she said.

'Keep him a moment, will you?'

'Yes, sir.'

C.J. leant forward and strummed on his desk.

'I want to talk to you about Harris-Jones,' he said.

'I think he was just a little drunk, C.J.'

'Yes, yes, not bothered about that,' said C.J. impatiently. 'The Letts-Wilkinson was drunk as well. Though I was not impressed with her dress. That sort of thing encourages hanky-panky.'

'Yes, C.J.'

'We aren't one of those firms where people can indulge willy-nilly in hanky-panky with their secretaries.'

'No. Quite.'

'Neither Mrs C.J. nor myself has ever indulged in hanky-panky with our secretaries.'

'I can believe that, C.J.'

C.J. turned the aluminium lamp onto Reggie's face. Reggie leant back in his chair, which made a noise like a fart. C.J. frowned.

'Sorry, C.J. It was the chair.'

'Very embarrassing. I've complained to the makers. Not at all the sort of thing we want at Sunshine.'

'Certainly not, C.J.'

'Do you think Harris-Jones is homosexual?'

'What? Good lord, no!'

'Hm. Spillinger does. Never had any complaints about him?'

'Never.'

'Never felt any stray fingers round your bum?'

'Good lord, no!'

'We'll have him in. I'd like you to stay.'

Reggie's heart sank.

David Harris-Jones knocked weakly, tottered over the

118

carpet, collapsed into a chair. He was wearing last night's crumpled clothes. He looked terrible.

'Cigar?' said C.J.

'No, thank you, C.J. I don't smoke cigars.'

'A-ha!' C.J. gave Reggie a meaningful look. 'Girl friend doesn't like the smell of them, eh?'

'Oh – I – cr – I don't actually have a girl friend at the moment, I'm afraid.'

'A-haa! You went to boarding school, didn't you, Harris-Jones?'

'Yes, C.J.'

'A-haa!'

Reggie stared at a stainless steel wall light, to avoid C.J.'s meaningful look.

'All of this arises out of last night's little shindig, Harris-Jones.'

'I'm sorry, C.J. I got drunk.'

'These things happen,' said C.J. 'Though they won't happen again. We're not one of those firms that believes in acting as a moral watchdog over you. Heaven forbid. Your private life is your own affair. Otherwise it wouldn't be private. Nevertheless, there have to be limits. I mean, just to give an example, we couldn't employ homosexuals. You might be sent to Russia. They'd play on your weakness, photograph you, blackmail you.'

David Harris-Jones said nothing.

'I wonder if you're altogether cut out for this kind of life,' said C.J. 'I mean perhaps you'd be happier in some other field. Running a boutique, for instance. Or opening a restaurant. Or you could have your own chain of hairdressing salons. There are plenty of avenues open for the gifted homosexual.'

David Harris-Jones's face turned from pale green to bright red.

'Are you? – look here – but surely – ' He managed with a supreme effort to get up from his pneumatic chair. 'You bastard!' he said. 'You bloody bastard!'

'Sit down!' barked C.J.

David Harris-Jones hesitated, then sat down. Reggie was sweating profusely.

'Why does the suggestion that you're a homosexual annoy you so much?' said C.J.

'Because — I don't know — I've nothing against them — some of my best friends — no, very few of my best friends — no, it's just that it's annoying because it's not true.'

'Fair enough,' said C.J.

'There's nothing wrong with being homosexual,' said David Harris-Jones. 'But I'm not.'

'Fair enough. Reggie, you're Harris-Jones's departmental head. Perhaps you'd like to have a word.'

'Yes. Er — certainly,' said Reggie. He felt a sudden desire to say 'parsnips'. For some reason he wanted to say, triumphantly, 'parsnips'. He mustn't. He must remain normal. He looked at C.J. Could C.J. see that he wanted to say 'parsnips'? Was that sort of thing visible? Control yourself, Reggie. 'You see, David,' he said. 'C.J. is naturally anxious, and so am I, to see that there is no hanky-panky connected with the firm.'

'Absolutely,' said C.J. 'I couldn't have put it better myself.'

'What C.J. was wondering, and I must say I agree with him,' said Reggie, and the words were as hard to swallow as a strawberry and lychee ripple, 'is whether it's suitable for a junior executive to wear underpants decorated with Beethoven.'

'Exactly!' said C.J. 'I didn't get where I am today by wearing underpants decorated with Beethoven.'

'What C.J. wonders, and I must say I wonder it as well,' said Reggie, 'is why you have a picture of Beethoven on your underpants.'

'I — er — I would have thought a man's underpants were his own affair,' said David Harris-Jones.

C.J. barked into the intercom, 'Get Webster for me.'

'I think what C.J. feels is that, although it is perfectly true that by and large a man's underpants are indeed his own affair, there could be occasions — in a traffic accident, for example – where this might not be so,' said Reggie reluctantly. 'I don't think it's altogether unreasonable to ask you to explain what after all are a somewhat unconventional pair of pants.'

'I admire Beethoven,' said David Harris-Jones angrily. 'I was in Bonn. I saw these pants. They had them in my size. They were seventy-three per cent Terylene. I bought them.'

'There, that wasn't so painful, was it?' said C.J.

'No, C.J.'

'Why don't you have a girl friend?'

'Well – you know – it's just that I – girls – er – opportunities in Haverfordwest weren't exactly – and I always – the truth is, women frighten me, sir.'

The intercom buzzed discreetly.

'Mr Webster is here,' said Marion.

'Send him in.'

There was a firm, yet not too firm, knock on the door.

'Come in.'

Tony Webster walked composedly, but not too composedly, towards them. He was wearing a double-breasted light grey suit and a pale purple floral shirt with matching tie.

'What would you do if I asked you to show me your underpants?' said C.J.

'I'd assume there was some good reason behind it,' said Tony Webster.

'Quite. Would you mind showing us your underpants?'

Tony Webster unzipped his trousers and pulled them down. His underpants were blue, but not too blue.

'Plain blue. An excellent colour,' said C.J. 'You see, Harris-Jones. A splash of colour, but not inconsistent with executive dignity. Well, I think no more need be said about that little incident.'

Tony Webster zipped up his trousers and the three of them left the room together.

Reggie sighed and mopped his brow with his handkerchief. David Harris-Jones sighed and mopped his brow with Reggie's dishcloth.

'That's my dishcloth,' said Reggie.

Tony Webster showed no surprise.

Reggie hurried out of the building. He had a lot to do during his lunch break.

He walked towards Waterloo Bridge and hailed a taxi.

'Parsnips,' he said.

'I don't know it. Is it a new restaurant?' said the taxi driver.

'When I say parsnips, I mean Bishopsgate,' said Reggie.

Davina was wearing dark glasses and looking extremely fragile. Uncle Percy Spillinger rang shortly after twelve.

'Hullo, my darling,' he bawled.

'Hullo.'

'The sun is smiling upon Abinger Hammer. Is it an omen? What is your answer, my little angel cake?'

'I can't speak freely here.'

'I haven't slept a wink all night.'

'I have to go now.'

'Say something to me, my treasure.'

'I must ring off.'

'What?'

'Give me a ring later.'

'What?'

'Give me a ring.'

'Straightaway. The best that Abinger Hammer can provide.'

Linda rang Worthing and caught her mother just before she went to the hospital. She told her all about Reggie's strange dinner party. Elizabeth said she'd come home as soon as the afternoon visiting was over.

Adam and Jocasta were looking at *Watch With Mother*, and Linda was sitting on the chaise longue. All three were naked.

'I didn't know whether to tell you,' said Linda.

'I'm glad you did,' said Elizabeth.

She put the phone down and watched the television. Lies. All lies. She switched it off.

'Hedgehogs aren't a bit like that,' she said.

*

Reggie had a busy lunchtime in the tall, narrow, crowded streets of the City. He visited eleven branches of his bank, and in each one he wrote out a cheque for thirty pounds, showed them his banker's card, and signed the cheque with his forged signature. He asked for the money in used fivers, saying the new ones sometimes stuck together.

When he had reached the end of his cheque book, he threw it in a waste-paper basket. He popped into the Feathers just before closing time. He was somewhat foot-weary, and he had three hundred and thirty pounds in his pocket.

The bar was empty except for Owen Lewis and Colin Edmundes.

'You're late,' said Owen Lewis.

'I'm having an efficiency drive,' said Reggie.

'Time and motion wait for no man,' said Colin Edmundes.

Reggie ordered two scotch eggs, forgetting that he hated them.

'Hey, I heard rumours you're giving Joan dick at last,' said Owen Lewis.

'That's a private matter,' said Reggie coldly.

'You old ram, you!' said Owen Lewis.

The scotch eggs tasted of sawdust.

'I hear Briggs and Woodcock are writing a musical,' said Owen Lewis.

'Yes,' said Reggie.

'The unspeakable in pursuit of the unsingable,' said Colin Edmundes.

Reggie left one and a quarter scotch eggs uneaten.

'Well, you pulled through,' said Elizabeth.

'So far.'

'You're going to be all right.'

She held her mother's hand. Her mother looked pale and elderly.

'Perhaps it would have been better if I'd gone,' said her mother.

'You're not to talk like that, mother.'

The Australian nurse wheeled the tea trolley round. She stretched a point and gave Elizabeth a cup.

'I shan't be able to come this evening,' said Elizabeth. 'Reggie's not well.'

'He's not strong. Mind you look after him.'

'Yes, mother!'

'That nurse is Australian. She has very dry skin.'

'Ssh, mother.'

'She can't hear.'

Elizabeth's mother sipped her tea and pulled a face.

'You'll feel better soon,' said Elizabeth.

'We'll see. Though I must say I have got faith in that doctor. He speaks so nicely.'

Elizabeth felt irritated. What had that got to do with it? Yet she checked her irritation. Hadn't she herself sounded rather like that, at the game reserve, about Adam and Jocasta?

Reggie was growing like his father and she was growing like her mother. She felt very close to her mother today, and yet also far away, like lying in bed when you weren't well and feeling tiny and enormous all at once.

Reggie's chrysanthemums were drooping in their cut-glass vase. The ward was filled with sunshine and flowers.

'She wants to rub oil into it,' said her mother.

'What?'

'Her skin. Nothing serious wrong with Reggie, I hope.'

I've believed in you all these years, God, thought Elizabeth. Please make it nothing serious. I want my Reggie.

A thin layer of high white cloud drifted across the sun. The afternoon was bright but hazy. Reggie was busy planning his speech for Friday. He hardly heard the trains rumbling past on the embankment.

Joan brought him tea and a macaroon. She didn't seem angry any more. There was so little time. So little time to spend with Joan, so little time to spend with Elizabeth.

'Can you come out this evening?' he said.

'Oh, I'd love to. I don't know. I don't know whether I can arrange it.'

'Can't your husband hold the fort? Can't you tell him you're working late?'

'I'll try.'

He couldn't get back into his speech. He rang Worthing but there was no reply. She was still at the hospital – or having tea with Henry Possett.

Oh, Reggie, you're supposed to have forgotten Henry Possett.

Joan was standing by his desk.

'It's all right for tonight,' she said.

His eyes met hers.

'Book us into a hotel,' he said.

The Elvira Hotel in North Kensington wasn't the Ritz. It was three early nineteenth-century houses knocked together. It had peeling stucco on the walls, and peeling walls underneath the stucco. But it was the twenty-seventh hotel Joan had tried, and the other twenty-six had all been full.

'I booked on the phone,' Reggie told the bored young desk clerk. 'Mr and Mrs Smith.'

The girl handed him the register to sign. She chewed gum constantly, and had Radio One playing on a transistor beneath the desk. He felt awkward. It was the dirtiness, the false name, the dull brown walls. It was unbearable when things turned out exactly the way you expected them to be.

He signed their names: 'Mr and Mrs Smith, of Birmingham.' Above their names in the register were Mr and Mrs Smith of London, Mr and Mrs Smith of Manchester, Herr and Frau Schmidt of Stuttgart, and Olaf Rassmussen, from Trondheim. Reggie felt sorry for Olaf Rassmussen, from Trondheim.

'Where's your luggage?' said the girl.

'We don't have any,' said Reggie, and he squeezed Joan's hand.

'You'll have to pay in advance. It's six pounds fifty with breakfast and ten per cent service.'

'I don't know if we're going to get good service yet, do I?'

'Service is included.'

'And we may not be staying for breakfast.'

'Breakfast is included.'

Reggie got out seven pounds, taking care not to show how much money he had in his pocket.

'I haven't got any change. Sorry,' said the girl.

'We'll wait,' said Reggie.

The girl went off reluctantly.

'Let's get upstairs,' said Joan. 'It's horrid here.'

'No. They're counting on that. It's a racket.'

An English couple wandered sadly into the foyer, on their way out. An Italian couple wandered wearily into the foyer, on their way in.

'Did you get to Madame Tussaud's?' said the Englishman.

'Yes. Madame Tussaud is good.'

'Yes. Very good.'

'Much good. Very many waxwork.'

Reggie was willing the Englishman to say something interesting to cheer up the weary Italians.

'Lots of waxworks,' said the Englishman.

'So many,' said the Italian woman, and they all laughed.

'Very like. Like what they are like,' said the Italian man.

'Good likenesses,' said the English woman.

'Yes. I am sorry. My English.'

'It's very good,' said the Englishman.

'No. I think not,' said the Italian man.

'Ah – well – *arrivederci*,' said the Englishman.

'Good-bye,' said the Italian man.

They all laughed.

Can passion, that hothouse plant, flower in this cold soil, thought Reggie.

'What's keeping that bloody girl?' he muttered.

'Come on,' said Joan.

'No. It's the principle.'

126

The girl came in slowly, with their change.

'About time,' said Reggie. 'About bloody time!'

'Room forty-eight,' said the girl. 'Fourth floor. The lift's stuck.'

They trudged up staircases increasingly narrow, on carpets increasingly threadbare.

Room forty-eight was a tiny box with ill-fitted cupboards of bulging brown hardboard. It overlooked a sooty parapet, stained with pigeon droppings.

They began to undress. Reggie watched Joan roll her tights back over the knobble of her much-desired knees. The slender thighs appeared, spindly arms, the exquisite breasts. He touched them, more out of sympathy than desire. He knew that he looked ridiculous with his hairy pale legs and paunch. He touched her neat little nose with his lips.

He knew that it would be no good. He was shaking, as if he was cold. He pulled back the blankets. They gave out a faint musty smell.

Damp. The sheets were cold and slightly damp, even in this heatwave. Olaf Rassmussen must have brought them, in his smack, from Trondheim.

'I'm afraid it isn't going to be any good,' he said.

She stood on his bare feet and held her body tightly against his.

'It'll be all right,' she said.

'Not here,' he said. 'It's too sordid here.'

'It doesn't matter,' she said.

'It does to me,' he said.

She sighed, and stepped off his feet. She sat on the cold bed and began to get dressed.

'An expensive five minutes,' she said.

'I'm sorry,' he said.

They got dressed in silence. In the corridor an American voice said, 'We went to the British Museum and saw the Crown Jewels.'

They walked down staircases increasingly wide, on carpets

decreasingly threadbare. Reggie put the key back on the counter of the reception desk.

'Thank you,' he said. 'The service was excellent. Breakfast was moderate. The bacon was good but the eggs were overdone and greasy. See it doesn't happen next time.'

The girl looked up at him with dead eyes. He handed her the fifty pence change that she had given him.

'Keep it,' he said.

They walked out into the evening sun.

'Why did you do that?' asked Joan.

'If that's her life, she needs it,' he said.

She put her hand in his and squeezed it. Desire, that hothouse plant, flowered. He pressed his thigh against hers. The pavements were hotter than the air, and a fine long sunset was beginning.

They went to an Indian restaurant and had mutton dhansak, ceylon chicken, mixed vegetables, fried rice, papadoms and two lagers each. They talked about all sorts of things and they were glad that they'd been born.

It was past midnight when he arrived home, stinking of curry, to find all the lights on and a very worried Elizabeth there.

'Where on earth have you been?' she said.

'Out,' he said.

'You stink of garlic.'

'I had a curry with some chaps from the office.'

'You look guilty,' she said.

'Me? No.'

He went into the kitchen and poured himself a glass of water. He was very dry.

'Ponsonby was starving. Haven't you been feeding him?' she said.

Ponsonby strolled into the kitchen with dignity.

'Tell Auntie Elizabeth what a good boy I've been while she's been away,' said Reggie.

Ponsonby miaowed curtly.

'How is your mother?' said Reggie.

'She'll pull through. She's tired.'

'It's only to be expected.'

Elizabeth gave him a long, serious look. Then she turned away.

'Linda rang me,' she said, putting on the kettle for some tea. 'She told me about your dinner party.'

'You should have seen their faces,' said Reggie.

'But, Reggie, why?'

'I felt like it,' said Reggie. 'It taught C.J. a lesson.'

'You can't go around teaching people like C.J. lessons.'

'Don't worry. He isn't angry.'

'Well, I don't know! Where's it all going to end?'

They took their cups of tea into the living room. They sat facing the television, even though it wasn't switched on.

'Why did you invite Percy?' she asked.

'I like Percy,' he said.

'Are you sure you're all right?' she said.

'I'll put a notice on the front gate, if you like: "Mr Reginald Perrin is all right. His condition is so satisfactory that no more bulletins will be issued until further notice."'

She smiled, a little sadly. Then she leant across and took his hands in hers.

'I love you,' she said.

They went upstairs. He lay on top of the bed and waited for her to come to him. She raised her eyebrows and he nodded and she went to make her preparations. When she came back they made love and it was very good and he didn't need to think about any artificial aids, not rollicking in haystacks or factory chimneys or a nude Wightman Cup or even Joan Greengross's breasts, but he thought of Elizabeth and he loved her. She moaned and writhed and he closed his eyes and grimaced and afterwards she said, 'You see. You're not impotent yet, you silly goose,' and he said, 'No. I'm not. I am a goose.'

She fell asleep and he lay there, listening to the clock striking and thinking how nice it would be just to stay with

Elizabeth, but he had work to do, he had souls to save, and if Elizabeth had seen his wide staring eyes she wouldn't have risen and fallen in her sleep like a sea reflecting the motion of a distant storm.

Thursday

Before he had his breakfast, Reggie went up into the loft and hid three hundred and twenty pounds, in used fivers, among the pile of faded curtains in his tuck box.

He ate a hearty breakfast. Elizabeth was much more relaxed now that their sex life had been resumed. In fact she had gone so far as to reward him with an extra egg.

He had a pleasant walk to the station, along the quiet streets of the Poets' Estate. The sky was grey but it looked as if the sun might break through at any moment.

In the eight-sixteen, rattling along, watching Peter Cartwright doing the crossword, Reggie thought about the cracked old woman. Who was she? What did she look like with nothing on? Did she ever clean her teeth? Did she ever look in a mirror? Who was Mr James Purdock, from Somerset? What traumas and personality inadequacies and hormone irregularities had conspired to turn her into a cracked old woman with hairy legs and a voice like an old rook? Had she ever slept with anyone? Did she know she wasn't normal? Was she happy?

They were almost at Waterloo. Over to the left he caught a glimpse of the Houses of Parliament, where they were busy plotting to foist a better Britain on us while we weren't looking. What plans had they for the cracked old woman? You'll be delighted, madam, to learn that we plan to build one thousand two hundred more miles of motorway, eighty miles of urban motorway, and by 1977 the whole of Europe will have achieved standardization of draught beer, pork pies and envelope sizes.

The train pulled in to Waterloo Station eleven minutes late, due to 'seasonal manpower adjustments'. Reggie knew what he must do. He walked slowly along the platform, in the dark respectable human river. His legs felt weak. He felt a sudden anxiety. Suppose she wasn't there?

But she was there. He walked casually towards her. His throat was dry.

'Excuse me,' she said. 'I wonder if you can help me. I'm looking for a Mr James Purdock, from Somerset.'

'I am Mr James Purdock, from Somerset,' said Reggie.

The old woman moved off, resignedly, to accost another commuter.

Reggie hurried after her, and plucked at her sleeve. She turned towards him.

'You don't understand me,' he said. 'You didn't hear what I said. I said I *am* Mr James Purdock, from Somerset. I'm the man you're looking for.'

She looked at him with staring, unseeing eyes.

'Excuse me,' she said. 'I wonder if you can help me. I'm looking for a Mr James Purdock, from Somerset.'

Joan was wearing a short red dress. It slid far up her thighs when she crossed her legs. She smiled at him out of playful eyes, and her lips were moist.

He dictated several letters. He didn't intend to ask her out again. He intended to remain faithful to Elizabeth until the end. But every now and then he paused to stroke her knees. It was the least he could do.

He found it difficult to concentrate on his work. The sun had still not broken through and he could feel the oppressiveness of the day. He kept wanting to use the wrong words, to say 'Dear Parsnip', or 'Yours Faithfully, a golf ball'.

Finally he could bear it no longer.

'Next one,' he said. 'To the Manager, Getitkwik Supermarts, Getitkwik House, 77, Car Park Road, Birmingham, BL7 EA3 5RS 9BD EAS JRV 4LD. Dear Sir or Madam. Your complaints about late deliveries are not only ungrammatical but also completely unjustified. The fault lies in your inability to fill in an order form correctly. You are a pompous, illiterate baboon. Yours faithfully, Reginald I. Perrin. Did you get that down?'

'I stopped. Did you mean it?'

'Of course. Take it down.'

He dictated the letter again. Joan looked at him in alarm.

'Next one. To the Traffic Manager, British Rail, Southern Region. Dear Sir. Despite my letter of last Friday, I note that you have taken no steps in the matter of the late arrival of trains at Waterloo. My train arrived this morning, as always, exactly eleven minutes late. It is becoming clear to me that you are not competent to hold your present job. You couldn't run a game of strip poker in a brothel. It would be obvious even to an educationally subnormal hamster that all the trains ought to be re-timed to take eleven minutes longer. You are living in a fool's paradise, all too typical of this country today. Yours faithfully, Reginald Iolanthe Perrin. P.S. During the pollen season Peter Cartwright's sneezing is rather offensive to those who, like myself, are allergic to sneezing. Once, Ursula having forgotten his tissues, he blew his nose on the special Rhodesian supplement of the *Guardian*. This might have been a sound enough political comment, but it was not a pretty sight. Why not divide compartments into Sneezers and Non-Sneezers? Got that?'

'Yes,' said Joan, looking at him with deep alarm.

'Anything wrong?'

'No. Oh no.'

As soon as Joan had left his office, Reggie realized the danger in sending the letters. He must continue to seem normal, or he would not be allowed to carry out his plans.

He rushed out into her office. She wasn't there, and nobody knew where she had gone.

Joan had gone to Doc Morrissey's surgery. She found the wizened medico in gloomy humour.

'Hullo, Joan. You find me in gloomy humour,' he said.

'What's wrong?'

'Middle age. Insecurity. Anxiety. One false move and I'm out.'

He swept a pile of splints off a chair.

'Well, well, it's nice to see you. What's the trouble? Chesty?' he asked hopefully.

Joan had been a bit chesty in the winter of 1967. He'd been able to examine her three times before it cleared up.

'It's not me,' she said. 'It's Reggie.'

'Oh.'

She showed him the letters, and told him what she knew of Reggie's recent behaviour. He stared gloomily at a diagram of the male reproductive organs.

'Do you know what's wrong with him?' she asked.

'Yes,' he said. 'Anxiety. Insecurity. Middle age. He's going mad.'

Doc Morrissey explored his left nostril with a hypodermic syringe.

'Should you do that?' asked Joan.

'No,' he said.

'What can we do?'

'Be nice to him. Give him as little to do as possible. Hope for the best. Sorry, Joan, I'm in a mood today. It *is* nice to see you. Would you like a drink? There's cough mixture, cod liver oil or I've quite a nice little mouth wash.'

'No, thank you.'

Doc Morrissey managed a smile.

'I'm not always such a misery,' he said. 'I've had a terrible morning.'

First there had been Leslie Woodcock from Jellies, convinced that his knees were enormous. Then Sid Bolton from Dispatch, who had stick-out ears, looked like Doctor Spock and was convinced he was the advance guard of a race from outer space, coming to take over the world. He'd been waiting in Dispatch for eleven years, and nobody else had come.

'Is there really nothing we can do?' said Joan.

Doc Morrissey waited while a particularly noisy train rattled past.

134

'Not really,' he said. 'Who's sane and who's mad? Cure somebody and they may get something worse. But you want to get off. Don't leave it so long next time.'

Reggie came back after looking everywhere for Joan, and found her sitting at her desk.

'Thank God you're back!' he said. 'Where've you been?'

'Shopping,' she lied.

'You haven't sent those letters, have you?'

'Not yet.'

'I meant those last two as a joke.'

'Oh. Good!'

'Yes. I think I almost took you in.'

'Yes.'

'Pretty good joke.'

'Yes.'

It was time to begin the next stage of his financial deception. He rang his bank.

'It's Reginald Perrin here,' he said. 'I'm afraid I've been a bit of a fool. I've gone and lost my cheque book and my banker's card . . . Yes, well, either I've been robbed or I've been very careless. I'm rather worried. I thought I'd better report it.'

He nipped out to the Feathers for a quick one and that made him feel better. He spent the rest of the morning preparing his speech, and then he had lunch with Roger Smythe from Public Relations.

'There's so much boozing involved in PR work,' said Roger Smythe. 'It gets you down. I need a drink.'

They sat in an alcove in the Axe and Rainbow. It had big Victorian windows and was scheduled for demolition.

Over their ham sandwiches and pints of gassy beer, Reggie gave Roger Smythe a brief outline of his speech. Of course he didn't tell him what he was actually going to say. If he had, there would have been no speech.

'I might be able to do something with it,' said Roger

Smythe. 'If you could make it a bit more controversial, it might even rate a paragraph in '*Dessert News*.'

Reggie thought he might be able to make it more controversial.

'This beer's foul. I need a quick whisky to pick me up,' said Roger Smythe.

They went up to the bar for their quick whiskies.

'Two earwigs, please,' said Reggie.

'Earwigs?' said the barmaid.

'Whiskies,' said Reggie.

Roger Smythe gave him a peculiar look. Careful, thought Reggie. You mustn't suddenly say 'earwigs' for no good reason.

'Earwigs?' said Roger Smythe.

'Rhyming slang,' said Reggie. 'Er — earwig's daughter, whisky and water.'

'I don't get it,' said Roger Smythe.

Elizabeth rang Jimmy from a public phone box inside Worthing Hospital. It was a cloudy, sultry afternoon.

She invited him round that evening for a drink, and asked him to talk to Reggie, man to man, and find out what he could about his mental state.

'Got you,' said Jimmy. 'Now, recap. Drink drink. General chit chat. Rhubarb rhubarb. Introduce subject of madness tactfully. Rely on me.'

After he'd left Roger Smythe, Reggie took a taxi to Jermyn Street. He went to an exclusive hairdresser's and bought himself a high quality dark wig, much longer than his own hair. Then he went to a theatrical costumier's and asked for a false beard.

'Oh yes,' said the assistant. 'A beard will suit you down to the ground.'

Reggie tried on a dark beard that matched his wig to perfection.

'Yes,' said the assistant. 'Oh yes. Très très distingué.'

*

When he got back to the office he found Davina sitting in his chair.

'Sorry,' she said, getting up. 'I was just wondering what it's like to be you.'

'You don't know when you're well off,' he said.

'Now, now. Don't be like that,' she said, sitting down opposite him and crossing the famous legs. 'You've got a better office than me, anyway.'

Reggie looked at the sad expanse of glass, the filing cabinets and the notice board with its eight postcards of Shanklin (IOW).

'I'm engaged to Percy Spillinger,' said Davina.

'What?'

'He proposed after your party. Yesterday he rang for an answer. I tried to put him off again. I said, "Give me a ring". It arrived this morning, recorded delivery.'

'My God. Can't you explain it was all a mistake?'

'It'd kill him.'

There was the sound of a crash outside. Reggie went to the window. A coal lorry had backed into C.J.'s Bentley. The shocked driver got out of his cab in slow motion action replay.

'I wondered if you could speak to him,' she said.

'Hullo, Percy,' he said. 'It's Reggie Perrin here.'

'They haven't locked you up yet, then.'

'No.'

'Joke.'

'Yes.'

'Good news, Reggie. Davina has consented to be my wife.'

'So I gathered. Percy . . .'

'Only one snag. She doesn't want to be buried in Ponders End. Perhaps you could prevail on her to change her mind.'

'Percy . . .'

'All my other wives are buried at Ponders End. Pity to spoil the ship for a ha-porth of tar.'

Joan came in with a pile of memos. He held the phone away from his ear and grimaced.

'Sorry, Percy, I didn't catch that,' he said.

'Sorry, Reggie, I didn't catch that.'

'I said I didn't catch that.'

'That's what I said.'

'Before that. What did you say before that?'

'I said, "What did you say?"'

'I didn't say anything.'

'Well can you persuade her about Ponders End?'

'I hardly think I'm the best man.'

'The what?'

'The best man.'

'Of course you can be best man. I feel very honoured that you should ask, Reggie.'

A flurry of telephone calls disfigured the grey, sullen afternoon.

Reggie rang Davina and told her that she couldn't break it off without hurting Uncle Percy Spillinger's feelings. He also told her that he was going to be best man.

Davina rang Uncle Percy Spillinger and told him that she would come over that evening to discuss the arrangements.

Maurice Harcourt rang Reggie and told him that the first consignment of exotic ice creams would be ready on July the eighth.

Elizabeth rang Reggie and told him that Jimmy would be calling in for drinks.

Terry Briggs from Dispatch rang about a mix-up concerning a consignment of damson pie mix which had failed to arrive at its destination – Newport (Mon). He also asked if Reggie had liked the synopsis of 'The Dessert Song'. Reggie told a white lie.

His bank rang with bad news. Seven cheques had come in, all cashed on his account in banks around the City for sums of thirty pounds. He expressed alarm and despondency.

Sid Bolton from Dispatch rang to say that half the consignment of damson pie mix had turned up in Newport (Pem).

Terry Briggs from Dispatch rang to say that the other half of the damson pie mix had turned up in Newport (IOW).

Reggie's head was hammering. He longed to be silly on the phone, to say, 'Damsons? Damsony-Wamsonies in the wrong Newporty-Wewporty? Oh, naughty boysy-woysies.' He only just managed to stop himself.

He remembered that there was a bottle of light ale in his filing cabinet. It had been left over one night when he'd been working late with Owen Lewis.

He took the beer, concealed in his inside pocket, and went into the toilet. David Harris-Jones was standing at the urinal.

'Hullo, David,' he said.

'Hullo, Reggie. I'm off to Hertfordshire tomorrow.'

'Good. Fine. Sorry, David, must rush. Nature calls.'

Reggie went into one of the cabinets and waited until David had left. Then he opened the door of his cabinet hastily, and stuck the bottle in the jamb. It opened quite easily.

He shut the door and poured the magic liquid down his throat. He'd never felt like that about a drink before.

He slipped out of the cabinet and dropped the empty bottle into the waste basket under the roller towel.

It was five-nineteen when he got back to his desk. He felt much better. He said goodnight to Joan. He felt sad. He knew that he would never see her naked breasts again.

Uncle Percy Spillinger's house was a handsome, three-storey early Georgian building in mellow red brick. Davina walked up a path of broken flagstones, past unweeded flower beds. She climbed a short flight of stone steps, flanked by two chipped Grecian urns. Her heart was beating anxiously, as she contemplated how best to break off the engagement.

Uncle Percy Spillinger kissed her delicately on the cheek and ushered her into the withdrawing room. A thick layer of dust covered everything in the house, and the handsome classical fireplace was filled with hundreds of used spills. Books lay everywhere, coated in dust.

Davina sat in a high-backed green leather chair. At her side was an embossed coffee table, scarred with burn marks.

'I've fixed the wedding for August the eleventh,' he said. 'Would that suit you, my little nut cutlet?'

'The thing is . . .' began Davina.

'Yes?'

'I fancy long engagements.'

'Oh.'

'It's a romantic time for a woman.'

'Oh, I see. I didn't realize. I've always gone in for whirlwind romances. I swept the second Mrs Spillinger off her feet. She was Burmese. She was the only Burmese wife I ever had. She was tickled pink at the idea of being buried at Ponders End.'

'Could we keep the engagement secret?' said Davina, blushing furiously. 'It's more romantic that way.'

'If you wish it, my dear,' said Uncle Percy Spillinger. 'You're a very romantic person.'

He broached a bottle of port, and then showed Davina his collection. She saw the finger that he'd bought in Basingstoke, the uniform of a full corporal in the catering corps, an inlaid ebony Japanese pith helmet, a Burmese wattle saucepan scourer, a clockwork haggis, the world's second largest riding boot, and many other curios.

'It's a very unusual collection,' she said.

'Of course it is. That's the whole point of a collection,' explained Uncle Percy Spillinger.

Soon it was time for Davina to take her leave.

'Do you think you'll be happy here?' said Uncle Percy Spillinger.

'Very,' said Davina.

He kissed her tenderly on the lips, and watched her as she walked carefully down the uneven path.

She turned to wave. He waved back. The smoke from his pipe was going straight up in the still evening air.

'Get many people going bonkers in your caper?' asked Jimmy.

'No more than anywhere else,' said Reggie.

'Glad to hear it,' said Jimmy.

Elizabeth was down the garden, weeding. Reggie and Jimmy sat in the big armchairs, at either side of the empty hearth, with whiskies at their elbows.

'Had an interesting talk from this head shrinker,' said Jimmy. 'Army lays on these talks. Keeps the chaps in the picture. Talked about neuroses. Ticklish little blighters, neuroses. Quite sound chaps, public school chaps some of them, suddenly get the idea they're deck chairs or ham sandwiches. You say to them, "Fancy a spot of billiards, old boy?" and they say, "Sorry. No can do. I'm a deck chair." Get much of that kind of thing in your caper?'

'No,' said Reggie.

'Hate to see anything happen to Elizabeth,' said Jimmy.

'Why should anything happen to her?'

'Quite. Absolutely.'

Reggie poured two more whiskies.

'Army says, "You're too old. You've helped defend the country. Now piss off." Get much of that?'

'No,' said Reggie. He wanted to say 'parsnips', but he knew that he mustn't.

'This trick cyclist told us about this African tribe. Pygmies. Ran around in the buff all day. Not a stitch. Two-foot-six, three-foot, that sort of crack. Never had an inferiority complex among the whole bang shoot. Never met anyone else, you see. Didn't know what little runts they were. Then in step these four missionaries, six-foot-three if they were a day, butter wouldn't melt in their mouths, come to save these chaps' souls. Know what happened?'

'No.'

'They all realized what little runts they were. They said, "Good heavens, we're absolutely minute. We're little runts. We're pygmies.' Out came their defensive aggression syndromes. That's what this trick cyclist reckoned, anyway, and he should know. Result: they had the missionaries for supper. Those four missionaries fed three hundred pygmies. Moral: depression, inferiority, all in the mind. Makes you think.'

'It makes you think: Who told that story if all the missionaries were eaten?' said Reggie.

'Yes. Good point. Nobody thought of that. Black mark for the regiment,' said Jimmy.

The light was beginning to fade. The room was dark and intense. Jimmy sipped his whisky.

'If you feel you're going off your chump, best thing to do, put your coat on and go straight round to the quack. That's what this trick cyclist cove said anyway. Age of enlightenment. Nothing disgraceful in being a nut-case. No stigma attached.'

'Absolutely,' said Reggie. 'But I'm not a nut-case, so you can relax.'

''Course you aren't. 'Course you aren't. Wasn't talking about you. God forbid. No, nothing wrong with your grey matter. Hit on the flaw in that pygmy story straightaway. Showed the whole regiment up.'

Jimmy looked out into the garden to make sure Elizabeth was still out of earshot. 'Could I ask a favour? Could you lend us something for breakfast? Been a bit of a cock-up on the catering front. Rather big sister didn't know.'

Reggie fetched egg, bacon, a tin of mushrooms, grapefruit, sugar, coffee and milk. Jimmy took them out to his car, and then they walked out on to the lawn. Elizabeth walked towards them, through the arch of rambler roses. She was wearing green gardening gloves and had a trowel in her hand. The light was fading fast.

'Well,' she said. 'What have you two gas bags been talking about?'

'Reggie's all right,' said Jimmy. 'He's as sane as I am.'

At intervals along the path there were little piles of weeds and dead roses, left there by Elizabeth.

'Very impressed with your garden,' said Jimmy. 'A-one ramblers. Top-hole bedding plants. Never get decent gardens in the army. Armies thrive on bad soil. Heath, scrubs, damned good for manoeuvres, no good for gardening. Never got me clematis established in BAOR. Antirrhinums a fiasco in BFPO thirty-three.'

A magpie stuttered across the sky towards Elizabeth Barrett Browning Crescent. Elizabeth put a bucketful of weeds on the compost heap. The steel of the sky turned imperceptibly to black.

Linda's voice rang out cheerfully.

'Hullo, everyone!'

'Hullo, Linda!'

'What's going on?'

'Nothing.'

'I just called round to see how you were,' said Linda. 'The car broke down. I've walked the last two miles. Tom's baby-sitting – he's got some nettle wine on the go. Phew, it's heavy! I'm sweating cobs.'

'Nonsense!' said Jimmy.

'Anyway, the exercise will do me good. I'm carrying too much weight.'

'Nonsense!' said Jimmy.

They strolled slowly round the garden, in the gathering gloom. Reggie found himself with Linda.

'You needn't have come, Linda,' he said. 'I'm not going mad.'

'Oh, father!'

Reggie smacked her bottom affectionately. The peace of the evening was shattered by the Milfords, starting their car with a roar, setting off to have a quick snifter at the golf club.

Elizabeth put an arm round Reggie, and Jimmy put an arm round Linda. She could feel his tough military thigh pressing against her as they walked, and she ran her hand gently over his left hip.

They sat on the terrace and Elizabeth made a pot of tea. Reggie had abandoned all plans of working on his speech. He'd get up early in the morning.

Jimmy offered to drive Linda to her car and see if he could sort things out.

*

At midnight Jimmy's torch packed up, and he still hadn't been able to get Linda's car to go.

'It's got me beat,' he said. 'What about the AA?'

'We aren't members. Tom says it's a waste of time now that they don't salute you.'

'It's too late to get a garage. Come on. I'll drive you home.'

He drove in silence for about five miles, then he turned down a narrow lane.

'Where are we going?'

The lane became a track. He drove over the dusty, bumpy ground and pulled up in a small pine wood at the edge of the golf course. He was breathing hard. He switched off the lights. Linda could hardly see his face in the darkness but she knew that his little red moustache no longer looked ridiculous. She felt his horny hand on her knee and she closed her eyes as a dreadful buzzing rushed through her head.

He helped her pull her tights down, and stroked her large smooth knee. He bent down and kissed her knee, and she kissed the top of his head. He couldn't believe that she wanted him. He was convinced that Malayan heat, North German cold, English battledress and Scotch whisky had turned his skin into a rough, objectionable hide.

He pressed his face into her sweaty thigh and gasped. He thought of Elizabeth, their mother ill in hospital, Tom, Reggie, his own wife, his children. He thought of his long struggle to behave like an officer and gentleman, keeping the flag flying in an increasingly hostile world. If he lost everything that he had become, he would lose himself. He felt desperately ashamed.

'This just isn't on, old girl,' he said.

She sighed, then squeezed his hand to show that she understood. He could hear her tights making little electric noises as she forced them on again. He straightened his clothes and gathered up his strength, ready to renew his old-fashioned fight to be an officer and a gentleman. He was a moral buffalo, doomed to extinction.

He started the car. The noise seemed obscenely loud in the still night.

'Ready, Linda?'

'Ready, Uncle Jimmy.'

Nice of her to say 'Uncle'. It made going home unsatisfied seem more bearable.

He drove her home, and didn't trust himself to kiss her goodnight. After he'd left her, he walked for more than two hours, past silent houses, in the moonlight.

Fate had dealt Jimmy some lousy cards. He had been just too young to fight in the war. He had discovered that he was going to be made redundant in his forties. He had been moved from rotten posting to rotten posting. His clematis had all died. His wife drank. But this was the lousiest card of all – that in return for promising to lead an upright life, bringing up the children, going to church, being kind to his men, faithful to his NCOs and affectionate to his family, in return for all this he had been given a passion, an almost irresistible passion, for fat women who sweated.

Howl of cat. Rumble of distant train. Reggie stretched his legs out further and further, until they seemed enormous. Elizabeth undid the cord of his pyjamas. Rustle of leaves. Return of Milfords from their snifter. Suddenly he had an awful fear that tonight it would be no good, that his John Thomas was a separate being, that it wouldn't respond, that it was Chapel, that it didn't really approve of the whole absurd messy business.

But it was all right, it was good, almost as good as last night. He eased himself gently out of ecstasy into calm, held a gentle hand on Elizabeth's right breast, caressed it gratefully, wishing he could explain to her that it was the last time, wishing he didn't have to deceive her.

Tomorrow his speech. Tonight, tired. Pyjama trousers crumpled beneath him. Too tired. Falling. Falling into sleep. Up early tomorrow. Falling.

'Goodnight, darling,' from Elizabeth.

'Good-bye,' from himself, far below.

Friday

So tired. He gave his limbs the relevant messages, telling them to hop out of bed and get things moving, but nothing happened. Mutiny. A general strike. 1926 all over again. His legs and arms had got him pinned down. His neck was in the thick of it, too.

Come on, lads. Let's have you. Wakey wakey rise and shine! I know you're fed up to the back teeth with being bits of me, always taking orders. Believe me, I'm tired of being the boss. I'm tired of the responsibility, so tired that I'm prepared to leave my wife, whom I love.

After tomorrow everything will be different. So what about it, limbs? See me through one more day, eh? Let's not have an energy crisis today.

Slowly the spasm passed. He got out of bed very gingerly. His legs felt weak. His head buzzed and on the way to the bathroom he thought he was going to faint.

He bent his head over the washbasin and poured cold water over it. This wouldn't do at all, not on the day of his big speech.

He opened the frosted glass window and gazed out over the back garden, gulping in the misty air.

He dressed carefully, dark suit, white shirt, brand new British Fruit Association tie, blue with the somewhat unfortunate symbol of two apples and a banana picked out in gold.

He climbed up into the loft, collected his £320 from beneath the old curtains in his tuck box, put some of the money in his wallet and distributed the rest around the pockets of his suit.

He went down into the kitchen. Elizabeth handed him his breakfast – two eggs, a rasher of bacon, and mushrooms.

'You're looking very smart,' she said.

He shrugged. He hadn't told her about his speech. It would only make him more nervous if she knew.

He had to force the breakfast down.

'Are you feeling all right?' said Elizabeth.

'I've got a bit of an earwig.'

'What on earth do you mean – an earwig?'

'Sorry. Not earwig. Headache.'

This was dreadful. At another time it might be amusing to call headaches earwigs. He couldn't imagine anything more boring than calling them headaches all the time. But not now.

She was watching him closely. He must apologize. Allay her earwigs. Not earwigs. Fears.

'Parsnips,' he said.

Not parsnips. Pardon.

'Parsnips?'

'C.J. asked if we could give him some parsnips,' he improvised feebly.

'What on earth does he want parsnips for?'

'He didn't say.'

This was terrible. She'd be calling the doctor before you could say parsnips. Not parsnips. Jack Robinson.

He finished his breakfast. Elizabeth gave him the parsnips. He picked up his briefcase, which contained the unfinished notes for his speech, the black wig and the false beard. He kissed Elizabeth good-bye, told her that he'd be working late that night and would see her at the hospital in Worthing the next day, and set off for the station. The mist was beginning to thin.

On his way to the station, Reggie was happy to report full cooperation from every limb. Even the potentially recalcitrant neck was doing its bit – to wit, joining the head to the body in such a way that the former could be swivelled upon the latter without falling off.

He stood at his usual place on the platform, in front of the door marked 'Isolation telephone'. The pollen count was low, and Peter Cartwright was blessedly free from sneezing.

On the train Reggie studied the programme for day three of the conference.

9.30 a.m.	Dr L. Hump, Lecturer in Applied Agronomy at the University of Rutland: 'The Role of Fruit in a Competitive Society'.
10.15 a.m.	Sir Elwyn Watkins, Chairman of the Watkins Commission on Pesticides: 'Pesticides – Salvation or Damnation?'
11.00 a.m.	Coffee.
11.30 a.m.	Special showing of the prize-winning Canadian Fruit Board Documentary: 'The Answer's a Lemon'.
12.30 p.m.	Lunch.
13.45 p.m.	R. I. Perrin, Esq., Senior Sales Executive, Sunshine Desserts: 'Are We Getting Our Just Desserts?'
14.30 p.m.	Professor Knud Pedersen, University of Uppsala: 'Aspects of Dietary Conscience'.
15.15 p.m.	Tea.
15.45 p.m.	L. B. Cohen, Esq., O.B.E., Permanent Under Secretary, the Ministry of Fruit: 'Whither a Multilateral Fruit Policy?'
17.15 p.m.	Open Forum.
19.00 p.m.	Dinner.
20.30 p.m.	Brains Trust.

At Waterloo he took good care to avoid the cracked old woman, and deposited his parsnips in a litter bin before leaving the station.

The sun shimmered sadistically through the great glass windows. The filing cabinets shone with green venom. Reggie's mouth was dry, his forehead stretched tight. He wanted to scream.

C.J. rang to wish him luck with his speech. Somehow he managed to speak normally, to use all the right words, to avoid saying, 'Earwig very much'.

He tried to work on his speech but the sentences wouldn't

148

form themselves. His bank rang to say that they had received four more cheques, each cashed in his name for the sum of thirty pounds. He expressed the necessary alarm.

At quarter to eleven he decided that he could bear it no longer.

'Well,' he said to Joan, sitting at her desk with nothing to do, because he had given her nothing to do. 'Well, I'm off.'

'Good luck with your speech,' she said.

He would never see her again, but he couldn't kiss her in the middle of the open-plan office.

'Good-bye,' he said.

'Well, off you go then if you're going,' she said.

Had she really no inkling?

Bilberry Hall was a long, white Regency building with green shutters, set in rolling wooded country between Potters Bar and Hertford. Reggie walked over the gravel to the front door with sinking heart and slightly unsteady feet. He had already drunk six large whiskies.

He was ushered into the spacious dining room. The tables had been arranged in three long rows, and there was a buzz of serious conversation from the dark-suited delegates. Above their heads hung the controversial International Fruit Year symbol – the intertwined fruits of all the nations.

Reggie took his seat and apologized profusely for his late arrival, which he attributed to a broken fan belt. He attacked his avocado vinaigrette vigorously, and caught everybody up half-way through the chicken *à la reine*.

'You missed a stimulating session this morning, Mr Perrin,' said Dr L. Hump, his neighbour on his left. Dr Hump had a round, bald head.

'Yes,' said Reggie.

Dr Hump filled Reggie's glass with rich, perfumy Alsatian wine.

'This'll give you Dutch courage,' he said.

Reggie took a big draught of the wine. He had suddenly lost his appetite.

'Sir Elwyn gave us a fascinating analysis of the pesticide issue,' said Dr L. Hump.

'You are Mr Senior Sales Executive Perrin?' said a serious man with blond hair, sitting opposite Reggie and eating a nut cutlet specially prepared for him.

'Yes.'

'I am Professor Knud Pedersen, University of Uppsala. You are giving a most stimulating talk to us, I think.'

'Let's hope so.'

Reggie's neighbour on his right introduced himself as Sir Elwyn Watkins. He signalled unobtrusively to a waiter to fill Reggie's glass.

'Dutch courage. Great advantage of you post-prandialites,' he said. 'You missed a very good little talk from Dr Hump. He touched mainly on the role of fruit in a competitive society. His thesis was, in a nutshell, that fruit should not be – indeed cannot be – less or indeed more competitive than the society for which – and indeed by which – it is produced.'

'That's very interesting,' said Reggie.

The walls of the dining room were hung with still lifes of fruit, and there were enormous bowls of fruit on the tables.

'Those pears are conference pears, and those apples are conference apples,' he said. 'Joke,' he explained.

During the sweet, Dr Hump and Sir Elwyn Watkins were engaged in conversation with their other neighbours. Reggie became acutely conscious that nobody was talking to him. He was Goofy Perrin again, Coconut Matting Perrin who feared that the girls would laugh at his thin hairy legs when he played tennis. He drained his third glass of Alsatian wine. His eyes met Professor Pedersen's. The author of the lecture on 'Aspects of Dietary Conscience' looked as if this little gathering was rather below his lofty intellect. Reggie smiled at him and tried to think of something stimulating to say, something worthy of consideration by the famous agrarian philosopher.

'You're Swedish, aren't you?' he said.

'Yes,' admitted the blond vegetarian patiently.

'I'm not Swedish,' said Reggie.

My God, I'm drunk, he thought.

'I wonder if you could pass me the earwig,' he said to Dr Hump.

'I beg your pardon?' said Dr Hump.

'When I say the earwig I mean the water jug,' said Reggie.

Dr Hump gave him a strange look. Then he gave him the water jug.

Reggie sat on the platform in the conference hall and faced a sea of two hundred and fifty earnest faces. Beneath the faces, on two hundred and fifty lapels, two hundred and fifty International Fruit Year symbols were pinned, and another huge International Fruit Year symbol hung threateningly over the speaker's rostrum. At the back of the platform there was a large mural representing the British Fruit Association – two huge red apples and a vast yellow banana.

The Chairman of the British Fruit Association, W. F. Malham, CBFA (Chairman of the British Fruit Association), rose to speak.

'Welcome back,' he said. 'We have had an excellent and fruity lunch (laughter). Now, if we can still concentrate (laughter), we come to what will undoubtedly be the high spot, the undoubted high spot, of our first talk this afternoon. I refer of course to none other than . . .' He hunted frantically for his notes. 'None other than . . .' He looked around for help but none was forthcoming. 'None other than our first speaker this afternoon. Indeed he is well-known to many of us, if not more, and his subject today . . . his subject today is the subject for which he is well-known to many of us. In fact he needs no introduction from me. So here he is.'

W. F. Malham, CBFA, sat down and wiped his red face with a large handkerchief. Reggie stood up. There was applause. He walked forward to the rostrum, desperately trying not to lurch. He tried to arrange his notes systematically.

'Thank you,' he began. 'Thank you very much, Mr Whatever Your Name Is.' There was some laughter and applause. W. F. Malham, CBFA, turned crimson. 'When they said to me,

"Reginald I. Perrin, you're a senior sales earwig at Sunshine Desserts. Would you like to talk on 'Are We Getting Our Just Desserts?'" my first thought was, What a pathetic title for a talk. And my second thought was also, What a pathetic title for a talk.

But I decided to come here, because what I have to say is important. Fruit these days is graded, standardized, sprayed, seeded, frozen, artificially coloured. Taste doesn't matter, only appearance. If a survey showed that housewives prefer pink square bananas, they would get pink square bananas.'

Reggie looked down at the people sitting in rows on cheap wooden chairs in the high, well-proportioned room. Behind them, through the windows in the north-facing wall of the house, he could see the tops of fine old oak trees.

'People are graded too,' he said. 'They're sorted out, the ones that look right are packed off to management training schemes. They're standardized, they're sprayed with the profit motive so that no nasty unmanagerial thoughts can survive on them, their politics are dyed a nice safe pale blue, their social conscience is deep frozen. I'm not so worried about the permissive society. I'm more worried about all those homogenized twits who decide that all their brewery's pubs should have green doors, or that the menu should say "eggs styled to choice" or something equally pathetic.'

He was doing well. Out of the corner of his eye he saw Professor Pedersen staring at him.

'I see Professor Pedersen's in the audience tonight,' he said. 'Let's have a big hand for Professor Pedersen.'

There was a surprised pause, then a smattering of applause, which grew slowly into a tolerable ovation. Professor Pedersen, greatly embarrassed, rose briefly to give curt acknowledgement.

'If we've ever complained about these things, we've been told we stand in the way of progress,' said Reggie, when the applause had died down. 'Progress. There's a word that begs the pardon. I beg your parsnips – I mean . . . *I* beg your pardon – it doesn't beg the pardon – it begs the question.'

He paused, totally confused. There was a groundswell of uneasy murmurings. He glared at the audience until at last there was silence.

'Where was I? Oh yes. Progress. Growth. That's another one. We must have growth. Six per cent per year or whatever it is. More people driving more washing machines on bigger lorries down wider motorways. More scientists analysing the effects of more pesticides. More chemicals to cure the pollution caused by more chemicals. More boring speeches to fill up more boring conferences. More luxury desserts, so that more and more people can enjoy a life increasingly superior to that lived by more and more other people. Are those our just desserts? Society functions best if I over-eat, so I buy too many slimming aids, so I fall ill, so I buy too many pills. We have to have a surfeit of dotes in order to sell our surfeit of antidotes. Well, it's got to stop.

'I hear some uneasy rumblings. I know what you would like to say to me, "What's your alternative, then?" That's rather unfair, you know, to stop me criticising the whole of western society just because I can't suggest a better alternative on my own.'

Reggie clasped the rostrum firmly, to stop himself swaying.

'Tell me this,' he said. 'What has progress done for the cracked old woman with the hairy legs? You can't tell me, can you?'

'What has it done for me? One day I will die, and on my grave it will say, "Here lies Reginald Iolanthe Perrin; he didn't know the names of the flowers and the trees, but he knew the rhubarb crumble sales for Schleswig-Holstein."

'Look at those trees outside. They'll all be pulled down soon to make underground car parks. But you try complaining. You'll be labelled as an earwig. Trees don't matter, people will say, compared with poverty and colour prejudice. So what will we end up with? Poor unloved black children who haven't even got any trees to climb. But I've good news for you. Half the parking meters in London have got Dutch parking meter disease.'

There were mutterings. Someone cried out, 'Get back to Desserts!'

'"Get back to Desserts," I hear you cry. "Get on with it." "Get your finger out,"' said Reggie. 'Well I knew a chap who could, because he bought a finger off a chap in a pub in Basingstoke, so that would be rather amusing.'

His head was swimming. He could feel himself sinking. He couldn't find the place in his notes. There was a buzz of conversation from the audience.

'We become what we do!' he shouted above the noise. 'Show me a happy man who makes paper tissues, and I will show you a hero who makes fondue tongs!

'You have a right to ask me what I believe in, I who am so anti-everything. I'll tell you. I believe in nihilism, in the sense that I believe in the absence of ism. I know that I don't know and I believe in not believing.' He could see earnest whisperings taking place in the front row. He hadn't much time to lose. 'For every man who believes something there's a man who believes the opposite. How many wars would be fought, how many men would have been tortured in this world, if nobody had ever believed in anything?

'"But that would be awful," I hear you cry. Well actually I don't, but that's what you would cry if you were listening. I deny it. Would the sun shine less brightly if there was no purpose in life? Would the nightingale sing less sweetly? Would we love each other less deeply? Man's the only species neurotic enough to need a purpose in life.

'Now I come to the question of earwigs, and when I say earwigs I mean a sense of values.'

Out of the corner of his eye he could see Dr Hump making signs to W. F. Malham, CBFA.

'Old Baldy Hump there. Why is he bald? Because he made a cock-up. He used pesticides on his head and hair restorer on his fruit trees. Now he's as bald as a coot and he's got a garden full of hairy plums.'

W. F. Malham, CBFA, leant over to him, red in the face, dripping sweat.

'I think we've had enough,' he said.

'Rubbish. I haven't finished.'

W. F. Malham, CBFA, looked at the front row of the audience and shrugged. Dr Hump beckoned him over. Sir Elwyn Watkins leant across Professor Pedersen to confer with Dr Hump.

Get the audience back on your side, thought Reggie. Win them over.

'Is there anyone here from Canada?' he thundered. 'Australia? Great Yarmouth? Anyone here from Tarporley? Hands up all those of you from Tarporley. All stand up and shake hands with the person on your right!'

'You're drunk!' shouted a greenfly prevention consultant.

'That's right,' said Reggie, swaying slightly, gripping the rostrum with both hands to steady himself. 'Shout at me. Pelt me with tasteless standardized tomatoes. Use your instant anger mix. I don't hate you. I want to help you. What is life for if not for those who have to live it?'

Dr Hump, Sir Elwyn Watkins and W. F. Malham CFBA, were advancing on him.

'Here he comes,' shouted Reggie. 'Old Baldy Hump, lecturer in applied manure at the University of Steeple Bumpstead!'

They were grabbing hold of him, politely but firmly. He writhed, shook them off.

'Get your hands off!' he shouted.

'Please, Mr Perrin,' implored Sir Elwyn Watkins, trying to steer Reggie off the platform without manhandling him.

'I haven't finished,' said Reggie.

'Thank you very much. Stimulating address,' said W. F. Malham, CBFA.

'Come on, you bastard,' said Dr Hump.

'Keep your hair on, Baldy!'

'A stimulating address. Should provoke discussion,' said W. F. Malham, CBFA.

Dr Hump's elbow caught Reggie in the genitals. He doubled up.

'He hit me in the balls,' he said.

'I'm sure we all learnt a lot,' said W. F. Malham, CBFA.

'Come on, now. Gently does it,' said Sir Elwyn Watkins.

Their firm hands were propelling Reggie towards the exit. He reached out to grab the rostrum but he was being dragged away from it.

'Come on, you bastard,' said Dr Hump.

'Easy does it, now. Fair do's,' said Sir Elwyn Watkins.

The three men propelled the struggling form of Reggie Perrin slowly towards the exit. W. F. Malham, CBFA, dripping with sweat, purple in the face, turned towards the audience, still holding one of Reggie's arms.

'Thank you for a very interesting and forceful examination of current issues, Mr – er – Mr – er – ' he said, and then the four of them disappeared from the platform in a tumble of legs and arms and collapsed in a heap in the corridor outside.

Reggie received another painful blow.

'He's hit me in the balls again!'

'Leave him be, Hump. Leave him be,' said Sir Elwyn Watkins, scrambling to his feet. 'Fair play.'

'He didn't call you old Baldy,' said Dr Hump, still lying on the floor, panting.

'I'm not bald,' said Sir Elwyn Watkins.

W. F. Malham, CBFA, got to his feet and dusted down his trousers. Reggie was doubled up in pain.

'The sooner we behave like academics, the better,' said Sir Elwyn Watkins to Dr Hump.

'Fuck off,' said Dr Hump.

'I'm going in there to make a statement,' said W. F. Malham, CBFA. 'Get him in the office. Give him some coffee. And no more monkey business, Hump!'

He went back on to the platform and held up his hand to still the excited murmuring. There were loud shushing noises from the assembly. For almost a minute the whole audience was going 'Sssh!' at each other. Then at last there was silence.

'Ladies and gentlemen,' said W. F. Malham, CBFA. 'A combination of the after effects of luncheon and of the heat has proved too much for Mr – for our distinguished speaker.

I'm sure I speak for us all when I say how sorry I am that a talk of penetrating brilliance, with which no doubt we all found something to agree, something to disagree, and plenty to provoke thought, which after all is what this conference is about, at least I hope it is, how sorry I am, as I say, how sorry I am sure we all are, that this talk has been cut short in its prime, as it were. I think probably the best thing now is to. . .er – to take a little break. We will resume again at fourteen-thirty hours p.m. when I am sure we are all looking forward with bated breath to what promises to be a high spot in our discussions, the long-awaited talk of Professor – Professor – of the distinguished Swedish Professor who will talk about a question that is on everyone's lips, the question of . . . as I say, the question that's on everybody's lips. And may I ask the staff, if they're present, which I believe they aren't, to see that the ventilation is increased. Thank you.'

The delegates streamed out on to the terrace to enjoy the quiet Hertfordshire sunshine. W. F. Malham, CBFA, hurried to the secretary's office. Reggie was slumped on a chair with his elbows resting on the secretary's desk. He looked distinctly green at the gills. Sir Elwyn Watkins and the secretary were standing over him solicitously.

'I've organized some coffee,' said Sir Elwyn. 'And I've got rid of Hump.'

Reggie said nothing. When the coffee came he drank three cups and then he asked for a taxi to take him home.

As they drove through Potters Bar he told the driver that he didn't want to go home, and gave him the address of the factory at Acton.

His mouth tasted foul, his head ached, and he felt sick. He'd been drunk. He had used the wrong words. He had insulted Dr Hump childishly. He had been heckled. He had asked if there was anyone there from Tarporley. He had failed.

He had one more task to perform – and this time there must be no failure.

*

When he got to Acton, he went straight to the canteen and had four cups of tea, to get the foul taste out of his mouth. He also bought three rounds of egg and tomato sandwiches, in case he was hungry later on. Then he went to the 'gents'. He sat on one of the lavatory seats, prepared for a long wait.

Up till half-past five there were people using the toilet. After that he was alone. His head still ached, and his stomach hurt. The only noises were the automatic flushing of the urinal every five minutes, and the gurglings of his digestive system.

He sat on the lavatory seat all evening. Nobody had seen him go in there. He wasn't expected back at work. Elizabeth wouldn't miss him until he failed to turn up in Worthing next day. In his briefcase there was a wig, a false beard, a mirror, and three rounds of egg and tomato sandwiches. In his pockets there were three hundred and fifteen pounds in used fivers.

It wasn't safe to move until he could be quite certain that he had the factory to himself, apart from old Bill, the nightwatchman. Reggie didn't expect much trouble from old Bill.

He hoped that Elizabeth would understand, and Joan, and the children, Linda and Mark. It was hard to accept that he would never see any of them again.

He ate one of his sandwiches. Slowly time passed. When the urinal had flushed sixty-three times, he judged that it was safe to leave.

Outside, it was dark. His legs had gone to sleep. He walked cautiously, quietly. His eyes began to grow accustomed to the dark, and the feeling returned to his legs.

He could see the outlines of the long dark blocks that formed the bulk of the factory. At night it looked more like a prison camp. He half expected searchlights and guard dogs, but there was only old Bill.

As he approached Bill's hut the door was flung open, and Bill limped out. He had a poker in his hand, clearly visible against the bright light inside the hut.

'Who goes there?' he shouted.

'It's me,' said Reggie. 'Mr Perrin, from Head Office.'

'Oh.' Bill shone his torch in Reggie's face. It almost blinded him. 'Blimey, you gave me a turn, Mr Perrin.'

'Sorry, Bill.'

Bill led him into the hut. As well as the torch and the poker he had been carrying a large bag of pepper.

In the hut there was a wooden table, a hard chair, a ring for making tea, a little stove and a small cupboard. On the table there were pictures of his wife and children.

'That was very brave of you, Bill,' he said.

'That's what I'm paid for, Mr Perrin.'

That's what you're underpaid for, thought Reggie.

Bill took a rusty kettle out of the cupboard. Reggie sat down. Bill went to the door and filled the kettle from a stand-pipe.

'A consignment of loganberry essence has to be sent to Hamburg urgently,' said Reggie. 'The ship sails from Southampton tomorrow. I've got to get that stuff down there.'

'I'm sorry. I've no authority to let you out,' said Bill.

'I'll give you the authority.'

'I'm sorry. I can't do it. I haven't got the authority to let you give me the authority, Mr Perrin.'

'I've got a PXB 43 and a PBX 34.'

'I see,' said Bill, reading the forms slowly.

The kettle whistled. Bill dropped six tea bags into a rusty enamel teapot.

'And I've got an open PXF 38 signed by C.J.,' said Reggie.

He showed Bill a blank order form on which he had forged C.J.'s signature that morning.

'It's blank,' said Bill.

'Of course it is. I fill in the details. Look. I'll do it now. One thousand packets of loganberry pie mix. Delivery to West Docks, Southampton. It's an open order form.'

'I see,' Bill poured twelve spoonfuls of sugar into the pot.

'I've got a PXL 2, double-checked through the computer.'

Reggie got out a fourth form and handed it to Bill. Bill

handed him a chipped blue mug. Then he spooned some powdered milk into the teapot, stirred vigorously, and poured tea into the mug.

'You drink that. I'll have mine afterwards,' said Bill. He examined the PXL 2 very carefully. 'Well, that all seems to be in order,' he said at last.

The sheer weight of forms, taken in conjunction with the mention of the computer, had become too much for a mere human being to resist.

'Thanks, Bill,' said Reggie.

He closed his eyes and took a sip of tea.

The rest wasn't too difficult. He took a key at random from the transport office and walked down to the garage. He slid back the heavy doors of the garage. Inside it was cool and there were patches of sticky oil on the stone floor. There were two rows of bright red lorries, with the words: 'Try Sunshine Flans – they're flan-tastic' painted on both sides in big yellow letters. There were double doors at the back of each lorry. On one door it said: 'Bring a suns into yo' and on the other door it said: 'little hine ur life', so that when the doors were closed the three-line message ran: 'Bring a little sunshine into your life'. Four lorries had been delivered with the message on the wrong doors, so that when their doors were closed they carried the message: 'Little bring a hinesuns ur life into yo'.

Reggie's key was for one of the two lorries shaped like jellies.

It didn't occur to him to go back and change the key. It didn't seem important.

He climbed up into the cab and examined the controls. He'd never been so high up in a vehicle before.

The lorry started first time. He switched on the lights, and drove it very cautiously out of the garage. He found it very difficult to judge its length.

He closed the garage door rapidly, and drove the lorry to the block where the fruit essences were made.

As he'd expected, the vat of loganberry essence was almost full. He fitted a hosepipe on to the back of the lorry, put the other end on to the vat, and switched on the pump. Within minutes the lorry was fully loaded with loganberry essence.

At ten past one in the morning Old Bill raised the automatic barrier, and the motorized jelly slid forward on to the open road.

Saturday

He thundered through Slough, the safety town. Maidenhead welcomed careful drivers and thanked them. The signs helped Reggie, high up in his cab, to feel that he was part of the great fraternity of the road.

Beyond Reading the outline of low hills was clearly visible in the moonlight. At Newbury he turned south on to the A34. The engine growled as the road climbed over the downs. The headlights picked out frightened rabbits at the roadside. They had never seen a moving jelly before.

The road dipped towards the head waters of the River Test. Reggie turned on to the minor road that led past C.J.'s cottage. The road dropped down on to the floor of the little valley.

Just before C.J.'s cottage there was a small wood on the right. He backed the lorry into the wood and reversed carefully down a narrow, bumpy track that led through silver birches towards the river. The engine was defeaning in the quiet night.

He switched the engine off. Far away in the sudden stillness a dog barked. He could hear the little river tinkling peacefully, with an occasional plop as a fish jumped.

He walked back to the road and approached C.J.'s cottage cautiously. No light was showing. Behind the cottage the old water mill was also in darkness. Here, in its luxurious converted rooms, C.J.'s guests would be sleeping now, where once there had been floury smells and whirring machines and slow, kindly men in white dungarees.

Reggie opened the wrought-iron gate carefully and tiptoed up the garden path. The cottage was half-timbered and thatched, with small, heavily-mullioned windows. In the silver moonlight it looked vulgar in its perfection, like an old-fashioned Christmas card.

He slipped his note through the letter box and crept away as carefully as he had come.

C.J. went down the narrow stairs in his purple dressing gown. The ninth step squeaked. He must get Gibbons to see to it.

It was still pitch dark, but it was time to be stirring, if they were to catch the best fishing.

He was surprised to see the note lying in the wire letter box. He pulled it out impatiently. On the envelope it said: 'C.J. Sunshine Cottage. By Hand'.

He slit the envelope neatly so that it could be used again, should war break out.

'The river is public property and should not be in private hands,' he read. 'The fish are not yours to kill. Nor are your employees. Possessions bring misery. Absolute power brings absolute misery. P.S. Blood will flow.'

Some nutter, thought C.J., as he switched the gas on underneath the kettle. There were nut-cases everywhere these days.

Who could it be? Doc Morrissey? Nothing that shrivelled-up oaf did would surprise him.

Blood will flow? Whose blood? He shivered.

He wished Mrs C.J. was there, so that he could talk to her. She didn't accompany him any more on these occasions. She got flustered by strangers, so he used outside caterers.

'I didn't get where I am today by having anonymous letters shoved through my letter box,' he told himself angrily.

He measured the tea carefully into the pot and poured boiling water over the tiny leaves.

'No. but I didn't get where I am today without making enemies,' he added grimly.

Reggie fitted the hosepipe on to the back of the lorry and put the other end into the little river. Then he settled down to wait.

Grey, unshaven dawn crept in from the east. A cool breeze began to stir the warm lethargy of the night. It was the time of day when trout and fishermen begin to feel hungry.

Doc Morrissey groaned, cursed C.J., tasted the stale claret and brandy that coated his mouth, crawled out of his soft bed, and slid his wizened white legs into a pair of gumboots three sizes too big for him. The tightness in his stomach wasn't just indigestion. It was a premonition of disaster.

The light grew stronger. On the river thin tongues of mist licked the clear waters, and there were haloes of mist over the hills.

Reggie rested. He gazed at the expensive waters, where fat exclusive trout lurked beneath smooth stones and waving green reeds. He munched his second egg and tomato sandwich.

C.J. had positioned himself downstream of all his guests. Immediately above him was old Hedley Norris, his mentor, half blind and half deaf now but still with a nose for trout. Beyond Hedley were L.B., S.T., E.A., and Doc Morrissey, getting hopelessly entangled in his equipment.

C.J. made a little tour of the lines, dispensing a joke here, an axiom there, making sure everyone had a flask of Irish coffee. Then he settled down to the serious business of fishing.

His spirits rose. This was his world, bought with his money. This was the proof that he wasn't just a crude self-made man, he was an English gentleman. He was using a fly of his own design, the brilliantly coloured Sunshine Blue Dun. His unpolluted waters were murmuring agreeably to themselves. The mists were beginning to lift over his downs. Not yet, he told his sun. We've fat trout to catch. Don't rise too fast today.

Reggie switched on the pump, and the loganberry essence began to pour into the river. On the opposite bank a herd of black and white Friesians watched with bored curiosity.

He ate his third egg and tomato sandwich. The essence

began to mingle with the waters of the river. Little currents of deep red slowly thinned and turned pink as they spread outwards. Then the whole river was pink. Soon it was a thick red stream that was running over the stained reeds. Reggie watched his loganberry slick for a few seconds, then turned and walked back towards the lorry.

He started the engine and drove cautiously to the edge of the wood. Nothing was coming. He slid out of the wood unobserved, and set off north, away from C.J.'s cottage.

Doc Morrissey saw the loganberry slick. E.A., S.T., and L.B. saw it, old Hedley Norris smelt it.

Finally C.J. himself saw it. The river was running red. 'Blood will flow'! Clouds of blood were pouring downstream. A cold vice gripped his heart. A madman was slaughtering his guests, cutting their throats, their thick blood pouring into the river. The soldier who had seen a colleague die because of C.J.'s hesitation in 1945. The relatives of the girl he had ditched in 1949. The people he had trodden on in 1951. The victims of his big purge in 1958. The sackings in 1964 after all the hanky-panky. Visions of all those who might bear grudges flashed into C.J.'s mind.

His face was white, his heart splitting down the middle. His guests were astounded at his reaction. He ran upstream, tripped over his rod, and fell headlong into the river. He cracked his head against a large stone which lay just beneath the surface. His last sight was of the thick, sweet loganberry waters of the river closing over his head. Then he passed out.

Old Hedley Norris, fishing on despite the noise and the strange sweet smell, had got a bite. He pulled. It wouldn't come. It was huge.

'I've got a whopper!' he shouted.

'It's C.J.!' cried S.T. 'It's C.J.! Don't pull!'

S.T. grabbed Hedley Norris's line and flung it into the river. Doc Morrissey rushed through the water shouting: 'Let me through! I'm a doctor! Let me through!'

'Where's my rod gone?' said old Hedley Norris.

Doc Morrissey lifted C.J. out of the water, and removed the hook from the side of his face. C.J. looked as if he was covered in blood, but most of it was loganberry essence.

S.T. helped Doc Morrissey carry C.J. to the bank. They laid him down. R.F. ripped a piece off his shirt. Doc Morrissey took it and bandaged C.J.'s face roughly. Then he knelt beside him and felt his pulse. When he stood up his expression was grim.

'He's dead,' he said.

C.J. opened his left eye slightly. He glared at Doc Morrissey.

'You're fired,' he whispered.

Reggie cut across on to the to A343 and drove south-west, making for the coast. The sun came up and it was going to be a glorious day. He drove to Salisbury, then took the A338 towards Bournemouth. He felt very conspicuous in the broad daylight. He didn't think anyone had seen him, but if they had he would be only too easy to trace. There couldn't be that many lorries shaped like jellies.

In the New Forest there were ponies wandering at the roadside. Outside Ringwood a lorry shaped like a huge bottle of light ale passed in the opposite direction. The driver waved, he waved back, expressions of mutual sympathy.

He parked in a lorry park in Bournemouth, and had breakfast in a self-service cafeteria. The breakfast had been kept under a hot plate, and the top of his fried egg was hard and green.

He was exhausted. He felt as if it was the end of everything.

C.J. lay unconscious in his bedroom at Sunshine Cottage. Glass cases on the walls contained stuffed trout.

The guests had dispersed. C.J.'s doctor had been summoned.

'I felt his pulse, and he felt dead,' thought Doc Morrissey, sitting glumly at C.J.'s bedside. 'Wishful thinking, that's what it was. The power of mind over matter. I might write a paper for the *Lancet* about it. But who'd be interested? Who'll be interested in me now? How will I ever get another job?'

As soon as the local doctor arrived, Doc Morrissey excused himself, packed his things, got into his car, and drove right out of the book in a northerly direction.

The doctor summoned C.J.'s daily woman and told her, 'He's got concussion. Aye. There's an awfu' lot of it about.'

He pronounced rest and quiet. He pronounced them in a thick Dumfries accent. Then he rang Mrs C.J. at her house.

'It's your husband,' he said. 'Dinna worry. He's not dead. Merely unconscious.'

Mrs C.J. fainted. As she fell she hit her head on the corner of a Finnish rosewood coffee table. Her daily woman picked up the phone and explained to the doctor what had happened.

'Feel her pulse,' said the doctor.

'It's thirty-eight,' the daily woman told him.

'Fine. Examine her pupils,' said the doctor.

'They're dilated,' reported the daily woman.

Mrs C.J. came to and announced that she had double vision.

'She's seeing double,' reported the daily woman.

'It's concussion. Aye. There's an awfu' lot of it about,' said the doctor.

The day passed slowly. It was extremely hot, and the tar melted on several roads.

It was very hot in Worthing. Elizabeth grew very worried when Reggie didn't turn up. She tried to hide her worry from her mother, but her mother could read her like an open book.

It was extremely hot in Meakers, where Reggie bought a pair of trousers and a shirt and tie. It was hot in Marks and Spencer's, where he bought underclothes and a suitcase, and it wasn't any cooler in Mr Trend, where he bought shoes, socks and a sports jacket.

It was hot at Sunshine Cottage, where C.J. had regained consciousness, to find that he was seeing double. And it was hot on the A30, where Mrs C.J. was also seeing double in the hired car that was speeding her towards C.J.

'Can't you go faster, driver? It is a dual carriageway,' she said.

'It isn't,' said the driver.

Reggie picked at his food in a self-service café in Bournemouth. Every now and then he came upon a chip amid the grease. At the next table there was a fat, middle-aged woman with livid, peeling skin. At Reggie's feet there was a suitcase full of clothes, and in his pockets there were two hundred and eighty pounds in used fivers.

As soon as it was opening time he went into a pub. He ordered a pint of bitter and sat at a table. The room was semi-circular. The bar counter was covered in bright red plastic and there was an orange carpet on the floor.

Reggie got out a pad of writing paper and began to write some letters.

Dear C.J.,

By the time you receive this letter I will be dead. I don't apologize for the loganberry slick as I hope it will teach you a lesson. I didn't get where I am today without realizing that you didn't get where you are today without needing to be taught a lesson.

By now you will have heard about my speech to the conference. I am sorry that I was drunk but I hope something of what I had to say got through. I am not optimistic but then only fools judge things by results.

I have decided to end my life because I cannot see any future for me. Obviously you could not continue to employ me even if I wanted you to and I don't imagine it would be easy to find other work. Please send my outstanding wages to Oxfam or any charity dealing with human suffering. I would like my pension annuities to be paid to my wife.

Be much nicer to Mrs C.J. She needs it.

   Yours faithfully,
     Reginald I. Perrin
     (Senior Sales Executive)

168

Next he wrote to Joan.

Dear Joan,

There is very little to say, except to thank you for everything and to say what happy memories of you I carry to my watery grave. I only hope you will be happy in the years to come.

I am sending this letter by second-class post because I want you to know that I am dead before you receive it.

With lots of love,
Reggie

He addressed the envelope and then began his third and last letter.

My dear Elizabeth,

By the time you receive this letter you will have heard the sad news. I'm sorry for any distress I've caused you. I suddenly started to see a lot of things very clearly and this coincided with the onset of what I suppose was a kind of nervous breakdown. I felt as if I was going sane and mad at the same time, but then the words sane and mad don't have much meaning. So few words do – blue, green, butter, kettle etc. Even blue is green to some people and some people can't tell butter from marge. I think kettle is safe enough. I've never heard of anyone being utensil-blind, unable to distinguish kettles from colanders.

I'm afraid I'm wandering. Sorry. This letter is for Linda and Mark too, as I hope we were a real family despite everything. Dear Linda, you must take care not to be too much under Tom's thumb. He needs to be influenced by you just as much as you need to be influenced by him. And don't forget that one of the main pleasures of childhood is rebellion. If you are too permissive with Adam and Jocasta, you'll force the poor blighters to turn to drugs and abortions in order to rebel.

I have no advice for you, Mark old thing, except to stick at your acting no matter how unsuccessful you are. I'm only sorry I made such a fuss about so many unimportant things. Length of hair, holes in socks, life's too short. The generation gap's a pitiful irrelevancy when you compare it to the real problems – the hunger gap, the colour gap, and the gaping hole that is the future.

Well, I must go now. I didn't do much in my life but in the last few days at least I've created a few surprises.

Dear Elizabeth, we never talked enough or loved enough or lived enough. Bitter waste. When did I last tell you that I love you? – which I do so very much. I love you all. Remember me not too sadly.

Lots of love,
Reggie

He addressed the envelope and was surprised to find that the pub was quite full. His beer had gone flat. He drank it rapidly. Then he walked out into the warm sunlight.

When Reggie hadn't reached Worthing by four o'clock, Elizabeth had driven home. Traffic was heavy, and it was gone seven before she arrived.

When she saw that he hadn't been home the previous night, she was really alarmed. She rang Linda, Mark and Jimmy. All three said they would come down immediately.

You can say what you like about the family – decry it as an anachronism if you must – but there's nothing quite like it when there's a spot of rallying round to be done.

The six-wheeled jelly moved along the A352 towards Dorchester and the setting sun. The downs rose handsomely on all sides.

There was some kind of delay ahead. He slowed down. He had almost pulled up when he saw the two policemen. His first wild instinct was to accelerate, swing on to the pavement or into the fast lane and surge through, but the instinct had been crushed by his natural lawfulness long before it had been translated into action.

He pulled up in the queue of traffic. His heart was beating fast. Keep calm Reggie, he told himself. Control yourself. Think things out.

If the police are looking for me, he thought, then they'll know I'm in a lorry shaped like a jelly. If they were looking

170

for a lorry shaped like a jelly, they wouldn't be stopping all these vehicles which bear not the slightest resemblance to a dessert of any kind, let alone a jelly. Ergo, they are not looking for me, and I have nothing to fear.

The queue of traffic edged slowly forward towards the police block – and Reggie realized that even if they weren't looking for him, one or two things could be hard to explain. He didn't have a licence to drive lorries. He had two hundred and eighty pounds in his pockets, in used fivers. In the back of the lorry there was a suitcase full of new clothes and a briefcase containing a wig and a black beard.

He edged forward until he was next in line to be examined. The policemen looked quite friendly. The older one signalled him on. He moved forward jerkily, betraying his nerves. There was sweat on his brow.

'Excuse me,' said the younger of the two policemen. 'We'd like to have a look in the back of your lorry.'

'Certainly, officer,' he said.

He stepped down from the cab and opened the moulded rear doors. They glanced in. They didn't seem at all interested in what they saw.

'Thank you, sir. Much obliged,' said the older policeman.

He drove on, hoping that they hadn't heard his sigh of relief. He had intended to make for the coast in these parts, but if there were police about he had better go further afield.

The two Mrs C.J.s thought that both C.J.s were looking tired. The two C.J.s thought that both Mrs C.J.s were looking worried.

'Blood,' said the two C.J.s. 'There was blood in the river.'

'It wasn't blood, dear,' said the Mrs C.J.s.

Two identical hired nurses brought in supper trays.

'There you are,' said the hired nurses. 'That'll do you good.'

The two C.J.s began to eat without enthusiasm. The two Mrs C.J.s sat on the side of the beds and watched.

'I'm sorry,' said the C.J.s. 'I'm sorry for everything.'

The Mrs C.J.s stared at them in astonishment.

'What?' said the Mrs C.J.s.

'Sit with me. Don't go away,' said the C.J.s.

The two Mrs C.J.s bent down and kissed the two C.J.s. Their four mouths met gently. Their eight lips touched tenderly.

Tom and Linda arrived first, dragging Adam and Jocasta. The children were excited but tired.

Elizabeth kissed Linda, then braced herself for Tom's garlicky, ticklish embrace.

The french windows were closed. Everything was quiet in Coleridge Close. Elizabeth looked pale and had bags under her eyes.

'No news?' said Linda.

'No,' said Elizabeth.

'Don't worry,' said Tom.

'Is Grandpa dead?' said Adam.

The mechanical pudding roared through Dorchester. The sun slipped lower towards the horizon.

The sunset came a few minutes earlier at Coleridge Close. Adam and Jocasta had been put to bed. Tom had rung the police, and a policeman was on his way to collect the details of Reggie's disappearance.

Elizabeth had made coffee. Every time they heard a noise she went to the front window to look out. Linda was sitting on the settee, looking tense. Tom appeared to have developed an intense interest in Mr Snurd's pictures of the Algarve.

It was several minutes since anyone had spoken.

'The cow-parsley's very prolific this year,' said Tom.

There was a stunned pause.

'I'll make some more coffee,' said Elizabeth.

'What did you say that for?' said Linda, when Elizabeth had gone into the kitchen.

'I was trying to take her mind off things,' said Tom.

'If you'd disappeared, it wouldn't take my mind off it to know that the horse-radish was plentiful this year.'

'Cow-parsley,' said Tom.

There was a sullen silence.

'It doesn't make things any easier if we quarrel,' said Tom.

'I'm sorry,' said Linda.

Tom walked over to the settee, bent over and buried his head in Linda's hair. At that moment the doorbell rang.

'I'll go,' said Linda.

Elizabeth hurried out from the kitchen.

'I'll go,' she said.

It was Jimmy.

'Sorry,' he said, as he saw their faces drop. 'It's only me.'

'Silly of me,' said Elizabeth. 'He wouldn't ring the bell.'

'Bad business,' said Jimmy. 'With you all the way. Count on me. Anything you need doing.'

He hugged Elizabeth, but he didn't kiss Linda.

'Er – sorry Sheila can't make it,' he said. 'Not – er – not too well.'

'I'll get that coffee,' said Linda. 'You sit down for a moment, mother.'

'I'll help,' said Jimmy.

Jimmy followed Linda into the kitchen. He was moving his lips in a tense, uncontrollable way.

'Sorry about Thursday,' he said.

'That's all right.'

He stared at the fridge as if it was the most interesting fridge he had ever seen.

'Can't think what came over me. Bad show,' he said.

'It doesn't matter.'

He walked over to the spin dryer, opened the lid and closed it again.

'Bad business, this,' he said.

'Yes.'

'He was one of the best, your father,' he said. 'Not that he's dead,' he added hurriedly. 'He's alive. Feel it in my water.'

Linda kissed him on the lips, then turned away and resumed her coffee-making.

When they went back into the living room. Elizabeth said, 'What's up with you two? You look as if you've seen a ghost. Now come and sit down. Tom's been telling me all about the origins of Morris dancing. It's very interesting.'

The whole western sky was burning. It was a scene to set shepherds dancing in ecstasy. The lane slipped gently down towards the shore, through a little village of chalets, bungalows and cottages. It ended in a car park. Entry was free now that the attendant had gone home.

Reggie pulled up and sat looking out over the sea. There were still a few other cars in the car park. Behind the car park there was a beach café. The owner was just putting up the shutters. There was a life-belt and a municipal telescope. An elderly man put a coin in and stared out at an expanse of magnified water.

There was a long sweep of shingle, and behind the bay the land rose gradually, a long slope of grass dotted with windswept shrubs. The village was at the end of nowhere. It was a suitable place to end a life.

The policeman had been and gone. It was dark, but Elizabeth still hadn't drawn the curtains when Mark arrived at half past eleven. He kissed his mother. His breath smelt of beer.

'No news?' he said.

'No.'

'I knew last Sunday he was trying to tell me something,' he said.

'I should have done more,' said Jimmy.

'We all should,' said Linda.

'I kept thinking, "It's nothing. It can't be. It'll be all right tomorrow,"' said Elizabeth.

'Is there any juice in the pot?' said Mark.

'I'll make some fresh,' said Linda.

'I'll help,' said Jimmy.

'Mark'll help,' said Linda firmly. 'Tea or coffee?'

'Tea,' said Mark, and he followed Linda into the kitchen.

'It's a bastard, isn't it?' he said.

'Yes.'

'It's a sod.'

'Yes.'

'Oh well, keep hoping.'

'Yes,' said Linda, with a sob in her voice.

'Come on,' said Mark. 'Cheer up. Mustn't lose your bottle.'

'No,' said Linda. She blew her nose on a piece of kitchen tissue.

Mark patted her on the bottom.

'Hullo, fatso,' he said.

Linda tried to smile.

'Hullo, shorthouse,' she said, ruffling his hair. 'How's work going?'

'Bloody awful,' said Mark.

'Didn't Wick work out?' said Linda.

'No.'

She laid out five cups on a tray and scalded the pot.

'I've got some work coming up next week,' said Mark.

'Oh good. What's that?' said Linda.

Mark looked sheepish. He picked a small tomato out of a bag on top of the fridge and popped it into his mouth.

'I'm playing the under butler in a play at Alistair and Fiona Campbell's barn theatre at Lossiemouth,' he said.

Linda poured the boiling water into the pot.

'Do you think father's all right?' she asked.

'I think he's gone off his nut, luv, that's what I think,' said Mark. 'Poor old bastard. Come on. Let's help make that tea.'

'I've finished,' said Linda.

They went back into the living room. Mark carried the tray.

A car came along the road and slowed down, but it was only the Milfords, returning from their snifter at the golf club.

It was dark now, and Reggie had the car park to himself. He changed into his new clothes in the back of the lorry, put his

175

old clothes into the suitcase with the beard and wig, and stepped out into the night.

He stood for a moment on the wall of the car park, listening to the waves crunching on the shingle and the little stones being sucked out by the undertow. In the village car doors were being slammed outside the pub.

Reggie stepped down on to the shingle and set off towards the west. It was hard walking.

He walked for about half an hour and then he felt he was far enough away from the village. He'd reached a cliff which towered above him in the darkness, rocky and jagged.

There was nobody about. There was no light except for the lights of Portland Bill away to the east, and the faint stars above, and the phosphorescence on the water.

Reggie felt acutely depressed. Could he face a life without Elizabeth? Had he really done anything at all worthwhile? Would he ever do anything worthwhile? Why not make it a real suicide after all? Why not prove he wasn't a fraud?

He took off his shoes first.

Sunday

Reggie stood naked and hairy under the cliffs and gazed at the placid sea. Tiny waves swished feebly against the shingle. A faint puff of wind came in from the west, and he shivered, although it wasn't cold. Far away, the beam of a lighthouse made an occasional faint flash on the horizon.

He didn't know if he dared to immerse himself in the water and hold himself down, gasping for breath, and then oblivion, a body on a beach, policemen and a mortuary slab, and a verdict of suicide while the balance of mind was disturbed, death was estimated at one a.m., he was a well-nourished man weighing thirteen stone eleven pounds, and there was evidence of semi-digested chips consistent with his having eaten a substantial meal eight hours before decease. And then he would be nothing, for he didn't believe in a life after death.

He stepped carefully over the shingle, and felt the water gingerly with his toe. It was cold, but not as cold as it looked. Soon he was up to his waist. He stubbed his right foot against a stone.

He looked back at the cliffs, towering above his two neat piles of clothes and his little suitcase with the wig and beard. That would be a mystery for the police.

He walked on, over stones and seaweed. Car headlights shone high up in the darkness behind him, and that little cluster of lights to the west must be Lyme Regis.

You don't really find life intolerable, he told himself. Killing yourself won't prove that you're not a fraud. Those cliffs have been there for millions of years. You're too ephemeral to be able to afford such a gesture.

He began to swim, in his jerky, laboured breast stroke. Then he swam on his back, looking up at the stars. He was alone in the great salt sea, and the universe looked cold.

He began to shiver and swam towards the shore. He was glad, on the whole, not to be dying just yet. He walked carefully up the beach to the little piles of clothes under the cliffs. There was nobody about to see him.

He hadn't brought a towel, so he jumped up and down, and rubbed his tingling body with his hands. Then he rubbed himself down with his new vest, and at last he was tolerably dry.

He shoved the sodden vest into his suitcase, and unwrapped his new shirt. It wasn't easy in the dark to make sure that he'd got all the pins out, but at last he was ready to put the shirt on. He was shivering uncontrollably now.

He pulled his new clothes over his sticky, salty skin. They felt stiff and unpleasant. He fitted the wig as best he could, then put the beard on.

He looked down at the pile of old clothes. 'Good-bye, Reggie's clothes,' he said, and then, 'Good-bye, old Reggie.'

He picked up the suitcase too violently, forgetting that it was almost empty. He overbalanced and fell in the shingle. A bad start to a new life, he thought, cursing and rubbing his elbow.

He set off along the beach, a tiny figure beneath the cliffs. Suddenly he remembered that he'd left all his money in his old clothes, so back he had to trudge. He took the money and his wallet and set off again. Then he realized that it would look suspicious if he didn't leave his wallet and some money in the old clothes. Only a compulsively mean man would take his wallet into the sea to drown beside him.

He couldn't leave any of the used fivers, for fear they'd be traced, so he left three pounds in notes and eighty-six pence in loose change. Off he went again along the beach.

Then his blood ran cold. He'd left his banker's card in his wallet. That would blow sky-high his story of losing the card. Back he trudged yet again.

178

He hunted through his wallet. Library ticket, dental appointment reminder, dry-cleaning counterfoil, the cards of three plumbers and a french polisher. At last he found it. He took it with shaking fingers.

He sat on the beach and tried to think if there was anything that he'd forgotten. God, he was bad at this. He'd never have made a master crook. When he had convinced himself that there were no more precautions he could take, he set off along the beach for the fourth time. Again he forgot that the suitcase was almost empty, and again he overbalanced. This time he didn't fall, but he almost twisted his ankle. His nerves were at their raw ends. He felt sure that somebody must have seen his comings and goings, some loving couple or insomniac coastguard.

He trudged back to the car park. There was the lorry shaped like a jelly, all alone now. There was the sleeping village.

He walked as casually as he could. His heart was pumping fast. It was absurd to feel so nervous. Murderers evaded detection for weeks on end, with the whole police force hunting them, and their photographs in every paper. And he had an advantage over them. They weren't masters of disguise, stars of the annual dramatic offerings of Sunshine Desserts.

He climbed slowly through this windswept ragbag of a place, even its diminutive flint pub lifeless and darkened.

There was a faint breeze just stirring the notice board outside the tiny chapel of green corrugated iron.

The houses were thinning out, just a few chalets and bungalows now. Still nobody about. Reggie was terrified of meeting anyone. He was afraid that his beard and wig were hopelessly askew.

He passed the last house, and began to climb the hill. His clothes were stiff, his new shoes were pinching and his skin felt damp and salty, but he walked more confidently now.

He heard footsteps and flung himself into the hedge. A drunk passed down the hill, barely five feet from him, weaving unsteadily, singing a monotonous and unrecognizable dirge.

Reggie set off again, more cautiously, ears alert. Soon the moon came up and its beam lit up a higher range of hills ahead of him.

He felt ridiculous. The grey trousers were narrow fitting and slightly flared. The shoes were brown suede. The jacket was green with gold buttons. The shirt was orange and had large lapels, and the kipper tie had a Gold Paisley pattern. Everything was too tight. Modern clothes were made for slim-fit men with girlish waists, tapered bodies and flared calves.

What must I look like, he thought, as he plodded along between the windswept hedges in the moonlight. I aimed at something rather distinguished, a sort of respectable Bohemianism. I must look like a trendy quantity surveyor.

The eastern sky began to pale. Vague shapes turned into trees. The hills ahead of him seemed to grow smaller. Sheep stared at him as if they had never seen a trendy quantity surveyor before.

He was very tired. His eyes were heavy, his legs ached. He felt cold, despite the mildness of the night.

He occupied his mind as he walked towards the hills by trying to think of a name for himself. Alastair McTavish? Lionel Penfold? Cedric de Vere Fitzpatrick-Thorneycroft?

Visibility was good. Every detail of the hills stood out with great clarity, and the sky was shot with high white cloud, tinged faintly with pink. Reggie sensed that the weather was on the blink. Arnold Blink? Barney Rustington? Charles Windsor? He couldn't go around calling himself Charles Windsor.

He came to a junction, where the lane forked. Could the signpost give him a clue to his new name? David Dorchester? Barry Bridport? Timothy Lyme-Regis?

He took the left-hand fork. Ahead of him he could see the narrow lane climbing up the range of hills. The tops of the hills were bare and chalky but their lower slopes were clothed in trees and he decided that he would rest for a while on their carpet of leaves.

Daniel Leaf? Beerbohm Tree? Colin Hedge?

Colin. He quite liked that. He felt an incipient colinishness. But Colin what? Colin Watt?

He approached a gate, and decided to call himself Colin the first thing he saw when he looked over the gate.

Colin Cowpat?

He climbed over the gate into the wood, a place of low trees cowering before the south-westerly winds. As soon as he was out of sight of the road, he sank down on to the ground and fell asleep.

He woke up with a start, listening to the screeching of alarmed jays. For a moment he didn't know who he was. He was a strange man in strange clothes with a ticklish face, lying on a bed of old leaves. Then it all came back to him.

God, he was tired. And hungry. How long had he been asleep? The sun was high in the sky.

He scooped a hollow out of the earth and buried his banker's card there. It should be safe from everything except moles and truffle hounds.

He brushed himself clean of leaves and twigs and ladybirds, and set off towards the lane. His legs were like lead.

He heard a car climbing up the lane, and stood behind a tree, pretending to pee, until it had passed. Then he clambered over the gate.

The lane climbed between high hedges. It was very hot. Brown birds flitted from bush to bush ahead of him. Sheep peered at him through brambles. The bright blue sky was flecked with confused mares' tails, as if a squadron of giant aeroplanes had been looping the loop. There was wind up there.

Who should he claim to be? A salesman? The suitcase suggested that. But what could he be selling, with his case empty? A suitcase salesman, with only one suitcase left to sell?

At last he reached the main road. He walked along it towards the west, until he came to a bus stop, set in a little lay-by. There was no time-table, and in any case he didn't know what time it was.

The holiday traffic whizzed past in both directions, an endless stream of caravans, roof racks, boats on tow, every now and then a plain ordinary car.

There was an ominous aura of buslessness. Reggie stood at the entrance to the lay-by and tried to thumb a lift. Most of the cars were full of kids, dogs, grannies and snorkelling equipment, but at last a buff Humber slid to an aristocratic halt. Inside were a well-dressed couple, with two chihuahuas.

'Can we take you somewhere?' asked the man.

Well, what do you think I was doing, thought Reggie. Thumb-slimming exercises?

'Yes, please. I'm making for Exeter,' he said.

'Hop in the back.'

Reggie hopped in the back. The car smelt of cigars, scent and chihuahuas. The control panel was made of varnished wood, and there was an arm-rest in the middle of the back seat.

'I nearly didn't stop. You looked too hairy,' said the man.

'We don't approve of hitch-hikers,' said the woman. 'Spongers, we call them.'

The road dipped and rose among the sharp Dorset hills. On the verges people were erecting elaborate picnics.

'What time is it?' Reggie asked.

'Quarter to twelve,' said the woman.

The chihuahuas barked at him.

'Don't mind Pyramus and Thisbe,' said the woman.

'Some kind of artist, are you?' said the man.

Reggie's spirits lifted. Well done, Reggie's disguise, he thought.

'I'm a writer,' he said.

'Ah. I thought so,' said the man.

'What kind of things do you write?' said the woman.

'Books,' said Reggie.

'What sort of books?' said the man.

'Stories,' said Reggie.

'What are you called? Would we know you?' said the woman.

'Charles Windsor,' said Reggie.

'That rings a bell,' said the woman. 'We must borrow one of your books from the library.'

'I've never written a book,' said the man. 'Often thought of it, but I've never got around to it.'

They stopped for a drink at the Smugglers' Inn, a low thatched pub on top of a hill, surrounded by a vast car park. At the side of the pub was a stall selling teas and ices. They left Pyramus and Thisbe in the car.

The landlord put on canned music in honour of their arrival. The pub was full of horse-brasses and hunting prints, and a notice above the 'gents' announced 'Here 'tis'.

They sat at a table by the open window. There was a fine view of the car park. Reggie was worried that they would find his appearance odd. It was the first time his beard and wig had been put to the test.

'How do you get the ideas for your books?' said the man.

'I don't know. They just come,' said Reggie.

'Interesting, isn't it, dear?' said the man.

They had two rounds of crab sandwiches each, and then they drove on. There were wisps of grey in the sky.

Now they were in Devon. Every cottage advertised 'Devon cream teas' and every guest house was called 'The Devonian'. The road wound and twisted through a tangle of wooded hills. There were frequent glimpses of the sea.

'Are you going on holiday?' said Reggie.

'Boating,' said the man. 'Golf. There's a lot of boating in Devon.'

'There's a lot of writing in Devon too,' said Reggie.

'I suppose there would be,' said the woman.

It didn't seem very long before they reached the Exeter by-pass.

'This'll do me nicely,' said Reggie.

He caught a bus into the city centre. There were fine old houses and a modern quarter. He tried several hotels before he found a room.

Inside the hotel it was deafeningly quiet. He signed his name 'Charles Windsor'. The desk clerk picked up his case and was so surprised at its lightness that he lost his footing, tripped and hit the gong with the suitcase. When he had picked himself up he looked at Reggie accusingly.

'I'm travelling light,' said Reggie.

The man led the way up the stairs. On the first floor landing they met a group of puzzled elderly people coming down to dinner.

'It can't be dinner, Hubert. We've only just had lunch,' said one of the women.

'I heard the gong, I tell you,' said a white-haired old man.

'I tripped and banged it by mistake,' explained the desk clerk.

He led Reggie to his room. Reggie heard the man say, 'I told you I heard the gong,' and the woman said, 'I knew it wasn't dinner,' and someone else said, 'Did you see that funny man with the beard?'

Reggie barely noticed his room. He was too tired and too hungry. He went out into the town and had egg, sausage, bacon, mushrooms, tomatoes, beans, chips and peas, bread and butter and four cups of tea.

'Mr Windsor,' said the desk clerk on his return.

Reggie took no notice.

'Mr Windsor!' called the desk clerk.

Reggie turned and went up to the desk.

'Sorry,' he said. 'I forgot that was me.'

The desk clerk gave him a strange look.

'Will you be taking dinner, Mr Windsor?' he said.

'No. I'm not feeling well,' said Reggie.

He went straight upstairs to bed and slept for fourteen hours.

Monday

It was shortly after tea-time when the last bus delivered the distinguished architect Mr Wensley Amhurst into the charming Wiltshire village of Chilhampton Ambo. Mr Amhurst was a bearded man with long black hair and a slow, dignified walk. He looked round the little square with every appearance of pleasure, and then disappeared into the Market Inn.

At the exact moment when Mr Amhurst was making his acquaintance with the comfortable recesses of the aforementioned hostelry, Chief Inspector Gate was conferring with his new assistant, Constable Barker. Mr Amhurst might not have been so happy if he had heard their conversation.

'The fact remains, sir,' Constable Barker was saying, 'that we don't have a body.'

'Maybe we never will. The currents round there are very variable,' said his superior. 'Look, Barker, we know he was a sick man. He'd stolen a lorry full of loganberry essence. He'd made a fool of himself at an important conference. He was drinking heavily. A lot of cheques had been stolen from his account.'

Chief Inspector Gate was a big, florid man whose hobby was double whiskies. Constable Barker was a few inches shorter, and his hobby was detection. Chief Inspector Gate's qualifications were that he was six foot tall. Constable Barker's were nine 'O' Levels and three 'A' levels.

'Couldn't he have written those cheques himself?' said Constable Barker, who was pacing nervously round Chief Inspector Gate's file-infested office.

'What for?'

'As the only way he could get some money to live on, without arousing suspicion. Off he goes, dumps the clothes on the beach, away to a new life.'

'But he has aroused suspicion – yours.'

Constable Barker blushed.

'Maybe I've been too clever for him, sir,' he said, as the rising wind rattled the window frames. 'Don't you agree, sir? Couldn't he have done that?'

'Of course he *could*. My auntie could have had balls, and then she'd have been my uncle. We have no evidence, Barker.'

'We have no body.'

'True. Sit down, lad. You're tiring me out.'

Constable Barker sat down and faced Chief Inspector Gate across his desk.

'Look, Barker,' said Chief Inspector Gate pompously, for he had no sons of his own. 'You've been reading too many books. Things like that only happen in books. In books the murder is committed by the least likely person – usually the detective. In life it's committed by the most likely person – usually the husband or wife. In books it's always the least likely person who commits suicide. In real life it's always the dead man himself.'

Constable Barker stood up, apologized, and sat down again.

'Couldn't this be the exception that proves the rule, sir?' he said.

'In books the exception that proves the rule is the rule. In life it's the exception. No, Barker. Forget it. Save us all a lot of trouble. Damn, it's raining!'

'I can't forget it, sir.'

'You're different from me, Barker. I joined the force because I was six foot tall. My cousin was four foot eleven. He became a jockey. He rode seven hundred and sixty-three winners on the flat. I'd have been a jockey if I'd been four foot eleven. I'd have ridden seven hundred and sixty-three winners on the flat. Life is all a matter of height.'

Chief Inspector Gate walked over to the window and looked out over the emptying main street of the seaside town. Nobody had brought umbrellas.

'But you've got a sense of vocation,' he said. 'That's why you always wear green socks and drink pernod.'

'I like green socks and pernod,' said Constable Barker.

'No. You're creating your mystique. They're Maigret's pipe and Hercule Poirot's moustache. You dream of the day when you'll be Barker of the Yard. I knew I could never reach the top, not with my name. Gate of the Yard. You try too hard. You see things that aren't there. British detection is based upon a sound principle – things are as they seem until proved otherwise.'

Chief Inspector Gate sat down again. Constable Barker sighed and stood up.

'I'm sorry, sir. I have a hunch that he's still alive.'

'A hunch? Your nine 'O' levels and your three 'A' levels and all your books on criminology, and you have a hunch?'

'Yes, sir.'

'That's different. A good policeman never ignores a hunch. All right, Barker. I'll tell you what we'll do.' It had grown unnaturally dark in the office as the storm deepened. 'We'll see if anyone can give us a description of the man who signed those cheques. We'll consult a handwriting expert. We'll go over that bloody beach with a toothcomb. If there's anything to find out, we'll find it out. All right? Satisfied?'

'Thank you, sir.'

'Come on, Barker of the Yard. It's going to piss down in a minute. I'll buy you a double pernod.'

The Market Inn was full but Reggie managed to get a room at the Crown.

'It's the last one, sir. Right at the back, I'm afraid. We're absolutely choc-a-bloc,' said the receptionist.

'Why are you so full?' said Reggie.

'We're always full, sir. This is a show place.'

'Is it?'

187

The receptionist looked surprised.

'Of course it is, sir. Name?'

'Wensley Amhurst,' said Reggie.

His room was small and impersonal. The carpet and bed-spread were bright yellow and the walls were white. There was a green telephone beside the bed.

He washed, opened the window wide, breathed in the warm Wiltshire air. There was a fresh breeze, and it smelt of rain. To the left, tucked away from the village, was a council estate, grey pebble-dash houses. They hadn't been there when he was a boy. In the background was farming country and beech woods.

He went for a walk around the village, working up his thirst, trying to walk like a distinguished architect. He didn't feel at all like a Wensley Amhurst yet.

It was all much smaller than he remembered. Stone houses, mainly, and a few half-timbered. Lots of thatch, immaculately kept.

He was drawn up Sheep Lane, towards the house where Angela Borrowdale had lived. He could still picture her riding breeches but not her face.

The house was an antique shop now. Chilhampton Ambo boasted three pubs, five antique shops, one grocers-cum-post office, and a boutique. Monstrous china dogs gazed out where once Angela Borrowdale, the unattainable, had sat.

Reggie had once sent her an anonymous note: 'Meet me behind Boulter's Barn. Tuesday. Nine p.m. An admirer.' She hadn't come, of course, and it gave him the hot flushes to think of that note now.

He wandered back down Sheep Lane, somewhat saddened. The old buildings were covered now with the little accessories of modern life – television aerials, junction boxes, burglar alarms. The little street was filled with middle-class married couples, walking slowly, wives slightly in front of husbands, admiring the antiques, popping into the little grocer's and buying a pot of local jam for only twopence more than the same jam would have cost in London.

Swifts and swallows flew high up in their grey paradise of insects. Reggie entered the Market Inn, where he had drunk his very first pint of bitter, long ago.

The public bar had gone, along with its darts and skittles. It was one big lounge, filled with reproduction antiques. The Italian barmen wore red jackets. Reggie ordered a pint of bitter and stood at the bar.

There were four young farmers at the bar, chatting cheerfully. The door opened and Reggie had a wild hope that it would be Angela Borrowdale. It was a pretty blonde with a hard face. The farmers greeted her with cries of 'Hullo, Sarah, how did it go?' and she said, 'We came third – Hollyhock made a nonsense of the water jump,' and they all said, 'Bad luck!' and Reggie felt very old and very lonely, and one of them said, 'Same again all round, Mario – and the usual for Sarah.'

A menu advertised smoked salmon sandwiches, prawn salads, and kipper patés. Touring couples sat in silence sipping medium sherry.

Reggie tried to be Wensley Amhurst, tried to feel natural, tried to forget that he was wearing a false beard beneath which his own hair tickled horribly.

'Nice day,' he said, in an upper-middle-class voice, which came out all wrong. The farmers turned and looked at him in astonishment. So did the unsuccessful Sarah. So did the Italian barmen. In the silence Reggie could hear the sound of teeming rain.

Wensley Amhurst finished his drink in silence, and hurried out into the rain. The big summer drops were bouncing back off the road. He pulled his jacket over his head and made a dash for the Black Bull, the venue of his second pint, long ago.

'Raining, is it?' said the landlord, laughing jovially at his wit. He was a big jovial man and he had a huge handlebar moustache.

'Pint of bitter, please,' said Reggie.

'Pint of cooking,' said the landlord.

The public bar had gone, with its darts and skittles. It was all one big bar now, its different areas separated by wrought-iron arches. The arches were festooned with plastic vines. A sickly blue and yellow carpet covered the whole floor space, and a stream of background music tinkled softly over its musical stones.

There was only one other customer, a thin gloomy man with a smaller, drop handlebar moustache.

'Lovely weather for ducks,' said the landlord.

'Yes,' riposted Reggie.

'Still, we can't complain,' said the landlord. 'We've done well. You a stranger here?'

'I haven't been here for twenty-five years,' said Reggie. 'I came here when I was a boy for my summer holidays.'

'I'm from Lowestoft myself,' said the landlord. 'It's a dump.'

'I came in this pub the first time I ever got drunk,' said Reggie. 'I was fifteen.'

The landlord glanced involuntarily at the number plate which said 'RU 18', and smiled.

'Bit different now, eh?'

'Yes,' said Reggie.

'Evelyn and I took the place over in '63, didn't we, Fizzer?'

'That's right, Jumbo,' said Fizzer. 'It must have been '63.'

'Frightful hole. No, I tell a lie, it was bloody well '62. Denise had her hysterectomy in '63, and we'd been here a year then.'

'That's right,' said Fizzer. 'It must have been '62.'

'We made a few changes, knocked the odd wall down.'

'What about the locals?' said Reggie. 'Don't they miss the darts and things?'

The landlord laughed jovially.

'Locals? What locals? The locals can't afford houses here. There's only the yobbos on the council estate. Touchy sods. Won't come in here just because I won't let them sit on the seats in their working clothes.'

'I think it's a pity,' said Reggie.

'So do I. So do I,' said the landlord. 'Don't get me wrong.

Nobody likes locals as much as I do. And darts, well, I threw a pretty decent arrow myself, in my day. But it takes up too much space. No money coming in.'

In the old days, thought Reggie, country life could be pretty grim. Now, with modern transport and electricity, it's becoming very pleasant – pleasant enought for all the working people to be forced out into the town.

'We get a damned good crowd in here,' said the landlord. 'Apart from that gloomy bastard over there. Old Dave Binstead's a regular. He's a lad.'

Reggie looked blank.

'The motor-cycle scrambler. He's here every night. Then there's Micky Fudge. You know him?'

'No,' said Reggie.

'You know. The band-leader. Micky Fudge and his Fandango Band.'

I decided on an identity. Wensley Amhurst. I felt better. No saying 'Earwigs'. No question of my legs failing to obey me.

'Vince Cameron, the film director, he pops in Saturdays. He's a lad. You know, he made *The Blob From Twenty Thousand Fathoms.*'

'I missed it,' said Reggie.

And then I chose to come to Chilhampton. Why? Wensley Amhurst, the distinguished architect, has no reason to go to Chilhampton Ambo. Can't I admit that Reggie Perrin is dead?

'Load of old stones in a field up beyond the village,' said the landlord. 'Load of weirdies came along last summer and had a festival, Druids or something. I said to them, "Piss off, you load of Druids." We get a decent crowd in here, apart from that bloody gloomy sod standing there. Of course we get the pouffes from the antique shops, but they're decent chaps. I say to them, "Come on, you bloody pouffes, drink up or piss off." They can take a joke.'

In my memory those summer holidays were an idyll. The exquisite agony of desiring Angela Borrowdale, the unattainable. She rode by, sometimes on the grey, sometimes on the

191

chestnut gelding, her riding breeches wide at the thigh, her whip in her hand.

We had P.T. first lesson in the afternoon at Ruttingstagg. I'd gone back to get my gym-shoes, which I'd forgotten, and I was going back along the corridor by the notice board and I saw the headmaster's daughter and I said, 'Hullo. Are you better?' and she went red and said, 'Much better, thank you. And I say, congrats on getting your shooting colours' and I put my hand right up her skirt. She ran off and I went to the gym. We did vaulting and then rope climbing. I was at the top of the rope when the summons came. I changed, gathered up my bundle of P.T. things, and went up to the headmaster's study. He made me wait outside for a few minutes although there was nobody with him. There was a smell of fishcakes and feet in the corridor.

'My daughter alleges that you put your hand up her skirt,' he said sternly.

'Yes, sir.'

'Did you?'

'Yes, sir.'

'Why?'

'I don't know, sir.'

'Come, come, Perrin, you can do better than that.'

'She said something nice to me, sir.'

'What did she say?'

'She said, "Congrats on getting your shooting colours," sir.'

'Do you always put your hands up girls' skirts when they say something nice to you?'

'No, sir.'

'Would you do that sort of thing at home?'

'No, sir.'

'Then don't do it here. We don't want dirty-minded little brats at Ruttingstagg. People think they can get away with it just because there's a war on.'

'Yes, sir.'

'You're expelled, Perrin.'

'Yes, sir.'

Mark had done better. He'd only been expelled for drinking.

'It's like talking to a brick wall,' said the landlord.

'Sorry. I was thinking,' said Reggie.

'I said, "Mad Pick-Axe" Harris comes in here Fridays. You know, the explorer chap on the television,' said the landlord.

'Oh, really?' said Reggie.

The door opened. Reggie looked to see if it was Angela Borrowdale, but it was a short, dapper man with a toothbrush moustache.

'Bloody hell, look what the cat's brought in,' said the landlord.

'Half of Guinness,' said toothbrush moustache.

'Half of diesel,' said the landlord.

'Lovely weather for ducks,' said Fizzer.

'Good-bye,' said Reggie.

The meal at the Crown was eaten in whispers. A dropped fork was a violent outrage. He had 'ravioli Italienne', which meant 'tinned', and 'entrecote garni', which meant with one slice of lukewarm tomato. The homosexual Spanish waiters had sound-proof shoes and double-glazed eyes.

After dinner the rain had stopped, and he walked up the lane and had a look at the old stone farm. Dusk was gathering, and the light had been switched on in the old kitchen of his schoolboy high teas. In front of the house there were two ugly new grain silos.

He wandered back into the village. The air smelt of drying rain. He entered the crowded hotel bar. There was a sign saying 'No Druids or Coach Parties'. It was only when somebody called her Angela that he recognized the artifically blonde middle-aged woman who was sitting on the end bar stool and behaving as if she owned the place. Her voice was hard and bossy, there were mean lines pulling down the sides of her mouth, and she wasn't wearing riding breeches. She looked straight at him, but she couldn't have been expected to see, in this bearded grotesque, any sign of the shy, clumsy youth of yesteryear.

Reggie sipped his whisky. Tomorrow Reggie Perrin would die, Wensley Amhurst would die, and his new life would begin in earnest.

Tuesday

The stone of the little Cotswold town was tinged with yellow. The Three Feathers was a gabled sixteenth-century building. Spells of bright sunshine were chasing away the flurries of rain. The receptionist had jet-black hair and huge grey eyes. When she smiled she might have been on location for a toothpaste ad., and when she said, 'Room number twenty-one, Sir Wensley,' it was in a voice that would not have disgraced a BBC announcer.

Small wonder, then, that she made such an impression on 'Mad Pick-Axe' Amhurst, the distinguished explorer, mountaineer, anthropologist, gourmet and sex maniac.

Reggie had been given a much better room now that he was knighted. The wallpaper was luxuriant with roses, and he had a private bathroom with green marble tiles.

He took a bath. There was a hand-held shower for washing the back, and he utilized this attachment to the full. Outside, thrushes and blackbirds were singing, and occasional spots of rain pattered against the frosted glass.

Reggie endeavoured to think as he imagined Sir Wensley Amhurst would think.

Sir Wensley Amhurst thought about the pretty receptionist. God, she'd look good in fawn riding breeches.

After his bath he settled in the lounge with a copy of the *Field* and ordered China tea and crumpets.

How would Sir Wensley use his considerable charms upon a pretty receptionist?

Reggie wandered over to her, adopting an almost imperceptible limp, a relic of a fall on the Matterhorn.

'Can you order me *The Times*?' he said.

'Certainly, Sir Wensley,' said the flashing smile.

'Er . . .'

'Yes, Sir Wensley?'

'Nothing.'

Sir Wensley limped through the stone jewel that was Chipping Hampstead-on-the-Wold. He limped past its four pubs, seven antique shops, three potteries, five boutiques, and its superior store selling local jams and herbal soaps. To him it wasn't a town, it was a tribal centre of the English middle class. His keen anthropological eye noted that there wasn't a coloured person in sight.

He acquired a bit more character with the purchase of a handsome locally-made walking stick. He limped up the lane past the magnificent early English church on to the open wold.

'Mad Pick-Axe' Amhurst sat on top of a stone wall and looked out over the fields. All this had once been a huge sheep run but most of it was under cultivation now. Sad, thought the reactionary explorer.

A finch, or was it a warbler, flew into a little clump of elms, or were they hornbeams? Let's just say a small bird landed on a big tree.

Reggie felt annoyed by his ignorance. Sir Wensley Amhurst would have known about such things.

He returned to the hotel, stopping on the way to consume two pints of foaming English beer. How often had he dreamt of beer like this as he cut laboriously through the mangrove swamps of the Amazon Basin with his pick-axe!

He smiled at the pretty receptionist, decided not to make his approach to her until after dinner, and enjoyed his traditional Cotswold meal of gazpacho, duck à l'orange and zabaglione.

After dinner a sallow young man was occupying the receptionist's booth, and he abandoned his plan of ordering early morning tea.

He went out for his after-dinner constitutional, and there,

coming towards him down the main street, was the receptionist. She had beautiful slender legs and her heels clacked
loudly. The surprise of seeing her took his breath away. She
said, 'Good evening, Sir Wensley,' and hesitated just percep-
tibly in her path. 'Good evening,' he said, and he hesitated,
then walked on.

He turned to watch her walk away from him. She went up
the road that led to the church and just before she disappeared
she turned and looked in his direction.

Bloody hell, thought Reggie, that wasn't 'Mad Pick-Axe'
Amhurst, who once had seven Chinese women in one
glorious night on the Shanghai waterfront. That was Goofy
Perrin.

He walked round a back lane, coming out at the end of the
road to the church. There was no sign of the receptionist.

He went into a pub on the hill by the church. It was packed
and smoky, and she wasn't there either.

He limped back to the hotel and went early to bed. He
couldn't sleep. His hatred of 'Mad Pick-Axe' Amhurst was too
strong.

Wednesday

It was shortly after tea-time when the last bus delivered Lord Amhurst into the charming Oxfordshire village of Henleaze Ffoliat. Lord Amhurst was a bearded man with dark hair and a gammy leg. He looked round the little square with every appearance of pleasure, and then disappeared into the Ffoliat Arms.

At this very moment, had Lord Amhurst but known it, Chief Inspector Gate was attempting to dislodge a particularly stubborn piece of wax from his right ear with the aid of a safety match. Two minutes later, however, a weary Constable Barker entered his office and sank gratefully into the chair proffered to him for just such a purpose.

'Nothing,' he admitted. 'The cashiers have been questioned at all the banks where the cheques were cashed. A few of them remember the man. If their descriptions are accurate, he was a tall dark fair-haired bald man of average height with a hooked Roman nose, one blue eye, one green eye and one brown eye.'

Chief Inspector Gate tossed his waxed match towards the waste-paper basket and missed.

'The handwriting expert thinks the signatures on the cheques are genuine forgeries,' he said. 'But he can't rule out the possibility that they're forged forgeries, in other words genuine.'

Constable Barker sighed.

'None of that proves anything either way,' he said.

'There's no motive. Perrin hasn't taken out any insurance policies lately.'

'Anything from the beach, sir?'

'Nothing much. There are no reports of any mysterious strangers. The only thing our chaps found on the beach was this pin.'

Chief Inspector Gate handed a small pin to Constable Barker. He examined it keenly. Then he stood up. He seemed excited.

'This could be a pin off a new shirt,' said Constable Barker. 'He could have been putting on new clothes.'

'He could have put on two enormous coconuts and done a moonlight impression of Raquel Welch,' said Chief Inspector Gate. He examined his ear with another match. 'It's not much to go on, is it?'

'I suppose not. But I've got a hunch that my hunch is right.'

Chief Inspector Gate threw the match towards the waste-paper basket. It landed bang in the middle, and he smiled with ill-concealed satisfaction.

'Possibly,' he said. 'But as far as our investigations are concerned, Reginald Perrin is dead.'

Reggie's room, now that he was a hereditary peer, was much better than the one he'd been given when he'd merely been knighted for services to the nation. He enjoyed a luxurious bath, utilized the disposable shoe-cleaning pads, sat in his comfortable armchair by the balcony door, and smoked one of Lord Amhurst's favourite cheroots as he admired the view. He looked out over a diminutive valley of small grassy fields. A low arched stone bridge carried a grassy farm track over a little river. Between the showers a bright sun shone. He had two hundred and twenty-five pounds in his pocket.

When he had finished his cheroot he took a turn round the aristocratic little town. There were four hotels, three pubs, five antique shops, six potteries, two boutiques and a suede boutique. He limped badly – the legacy of an accident on the

Cresta Run, where he had been a distinguished performer in the two-man bobsleigh.

He limped back across the square, filled with parked cars and coaches, and entered the Ffoliat Arms. Its handsome three-storey frontage was covered in Virginia creeper.

He crossed the foyer, threading his way between suits of old English armour, and entered the bar. It was beset rather than decorated by antlers.

The bar had six occupants. Four of them were Americans, the fifth was an attractive blonde, and the sixth was his son-in-law Tom. Tom was sitting at a corner table with the attractive blonde. Reggie almost forgot that he was supposed to be Lord Amhurst. Then he recovered himself, ordered a whisky and soda, and limped to a table as close to Tom as he dared. He sat beneath a magnificent set of antlers. His heart thumped, but Tom gave no sign of recognition. He was drinking white wine. So was his blonde companion.

So, thought Reggie, fear giving way to anger, this is how you treat my daughter, you swine.

'It's a very lovely house indeed,' Tom was saying. 'It's got charm and distinction. Now let's just see. Four recep., six bed., three bath. Stables. Seven acres. I'd have thought we'd be thinking in terms of at least sixty-five thou.'

'Fine,' said the blonde, who looked about thirty and had slightly plump arms and legs. She had a deep tan, and she was wearing a low-cut green and white striped dress. Tom was staring straight at her luxuriant cleavage.

'You have a wonderful staircase,' he said. 'Marvellous mouldings.'

'Thank you,' she said.

Tom's next words were drowned in a burst of American laughter. When it died down Reggie heard him say, 'I love stone houses. I'm very much a stone person.'

'I adore stone,' said the cleavage. She became aware that Reggie was watching them, and tossed her head haughtily. 'Can I buy you a drink?' she asked Tom.

'No, really, I must be going, Mrs Timpkins,' said Tom.

'Call me Jean,' said the cleavage. 'I hate that name Timpkins. It reminds me of my husband.'

Tom looked slightly embarrassed. Jean picked up their glasses.

'No, really,' said Tom. 'I must be getting home. It's fifty miles, and my wife'll have dinner ready.'

Reggie felt a glow of warmth towards Tom.

'Just a teeny one,' said Jean.

'All right, just a teeny one, Mrs Timpkins,' said Tom, and Reggie forgave him his extra drink in gratitude for his calling her Mrs Timpkins.

He had an uncontrollable urge to speak to Tom. He walked over to his table.

'Excuse me,' he said. 'Aren't you Tom Patterson?'

'That's right,' said Tom, surprised.

'You don't remember me, do you? I'm Lord Amhurst.'

'I knew I'd seen you before, but I couldn't place you,' said Tom.

'We met at a party somewhere. Your charming wife was with you.'

'Oh. You met Linda?' said Tom, pleased.

'Do you mind if I join you?' said Reggie.

'Not at all.'

Reggie sat beside his son-in-law, who clearly didn't recognize him. Jean returned with Tom's teeny one. They were introduced.

'I'm afraid I'll have to rush away in a moment, Lord Amhurst,' said Tom. 'We've had a spot of bother in the family.'

Reggie frowned. He felt his presumed suicide deserved a stronger description than 'a spot of bother'.

'I'm sorry to hear that,' he said.

'My father-in-law killed himself at the weekend,' said Tom.

'Oh dear! How awful,' said Jean. 'How did it happen?'

'They found his clothes piled on the beach.'

'Have they found the body?'

'Not yet,' said Tom.

201

'I think it's awful when things like that happen,' said Jean. 'I think tragedy's terribly sad.'

Tom left soon after that, promising to give his wife Lord Amhurst's sincerest condolences.

The bar was filling up. Four Japanese came in and ordered beers. They looked at the barman blankly when he said, 'Keg or cooking?'

Jean smiled at Reggie. He smiled back.

'You don't remember me, do you?' she said.

'Er – no, I'm afraid I don't,' said Reggie.

'I met you at Lady Crowhurst's. At least I think it was Lady Crowhurst's.'

The head-waiter approached them, with a large menu.

'Will madam be dining with his lordship?' he asked.

Jean looked away expectantly.

'I'd be delighted if you'd take dinner with me, Mrs Timpkins,' said Reggie.

She ordered smoked salmon and fillet steak. Reggie felt that he couldn't afford to be Lord Amhurst for long.

The dining room had dark green wallpaper and big windows overlooking a lawn. Lord Amhurst had been given the best table. The four Japanese were sitting by the door.

'Why are you selling your house?' said Reggie.

'Because my husband lived there,' said Jean.

Their smoked salmon arrived. Jean chewed it with her big white teeth.

'How is Lady Amhurst?' she asked.

'There is no Lady Amhurst,' said Reggie.

'It was awfully sad about that poor man,' said Jean. 'Killing himself like that. I hate death. It's so morbid. I mean, it makes you guilty, sitting here enjoying your smoked salmon while he's lying at the bottom of the sea, decomposing.'

'He'll have been eaten by fish by now, Mrs Timpkins,' said Reggie, and Jean hesitated momentarily in her attack upon the smoked salmon.

'Please call me Jean' she said.

'My friends call me Jumbo,' said Reggie.

Their fillet steak arrived.

'I feel awfully guilty, being so rich and idle,' said Jean.

'You ought to get a job,' said Reggie.

'I wouldn't know how to,' said Jean.

Reggie could hear a flood of voluble Japanese, in which the words 'spinach' and 'steak and kidney pie' stood out strangely.

'Jumbo,' breathed Jean, under the mellow influence of the claret. 'How did you get your limp?'

Reggie described his accident. He described the raw thrill of the bobsleigh, the Cresta Run on a crisp morning. He saw her breasts heave. He looked at her unnaturally blonde hair and her wide, shallow nose, her aggressive teeth, her ebony shoulders, the deep sticky slit between her breasts as she ate her tossed green salad, and he thought, 'Last night you were reduced to speechlessness by a dark fragile receptionist. Today you have this lioness for the taking. She would let you have her in her six bdrms, four rcp and three bthrms, not to mention the stbls. She would let you have her because you're a hereditary peer, because of your limp, because of the Cresta Run. But you don't want her, because you aren't Lord Amhurst, you don't limp, you've never been on the Cresta Run, and you love Elizabeth.'

Thursday

When Reggie woke up the sky was blue, sheep were bleating, and innumerable birds were singing. It was twenty-five past six, and he knew that he must go home.

He washed, dressed, and went for a brief limp before breakfast. Pools of water lay in the gutters, and there was a distant clink of milk bottles.

He went down the little street, out into the country, a country of dry-stone walls and beech trees. Rooks cawed and a kestrel hovered. The road ran beside a disused railway line.

Would he reveal himself to Elizabeth? He didn't know. All he knew was that he must go back. And he needed a new identity. Lord Amhurst must be returned to the oblivion whence he had come.

He limped back to the hotel, and consumed a large breakfast of cornflakes, smoked haddock and poached egg. He paid his hefty bill and went to catch the bus. Jean Timpkins roared up in her open sports car with a fawn scarf round her head. She looked older in the mornings, and Reggie felt unable to refuse her offer of a lift to Oxford.

'Don't you have a car?' she said.

'I'm a bus enthusiast,' he said. 'I'm President of the Bus Users' Association.'

She kissed him quickly. She smelt of expensive scent.

'I'm sorry your leg was playing you up last night, Jumbo,' she said. 'How is it this morning?'

'Much better, thank you, Mrs Timpkins,' he said.

She drove extremely fast. His eyes and nose ran as the wind streamed past his face. The lines of trees flashed past.

He tried to hide his nervousness and his streaming eyes. He was painfully aware that he wasn't presenting a convincing picture of an erstwhile bobsleigh enthusiast.

Suddenly, his wig blew off. Jean slammed on the brakes. He ran back for it, and found it lying on the verge. He dusted it down, brushing off the wood-lice. Then he fixed it in position again. He gave Jean an embarrassed smile.

'Why wear a wig when you're not bald?' she asked.

'Vanity,' he said.

He held his wig on his head as she roared to Oxford. She pulled up at the bus station. He thanked her and blew his nose. She didn't kiss him good-bye.

She was the last person to see Lord Amhurst alive. By the time he reached the railway station he was already Jasper Flask.

Jasper Flask, theatrical agent, reached Paddington Station shortly after mid-day. He wandered through the crowded streets of London. His gait was slow, leisurely, aloof. He held his body stiffly and rolled his hips with a slight swagger.

He crossed Oxford Street and plunged into Soho. He crossed Charing Cross Road. Soon he was in Covent Garden.

He went into a pub and bought himself a half of draught lager and a turkey sandwich. He sat in a corner, by the fruit machine. All around him were market traders, opera singers, scene shifters, theatrical hangers-on, and tourists. Jasper Flask, theatrical agent, should be at home among this motley crowd.

An argument broke out between two market traders.

'There's no taste in nothink any more,' said one. 'You take Ghanaian oranges. They don't taste of nothink. Not like in the old days when you got your Gold Coast oranges.'

'What are you talking about?' said the second man. 'Ghana is the bleeding Gold Coast. It's the same difference.'

'I'm not saying it isn't, Jim. I'm saying your Ghanaian oranges doesn't taste of nothink. It's the same with your asparagus.'

'Wait a minute, hang about, asparagus, that's a luxury bleeding commodity.'

Reggie wanted to join in. This was his subject.

'Not any more it isn't,' said the first trader. 'That's my point. You get it all the year round. After your English you get your Bulgarian asparagus. After your Bulgarian you get your fucking Liberian asparagus. It's not got the same taste, Jim.'

'Don't fucking give me that. Listen, we've got a consignment of gooseberries . . .'

'Gooseberries? I'm not talking about bloody gooseberries.'

'Wait a minute. Listen, will you? They're Mongolian gooseberries, aren't they? Course they are. But you wouldn't know if you wasn't told.'

'What are you talking about? I'd know in the dark they was Mongolian. Listen, have you got your own choppers?'

'What?'

'Your own teeth. Have you got them?'

'Course I bloody haven't.'

'Well, you don't know what you're fucking talking about, then, taste, if you haven't got your own choppers.'

There was an angry pause. Reggie seized his chance.

'I agree,' he said. 'It used to be much better when there were different seasons.'

The two men gave him a strange look.

'All I'm saying,' said Reggie, 'is that the stuff seemed to taste better when you only got it for a few weeks. Whether it really did taste better is another matter.'

The conversation was over. The man called Jim went to the bar to buy drinks. Silence fell between Reggie and the other man. Soon he left the pub.

He crossed the Strand and went over Waterloo Bridge. Over the Houses of Parliament the clouds were double-banked.

The grimy street beside the railway arches was quiet. C.J.'s Bentley was parked in its usual spot. The clock on the tower of the Sunshine Desserts building still said three forty-six. The lift was still out of order.

He walked through the foyer so purposefully that the receptionist didn't like to stop him. He climbed the stairs and entered the open-plan office on the third floor.

The girls were all still there, clacking away at their typewriters. It seemed amazing that all this should be unchanged.

Joan was seated at her desk. She looked outwardly placid. What had he expected? Deep bags under the eyes? Horrible bald patches? Evidence of slashed wrists?

The postcards of Pembrokeshire were still there, to remind him that he really had existed.

'My name is Perrin,' he said, in a slightly less clipped version of his Lord Amhurst voice.

'Perrin?' she said, and he fancied that she turned a little pale.

'No, sorry. *My* name is Flask. I have an appointment with Mr Perrin. *His* name is Perrin. I spoke to him last week and arranged to call in.'

'I'm afraid Mr Perrin isn't with us any longer,' said Joan, whose dress reached down to her knees. 'Perhaps you'd like to see our Mr Webster instead?'

'It's a personal matter,' said Reggie. 'Is there anywhere I can get hold of Mr Perrin?'

'I'm afraid not,' said Joan. She explained the tragic circumstances of Reggie's disappearance. 'I'm sorry. There's not much I can do.'

'No, there isn't,' said Reggie.

He walked away, slowly, vaguely disappointed, as if he had wanted to be recognized. He visited Davina's office next.

'I have an appointment with Miss Letts-Wilkinson,' he said. 'The name is Flask. Jasper Flask. Entrepreneur.'

'I'm afraid Miss Letts-Wilkinson has been called away,' said her secretary.

Davina sat at the bedside. Uncle Percy Spillinger's breathing was laboured. His wardrobe doors were open. Davina closed them quietly. It didn't seem right that his last moments should be witnessed by all his suits.

He awoke with a jerk, saw Davina and smiled.

'I've been making a list of wedding presents that we might ask for,' he said in a weak voice. 'Do we want an early morning tea machine?'

'That would be nice,' said Davina.

'I thought we'd need a canteen of cutlery,' said Uncle Percy Spillinger. 'And a cheeseboard. And a set of tongs.'

'Don't tire yourself,' said Davina.

'Herb rack. Garden roller. *Radio Times* holder,' said Uncle Percy Spillinger.

'Lovely,' said Davina.

'Listen to those damned dogs,' said Uncle Percy Spillinger.

Davina listened. She could hear no dogs.

The wardrobe doors opened again with a shuddering groan. Again Davina shut them.

'It's no use. The catch has gone, and the floor slopes,' said Uncle Percy Spillinger.

'Never mind,' said Davina.

'Bathroom scales,' said Uncle Percy Spillinger. 'Folding chair. Liquidizer, oblique stroke, grinder.'

'That would be nice,' said Davina.

Uncle Percy Spillinger nodded off. Davina held his hand. The wardrobe doors opened, and she didn't bother to shut them. It was very quiet in the old room with the threadbare carpet and the dusty oak chest of drawers.

Uncle Percy Spillinger awoke with a start.

'Blast those dogs,' he said. 'Listen to them.'

Davina listened and heard nothing.

'Damn them!' he said. 'Why can't they leave me alone?'

Davina patted his hand and he smiled.

'Draught excluders,' he said. 'Shoe box with optional accessories. Kiddies' chair with wipe-clean feeding tray.'

Davina blushed.

The doctor called, felt Uncle Percy Spillinger's pulse and gave Davina a pessimistic glance.

'Heated dining trolley with teak veneer finish,' said Uncle Percy Spillinger.

'Absolutely, old chap,' said the doctor.

'Watering can with assorted sprays and nozzles,' said Uncle Percy Spillinger.

'He's rambling,' whispered the doctor to Davina. 'Phone me if he gets worse.'

When the doctor had gone, Davina gulped and said: 'Shall we fix a date for the wedding now?'

Uncle Percy Spillinger smiled.

'I rather like September the eleventh,' he said.

'That would do fine,' said Davina.

Uncle Percy Spillinger lay back on his pile of pillows.

'September the eleventh,' he said. 'Two-thirty p.m. And afterwards at the house.'

He closed his eyes. His breathing grew steadily worse. He was dead before the doctor arrived.

'He wasn't on the National Health,' said the doctor.

'Send your bill to me,' said Davina coldly.

She pulled the top sheet over Uncle Percy Spillinger's head.

'I'd better get on to the undertakers,' she said. 'It's essential that he be buried at Ponders End. Nothing less will do.'

At half past five Reggie went to the Feathers. He sat on a bar stool at the end of the bar normally frequented by the Sunshine Desserts crowd.

He ordered a double whisky and a fat cigar and tried to look as much like Jasper Flask as possible. He had a compulsion to find out what things were like when he wasn't there. All his life he had been constantly present. Perhaps that had been the whole trouble. Absence makes the heart grow fonder. Now, when he was absent, he might like himself better.

The thirsty invasion began. Leslie Woodcock from Jellies came first, holding his legs further apart than ever. Then came Owen Lewis, Tim Parker and David Harris-Jones. They were followed by Colin Edmundes from Admin., whose reputation for wit still depended on his adaptation of existing witticisms. Then came Tony Webster and his dolly bird. Tony displayed no sign of emotion towards her. She was just something that came with his life, like Green Shield stamps.

Jasper Flask ordered another double whisky. After a few minutes, the talk turned to the Reggie Perrin affair.

'It's strange to think,' said Leslie Woodcock, 'that this time last week he was no further from me than you are now.'

'I wonder why he did it,' said Tim Parker from Flans.

'Bird trouble,' said Owen Lewis. 'His wife found out he was banging the Greengross.'

Reggie had to concentrate hard on being Jasper Flask.

'I – er – think he was at the sort of age when you wonder – you know. I mean, after all, he could have felt he was going to get the push,' said David Harris-Jones.

'There but for the grace of Mammon go I,' said Colin Edmundes.

'Who are you talking about?' said Tony Webster's dolly bird, returning from the loo.

'My boss, the one I told you about,' said Tony Webster.

'Oh, the one who snuffed it,' she said.

Jasper Flask's hands twitched.

'I think London can get you down,' said Tim Parker.

'A man who isn't tired of London is tired of life,' said Colin Edmundes.

'Tell me, Tony,' said Leslie Woodcock. 'You saw more of Reggie than I did. What did you make of him, as a person?'

Reggie waited breathlessly, while Tony Webster considered the question from every angle.

'I don't really know,' said Tony Webster, and the way he spoke made his answer sound intelligent and thoughtful. 'He was sort of difficult to sum up, if you know what I mean.'

There was a pause.

'I see Virginia Wade got knocked out at Wimbledon,' said Leslie Woodcock.

Jasper Flask, theatrical agent and entrepreneur, downed the remainder of his double whisky, stubbed out the sodden butt of his cigar, and left the pub.

210

He walked briskly to Waterloo, maintaining his Jasper Flask walk throughout.

The cracked old woman with the hairy legs approached him.

'I wonder if you can help me?' she said, in her deep, cracked voice. 'I'm looking for a Mr James Purdock, from Somerset.'

'I'm awfully sorry,' he said. 'I'm afraid I can't.'

He caught the six thirty-eight.

Opposite him sat a man of quite extraordinary normality. What are your secret thoughts, thought Reggie. Do you believe that your knees are enormous? Or are you convinced that your elbows are a laughing stock? Do you have an uncontrollable horror of vegetable marrows? When you see spittle on the pavements, do you have a grotesque temptation to bend down and lick it up?

What about your sex life? Are you only really turned on after you've seen a hat-stand? Do you have to dress up in a Saracens' rugby shirt and muddy boots?

Or are you just as normal as you look?

Reggie began to feel increasingly nervous as he got nearer home.

The train was eleven minutes late. The loudspeaker announcement explained that 'someone has stolen the lines at Surbiton'. The sky had cleared of cloud, the wind had dropped, but there was a distinct chill in the air.

He walked along Station Road, up the snicket, up Words-worth Drive, turned right into Tennyson Avenue, then left into Coleridge Close.

Mr Milford was in his garden, staring at his roses. Reggie's house looked completely lifeless.

There it was, well-preserved, eloquent of affluence. Only an unusual incidence of dead heads on the rose bushes revealed that anything abnormal was afoot.

Of course. Elizabeth was in Worthing. Visiting her mother. Seeing Henry Possett?

He walked back up the road once more, staring at the

house as he passed. There it sat, so solid, as if none of this had really happened.

He walked on towards the station. On the way he said farewell to Jasper Flask. He wasn't sorry to see him go.

Friday

Signor Antonio Stifado stood at a bus stop opposite the hospital. Several buses passed, but he did not hail them. He was a tall, rather heavily built man and he had a big black beard. The evening sun shone on his jet-black hair.

Signor Stifado had arrived in Worthing that afternoon from London, where he had passed a disturbed night in a hotel in Bloomsbury. He had a hundred and ninety pounds in his pockets, in used fivers.

There were disadvantages in pretending to be a foreigner. Everything suddenly became very expensive. People shouted at you, as if they expected all foreigners to be deaf. But there was also one advantage. It needed concentration. It occupied the mind. It had prevented Reggie from getting too nervous.

Elizabeth's car was parked in the main road outside the hospital, less than fifty yards from the bus stop.

Would he dare? It needed courage to admit that you hadn't really committed suicide.

It would mean Elizabeth had done all that mourning under false pretences.

The trickle of departing visitors was becoming a flood. Visiting time was over.

There she was. And there beside her was Linda.

And there was Henry Possett.

They had reached the main gate. They were waiting to cross the road. Reggie could hear his heart pumping. He walked towards them. He had no idea what he was going to say. The traffic noises sounded far away but very loud. The sun seemed unusually bright.

All he had to do was rip off the beard and wig and say, 'Hullo, darling. It's me. I'm awfully sorry about what happened. I always was a bit of an arse.'

How beautiful Elizabeth was, and how tall Henry Possett was.

It might be too much of a shock. It might kill her.

'Excuse me,' he said, 'which is way to middle town?'

'Middle town?' said Henry Possett.

'Middle town. Centrum. Centre ville.'

'Oh, the town centre!'

'Centre town. Yes, please,' said Reggie.

They directed him. Elizabeth was close enough to touch. Soon they would move on. He must detain them.

'Thank you. I have hotel here, Littlehampton,' he said.

'This isn't Littlehampton. This is Worthing,' said Linda.

'Oh. Excusing me. Wort things,' he said.

'Worthing.'

'Worth thing. Oh. This Worth thing, has it much far from Littlehampton?'

They told him how to get to Littlehampton. Elizabeth looked pale. It touched his heart to see how pale she was.

'Wait a minute,' she said. 'If we run you home, Henry, we can take this gentleman to the station.' She turned to Reggie and shouted, 'We can take you to the station.'

'Oh. Is most kind. But is no need,' said Reggie.

He sat in the back seat of his car. Elizabeth changed to second gear too soon.

'How was your mother?' said Henry Possett.

'Much more like her usual self,' said Elizabeth. 'How about your sister?'

'They're very pleased with her,' said Henry Possett.

'Are you on holiday?' said Linda to Reggie.

'Yes, I take a vacations,' said Reggie.

'How are you liking England?' said Henry Possett.

'Oh. *Molto bene*. Much well. England, beautiful. Devon, beautiful. Bognor Regis, beautiful. But – er – she is – how you say – much costing,' said Reggie.

214

'Very expensive,' said Henry Possett.

'*Si. Si.* Expensive,' said Reggie.

They had to wait at a level crossing. Henry Possett tried a sentence in fluent Italian. Reggie didn't understand a word of it.

'Oh. You speak Italian. Bravo,' he said. 'But I in England only English speak, yes? Because I learn. Yes?'

'Yes,' said Henry Possett.

'I didn't know you spoke Italian, Henry,' said Elizabeth.

A twelve-coach electric train crossed the level crossing. Motorists who had switched their engines off switched them on again.

'Italian, Greek, Yugoslavian, French, Swedish and Danish,' said Henry Possett.

'Oh. This is good. I hear English mens no speaking much foreign,' said Reggie.

The line of cars began to move.

'Plus a smattering of Urdu and a little functional Swahili,' said Henry Possett.

They crossed the level crossing and turned into the station forecourt.

'Thank you very much,' said Reggie.

Henry Possett insisted on accompanying him to the station. There was a train for Littlehampton in three minutes.

Henry Possett waited by the ticket office to make sure he got on the train all right, so he had to go to Littlehampton. When he got there he took a taxi back to his hotel in Worthing. He hurried upstairs, terrified that he would meet Henry Possett or Elizabeth in the bar.

He stayed in his room all evening. He sat at his little writing desk and wrote two letters on hotel notepaper.

The first letter was to Elizabeth.

My dear Elizabeth,

By the time you receive this letter I shall be alive. Please forgive me for deceiving you in this way, but I could see no other way out at the time. Now I realize that I cannot live without you. This

215

evening I posed as an Italian and you gave me a lift to the station. It was so thrilling to be near you, in the same car, our car, on which incidentally I couldn't help noticing that the road tax had run out. When you changed to second gear too soon I almost spoke. I realize that I shall have to look for a new job and I daresay that since I have rejected ambition and have no desire to work in a competitive industry again we will have to live in straitened circumstances. This will not matter to me, but I shall of course understand if you do not wish to continue our life together, but I do hope that you will.

With all my love,
Reggie.

He read the letter through three times, then crumpled it up and threw it in the waste-paper basket.

His second letter was also to Elizabeth.

My dear Elizabeth,

I am writing this to tell you that I am not dead, and that I love you and always will. Today when I posed as an Italian and got a lift in your car I knew that what matters most is your happiness. Too many things have changed for me to be able to offer you happiness. I no longer feel able to deliver the goods in the manner expected of me by society. I have no desire to return to industry and support you in the manner your mother would think right. I cannot believe in the expansion of industry, the challenge of the Common Market, any of the clap-trap. I see things now with a new clarity. So much seems utterly ridiculous. The shape of this pen strikes me as ludicrous. I can't take the male sexual organs seriously. The sight of a pumice stone would be liable to drive me hysterical. Ambition seems to me totally ridiculous. When people take themselves too seriously, I shall be tempted to say 'I love you earwig'. I can never again look at your mother without thinking of a hippopotamus.

In these last days since my fake suicide – I apologize for the distress it must have caused you and for hoping that it has caused you distress – in these last days I have adopted several personalities. Charles Windsor, Wensley Amhurst, Sir Wensley Amhurst, Lord Amhurst, Jasper Flask, Signor Antonio Stifado. Shadowy figures, without past or future, yet real enough to those who met

216

them. It is tempting to think of myself as a shadowy figure, like them, yet the truth is very different. For me the problem of identity is not that I do not know who I am. It is that I know only too clearly who I am. I am Reginald Iolanthe Perrin, Goofy Perrin, Coconut Matting Perrin. I am absurd, therefore I am. I am, therefore I am absurd.

Tomorrow I shall adopt a permanent name, seek out a new life. It won't be easy to forget, but I have got to make it work. It is hard to know that I shall never see you again, and that I can't even send you this letter, and you will never receive my best wishes for the future.

With all my love,
Reggie.

He read the letter three times, crumpled it up, and threw it in the waste-paper basket.

That night, tucked up in his hotel bed in Worthing, with the sea lying dark and placid not a hundred yards away, Reggie thought: 'Well, I'm in a mess, but at least I've stirred my life out of its predictable course.'

Then he wondered if a psychiatrist would say: 'On the contrary, this is exactly what I would have expected from you.'

We can never escape our destiny, he realized, because whatever happens to us becomes our destiny.

It had all been a terrible mistake.

July

The rain fell steadily, good grey nonconformist Sunday rain. It soaked the backs of cats and dribbled down the instruments of Salvation Army bands. It reduced American tourists to pulp and splashed mud over the jeans of protest marchers. It was soft, relentless and dirty.

Reggie lay on his bed and watched a patch of damp spreading across his ceiling. He was in a cheap hotel near King's Cross and his name was Donald Potts. He had one hundred and sixty-five pounds in his pocket, in used fivers, and he was an outcast.

He had taken off his false beard. There was no need of it now that his real beard had grown.

He went over to the mirror and examined himself. He was shocked by what he saw. He was going grey. He pulled off his wig and underneath it the hair was streaked with grey. Even the hairs on his chest were going grey. The lines on his face had deepened, and the skin was sagging. He realized with a shock that he would pass for fifty-six, rather than forty-six. This wasn't the new life that he had promised himself, free from care.

Was it just the effect of the strain that he had been through, or had he taken on some of the years of Lord Amhurst and the rest? He shivered with horror. Perhaps he would continue to grow old at this rate. Perhaps in a month he would look like an old man of seventy-six. He began to shake uncontrollably.

He was alone, utterly alone. No family. No friends. Not even a friendly bank manager in the cupboard. He began to cry. He lay on his bed and wept, until there were no more tears and he was exhausted and empty.

This wouldn't do. This way lay madness. He took a grip on himself and went for a walk. For three hours he walked through the streets in the glistening rain. He trudged across Regent's Park and the open space soothed him. He would like to work in an open space like that.

He had steak and chips in a comfortless café and two pints of tasteless chemical beer in a tall, dark, shabby pub. By the time he went to bed his mind was made up. He would become a park keeper.

The thought calmed him. The new life was beginning at last. The decision had been made. He was going to be Donald Potts until he died.

Cats fought, diesels hooted, the wind howled, traffic roared, men shouted, women screamed, water pipes gurgled, dustbin lids crashed to the ground, milk bottles rolled down steps on to pavements, ambulances wailed, and Donald Potts slept.

In the morning he was Reggie again, playing at being Donald Potts. He bought some writing paper, went to the reference library and wrote to the parks departments of twenty-two London Boroughs. He was careful to make the letters suitably illiterate.

The reference library smelt of floor polish. One very old woman was hunting through the railway timetables, although she would never go anywhere again. Another old woman suddenly shouted, 'Bastards. Bastards. Shits,' and then retired into silence. One old man had a compulsive snort. As he listened to the compulsive snort Reggie thought about that old man's life. His first rattle, his first step, his first word, his first wank, his first woman, his first conviction, his first stroke, his first compulsive snort. The history of a man.

He wanted to shout to the old people, 'I am free. I have joined you. I am one of you. I shall suffer with you.'

Instead, he went out quietly and posted his twenty-two letters.

*

219

Tuesday was dry. Wednesday was dry, but in the evening it rained. On Thursday there were showers. On Friday he got his first replies. Six boroughs had no vacancies, but Hillingley suggested that he present himself at the council offices at eleven-thirty on the following Wednesday.

He spent the evenings in pubs, talking to people who looked as if they might be members of the criminal fraternity. A man called Kipper introduced him to a man called Nozzle who knew a man called Basher who knew a forger who was prepared to present Donald Potts with a birth certificate and all the documents necessary for starting a new life. It set Reggie back a hundred pounds.

He prepared for his interview thoroughly. He bought a faded second-hand suit. It was two sizes too large in some places and three sizes too small in others.

On his way to catch the Tube he stepped in some mud, smearing it carefully over his boots and up the inside of his trouser legs. A policeman gave him a suspicious look and he disappeared hastily into the subway.

The sun was shining when he reached Hillingley. It was an area of large housing estates broken by windswept open spaces and occasional industrial areas.

The council offices were a large L-shaped red-brick building situated in a corner by some traffic lights. A clock above the main door indicated that it was eleven twenty-seven. Reggie ran his hand through his hair to disarrange it, and presented himself at the reception desk.

'I've got an appointment to see Mr Thorneycroft,' he said.

'What name shall I say?' said the girl.

'Say Potts,' said Reggie.

He was sent to an office on the third floor, at the rear of the building. Mr Thorneycroft was a thin man with a long sad nose.

'Why do you want to work in our Parks Department?' he said, when Reggie had sat down.

'Well, I – er – I like the open air life,' said Reggie, adopting a Cockney accent in the best traditions of the Sunshine Desserts Dramatic Society.

'Do you have much experience of gardens?'

'I done a lot of odd jobs in gardens.'

'What job do you have at the moment?' said Mr Thorneycroft.

'I'm temporarily unemployed, sir.'

'I see. What was your last position?'

'I been working for myself. Doing odd jobs.'

'What sort of jobs?'

'You name it, I done it.'

'I'd rather *you* named it, Mr Potts.'

'Decorating, gardening, tiling, guttering, perching.'

'Perching?'

'Gutter-perching. Perching on gutters,' said Reggie desperately.

'Perching on gutters, Mr Potts?'

'To repair roofs.'

'I see. Do you have any references?'

'No, sir.'

'Good. Splendid. What sort of gardening do you like best, Mr Potts?'

'My speciality, sir, is lawns, flowers, vegetables and plants.'

'I see.' Mr Thorneycroft made a note on a piece of paper. He liked interviewing. 'Hedging?'

'As and when needed, sir.'

'I see. Compost?'

'I can turn my hand to it.'

Mr Thorneycroft looked down at the floor.

'Have you ever been inside?' he said in the tones newsreaders use for disasters.

'I'd rather not talk about it, sir.'

'That's not much of an answer.'

'I've paid for what I done.'

'What did you do?'

'Twenty-eight days.'

'Yes, but what crime did you commit?'

'Embezzlement, sir.'

'I see. Fine.'

'But I've learnt my lesson, sir. I've turned over a new leaf.'

'Yes, and if you get the job with us you'll be turning over lots of leaves.' Mr Thorneycroft laughed. It was like a knife sawing through concrete. Then he became serious again. 'Do you drink, Mr Potts?'

'I wouldn't say I never indulged, sir.'

'Fine. Fine.'

'But not to excess, sir. Leastwise, not any more.'

'I see.'

Behind Mr Thorneycroft was a large calendar with a picture of Balmoral Castle and the legend: 'Queen's Garage, 19–23 Parkside, Hillingley.' The dates of Mr Thorneycroft's holidays were ringed in red ink.

'I lost my Doris over that.'

'Doris?'

'My wife, sir, as was. I lost her on account of the drinking and the embezzlement.'

'I see. Well that's all very satisfactory, Mr Potts. It sounds as though you're just the man we're looking for. We need an under-gardener at the North Hillingley Mental Hospital. How does that strike you?'

'Well, I had thought more of parks.'

'We don't have any vacancies in parks.'

'I'll be happy to give it a try, sir.'

'That's the spirit.' Mr Thorneycroft stood up. 'I'll send you to see our Mr Bottomley. He's the head gardener. If you hit it off with him, you can start Monday.'

Reggie did hit it off with their Mr Bottomley, so he started Monday. He knew they must be desperate for staff, yet he felt as proud of landing the job as he had ever felt in his life.

The search for lodgings in the Hillingley area proved a problem. Mrs Jefferson of Carnforth Road took one look at him and said, 'The vacancy's gone.' So did Mrs Riley of Penrith Avenue. Mrs Tremlett, of Aspatria Drive, said, 'I don't

222

hold with beards. I've nothing against them as such, but I don't hold with them, and that's the end of the matter.' Mr Beatty, also of Aspatria Drive, said, 'Ma's visiting the grave, but I don't think you're quite the sort of thing she had in mind.'

Finally he found a room in the home of Mr and Mrs Deacon of Garstang Rise.

'We've never had lodgers, not so's you'd speak of,' said Mr Deacon. 'But there's the boys gone, and the inflation, and Mrs Deacon's legs, and we're none of us getting any younger as regards that.'

'I think I'll be very happy here,' said Reggie.

'This is a happy house, Mr Potts,' said Mr Deacon. 'And as regards the lights going off suddenly, don't worry. They only do that when we watch BBC2.'

Reggie's room was tastefully furnished, with shocking pink and cobalt blue the predominating features of the colour scheme. The smallest room in the house was situated at the top of the stairs. It had a mustard yellow lavatory-brush receptacle and matching holder for the spare toilet roll. From his window Reggie could see most of Garstang Rise, and a small stretch of Egremont Crescent.

Mr Deacon took him to the Egremont Arms, while Mrs Deacon watched 'Alias Smith and Jones' in the dark.

'I'm glad you're here. It's company for Mrs Deacon. She gets a bit down at times. It's the inflation. It's gone to her legs,' said Mr Deacon.

The pub was vast and had a large car park. In the public bar there was a darts board and in the lounge bar there was a pop group but Mr Deacon and his cronies patronized the saloon. The tenor of their discourse was nostalgic. Hillingley wasn't what it was, nor was the nation, that was their theme.

'This country's had it,' said Mr Deacon.

Reggie expressed his regret for the passing of the steam engine, the brass bedstead and the pyjama cord.

'This country's had it,' said Mr Jefferson.

'What's your opinion as regards women and where they used to keep their hankies?' said Mr Deacon.

'How do you mean?' said Reggie.

'Don't let the talking stop the drinking,' said the landlord.

'Well,' said Mr Deacon. 'What's your opinion as regards my teacher keeping her hanky right up her knickers, which was blue?'

'I ain't got no opinion as regards that,' said Reggie.

'I don't blame you. Same again?' said Mr Deacon.

One evening, shortly before eight o'clock, as Reggie was reading the *Evening Standard* with his feet up, there was a knock at the door.

'Come in,' he said, putting his feet down hastily.

It was Mrs Deacon.

'I'll come straight to the point,' she said. 'You're coloured, aren't you?'

'Of course I'm not,' said Reggie. 'I'm just a bit sunburnt from the open air life, that's all.'

'Not that I'm prejudiced,' said Mrs Deacon. 'But it's the religious side, isn't it? You have your customs, we have ours.'

'Mrs Deacon, I'm not bleeding well coloured.'

'It's Mr Deacon I'm thinking of. It's his legs. The inflation's hit them very badly. He has a hard day down the electricity. You can't expect him to sit there facing Mecca while he has his tea. He wouldn't stand for it.'

'Mrs Deacon, I am as white as you are and prejudice is an ugly thing,' said Reggie.

Mrs Deacon grabbed his paper and tore it right through Sam White's revelations about Aristotle Onassis.

'You nig-nogs are all the same,' she said, and with that she left the room.

Some minutes later there was another, milder knock on the door. It was Mr Deacon. He seemed uneasy.

'You've done it now,' he said. 'Mrs Deacon's an emotional woman. It's a lonely life for her. Donald. Garstang Rise isn't Paris.'

'I realize that,' said Reggie, 'but she called me a nig-nog.'

'You don't want to worry as regards that. She won't let her own brother in the house. Says he's a Sikh. She claims she looked in his front room and saw him wearing a turban.'

'Was he?'

'Course he bloody wasn't. He'd just washed his hair, hadn't he? He'd got a towel round his head. It's all a pigment of her imagination, Donald, but it's what I've got to live with. It's the cross I've got to bear. You're the first man she's allowed in the house for eight years. I thought it was going to be all right at last.'

'I'm very sorry, George.'

'Don't worry as regards that. It's not your fault. But it's no life for me. I can't invite me friends in and have her accusing them all of being Parsees. I've done everything for her, redecorated, rewired the house with my own bare hands.'

The room was plunged into darkness. Mr Deacon consulted his watch.

'She's watching "Call My Bluff",' he said.

'I think I'd better look for somewhere else,' said Reggie.

'I think you had as regards that,' said Mr Deacon.

Two days later Reggie moved into Number thirteen, Clytemnestra Grove, on the other side of the borough. It was a two-storey house, converted into three flats. Miss Pershore of the Scotch Wool Shop lived on the ground floor, and Mr Ellis, an upholsterer, occupied the first floor front. Reggie had the first floor back.

'I think I'm going to be very happy here,' said Reggie.

'This is a happy house, Mr Potts,' said Miss Pershore.

August

August came in like a leaping gazelle and went out like a pregnant ant-eater. Which is to say that it began with high hopes of a golden climax to the summer and ended in childish tears, endless inspections of sodden wickets, and record losses on municipal deck chairs.

Reggie's August began with hopes of a new life. It ended with his being driven back inexorably towards his old one.

The North Hillingley Mental Hospital was a large rambling building of dark Cambridgeshire brick. It had an imposing central tower in the French style. The spacious gardens were surrounded by a high brick wall topped with fragments of broken glass in many colours.

Reggie did his work to the satisfaction of all concerned. When it was expected of him that he mow a certain lawn, he did in fact mow that lawn. If a drooping hollyhock had to be secured to a wall with a nail and strong garden twine, Reggie would secure that drooping hollyhock to that wall with a nail and strong garden twine. Mr Bottomley found no fault with him.

From time to time various patients spoke to him. One of them told him that the curfew had been fixed for seven p.m. and the Arabs would attack before dawn. Reggie thanked him for his timely warning.

A second man informed him that the district commissioner would be stopping off at his bungalow next day, and invited Reggie to join them for a spot of tiffin. He accepted the invitation with alacrity.

One day of rain squalls and high winds a patient watched

him bedding out plants for several minutes, and then said, 'Those are plants.'

'Thank you very much,' said Reggie politely.

'Any time,' said the patient.

Five days a week he took sandwiches to work, did his stint in the gardens, downed tools at five-thirty, had a quick drink with Mr Bottomley, returned to his brown room full of bulky furniture, cooked himself some food out of tins or packets, read a book and went to bed. His health was good, although his hair grew steadily greyer.

At weekends he went to the Clytemnestra, and had a few pints of light and bitter. Occasionally he met Miss Pershore or Mr Ellis there.

One Thursday afternoon Joan Greengross visited the Mental Hospital. Reggie was cutting dead heads off rose-bushes. Around the lawns were luxuriant flower beds and fine old oak and beech trees. Outside the walls traffic thundered ceaselessly. Inside, all was peace and quiet in the afternoon sun. Several patients were playing tennis. And suddenly there she was, with her trim legs and her blue lightweight coat bulging pointedly over her breasts. Reggie's heart stood still, and he snipped two splendid Queen Elizabeth roses off in his astonishment.

How did she know that he was here? Why should she visit him in the afternoon?

She walked past him up the drive, not recognizing him in these surroundings, in his gardening clothes, with his long grey hair, grey beard and lined, tanned face.

She disappeared through the visitors' entrance. He busied himself in his work, but his heart was racing. All pretensions towards being Donald Potts were gone.

A few minutes later she reappeared, pushing a wheelchair. In it was a middle-aged man whose mouth hung half-open. Reggie watched her as she wheeled the pathetic figure along the gravel path towards the tennis courts. Then he went up to a male nurse, who was settling old ladies in wicker chairs on the terrace.

'Who was that man in the wheel-chair?' he asked. 'Only it looked like an old friend of mine. Lewis, he was called. Owen Lewis.'

'That's Mr Greengross,' said the male nurse. 'He's been here ten years. He suffered brain damage in an accident.'

Reggie was badly shaken. After work that day he drank four pints. All that time she had been with him at Sunshine Desserts, all that time she had talked about her husband, and never once had he suspected, and he had meddled with her deepest emotions, in his blundering ignorance. He felt physically sick.

When he got home Miss Pershore met him in the hall.

'You've been indulging,' she said.

'I was upset,' he said. 'I saw a ghost from my past today.'

'It's funny,' she said. 'I'd never imagined you as having a past.'

He had no stomach for his instant chicken dinner in his remorselessly brown bed-sitting room. He went to bed early but he didn't sleep.

He had wild thoughts of going to see Joan, of revealing his identity to her. But it wouldn't do any good. There could be nothing further between him and Joan.

He buried his head in his pillow and let the tears flow, and he murmured just one word. It wasn't 'Joan'. It was 'Elizabeth'.

The following night Reggie had a dream so vivid that when he woke up he could remember every detail.

He was digging in a huge formal garden, with rows of statues and hundreds of fountains. Joan was wheeling her husband along in the hot sunshine. She was entirely naked. Her pubic hair had been shaved off except for a tiny triangle, and she had three breasts, a small one nestling between two huge ones. The doctor was walking in the grounds. His name was Freud. He nodded to Reggie and pointed at Joan. 'Very revealing,' he said, and laughed. His laugh was like a knife sawing through concrete.

Joan's husband opened his half-open mouth until it was a great gaping hole. He had no teeth. Suddenly he screamed. An enormous noise like a siren came out of his mouth. It rose and fell. Reggie knew immediately what it was. It was the four-minute warning, but it wasn't for a nuclear attack, it was for the end of the world.

The cry 'The end of the world!' went up. People were running on all sides. Some of them were throwing themselves into the fountains. Reggie could hear a lark singing. Adam and Jocasta were crying.

'What is it?' Adam asked.

'It's the end of the world, dear,' said Linda. 'We're all going to be blown up.'

C.J. hurried past them. He seemed angry.

'I didn't get where I am today by getting blown up in the end of the world!' he shouted.

Reggie saw Mark and Henry Possett among the crowds. Henry Possett was undressing quite calmly. Mark was leaning against a Grecian urn. He was wearing a T-shirt and jeans. Elizabeth, who was naked, said, 'I do think you might have put on clean socks, today of all days,' and Mark said, 'How was I to know it was going to be the end of the world?'

Tony Webster ran past them. Tears were streaming down his face. He threw himself into one of the fountains, crying, 'I've no prospects.'

Henry Possett hung his clothes on a statue and lay down with Elizabeth on the rabbit-cropped grass. They began to make love. Reggie watched them. The lark sang louder and louder, but nobody listened. Henry Possett shouted in ecstatic Urdu as their love-making grew more and more passionate. Joan was frantically building a stone shelter round her husband's wheel-chair. Dr Freud threw himself into the fountains. The jets of water grew higher and higher, the wind sent the spray swirling over the lawns, the lark grew louder still, Henry Possett's Urdu groans grew more and more triumphant, people were running and screaming, there was a rumbling, Reggie braced himself against the force of the explosion.

It was hot, with a heat that seemed to be composed entirely of noise. The ground was smoking. Stones were hurled in the air. The lawns buckled and caved in. The earth's crust was opening. Reggie was sinking into the hot, smoky earth. It was deafeningly hot now. He was falling, falling through smoke and space and heat, down, down, away from the heat and the noise. It grew quiet now, cool and dank. He was on a playground slide. He could hear all the noise receding far away. He slid for several miles. Below him there was light. The slide began to level up. Suddenly he was in the open air. The slide deposited him quite gently upon a perfect lawn. He stood up. He still had his spade in his hand. He was in a huge, formal garden, with rows of statues and hundreds of fountains. Joan was wheeling her husband along, in the hot sunshine. She was entirely naked. Her pubic hair had been shaved off except for a tiny triangle, and she had three breasts, a small one nestling between two huge ones. Already, faintly, far away, Reggie could hear the lark. This repetition was far more frightening than anything that had gone before. 'I've been here before!' he shouted. 'I've been here before!' But nobody took any notice.

And then he was awake, shouting, 'I've been here before!' Sweat was pouring off him and his bed-clothes were all tucked up round his neck.

When Miss Pershore waylaid him in the hall next morning, he asked her if she had heard him shouting.

'So that's what it was,' she said. 'I thought I was dreaming.'

'No, I was dreaming,' said Reggie.

'Come in and have a spot of lunch with me, and we can watch the one-thirty at Wincanton,' said Miss Pershore. 'I don't believe in gambling, but a little flutter never did anyone any harm, and one of my friends from the Chamber of Commerce has given me a red hot tip.'

'I can't today, thank you,' said Reggie, 'I have a prior engagement.'

*

The prior engagement was not a success. It consisted of a visit to see Elizabeth, but his courage failed him as he walked through the Poets' Estate, wandered along those wealthy streets, looked at those tranquil houses. He walked down Coleridge Close and went straight past the house, pausing only to avoid being run over by the Milfords as they set off for their snifter at the nineteenth.

A few minutes later he walked back along the other side of the road. He looked across at his house. How enormous it seemed now, compared with Number thirteen, Clytemnestra Grove. He could see no sign of life, and he knew that he would never dare to reveal himself to Elizabeth.

He must keep away. He must find the strength to keep away. He couldn't keep walking up and down Coleridge Close, a desperate furtive figure.

If Reggie didn't see Elizabeth, it is equally true to say that she didn't see him. She was busy in the kitchen, for she had six people coming to Sunday lunch, and it was the first time she had entertained since her bereavement. Her mother was coming, and Mark, and Linda and Tom, and Henry Possett and his sister Vera.

Henry Possett worked for the government. His job was hush-hush. He spoke several languages. No doubt he was used to eating frightfully sophisticated meals. So Elizabeth was going to great lengths to make the lunch a success.

A strange thing was happening to her as she sliced the aubergines and washed the baby marrows. She had been bracing herself for an ordeal, for putting a brave face on things, but now she was actually beginning to enjoy her preparations. For the first time since Reggie's death, she was actually looking forward to a social occasion, albeit apprehensively.

Sunday morning was misty, grey and cool, almost a winter's morning. She wished it was nicer for them.

Mark was the first to arrive. He was quite respectably dressed, in flared grey trousers, brown corduroy jacket, and a tolerably clean yellow shirt. She wanted to ask him to speak nicely in front of Henry Possett, but she was frightened that if she did he would speak worse on purpose.

The Worthing contingent arrived next. Henry Possett was wearing a lightweight fawn suit and a check shirt. Mark looked terribly short beside him. Why did he always have to be so short?

Mark did the drinks while Elizabeth saw to some last-minute things in the kitchen.

'Can I help?' said Vera.

'No. You're to relax,' said Elizabeth.

Vera Possett seated herself carefully on the sofa. She was handsome in a rather severe way. She didn't resemble Henry except in the thinness of her lips. She was manageress of an employment agency. There had once been talk of an American, but it had come to nothing and nobody had ever liked to ask.

'Tell me all about the theatre, Mark,' she said.

'I can't afford to go,' said Mark.

Over by the piano, Elizabeth's mother had cornered Henry Possett, and was having a word in his ear.

'How do you think she's looking?' she said in a loud theatrical whisper.

'Elizabeth?' he said. 'She seems to be bearing up.'

'Yes, but she needs to be taken out of herself,' she hissed. 'I mean it must have been a shock.'

'Yes.'

'I mean she must wonder sometimes if she was in any way to blame. Not that she was, of course. Reginald always had been delicate.'

'Suicide is hardly the preserve of the delicate,' said Henry Possett.

'Well I think these things often go hand in hand. I don't want to speak out of turn, and I *was* very fond of Reginald, we all were, naturally, but I know that you and Elizabeth were friends, and I don't think she ought to be allowed to dwell on things too much, if you know what I mean.'

232

'Yes,' said Henry Possett. 'I do.'

Mark interrupted them, bearing olives and squares of cheese. Elizabeth's mother popped into the kitchen. Elizabeth was testing the joint with a fork.

'It's going to be late,' she said. 'I think the pressure's down.'

'How do you think Henry's looking?' said her mother.

'Very well.'

'Of course he's not strong. I think he's rather under his sister's thumb. It would do him good to get out more.'

The subject of their conversation was at that moment talking to Mark.

'Tell me all about the theatre, Mark,' he said.

'I can't afford to go,' said Mark.

It was a relief when Tom and Linda arrived.

'Sorry we're late,' said Linda. 'We did rush. Phew, I'm in a muck sweat!'

Henry Possett's eyebrows barely registered his distaste. Drinks were served, and introductions effected. There was an animated discussion about Worthing and its environs. Tom intimated that he and Linda weren't seaside people.

Elizabeth apologized for the delay. She's as nervous as a kitten, thought Linda.

At last lunch was served. They all took their places in the dining room. The napkins on the oval walnut table matched the dark green wallpaper. Elizabeth suddenly felt ashamed of Mr Snurd's pictures.

'Who did your pictures?' said Henry Possett.

'Our dentist,' said Mark.

'I'm sorry it's such a rotten day for you,' said Elizabeth.

'Henry likes mist,' said Vera Possett. 'Sometimes I think he's only really cheerful when he's feeling melancholy.'

'That's very unfair,' said Henry Possett. 'But I must admit I do find the hot climates rather monotonous.'

'Heat brings me out in great red lumps,' said Tom. 'They don't irritate much, but they're unsightly.'

Linda gave him a look, but he didn't notice.

'Lindyplops and I went to Tunisia before the children came along,' he said. 'And we both came out in great red lumps.'

'This ratatouille is delicious,' said Henry Possett.

'Marvellous,' said Tom.

'I just followed the recipe,' said Elizabeth.

'How's work coming along, Mark?' said Linda.

'I've got a part in a West End play,' said Mark.

'Oh how wonderful!' said Elizabeth. 'Darling, why didn't you tell us?'

'It's only a small part,' said Mark.

'You've got to start somewhere,' said Vera Possett.

Mark served the wine while the women helped to fetch the main course. He couldn't get the cork out.

'Blast and damn it,' he said.

'Let me help,' said Henry Possett.

Henry Possett eased the cork out without difficulty.

'Evidence of a mis-spent life,' he said.

Elizabeth brought in the roast beef.

'It's only roast beef, I'm afraid,' she said.

'Henry loves beef,' said Vera.

'The roast beef of old England,' said Elizabeth's mother.

'You carve, Mark,' said Elizabeth.

'I can't carve,' said Mark.

'Offer, Henry,' mouthed Vera.

'Oh. Well – I'll carve, if you like,' said Henry Possett.

'I'll carve,' said Tom.

'It's been decided now,' said Linda. 'Henry'll carve.'

Henry Possett carved beautifully. The beef was delicious.

'What have you done with the dustbins?' said Mark to Linda.

'Dustbins? Is that rhyming slang – dustbin lids – kids?' said Henry Possett.

'Yes,' said Mark coldly.

'Fascinating,' said Henry Possett. 'Oh, I'm sorry I interrupted. What have you done with the dustbins?'

'We've farmed them out to some friends,' said Tom.

'It's not overdone, is it?' said Elizabeth.

'Perfect,' said Henry Possett.

'Lovely,' said Vera. 'I wish I could get my potatoes as crisp as this.'

Mark went round topping up the glasses.

'What a nice cruet set. I don't think I've seen it before, have I?' said Elizabeth's mother.

'Reggie bought it. He had good taste,' said Elizabeth.

The mention of Reggie brought a temporary halt in the conversation.

'What a lot of crime there is these days,' said Elizabeth's mother. 'I blame the Labour Government. Don't you, Mr Possett?'

Henry Possett put his glass down and smiled.

'I don't discuss politics at meal times,' he said. 'I never mix business with pleasure. Though I must admit I can usually be prevailed upon to mix pleasure with business.

Elizabeth and her mother laughed excessively.

'I don't see how you can say that,' said Mark. 'You can't just separate life and politics. I *am* left wing. I can't suddenly forget that this is a bloody awful world because somebody serves a meal.'

He avoided everyone's eye and cut his beef viciously.

'I heard a very funny joke on Friday,' said Tom. 'I don't usually tell jokes but this one was so funny. At least I thought it was funny. Now I must get it right.' Suddenly he remembered Linda warning him not to be a bore. 'No,' he said. 'It's not all that funny.'

'Oh come on!' said Henry Possett. 'We're intrigued now!'

'Don't make him tell it if he doesn't want to,' said Vera.

'No, you see, the thing is,' said Tom, 'I've just realized that you wouldn't really understand it unless you were an estate agent. And none of you is.'

'Well, if you've all finished, I'll clear away,' said Elizabeth.

Everyone except Mark helped to clear away the plates. Elizabeth brought in the mousse, Henry Possett the cream, Tom the cheese and Linda the biscuits.

'Well, that was a wonderful lunch,' said Henry Possett when they had finished.

'We'll leave the washing up,' said Elizabeth. 'You're all to enjoy yourselves.'

'All right, but Linda and I will clear away,' said her mother.

When she was alone with Linda, she said: 'Well?'

'Well what?'

'What do you think?'

'What about?'

'Henry, of course. Do you think he'd do her good?'

'Mother? Yes, I suppose he would. It's a bit soon, though, isn't it?'

'It's never too soon to start.'

They piled plates and glasses on to their trays. Mark had left half his cheese and biscuits.

'You don't think there's anything wrong with him, do you?' said Elizabeth's mother.

'Wrong?'

'You're being stupid today, Linda. Wrong. You know. Wrong. Something not quite right about him. I can't put it much plainer than that. I mean, I know he went out with Elizabeth once but I mean he's never married.'

'Oh, I see. Good God, no! He's not queer. Can't you tell?'

'I haven't had much experience of that sort of thing,' said her grandmother huffily.

'No, I think he's just a bit ascetic,' said Linda.

'Good lord, what do they do?'

'They practise self-denial.'

'It doesn't sound very healthy to me. They'll go blind,' said her grandmother.

Linda and Tom left as soon as they had finished their coffee. Mark followed soon after.

'Sorry I lost my bottle with the lipless wonder,' he said to Elizabeth at the door. 'I'm afraid he gets on my wick.'

'It doesn't matter,' said Elizabeth.

'How are you off for bread these days?' he said.

'I could let you have a loaf.'

'Not bread. Bread. Dough. The old readies.'

'Oh. Well, really Mark, aren't they paying you for this play?'

'Yeah. I'm just a bit short of the old readies, that's all. I'll pay you back. You know that. I mean, I only need a tenner.'

Elizabeth gave him a tenner, waved good-bye, and returned to her guests.

'Vera, I've something I want to show you,' said her mother, and she led Vera out of the room.

Elizabeth smiled.

'Well, she's got us alone,' she said.

'Yes,' said Henry Possett.

There was a pause. Henry Possett seemed tongue-tied.

'Would you like to come to a concert some time?' said Elizabeth.

'Well – er – yes, that would be lovely,' said Henry Possett.

Reggie made another determined effort to forget his old life. All week he laboured in the gardens, the hours passing more and more slowly. He didn't see Joan Greengross again, but he saw her husband being wheeled round the garden on more than one occasion.

The following Friday night, in the Clytemnestra, Miss Pershore drank too much Guinness.

'My friends from the Chamber of Commerce won't take no for an answer,' she explained to Reggie as he escorted her home through the sodium mist of a suburban night.

She invited him in for a cup of coffee, and he didn't like to refuse her in that condition.

She had big armchairs with drooping springs and faded floral loose covers. Her lounge was full of bits of crochet work which she had done over the years. She was fifty-three years of age, and had four cats.

Reggie thought of Elizabeth and wondered what on earth he was doing here. He was feeling tired. It was hard work, remembering all the time to talk like Donald Potts and not like Reggie Perrin. But he was determined to be polite to Miss Pershore.

She took a long while to make the coffee, but at last it was ready. They sat in the drooping armchairs, and she told him about her family life, in the days of long ago. Her father had been a draper in Great Malvern, and a stalwart of the local Chamber of Commerce. She talked about the jolly Christmasses, the close-knit family days, before she became a virgin and a spinster.

'You may not believe me, Donald,' she said, her voice thick with Guinness. 'But I have never given myself to a man.'

'I believe you,' he said.

'Mr Right never came along,' said Miss Pershore. 'I always was particular. Particular to a fault, some would say.'

Reggie demurred.

'I would never have dreamt of giving myself to riff-raff,' she said.

'Quite right,' said Reggie.

The Radio Big Band, conducted by Malcolm Lockyer, provided a suitable accompaniment to their evening beverage.

'Now take Mr Ellis upstairs,' said Miss Pershore. 'He's a nice man, but not out of the top drawer. You can't imagine him in the Rotary Club.'

'He's all right,' said Reggie.

'I'm no snob,' said Miss Pershore. 'But there are such things as standards.'

'You're right there, Miss Pershore.'

'Call me Ethel.'

'Ethel.'

Miss Pershore stood up and peeped out of the curtains.

'It's starting to rain,' she said.

She sat down on the settee.

'Do you think I have missed life's greatest experience, never having given myself to a man?' said Miss Pershore.

'It all depends what you want out of life,' said Reggie.

Miss Pershore patted the settee beside her, but Reggie

pretended not to notice. One of the cats jumped up, but she shoved it off.

'You're so right, Donald,' she said. 'The inner life is so much more rewarding.'

'Ta very much for the coffee, Ethel. I'm ready for my pit,' said Reggie, stretching and yawning.

In the morning Miss Pershore waylaid him in the hall when he came down to get his milk.

'I want to thank you,' she said. 'I had too much to drink, and you didn't take advantage of me.'

'That's all right,' said Reggie.

'I was yours for the taking, and you desisted.'

'It was nothing.'

'You have the hands and body of an under-gardener, but you have the heart and soul of a gentleman,' said Miss Pershore.

'Well, ta very much, Ethel,' said Reggie, embarrassed.

Mr Ellis came downstairs for his milk. He was in his vest, and his biceps rippled.

'Good morning, Mr Ellis,' said Miss Pershore. 'And it is a nice morning.'

'They gave out rain later,' said Mr Ellis.

When he bent down to pick up his milk, they could see a slit along the seam of his trousers.

Mr Ellis went upstairs, whistling gloomily. Miss Pershore sighed.

'He has the body of a Greek God, and the heart and soul of an upholsterer,' she said.

'Well, I must go and get my breakfast,' said Reggie.

'Come and have a spot of lunch, and we can watch the one-thirty at Market Rasen,' said Miss Pershore. 'A friend from the Chamber of Commerce has put me on to a good thing.'

'I'm afraid I have a prior engagement,' said Reggie.

The prior engagement consisted of walking round the streets of Hillingley until it was safe to go home again.

*

It was one-thirty in the morning, and fourteen policemen were drinking after hours in the back bar of the Rose and Crown. Twelve of them were swapping Irish stories at the bar, but Chief Inspector Gate was losing doggedly on the fruit machine, and Constable Barker was trying to get his attention.

'I think I'm on to something,' said Constable Barker.

'Bloody hell. Every time I get a "hold" there's bugger-all to bloody well hold. I don't know why I play this machine,' said Chief Inspector Gate, whose face was flushed with whisky.

'All I want to do is carry on the search,' said Constable Barker.

The fruit machine stopped with a clang. Chief Inspector Gate had got an orange, a plum and an apple.

'I give up,' he said. 'Now listen, lad, I want a word with you. Come over into the corner.'

Constable Barker and Chief Inspector Gate sat in the far corner of the darkened bar. A roar of laughter came from the policemen at the bar.

'Listen, Barker,' said Chief Inspector Gate. 'Your evidence amounts to the square root of bugger-all. You find a couple who pick up a rather strange author named Charles Windsor.'

'There is no author called Charles Windsor.'

'They drop this pseudo author at Exeter. He stays a night in a hotel and disappears. He's described as looking like a quantity surveyor who's trying to be trendy. That description might or might not fit Perrin. The clerk at the hotel thinks he was using a false name, but isn't sure. Handwriting experts are undecided about his writing being the same as Perrin's. Big deal. What do you want me to do – get a warrant to search Devon?'

'There's many a case been solved by the persistence of one man. Patient, determined, single-minded, he stalks his prey.'

'I'll stalk you if you're not careful. This isn't a mass murder. It's not worth it.'

'It's all right if I go on making enquiries in my spare time, is it, sir?'

'Knock it off, Barker. The case is closed.'

'You must admit that Charles Windsor might be Reggie Perrin.'

'Yes, and next Christmas my Uncle Cecil may stick his wooden leg up his arse and do toffee apple impressions.'

Sgt Griffiths put a twopenny piece in the fruit machine and got the jack-pot.

'Did you see that?' said Chief Inspector Gate. 'Jammy Welsh bastard. I put all the money in and he gets it out. Come on, Barker, forget the case and have another Pernod. I don't know why you drink that stuff. Doesn't it make your piss green?'

But Barker of the Yard did not reply. He was too busy working out the next move in his quest for Reggie Perrin.

Bursts of heavy rain drenched Hillingley and Reggie's boots were caked with mud. Thunder and hail and lightning tore the end of the summer to shreds, and the lowest August temperature since records began was recorded at Mildenhall, Suffolk.

'I can't go back,' thought Reggie as he dug and raked. 'I can never go back.'

By Thursday the depression had moved away towards Scandinavia, and was battering at the doors of pornographic bookshops, but there were still unseasonal strong winds at Hillingley, tossing the tops of the diseased elms.

'I must go back,' thought Reggie as he mowed and pruned. 'I will go back.'

He would reveal himself to Linda. He would approach Elizabeth through Linda. He would have a migraine tomorrow. Tom would be at work and the children would be at nursery school, learning progressive socially-conscious non-racial nursery rhymes. Tomorrow he would find Linda alone.

For a long time the next morning Linda was alone. The nursery school was still on holiday but Adam and Jocasta had been taken to Eastbourne by the Parents' Co-operative run

by a neighbouring solicitor's wife to take everybody's loved
ones off their hands from time to time. Linda lay in her bra
and panties, the fat curves of her legs draped over the carved
arm of the chaise longue. Her mother had rung to tell her
about her concert trip with Henry Possett. He had taken her
to a splendid restaurant. It had really done her good to get
out. It was no use dwelling on things.

A car crunched to a halt in the drive.

'I'll have to go now, mother. Someone's coming.'

She rushed upstairs and put on a dress. The doorbell rang.
She opened Jocasta's bedroom window and shouted out, 'I'm
coming,' and then she recognized Jimmy's rusty old car and
her heart missed a beat.

She opened the door to him. She was bare-footed and bare-
legged. Jimmy looked older.

'Hullo. Long time no see,' he said.

'Come in,' she said.

He came in.

'Sorry about the mess,' she said. 'I haven't got round to
things yet.'

Jimmy sat down on the sofa. Linda sat on the chaise
longue.

'Fact is,' Jimmy said. 'Bit of a cock-up on the catering
front.'

'Would you like some coffee?' said Linda.

'Please,' said Jimmy.

He followed her into the kitchen. She glanced at his
trousers. They were bulging. She put the coffee on. Her hands
were shaking.

'It's only instant,' she said.

'Fine,' said Jimmy.

The kitchen was large and looked out over a handsome
garden, with beds of rare shrubs round the lawn. At the
bottom of the garden was Tom's folly, a little Gothic tower.

Jimmy leant against the fridge. There were rows of stone
jars containing spices and herbs, and on the floor there were
three large containers in which home-made wines were

242

working. On the top of the pile of dishes in the sink were two little plates with stories in pictures on them.

'What sort of thing do you want, Jimmy?' said Linda.

'Owe you an explanation,' said Jimmy. 'Fact is, cock-up. Too old for army. Leaving.'

'Oh, Jimmy.'

'Putting money aside. Saving. Got to buy a business, Linda.'

'I suppose so. What'll you do?'

'Don't know. Thought of canal boats. No idea, really. Not got a lot of money. Give Sheila housekeeping. Spends it. Booze. Always bloody booze. Excuse language. Oh, thank you.'

'I haven't sugared it.'

'Of course you know Sheila's trouble. Well-known. Easy lay.'

'Oh, Jimmy!'

'No. Common knowledge. Few drinks, she's anybody's. Poor bitch can't help it. Excuse language.'

'Come and sit down, Jimmy.'

'Yes. Sorry.'

They went into the living room. Linda sat on the chaise longue, and moved up to let Jimmy sit beside her, but he sat in a chair.

'Children not here?'

'They've gone to the seaside.'

'Tom?'

'He's working. We're all alone, Jimmy.'

'Anyway, thing is, Sheila's money gone, mine gone too, mess expenses and what have you, no chow. All alone, eh?'

'It's all right, Jimmy. There's lots I can give you. Yes, all alone.'

'Thanks. Horrible, having to tell you. Oh, Linda. Linda!' He rushed over to her and buried his face in her legs. He kissed her just above the knee. 'Oh, Linda, you're beautiful. Beautiful. I want you. Oh, Linda, I want you.'

Linda leant forward and kissed the top of his head.

'You can have me, Jimmy darling,' she said.

They went upstairs and undressed each other and clambered into the unmade bed. Linda was overwhelmed with tenderness towards Jimmy. It wasn't love. It was sympathy. Her physical desire was an ache to give pleasure. She even felt at that moment that Tom would approve and the children would approve if they could understand. Mummy's having sex with Uncle Jimmy because Mummy's nice. She felt Jimmy on top of her and inside her. She felt his release from a suffering that she herself had also endured on his behalf. He was happy, he told her that he was happy. He was proud, she could feel that he was proud.

Afterwards she felt sick. Here, in Tom's bed, in her own home, with her uncle. Jimmy lay absolutely still, here in her bed, in the Thames Valley, on Friday morning, when decent housewives were busy buying fish. Linda stroked his hard, leathery, freckle-flecked back very gently. He must never know what she was thinking.

'Imagined that,' he mumbled. 'Never thought, never thought you'd let me. Imagine lots of things, never happen. Imagined telling you you're beautiful. Never thought I'd hear myself say it.'

'I'm not beautiful, Jimmy.'

She felt him grow tense.

'Must go,' he said. 'Not right. All wrong.'

'No, Jimmy,' said Linda. 'It wasn't all wrong.'

They began to dress. All she wanted was to get him out of the house.

'Jimmy,' she said. 'It can't happen again. It mustn't. I can't let it. But I'm glad it's happened. Truly!'

She forced herself to kiss him, very quickly, on the lips. She could barely repress a shudder of revulsion.

They went downstairs. She gave him eggs, bacon, pheasant paté, Greek bread, a tin of partridge in red wine, half a cold chicken, sausages, butter, jam, baked beans, baked beans with frankfurters, a packet of frozen faggots, a green pepper, and fresh beans.

'Thank you, Linda. Saved my life,' he said.

They loaded his car.

'If you ever need money, please come to us,' said Linda. 'Don't be ashamed. There's nothing to be ashamed of.'

'No. None of it's my fault. Fate. Rotten business,' said Jimmy. 'Better not kiss you. Someone might see. Well, thanks again. And for the nosh. Well, mustn't stay. Be in the doghouse.'

'Bye bye, Jimmy.'

'Well, thanks again. Cheerio. Toodlepip.'

He got into his car. Linda walked to the white gate in the high box hedge and opened it. Jimmy drove out, and waved good-bye. Linda waved back until his car was a speck.

There were tears in her eyes, for Jimmy and herself.

She shut the gate and walked back to the house. She must change the sheets.

O, Tom, Tom, I do love you. I love you in all your absurdity. I'll never tell you about this. You'd be abominably hurt. But will you know? Can I conceal it? Does treachery smell?

Oh – pulling off the old sheets – I did it partly at least for the best of motives. Partly. A mish-mash of motives. Also, admit it, a thrill because he was my uncle. Oh God. Oh, Tom – putting on the new striped sheets, Tom will wonder why I've changed them – oh, Tom, Tom, Tom, I love you. I do, I do. I will, I will. I must.

The doorbell rang. Who could this be? Not Jimmy again. Let it not be Jimmy again.

A tall man with grey hair and a grey beard stood in the porch. He was wearing a new suit.

'Hullo,' said the man.

'Oh!' said Linda. 'Have you come about the boiler?'

'No,' said the man.

'Oh. Was I expecting you?'

'Definitely not,' said the man. 'Most definitely not.'

'Oh.'

'Don't you know me?'

Linda gave him a searching look. There was something familiar about him.

'I'm sorry. I can't place you,' she said.

'I'm not surprised,' said the man.

The shadows cast by small clouds were passing swiftly over the expanse of gravel outside the front door. In the centre of the gravel was a circular bed of small shrubs and ferns.

'Are you alone?' said the man.

He looked nervous. It crossed Linda's mind that he might be a sex maniac. But she would be able to smell it, if he was. She smelt trust from this man. She liked him.

'Don't be afraid,' he said.

'Who are you?' she said.

'This may be a bit of a shock,' he said. 'It's me, Linda. Your father.'

She just stood and stared foolishly.

'It's me,' he said. 'I didn't kill myself.'

Linda felt incapable of any emotion except shock.

'I saw Jimmy leaving,' he said.

'Yes,' she said. 'He – er – '

'He had a cock-up on the catering front?'

'Yes.'

'May I come in?' he said.

'Yes, of course. Sorry.'

She led him into the living room. She was numb.

'I'm sorry it's such a mess,' she said.

'That's all right,' he said.

He sat down on the chaise longue. He looked out of place and awkward. She could see now that it was him, but he had changed. He seemed grey and shrunken.

The delayed shock sapped all the strength from her body. She realized with horror that she hadn't kissed him and hadn't taken in a word of the story he was unfolding.

'So that's it, and here I am,' said Reggie.

'Yes.'

'I want to tell your mother, but I don't dare. I wondered if you could sort of pave the way,' he said.

'I'll make you some coffee,' she said.

He followed her into the kitchen.

'I thought you might be able to make it less of a shock,' he said. 'Coming from a woman, I mean.'

'Yes, all right. I'll tell her,' she said.

'I just can't,' he said. 'I feel such a fool.'

Linda rushed up to him and hugged him. Tears sprang to her eyes. She began to shake. Day after day of routine, then this, in one morning, first Jimmy and then this, one ordinary Friday morning, with the new one-man buses passing the front gate every twenty minutes as usual.

'Oh by the way,' he said, as they drank their coffee. 'I met Tom at Henleaze Ffoliat, when I was posing as Lord Amhurst. He didn't recognize me.'

He told her how anxious Tom had been to get home to her, and how loving he was. She burst into tears.

'I understand. It's a delayed reaction,' he said, patting her head ineffectually. 'It's the shock of seeing me.'

He poured them both a glass of turnip wine.

It was Tuesday before Linda got a chance of seeing Elizabeth, because Elizabeth had gone down to Worthing for a long weekend.

Linda hadn't told Tom about Reggie. She'd been intending to, but somehow she couldn't start. Perhaps it was because it had happened so soon after Jimmy.

She sat in the Parker Knoll chair. Elizabeth had made a pot of tea, and there were chocolate biscuits. Her mother looked almost as nervous as she did.

'I've something to tell you,' said Linda.

'I've something to tell you first,' said Elizabeth. 'I'm going to be married.'

'What?' said Linda, standing up abruptly.

'Don't look so shocked. It's only to Henry Possett.'

Linda sat down again.

'You're shocked,' said Elizabeth. 'You think it's too soon.'

'It's not that.'

'It would be if it was a stranger. But I knew Henry before I

247

knew Reggie. He's the only person I could ever marry, after Reggie.'

'It does seem a bit quick. I mean . . .'

'What?'

'Nothing.'

'I thought about it a lot before I proposed.'

'*You* proposed?'

'Oh yes. On Worthing pier. He'd never have dared propose to me. We're keeping it a secret for a while of course. It wouldn't be seemly to announce it so soon.'

'I suppose not. Well, congratulations, mother.'

'Thank you. I hope you'll feel pleased when you get used to the idea.'

'I expect I will.'

Linda kissed her mother, and Elizabeth insisted on broaching a bottle of hock.

'Now,' she said, when she'd poured out the wine. 'What was your news?'

'My news? Oh. Oh yes. Jocasta has two new teeth.'

'Oh. Marvellous. Oh, by the way, I thought it best – and Henry agrees – and the vicar's perfectly willing. We're going to hold a memorial service for Reggie.'

September

'Oh,' said Reggie. 'Well that's that, then.'

'Yes,' said Linda. 'I'm afraid so.'

'I hope she'll be very happy,' said Reggie.

'Yes,' said Linda.

'How can she marry somebody with such thin lips,' said Reggie.

It was Friday morning. The children were back at nursery school, and Reggie had taken the morning off. He was wearing his gardening clothes, so that he could go straight on to the mental home afterwards.

Linda poured him a glass of sultana wine, and they went out into the garden. It was a day of mild September wistfulness.

They sat on the rustic seat, under an apple tree.

'Cheer up, father,' said Linda.

'I love your mother,' said Reggie.

'You'll get over it,' said Linda.

Reggie picked up a windfall and hurled it savagely into the rare shrubs.

'They're holding a memorial service for you,' said Linda.

'Good God.'

'Next Thursday. Your brother's coming down from Aberdeen.'

'Good God.'

'There's a piece in this morning's local paper about it.'

'Good God.'

There were fluffy toys and overturned lorries lying on the lawn.

'I'll have to come to that,' said Reggie.

'What? You can't go to your own memorial service,' said Linda.

'I should have thought I above all people had a right to be there.'

'People will recognize you.'

'No, they won't. You didn't. Nobody has. I'm at the bottom of the sea as far as they're concerned.'

'I don't like the idea of your going,' said Linda.

'I'm going to be there – and that's all there is to it,' said Reggie.

A hedge sparrow was watching them from the roof of the folly.

'I wonder if I'll ever marry,' said Reggie. He stood up. 'Come on,' he said. 'I want to see that article. It's not often I get my name in the paper.'

'It isn't exactly your name,' said Linda.

She led him into the living room and handed him the paper. She poured another glass of sultana wine while he read.

MEMORIAL SERVICE FOR CLIMTHORPE MAN

There is to be a memorial service for the local businessman who was presumed to have drowned himself after his clothes were found piled by the sea on a beach in Dorset in June.

He is Mr Reginald I. Perry, who lived in Coleridge Close, Climthorpe.

He is Mr Reginald I. Perry, who lived piled by the sea on a beach in Dorset in June.

At the time of his death an official of the well-known London firm of Sunshine Desserts stated that Peppin had been 'over-corked'.

A police spokesman told us today, 'We have no reason to suppose that Mr Peppin is not deaf, although his body has never been found.'

The memorial service will be piled by the sea on a beach in Dorset in June.

'It's a fitting obituary,' said Reggie.

'Oh, father!' said Linda.

A car pulled up on the gravel outside. A door slammed tinnily. There were loud footsteps. The bell rang firmly.

'Don't worry,' said Linda. 'Whoever it is, I won't let them in.'

It was Major James Anderson, serving his last month with the Queen's Own Berkshire Light Infantry.

'Come in, Jimmy,' she said.

She led him into the living room. He was in uniform, and wearing his medal. She saw Reggie stiffen with shock. She only hoped Jimmy wouldn't recognize him.

'I have the plumber here,' she said. 'Uncle Jimmy, this is the plumber. The plumber, this is Uncle Jimmy.'

They shook hands.

'Watcher, mate,' said Reggie, and he knocked back the remains of his sultana wine. 'Yeah – well – I'll be off then, lady. Ta for the vino. I don't think you'll have any more trouble in so far as your ballcock. And I've cleared your persistent drip. That'll be six pounds seventy-five. I'd like it in cash if you don't mind, lady. I don't declare everything to the tax people, why should I, nobody else does.'

Linda handed her father six pounds seventy-five.

'I'll see you out,' she said.

When she opened the door she could see the sadness in Reggie's eyes. She wanted to kiss him good-bye, but Jimmy might be surprised if she kissed the plumber.

She returned to the living room, and offered Jimmy a glass of sultana wine.

'Bit early for me,' he said. 'Just a small one.'

She poured out the drink.

'Do you usually give your plumber sultana wine?' said Jimmy.

'You have to give them things these days, if you want to keep them,' said Linda. 'My french polisher has smoked salmon sandwiches.'

251

She sat on the chaise longue. Jimmy sat in the rocking chair. He rocked cautiously, stiffly, regimentally.

'Just came round, apologize,' he said.

'There was no need,' said Linda.

'Nonsense. Bad business. Your own uncle. Almost like incest. Chaps cashiered for less.'

'Really, Jimmy, it's over and done with,' said Linda.

Jimmy came over and sat on the chaise longue beside her. He put his hand on her right knee.

'It's all right,' he said. 'I'm only apologizing.'

He caressed the smoothness of her leg through a small hole in her tights.

'I love you,' he said.

She led the way upstairs, and they made love on the striped sheets. Linda was on fire and Jimmy groaned hoarsely as they reached a marvellous climax together.

Afterwards they dressed in silence and didn't look at each other.

'Only came round to apologize,' said Jimmy. 'Sorry.'

'Don't be silly,' said Linda.

'Chap comes round to say, "Sorry. Bad show". Does it again. Shocking show,' said Jimmy.

'Well at least let's try and enjoy it,' said Linda. 'Let's not ruin it with guilt.'

'Quite right. Sorry. No guilt. Enjoyed it. Enjoyed it very much. Wouldn't mind doing it again,' said Jimmy.

'No,' said Linda. 'Now, can I get you some food?'

'Lord no, didn't come round for that. Unless you've got the odd scraps.'

'I'll see what I can find,' said Linda.

'Last consignment much appreciated. Literally saved our bacon,' said Jimmy. 'Top-hole pheasant paté. General verdict – yum-yum.'

Linda gave him cold roast beef, hare terrine, bloaters, instant coffee, a smoked trout, six oranges, half a pound of Cookeen and a damson pie.

He kissed her decorously on the cheek, ran his hand briefly over her stomach and heard her gasp.

'Don't come to apologize again,' said Linda.

'No. Sorry. Take it as read,' said Jimmy, and he drove off through the gate.

He limped back, carrying the remains of the gate.

'Awfully sorry,' he said. 'Bad show. Blasted plumber must have closed it. Pay for a new gate. Insist.'

'I want you to come to the Memorial Service,' said Elizabeth.

'Oh, I couldn't. It wouldn't be right,' said Henry Possett.

The scene was an expensive London restaurant. It was pink. They had been to the second night of Mark's play.

'I agree we shouldn't announce our engagement yet,' said Elizabeth, 'but I don't want to hide you away. I'm not ashamed of loving you. It doesn't make any difference to what I felt for Reggie.'

'Well, all right, then,' said Henry Possett.

An ancient, white-haired waiter brought their chateaubriand.

'Poor Mark,' said Elizabeth.

'I thought he said his line very well,' said Henry Possett. 'He didn't fluff a single word.'

'I'm glad we didn't tell him we were going, though. He's so sensitive.'

After their meal she drove Henry to his pied-à-terre off the Brompton Road, which he shared with four other people on a rota basis, thus enabling them all to have a late evening in London every week.

He didn't invite her in for a cup of coffee.

Reggie crept out of Number thirteen, Clytemnestra Grove at six-thirty a.m., in order to avoid Miss Pershore. He was wearing his new suit and doing his best not to look like Donald Potts. He was Martin Wellbourne, an old friend of the deceased, whom he had not seen for many years, having sequestered himself in Brazil following an amorous disappointment in Sutton Coldfield.

It was a cool, misty morning. He had breakfast at Waterloo Station, rang to tell Mr Bottomley he had a migraine, and waited in the station forecourt until it was time to catch his train to Climthorpe.

Soft music played over the loudspeakers and the cracked old woman was busy accosting people. Reggie was nervous. Supposing somebody did recognize him? They shouldn't, with his grey hair, beard, lined face, deep tan, slimmer build, more erect posture, and the subtle changes of voice and mannerism which he had adopted. But supposing they did?

The train was almost empty, and he couldn't see any other mourners. The sun came out shortly after Surbiton. They were going to have a nice day for it.

The service was just about to commence when Reggie entered the church. He sat at the back, as you should do at your own memorial service.

The Victorian church was tall and dark, conceived more in righteousness than love, more in sorrow than in anger.

The few mourners in their subdued clothes seemed a pitifully small group in this great vault.

Elizabeth was there, of course and Linda and Tom, with Adam and Jocasta looking puzzled and over-awed. Linda looked round, saw him, and gave no sign. She looked very nervous.

There was Henry Possett, in an immaculate dark suit, with a striped shirt, and white collar. Reggie hadn't expected him to be there.

His eyes roamed round the dimly-lit nave. There was Davina, dressed in silky pink, with a black arm band.

Reggie was surprised to see C.J., who was accompanied by Mrs C.J.

There was Jimmy, and Reggie was amazed to see that Sheila was with him.

There was no sign of Mark.

His heart gave a little jump as he saw his elder brother

254

Nigel, the engineer, whom he had loved and admired so much. Reggie hadn't seen him for nine long years.

That must be Fiona beside him, in the fur. His brother's first wife had been Danish, his second French, yet he had always seemed to Reggie to be an insular man. Men who took foreign wives often were. Perhaps it was a form of self-protection.

There she was, his mother-in-law, in black coat and simply enormous navy blue hat with a black band, steeped in the enjoyment of mourning, the hippopotamus shedding crocodile tears.

Where was Mark?

Joan Greengross wasn't there but that was only to be expected.

There was an unnatural chill in the church, as if central cooling had been installed.

High up, a sparrow was flying from ledge to ledge.

The friendship department was represented by two friends of half a lifetime – Michael Wilkinson and Roger Whetstone. Yet in the last year or two Reggie had hardly seen either of them. Oh, the waste.

The Rev. E. F. Wales-Parkinson entered. There was a moment of uncertainty. Nobody knew what to do, never having been to a memorial service before.

Then they all stood up.

'Let us pray,' said the Rev. E. F. Wales-Parkinson.

They all knelt.

Reggie didn't listen to the words. Prayer had no efficacy as far as he was concerned.

He watched the mourners. Jimmy was concentrating with strong devotion. Tom was watching the sparrow. Linda was trying to stop Tom watching the sparrow. Nigel was concentrating hard on simulating deep concentration. Elizabeth moved her head instinctively in the direction of Henry Possett, for moral support. Michael Wilkinson and Roger Whetstone weren't kneeling, they were just sitting forward

255

and crouching. C.J. appeared to be kneeling, getting his knees dusty.

A hymn followed. Everybody stood up. Mark entered the church during the first verse and spent the whole hymn trying to find the number. He found it in time to sing the last line.

Jimmy bellowed, his fervency exceeded only by his tune-lessness. Beside him Sheila twitched rhythmically. Elizabeth's lips moved but no sound came out. Davina sang piercingly. Michael Wilkinson and Roger Whetstone murmured incomprehensibly in embarrassment. The sparrow cheeped monotonously. The Rev. E. F. Wales-Parkinson sang some lines very loud, others not at all.

Nigel read the first lesson. He read in a stiff, staccato voice, rendering it all meaningless. The sparrow cheeped throughout, and Adam and Jocasta were beginning to talk.

There were more prayers, then the second lesson was read by C.J. He went to the other extreme, investing the words with too much emotion, too much dignity, too much sonorance, too much sincerity. He gave the impression of a man who hadn't got where he was today without knowing how to read the second lesson.

C.J. rolled to his conclusion. He paused. 'Here endeth the second lesson,' he thundered. He closed the great bible carefully, like a celestial Eamonn Andrews saying, 'Reggie Perrin, that was your life.'

Stop being so tart, Reggie, said Reggie to himself. Stop criticising. But I can't help being tart, because I'm moved. We're singing a hymn now but I'm not conscious of the words. I am only conscious of the people. I am moved by Jimmy's simple warmth, at knowing that Mark is upset, at watching Elizabeth and knowing that she loved me truly, at knowing that I must live the rest of my life away from her. I am moved that all this gathering is for me, goofy old me, and I am moved not only with pride but also with shame, because of all the empty pews, because this is such a pathetic occasion. I am moved with wonder at the existence of religious belief, which seems to me so truly extraordinary and so far beyond my capacity. Add to this my fear of recognition, and it's no wonder if I take refuge in criticism.

The hymn was over. The Rev. E. F. Wales-Parkinson was climbing the pulpit steps. They all sat down.

The congregation cleared their throats, as if it was they who were going to speak. The sparrow flew over them and landed on a window ledge in the north aisle. Adam said, 'Is it over?' loudly and Linda whispered, 'Not yet, dear. The man's going to speak to us.'

The Rev. E. F. Wales-Parkinson waited patiently for silence.

'"Here are the gumboots you ordered, madam,"' he began. '"Here are the gumboots you ordered, madam." A strange choice of text, perhaps. It comes not from the Old Testament, not from the New Testament, but from a play I saw on Tuesday night. We are gathered here in memory of Reginald Perrin — Reggie to his many friends — for Reggie was nothing if not a friendly man. I went to see this play, because Reggie's son Mark was appearing in it, and also because I thoroughly enjoy a visit to the boards.

'Mark's part in the play was not a large one. He had just one line. Yes, you've guessed it. "Here are the gumboots you ordered, madam."'

Reggie glanced at Mark, who was looking down at the floor in deep embarrassment.

'Just one line,' said the Rev. E. F. Wales-Parkinson. 'Yet, a vital line, for if the lady had not received the footwear in question, she would not have gone out into the farmyard mud on that wild night, she would not have been ritually slaughtered by the maniacal cowman, and there would have been no play.'

'Cheep, cheep,' said the sparrow.

'It was a line, too, that was delivered by Mark with rare skill. He wrung every possible drop of emotion from it. He became that servant, handing over the gumboots and then retiring, wistfully, to the periphery of life's stage.

'I chose this text for several reasons,' said the Rev. E. F.

Wales-Parkinson. 'Firstly, because I have a sneaking feeling that Reggie would have liked it. He was a man with a taste for the unexpected. And I chose this text because I think that Reggie himself had an innate sympathy with those on the periphery of life. Beneath the cloak of cynicism which he sometimes donned there beat a kindly heart, a heart very much in sympathy with the underdogs, the misfits, the backroom boys, the providers of life's actual and metaphorical gumboots.

'Thirdly, I chose this text because in remembering Reggie Perrin, what better memorial can there be than the human one, a son of whom he may be justly proud?

'We think also today of Elizabeth, a brave woman much loved by us all, whose good works in this parish have been legion. We offer her our sympathy in her time of loss but we also hope that she can draw strength and happiness from the memory of Reggie Perrin.

'And we think too of Linda, whose vocal skills once graced our choir here in this very church. Linda is married now, she has a fine husband, and they in their turn have two fine children.'

'I wanna go home,' said Adam.

'One of the most attractive aspects of Reggie's character was his love of children,' said the Rev. E. F. Wales-Parkinson. 'But of course he was not only a family man. I am not qualified to speak of his contribution to British industry. He worked, in his characteristically self-effacing way, half a lifetime for one firm. Loyalty was a virtue he prized highly. Let us not forget that. And it is a measure of the esteem that is inspired by loyalty that the managing director of his firm has taken time off to be with us today. That speaks louder than anything I can say.'

Jocasta began to howl, louder than anything the Rev. E. F. Wales-Parkinson could say. Tom and Linda whispered together for a moment, then Tom led Adam and Jocasta out. Everybody turned to watch them, except Linda, Elizabeth, Henry Possett and Jimmy.

258

'It would be presumptuous of me to speculate on the reasons behind this tragic death,' said the Rev. E. F. Wales-Parkinson. 'It may well be that the rat-race had become increasingly distasteful to this least ratlike of men. It may be that his conscience could not rest at peace in a world that knows very little peace.'

Reggie caught his mother-in-law staring at him as she turned round to count how many people were there. He didn't think she had recognized him. Probably she was just wondering who he was.

'Reggie did not call himself a Christian. He did not visit this church,' said the Rev. E. F. Wales-Parkinson. 'But when I called at his delightful house I was always assured of a friendly reception from him. Indeed he liked nothing better than the cut and thrust of ethical debate. "What about that earthquake last Tuesday, padre?" he'd say. "How do you explain that one away?" A jocular remark, and yet one was left with a glimpse of the feeling that it cloaked, of the real concern for the moral problems of this day and age.'

'Cheep, cheep,' said the sparrow.

'It may seem paradoxical that a man of so strong a conscience should not call himself a Christian,' said the Rev. E. F. Wales-Parkinson. 'It is I think a paradox that we would do well to ponder on. We Christians do not have a monopoly of conscience, any more than the secular world has a monopoly of sin.

'Let us all examine our consciences, and ask ourselves if we are aware enough, if we care enough, if we do enough. Would *we* be able to say, with dignity and without envy and resentment, "Here are the gumboots you ordered, madam"?

'But let us also take some comfort in our religion, in our faith. There is a sense in which Reggie Perrin is not dead. He is, in a real and meaningful way, here with us today, in this very church, at this very time.'

Reggie's blood ran cold. Linda instinctively looked round towards him. They sang a hymn, the Rev. E. F. Wales-Parkinson said a final prayer, and the memorial service was over.

259

The September sunshine seemed very bright after the church. Reggie shook hands with the vicar.

'I don't think I . . .' began the vicar.

'I was an old friend,' said Reggie.

'Thank you so much for coming,' said the vicar.

Reggie approached Elizabeth. He could see Linda watching him nervously, and he could feel his heart pounding.

'My deepest sympathy, Mrs Perrin,' he said.

'Thank you,' said Elizabeth. 'I don't think I . . .'

'Martin Wellbourne,' said Reggie. 'I'm an old friend. We lost touch.'

'Well it's always a pleasure to meet an old friend of Reggie's.'

'I was shocked when I read the announcement,' said Reggie. 'I felt I must come. I do hope you don't mind.'

'I'm very glad you did,' said Elizabeth. 'I'm having a few people back to the house. I do hope you'll be able to join us.'

And so he entered his own house once again. Ponsonby miaowed and rubbed against his leg.

'She's taken to you,' said Tom.

'It doesn't mean anything with cats,' said Reggie.

'I don't get on with cats,' said Tom. 'I'm a dog person.'

There was an excellent selection of cold foods laid out on the dining room table. A choice of red or white wine accompanied them. Reggie had never questioned the propriety of eating and drinking on such occasions, but now he wasn't certain that he really liked being sent on his way with prawn and chicken vol-au-vents.

He took two vol-au-vents and a sausage on a stick, because they were there. Then he introduced himself to Linda.

'I haven't seen Reggie for over twenty-five years,' said Reggie. 'I sequestered myself in Brazil, following an amorous disappointment in Sutton Coldfield.'

'Ah, the cat lover,' said Tom, joining them by the drinks trolley.

Reggie was formally introduced to Tom.

'These scampi concoctions are delicious,' said Tom.

Through the french windows, Reggie could see Adam and Jocasta chasing Ponsonby round the garden.

'You believe in introducing your children to death rather young,' he said.

'We're bringing them up to accept it as quite natural,' said Tom.

'Yes. People do get such a thing about death,' said Linda.

'Death ruins lots of people's lives,' said Tom. 'We saw a dead hedgehog last week, and Jocasta really showed a very mature attitude.'

'Yes, darling, but I don't think she really grasps the implications. She's only two,' said Linda.

'You weren't there,' said Tom. 'She knows what it's all about.'

'Sad thing, death,' said Jimmy, passing by on his way to collect another drink.

'This is Elizabeth's brother Jimmy,' said Tom. 'Jimmy, this is Mervyn Wishbone.'

'Chap pegs out, everybody comes round, nosh nosh, gurgle gurgle, waffle waffle. Odd,' said Jimmy.

'Yes. Very odd,' said Reggie.

Sheila came threading her way through the gathering towards the drinks trolley. Jimmy put his arm round her with a gesture that said, 'Got you.'

'I was just getting a drink,' she said.

'Do you really need another one?' said Jimmy.

'Yes, I do,' she said, rather loudly.

'All right,' said Jimmy hastily.

When she'd got her drink, Jimmy introduced her to Reggie.

'Darling, come and meet an old friend of Reggie's, Melvyn Washroom,' said Jimmy.

Reggie shook hands.

'Well, it's a nice day for it,' said Sheila.

'Yes.'

'I always say it makes all the difference.'

'Yes. Yes, it does,' said Reggie.

'Mr Washroom has lived in Peru,' said Jimmy.

'Brazil,' said Reggie.

'Brazil. Sorry. Memory like sieve,' said Jimmy.

'It must be very interesting, living in Brazil,' said Sheila.

'It is,' said Reggie.

'Come on, dear. Circulate,' said Jimmy.

'I want to talk to Mr Washroom,' said Sheila. 'You circulate.'

'Now come on, dear,' said Jimmy.

'I'll shout,' said Sheila.

'Sorry. Right. I'll circulate,' said Jimmy, and he wandered off hastily towards the french windows.

'Let's have a refill,' said Sheila.

'I don't think we ought to drink too much,' said Reggie. 'I don't think there's much left.'

'Reggie didn't like me.'

'Didn't he?'

'None of his family liked me. They had it in for me from the start.'

'Really, I don't think . . .'

'You don't know. You weren't there, Mr Washroom.'

'That's true.'

Jimmy returned and took Reggie by the arm.

'Come and meet Reggie's brother, Mr Washroom,' he said, and he led Reggie firmly across the room towards Nigel and Fiona. They were standing in isolation by the piano.

'This is an old friend of Reggie's, Melvyn Washroom,' said Jimmy. 'Reggie's brother Nigel, and Fiona.'

They shook hands. Nigel's hands were cold. So were Fiona's.

'My brother told me a lot about you,' said Nigel.

Reggie was shocked by Nigel's lie.

'Really. That's intriguing. What did he say?' he said.

'He just said how highly he regarded you,' said Nigel.

'I never met him,' said Fiona. 'Aberdeen is a long way off.'

'Reggie and I didn't see a lot of each other. We were never close,' explained Nigel.

You may not have been, thought Reggie, but I was.

'Different temperaments, I suppose,' said Nigel.

The hippopotamus was bearing down on them.

'I must meet the intriguing stranger,' she said.

'This is Mrs Anderson, Elizabeth's mother. An old friend of my brother's, Melvyn Windscreen,' said Nigel. He glanced at his watch. 'We ought to move around and do our stuff if we want to be getting along,' he murmured to Fiona. 'Excuse us, will you?' he said. 'We've got to get all the way back to Aberdeen.'

They moved off to speak to Elizabeth.

'I've been hearing such a lot about you,' said his mother-in-law. 'You've been very cruel to us all, burying yourself away in the Argentine.'

'Brazil,' said Reggie.

'They're all the same to me,' she said. She removed Nigel's glass from the piano top. 'It must have been a great shock to you to hear about poor Reginald.'

'Yes, it was,' said Reggie.

Adam and Jocasta came in through the french windows.

'My daughter was considered quite a catch in her day.'

'I can imagine.'

There was a sudden hoot and everyone looked round. It was Jimmy, leading the children out through the french windows and pretending to be a railway train.

'So you've denied us all your company, you naughty man, just because you were jilted in Merthyr Tydfil.'

'Sutton Coldfield,' said Reggie.

'I knew it was something to do with mining,' said his mother-in-law.

'I must say his wife is very lovely,' said Reggie.

'Well of course I don't approve of her bringing that man here,' she boomed confidentially — why is it that the people who indulge in the most asides so often have the loudest voices? 'Of course he's a very nice man but some things just aren't done. I mean Reginald is still practically warm.'

'Quite,' said Reggie.

His mother-in-law introduced him to Mark.

'This is Mr Melville Windpipe,' she said.

'You're the actor, aren't you?' said Reggie.

'That's right. Stupid, I thought that sermon was.'

'I think Reggie would have rather liked it,' said Reggie.

In the garden, Jimmy was being forcibly shunted on to a flower bed.

'How's the play doing?'

'It's folding on Saturday.'

'Oh dear. What'll you do then?'

'I've got another part lined up.'

'In the West End?'

'Not exactly. It's a new experimental tea-time theatre in Kentish Town. It's a twelve-minute play called "Can Egbert Poltergeist Defeat the Great Plague of Walking Sticks and Reach True Maturity?"'

'What do you play?'

'I play the hat-stand. Let's get some nosh.'

They went into the dining room and helped themselves to egg and cress sandwiches and sausage rolls.

'Your father was an awfully nice chap,' said Reggie.

'Yeah.'

What sort of a reply was that? 'Yeah.' Couldn't Mark do better than that? What about, 'When they made my father, they threw away the mould'?

They went back into the living room.

'Can I get you another kitchen?' said Mark.

'Kitchen?'

'Kitchen sink. Drink.'

'Oh. Thank you.'

Nigel and Fiona came past to fetch their coats and he said, 'Good-bye,' and Nigel said, 'Good-bye, Mr Windscreen,' and Reggie said, 'It was nice to meet you – and your lovely earwig,' and Nigel said, 'Earwig?' and Reggie said, 'When I say earwig I mean your wife,' and Nigel gave him a strange look and went to fetch the coats, and Fiona smiled like a dark mysterious loch.

Mark brought Reggie his drink and introduced him to the C.J.s.

'Any friend of Reggie Perrin is a friend of Mrs C.J. and myself,' said C.J. 'When they made Reggie Perrin, they threw away the mould.'

But I don't want to hear it from you, C.J., thought Reggie.

'We owe a great deal to Reggie,' said C.J. 'He opened our eyes. Sunshine Desserts will be a better and a happier place as a result.'

'I'm very glad to hear it,' said Reggie.

C.J. introduced him to Davina.

'I owe a great deal to your friend,' said Davina. 'He introduced me to my late fiancé. He was Reggie's uncle. He was a gorgeous old man. He left me this super house in Abinger Hammer. I'm leaving Sunshine Desserts and opening a gorgeous little curio shop. I've got some marvellous stuff. All the up and coming things. Burmese wattle saucepan scourers. Japanese ebony pith helmets.'

'I'm very happy for you,' said Reggie.

'I only wish my late fiancé was alive to share it,' said Davina.

Reggie circled round the room, getting closer to Elizabeth without actually arriving. Jimmy came in again, somewhat puffed after pulling a freight train all the way from Bristol Temple Meads to the forsythia. Reggie saw Linda smile at him and thank him gratefully. Linda had always had a soft spot for Jimmy, he thought.

Jimmy came over to him. 'Rum, isn't it? Chap kicks the bucket, down come the vultures, nosh nosh, gurgle gurgle, rhubarb rhubarb. Makes you think.'

'Yes.'

Jimmy led Reggie into a corner by the standard lamp and said in a low voice, 'Owed a lot to Reggie. Saved my life. Rum story.'

'How do you mean?' said Reggie.

Jimmy took a gulp of white wine.

'Told you too much already,' he said.

'This is a charming house, isn't it?' said Reggie.

'Saved my life,' said Jimmy. He looked furtively round the room. Sheila was chatting up Roger Whetstone by the french windows. Nobody was within earshot.

'Fact is, wits end,' he said. 'Domestic hoo-has. Then army says, "Thank you for defending freedom. You're forty-four. Piss off."'

'I'm sorry to hear that,' said Reggie. 'What's all this about my saving – about my friend saving your life?'

'Told you too much already,' said Jimmy.

'Look. There's an albino blackbird over there,' said Reggie.

'Got it all worked out. Throw myself in front of train. Then this business blows up. Reggie drowned. Well, couldn't do it. Next day, my body, Bakerloo line, just not on. Too much for Elizabeth. Straw that broke camel's back.'

'Are you glad you're still alive?'

'Yes and no. Swings and roundabouts.' He lowered his voice still further. 'While there's life I'm near to her,' he said.

'Who?' said Reggie.

'Told you too much already,' said Jimmy. He led Reggie over towards the drinks trolley. On the way they met Henry Possett.

'You know you remind me of Reggie,' said Henry Possett.

'Rubbish,' said Jimmy.

Reggie could see Linda freeze in mid vol-au-vent.

'Take away the beard and you'd be very similar,' said Henry Possett.

'By jove. See it now,' said Jimmy.

'People used to say we were rather alike,' said Reggie. 'They called us the terrible twins.'

'You're a bit slimmer, of course,' said Henry Possett.

'And older,' said Jimmy. 'I mean – well – not exactly older. Less – less young.'

'We were very much the same age, actually,' said Reggie. 'My appearance is the result of the Brazilian climate.'

'Tricky chap, the climate,' said Jimmy. 'Not surprising some of these foreigners are a bit odd. Daresay I'd be a bit odd if I lived in Helsinki or Dacca. Excuse me, chap over there monopolizing my better half. Rescue operations.'

Elizabeth joined Reggie and Henry Possett.

'I'm afraid I've been neglecting you, Mr Wellbourne,' she said.

'Not at all,' said Reggie.

'It was so good of you to come.'

'Not at all,' said Reggie.

'Well at least we had a nice day for it,' said Elizabeth.

'Yes. Very nice,' said Reggie.

'I think people are beginning to break up,' said Henry Possett.

'I'd better go and do my stuff,' said Elizabeth.

'Well, that's that,' said Henry Possett.

'Yes,' said Reggie. 'That's that.'

People were indeed beginning to go. Reggie didn't want to leave. This was his house. It was his garden. Ponsonby was his cat. He belonged here.

He left quickly, not even trusting himself to say goodbye to Elizabeth. Jimmy was just getting into his car, which was badly dented. He was carrying a brown paper bag. The bag burst and a stream of vol-au-vents and sandwiches slipped out on to the pavement. He began to pick them up frantically.

Reggie looked the other way and set off down Coleridge Close.

'Mr Wellbourne!'

Swallows were gathering on the telegraph poles.

'Mr Wellbourne!'

He turned round. Elizabeth was standing at her gate.

'Mr Wellbourne!'

He walked back to her.

'I didn't know you were going, or I'd have spoken before,' she said. 'I don't expect, if you've been in Brazil, that you know many people in this country.'

'No. Not a lot.'

'I wondered if you'd like to come round and have dinner one night, if that wouldn't be too boring for you.'

267

October

It was a very pleasant dinner party. The only other guests were Linda and Tom. Reggie and Elizabeth seemed to hit it off from the start. Reggie kept them fascinated with his tales of life in Brazil. They drank Linda and Tom's prune wine.

After dinner Reggie said, 'Well, I haven't enjoyed an evening so much for a long time.'

'You've helped to take me out of myself,' said Elizabeth.'

Linda's eyes flashed warnings at Reggie.

Elizabeth drove Reggie to the station. He had great difficulty in restraining himself from kissing her.

'You can't have seen much of England recently,' she said. 'I wondered if you'd like to go for a drive one day, if it wouldn't be too boring for you.'

Reggie walked wearily up the steps that led to the front door of Number thirteen, Clytemnestra Grove. It had been a strenuous day of transplanting young fruit trees in the gardens of the North Hillingley Mental Home. He barely had the energy to get his key out.

'Caught you,' said Miss Pershore, as he crossed the hall.

'Hullo, Ethel.'

He picked up his pint of milk.

'You've been avoiding me,' said Miss Pershore.

'Rubbish.'

She was blocking the foot of the stairs, her chins sticking out pugnaciously.

'I will not be trifled with,' she said. 'I'd expected better manners from you. Hiding yourself away, borrowing all those books on Brazil from the library, emigrating the moment my back's turned!'

'I'm not emigrating, Ethel. Honest. Look, tell you what, we'll go down the Clytemnestra Friday.'

'My friends from the Chamber of Commerce expect me to drink with them on a Friday,' said Miss Pershore loftily. 'What about Saturday? Why don't you pop in and see the one-thirty at Haydock Park?'

'I can't,' said Reggie. 'I've got a prior engagement on Saturday.'

'Prior engagement my foot!' said Miss Pershore. 'More like another woman.'

The pale golden sunshine of early October shone upon stone and timber, thatch and tile. The acrid smoke from burning stubble drifted across the lanes. The sun burnt on broken bottles in hedges and shone with a silvery sheen on the bellies of poisoned fish in the canals. It flashed off the radar screens of secret defence establishments and glinted on aeroplanes high in the blue white-wisped sky. Reggie wanted to kiss Elizabeth on her wide lips and large soft eyes. He wanted to run his hand up her broad, strong, mature thighs and melt in the liquid writhing of lips like Waterloo Station on war-time evenings.

They leant over a gate and watched wood-pigeons ransacking a field. Reggie's thigh was touching hers. He slipped his hand into hers. Nothing was said. He tickled the palm of her hand gently with his nails. She didn't respond, nor did she push his hand away.

They had a drink in a country pub. It was unspoilt. They played a game of darts. There was a big pit in the board around the treble twenty, but very few of their darts went anywhere near the treble twenty.

When they got back in the car, Reggie wanted to plunge his face into the folds of her light green dress. Instead he got out the map and directed her to a restaurant at which he had booked dinner.

It was expensive. He could ill afford to pay for it on his under-gardener's wages.

When she dropped him off at a station suitable for catching a fast train to London, Elizabeth said, 'I really did enjoy myself. It was almost like being with Reggie again.'

In the pink restaurant, at Henry Possett's favourite table, Elizabeth dabbled perfunctorily with her artichoke vinaigrette.

Henry Possett speared a snail, and removed it carefully from its shell.

'What's wrong?' he said. 'You're not yourself tonight.'

'I want to break off the engagement,' she said. 'Oh, Henry, I'm so sorry.'

He held the snail poised in mid-air. His face was a state archive, in which his emotions had been classified top secret.

'It's Martin Wellbourne, isn't it?' he said.

'Yes, I suppose it is,' she said.

The waiter misinterpreted their mood and enquired anxiously whether everything was all right.

'Yes. It's all perfect,' said Henry Possett angrily. He smiled at Elizabeth. 'Martin's your type,' he said.

'I suppose so,' she said. 'I'm terribly sorry, Henry.'

Henry Possett popped the snail into his mouth. He chewed the gritty, rubbery flesh very delicately, as if shrinking from the vulgarity of his cruel sophistication.

'I've been worried about getting married, if the truth be told,' he said quietly, when he had finished eating the snail. 'I haven't been sleeping well. I couldn't help wondering how I would measure up to Reggie so far as the physical side of marriage is concerned. I'm not a physical person. I once went to a strip-tease in Istanbul, during the international conference on reducing waste effluent. I found the allure of such entertainment totally mystifying. I don't know if I could live happily in close contact with another person. I'm a creature of habit. I have my books, my languages, my work. I play my recorder. Vera and I suit each other. Our modes of life dovetail

270

beautifully. I don't know what would have happened to Vera. I expect it's all for the best.'

He speared another snail and ate it slowly.

'Finished?' said the waiter.

'Finished,' said Henry Possett.

'I'm terribly sorry,' said Elizabeth.

The first kiss between Elizabeth and Martin Wellbourne took place on the sofa in Elizabeth's living room. Ponsonby was their only witness.

Reggie had used a small amount of scent, in order not to smell like Reggie.

'It's odd,' said Elizabeth. 'Until yesterday I was engaged to be married to Henry Possett, yet I don't feel guilty about that. I feel guilty towards Reggie.'

'I don't think he'd mind,' said Reggie.

'How can you tell?' said Elizabeth.

Ponsonby joined them on the sofa. On the television Malcolm Muggeridge was talking with the sound turned down.

'If I was Reggie, and I was able to watch what's going on in this room,' said Reggie, 'I think I'd be rather proud at seeing how much you had loved me.'

'Oh yes, I did love him,' said Elizabeth. 'Oh, Martin, and now I love you. Is that terrible?'

'No,' he said. 'Elizabeth?'

'Yes.'

'Will you marry me?'

When Linda heard the news of the engagement, she drove straight round to Clytemnestra Grove and rang the bell beneath which it said 'Potts' on an untidy strip of dirty white paper.

'You shouldn't have come here,' said Reggie, who had a cold coming on.

He led her up the bare brown stairs and into his ungainly brown room. She refused to sit down.

'You can't marry mother, father,' she said. 'It'd be bigamy.'

'It can't be bigamy,' said Reggie. 'I'm the same man both times.'

'Mother doesn't know that,' said Linda. 'It's bigamy as far as she's concerned.'

'She doesn't know I'm still alive,' said Reggie. 'It isn't bigamy as far as anyone's concerned.'

He made a cup of Camp coffee on his grimy gas ring.

'Can't you tell her the truth?' she said. 'That's what you wanted me to do earlier.'

'Things are different now,' said Reggie. 'She's in love with Martin Wellbourne. I daren't destroy that.'

'It's not right,' said Linda stubbornly.

'I know she'll be happy, and that's what matters,' said Reggie.

'She'll know,' said Linda. 'Women sense these things. You can't hide it from your own wife.'

'I'll be different in every way, Linda. I'll eat differently, live differently, talk differently, sneeze differently, cough differently. I'll become Martin Wellbourne. I look different already. I'm greyer, slimmer, I'll have electrolysis, I'll use after-shave and scent. My body won't look the same, feel the same or smell the same.'

'Some parts will,' said Linda.

'Elizabeth won't examine me under a microscope,' he said. 'You forget that as far as she's concerned I'm dead. In her own mind, she knows I'm dead. The possibility just won't occur to her.'

'I still think you're behaving badly and irresponsibly, father.'

'What about your mother?'

'What do you mean?'

'What about her behaviour? She shouldn't be falling in love with me so soon after my death. It's not very flattering.'

He looked at the horrible, bulky, brown furniture that went with Donald Potts. Soon all that would be gone for ever.

'Are you warm enough?' he said.

'It is a bit chilly,' said Linda.

He lit the gas fire.

'Do you and Tom have separate bank accounts?' he asked.

'Yes. Why?'

'Can you lend me £200?'

'What for?'

'To set myself up as Martin Wellbourne I need documents and things.'

'I'm sure it's all against the law,' said Linda.

'Haven't you ever done anything illegal?' said Reggie.

Linda blushed.

'What'll you do for a living?' she asked.

'I'll live off your mother. There's my savings, my life insurance policies, my pension. We'll manage.'

'Won't you feel humiliated?'

'Of course not. It's my money. I'll be marrying into my own money. And don't worry, old girl. Our secret is safe.'

He didn't accompany Linda downstairs, for fear that he would meet Miss Pershore. But in the morning, when he went downstairs to collect his milk, she was there.

'She's young enough to be your daughter,' she said coldly.

Donald Potts disappeared off the face of this earth without a flicker of surprise or interest. Society does not mourn for the under-gardeners at its mental homes.

Martin Wellbourne took rooms in Kensington and acquired the necessary documents from his forger. He wrote himself a few glowing references from his Brazilian employers.

He went down to Coleridge Close every evening, despite a streaming cold. He was rather proud of his new sneeze, and it proved a great success. He told Elizabeth all about his family, how he was an only child, his mother and father had been killed on holiday in Turkey, when their mule was in collision with a bus, how his fiancée had been drowned in a mangrove swamp before his very eyes, and all his family trophies and snapshots had been burnt in a gas mains explosion in Chorlton-cum-Hardy.

'You've had your share of tragedy,' said Elizabeth.

'One soldiers on,' he said.

After they had eaten their supper they sat in the dark, the room lit only by the flickering smokeless fuel in the grate.

'Will you be happy to live here?' said Elizabeth.

'It's lovely,' he said. 'Reggie's taste was very similar to mine.'

'You're alike in so many ways,' said Elizabeth. 'But deep down you're very different.'

'How do you know?' said Reggie.

'Feminine intuition,' said Elizabeth. 'We women have a sixth sense about these things.'

Reggie walked across the thick carpet of C.J.'s office towards the pneumatic chairs. The Bratby and the Francis Bacon were still there, but the picture of C.J. at the Paris Concours Des Desserts had gone. The cult of personality was over.

'Nice to see you again, Mr Wellbourne,' said C.J., shaking his hand. 'Sit down.'

Reggie sat down. His chair hissed at him.

'I could have sworn you were called Windpipe,' said C.J.

'That was a mistake,' said Reggie.

'Good. Fine,' said C.J. 'Now, I'll come straight to the point. Cigar?'

'No, thank you.'

'No formality, please, Melvyn. Call me C.J.'

'My name's Martin, C.J.'

'Even better. Where was I?'

'You were coming straight to the point.'

'Absolutely. Are you sure you won't have a cigar?'

'Really, no.'

'Mind if I do?'

'Not at all.'

C.J. lit his cigar.

'I'll come straight to the point,' he said. 'I met you at Elizabeth's, I liked what I saw, I liked the fact that you had come straight from Brazil, uncluttered with preconceptions about modern British industry. I've got a job for you.'

'Well, that's very kind of you,' said Reggie. 'But I'm not sure it's quite what I have in mind.'

'Don't fancy the grind of office life, eh? Don't want to give your life to desserts?'

'Frankly, no.'

'It isn't anything like that.'

A tug hooted on the river.

'What's business all about, Wellbourne?' he said. 'Profits? Not a bit of it. Products? Don't you believe it. Our overall sales, across the whole spectrum, were down 0.3 per cent last month.'

'I'm sorry to hear that, C.J.,' said Reggie.

'I couldn't care less myself,' said C.J. He walked over to the window and gazed out. 'London's river,' he said. 'As English as Yorkshire Pudding. A grimy snake worming her way to the sea. I love it. The smell of salt and mud. Barges piled with timber. The harsh cries of herring gulls. It was here before we came here. It will be here long after we have gone. We are but specks in the infinite, Mrs C.J. and I. So why worry about profits?'

C.J. sat down again. Reggie looked at him in amazement.

'Happy employees, that's what business is all about,' said C.J., and he paused to relight his cigar. 'But unfortunately all these falling sales, these shrinking dividends, a fiasco we had recently, a damn fool scheme for selling exotic ices, all this is undermining staff morale. There are danger signals, chaps starting to think their knees are enormous, the usual sort of thing.'

'I'm sorry to hear that,' said Reggie.

'I have reasonable private means, Martin,' said C.J. 'And I intend to live more moderately. Possessions bring misery. I am selling various of my properties. I'm buying a smaller house. With my own money I am setting up a foundation to provide a full range of social services and social functions for all my staff and their dependants.'

'It sounds a very good idea, C.J.,' said Reggie.

'It's the kind of project Mrs C.J. and I are in industry for,' said C.J. 'Now we are going to appoint a director, with a salary of six thousand pounds per annum rising to seven thousand pounds after one annum. How would you like to have a crack at it?'

'Well I've never done anything like it before,' said Reggie.

'Nor have we,' said C.J. 'That's why you're the man for the job.'

'I'd love the job,' said Reggie.

C.J. stood up.

'We need a name for the organization,' he said.

'I suppose we do,' said Reggie.

'I didn't get where I am today without calling it the Reggie Perrin Memorial Foundation,' said C.J.

'My name's Constable Barker,' said the intense young man at the door of Reggie's Kensington flat.

'Oh. Yes,' said Reggie.

'I've caught you at last,' said Constable Barker.

Reggie froze. So this was it.

He led Constable Barker into the living room. It was comfortable in the impersonal way of furnished flats. Whatever could conceivably have a tassel, had a tassel.

'I need a drink,' said Reggie. 'Will you join me?'

'No, thank you. I only drink Pernod on duty,' said Constable Barker, who was wearing green socks.

'Well, there's not much I can say,' said Reggie, pouring himself a large whisky from the cut glass decanter.

'I suppose not,' said Constable Barker. 'You hadn't seen him for many years, had you?'

'Who?' said Reggie.

'Mr Perrin. That's who we're talking about, isn't it?'

'Oh. Mr Perrin. Yes. Of course,' said Reggie.

'You were a close friend of his, weren't you, Mr Wellbourne?' said Constable Barker, who looked ill-at-ease in his armchair.

'Oh. Yes. Yes, I was. Very close. Yes,' said Reggie.

'He isn't dead,' said Constable Barker.

'What? Not dead? You mean . . . he's still alive? But . . . that's incredible.'

Careful, Reggie, don't overdo it in your relief. This man is a fanatic, but he's for real.

'He booked into several hotels under the names of Charles Windsor, Sir Wensley Amhurst and Lord Amhurst.'

This young man has talent. He's dangerous. He must be dealt with.

'But why?' said Reggie. 'Have you any idea why?'

'No, and I can't prove any of it, but I'm sure of it, as sure as I am that your name's Martin Wellbourne.'

'Quite. And what do you want me to do?'

'I just wondered if you could tell me anything that might help?'

A police siren blared its way down Kensington High Street. Constable Barker swelled with pride.

'Even if your far-fetched theory is right, constable, why not leave this man in peace?' said Reggie.

'That's not the spirit that's made the British police force the finest in the world,' said Constable Barker. 'I've lost the trail, but I'll find it again. I'll find it, if I have to go to the ends of the earth.'

'Ends of the earth,' said Reggie. 'You may just have to at that.'

'What do you mean by that, sir?'

Reggie poured himself another whisky.

'It was something he said to me once at Cambridge, over a drink,' said Reggie. Constable Barker leant forward eagerly. 'I must try and remember the exact words. He said, "Martin, there's one place I've always wanted to go to. I know nothing about it. It's just a place on the map. But it's become an obsession. One day I'll go there. I must. I might even end my days there."'

There was a moment's silence, apart from the muted roar of the traffic far below them.

'Do you remember what that place was, sir?' said Constable Barker.

'I do indeed,' said Reggie. 'It was a place called Mendoza, in the Argentine.'

'Thank you very much indeed, sir,' said Constable Barker.

On the last day of the month, a day of Scotch mist and condensation, a small family party gathered at the home of Mrs Elizabeth Perrin, widow of Mr Reginald Iolanthe Perrin.

The purpose of the party was to celebrate in an intimate manner the impending nuptials of Mrs Elizabeth Perrin and Mr Martin Wellbourne.

The guests were Linda, Tom, Mark, Jimmy and Elizabeth's mother. Jimmy's wife Sheila was unable to attend owing to 'illness'.

The curtains were drawn on a gently sodden world. The smokeless fuel glittered in the grate, and there was a splendid array of liquid and solid refreshments laid out on the trolley.

Elizabeth stood with her back to the fire and faced her guests. She looked beautiful and dignified in a long, black, sleeveless dress which emphasized the golden harvest that was her hair.

'I'd like to say a few words,' she said. 'As you know, I've decided – Martin and I have decided – oh, gosh, what am I saying, I'll be in trouble – come here Martin.'

Reggie shook his head.

'He's shy,' said Elizabeth, laughing. 'Come on!'

Reggie stood up and joined her by the fire. He was pulling at his beard in his embarrassment. Elizabeth put her arm round him.

'No doubt some people will say that I – that we – are being a little hasty,' said Elizabeth. 'So I'd like to say now that I'm sure that my dear Reggie wouldn't have wanted me to live in the past. Nothing I do can bring him back again, and there's no point in pretending that it can. You all know Martin, he was a friend of Reggie's, and I'm sure that if Reggie was alive he'd be pleased that – well of course if Reggie was alive I wouldn't be – oh dear. Anyway I don't know why I'm making a speech really – sorry – anyway there's heaps to drink.'

'Bravo! Congratulations!' said Jimmy.

'Congratulations,' echoed Tom and Linda.

Mark remained silent.

They all replenished their glasses.

'Meant it,' said Jimmy to Reggie. 'Sincerest congratulations.'

'Thanks,' said Reggie.

'Reggie, nice chap, bit of an odd-ball. You, steadier, different kettle of fish.'

'Thanks,' said Reggie. 'How are you finding things in civvy street?'

'No joy yet,' said Jimmy. 'Trying to set up a business. Long job.'

Linda joined them by the fireplace and Jimmy tapped her on the bottom.

'Can I get you another drink, father?' she said.

Reggie saw the horror in her eyes as she realized that she had called him 'father'.

'Bravo!' said Jimmy. 'You called him father!'

'I hope you didn't mind,' said Linda.

'Not at all,' said Reggie.

'She likes you. Half the battle,' said Jimmy, as Linda fetched herself another drink. 'Other half could be stickier. Storm cones hoisted.'

He indicated Mark, glowering on the sofa. Reggie moved over to do battle.

'Mind if I join you?' he said.

'Please yourself.'

'I do hope you'll come and visit us regularly,' he said.

'That depends, doesn't it?' said Mark.

'Yes, I – I suppose it does,' said Reggie. 'But anyway I just thought I'd tell you that you'll always be very welcome.'

'Ta,' said Mark. 'Excuse us, will you?'

'Yes. Fine. Absolutely. Carry on, please,' said Reggie.

Tom came and took Mark's place on the sofa.

'Congratulations,' he said.

'Thank you,' said Reggie.

'Welcome to the club,' said Tom. 'The marriage club, I mean.'

'Oh. Thank you.'

'It's a happy state, matrimony.'

'I'm glad to hear it,' said Reggie.

'I'm a marriage person,' said Tom.

'Your wife's a lovely girl,' said Reggie.

'Lovely. Looks a real picture,' said Jimmy, who was standing behind the sofa trying not to look as if nobody was talking to him.

Elizabeth went into the kitchen to get some sandwiches.

'Let me help you,' said Jimmy. 'Reinforcements on the solid refreshment front.'

'I'll go,' said Mark.

'No. I insist,' said Jimmy.

'Let Mark go,' said Elizabeth's mother.

'Oh. Penny's dropped. Secret chinwag. Sorry,' said Jimmy.

In the kitchen Elizabeth said, 'I hoped you'd be pleased. I know you didn't like Henry.'

'This one's better than him,' admitted Mark. 'But you know what you're doing, don't you?' He picked up a quarter of chicken sandwich and pulled it systematically to pieces as he spoke. 'You're trying to relive your life with father.'

'You're probably right,' said Elizabeth.

'There's no need to sound so sarcastic,' said Mark.

'I wasn't meaning to be sarcastic.'

'Oh no.'

'I'll wear a little card that says, "I'm not being sarcastic" if you like.'

'There you go again. Look, I'm just thinking of you. It's no skin off my shonk who you marry.'

'Come on,' said Elizabeth. 'Wheel the trolley in. Offer the sandwiches round. And try and smile.'

The moment she had a chance Elizabeth steered Reggie

into the corner by the piano and said, 'Go easy on Mark, Martin. He's upset.'

'I don't intend to bite him,' said Reggie.

'There's no need to be sarcastic,' said Elizabeth.

'I'll put a notice on the garden gate, if you like,' said Reggie. 'Mr Martin Wellbourne is now almost free of sarcasm, and irony has not developed. No further bulletins will be issued.'

'You sound just like Reggie,' said Elizabeth.

A few words passed between Reggie and his prospective mother-in-law.

'I suppose I'm old-fashioned, but I must say this is all a bit hasty for decency, in my opinion. Still, you're not youngsters. You're old enough to be your father. You know what you're doing, I suppose. Elizabeth's my daughter, when all's said and done, and provided she's happy, that's the main thing,' were the words that passed from his prospective mother-in-law to Reggie.

'Yes,' was the word that passed from Reggie to his prospective mother-in-law.

'I must be off,' said Mark. 'I've got a day's filming tomorrow. Only a little part. I play a man who's been turned into a pig by a mad scientist. I'd better get off home and learn my grunts.'

'It's a pity you have to go so early,' said Reggie.

'I think it's a good thing,' said Mark. 'It'll give you all a chance to discuss me.'

Linda accompanied him to the door.

'You're being silly,' she said. 'They aren't going to discuss you. You aren't that important anyway. You want to grow up.'

'Yes, that's right, you're very grown up,' said Mark. 'And you're being frightfully sensible. Sensible grown-up big sister Linda. You want to watch it. I'm very worried about you, face ache.'

When Linda went back into the living room, they were all discussing Mark. She didn't listen, she couldn't listen. Was she being sensible? Was what she was going to do sensible, or was it the most foolish thing she had ever done?

'I'm going to make some coffee,' she said.

'I'll help,' said Jimmy.

'Can I help, squerdlebonce?' said Tom.

'No. Mother'll help, won't you, mother?' said Linda.

'Oh, I see. Chinwag time again. Off you go, nobody's noticed anything,' said Jimmy.

Reggie gave Linda a questioning look. She met it blankly. Elizabeth followed her into the kitchen. Everyone sensed the sudden tension.

In the kitchen, Linda said, 'I don't know how to put this.'

'What?' said Elizabeth, as she filled the kettle.

'Oh, mother, it's Martin.'

'What about him?' said Elizabeth quietly.

'He's not what he seems.'

'Are you trying to tell me he's got a past?'

'Not in that sense, no.'

'Another wife?' said Elizabeth, smiling ironically.

'Not exactly. Oh mother . . .'

'Linda darling, I think I know what you're going to say.'

'What?'

'You can fool some of the people some of the time, you can even fool all the people all the time, but you can't fool a wife.'

'You mean you know?'

'S'sh. Keep your voice down. They'll hear us.'

'Have you known all along?'

'Quite a while. Now come on, let's make that coffee.'

Elizabeth began to get the cups out but Linda didn't move.

'I do think you might have told everyone before tonight,' said Linda.

'Oh, but I'm not going to tell them.'

'What?'

'Hush, dear. Get me the coffee.'

Linda handed her the tin of coffee like an automaton.

'I think it's going to work out very well with Martin Wellbourne,' said Elizabeth.

282

'But it's a lie,' said Linda.

'Yes, it's rather fun, isn't it?' said Elizabeth.

'But, mother . . .'

'Oh why do children always have to be so boringly puritan about their parents?'

'It's not that, mother, but it's a ridiculous situation.'

'If it works, it isn't ridiculous. This may be hard for your pride, Linda, but just because I'm your mother it doesn't mean that I'm going to behave like an ageing girl guide.'

'But what about Mark?'

'Yes, he's furious, silly boy. It's rather funny, isn't it?'

'But mother, you're his mother.'

'Yes, it's shocking, isn't it? Now come on, let's take this parsnip in.'

'Parsnip?'

'Parsnip, coffee. Perrin, Wellbourne. What does it matter what we call things?'

Elizabeth picked up the tray of coffee and moved towards the door.

'But mother . . .'

'I don't want any more "but mothers". Our marriage wasn't working all that well. Now it is going to work. Now come on, be sensible enough to be silly.'

'But, mother . . .'

'Linda, you wouldn't do me out of my wedding day, would you? It's the greatest day in a woman's life. And think of the honeymoon. You wouldn't want me to miss the romantic experience of a lifetime. And then there are the presents. I can't wait to open all the presents. I do hope you and Tom are going to give us something really exciting.'

Linda gave up, and they took the coffee in, and Jimmy said, 'That was a chinwag and a half,' and Reggie raised his eyebrows at Linda and she shook her head and Elizabeth said, 'We've been talking presents,' and Elizabeth's mother said, 'You must make a list. It may not be so romantic, but it avoids duplication, that's what I always say,' and Reggie said, 'Oh this is nice. I feel as if I've known you all for a long time,' and

Tom said, 'That's what life's all about. People. We're people people,' and Jimmy said, 'Word in your ear, old girl. Bit of a cock-up on the old c.f. All scraps and swillage gratefully received,' and Linda remembered that they'd brought a bottle of wine and forgotten it, and Tom fetched it and they toasted the happy couple in fig wine, and Tom told a story which nobody understood, but they laughed, and went home happy, and that's about it, really.

Epilogue

The February gale, sweeping in off the English Channel, caused a portion of chimney cowling to crash through the kitchen window of Constable Barker's flat. At the time Constable Barker was dropping a fivepenny piece into a large glass pickling jar. When he had enough fivepenny pieces he would set off for his holiday in the Argentine.

The same gale caused a plastic bag to get caught round the exhaust of a Rentokil van in Matthew Arnold Avenue, Climthorpe, at the exact moment when Reggie and Elizabeth were driving past on their way to the crematorium.

There was only one other car in the car park, yet Elizabeth parked right alongside it.

They walked slowly towards the crematorium building. Pollarded limes cringed before the probing wind. Decaying leaves chased each other half-heartedly across the sodden lawns, which were pocked with slivers of earth cast up by worms. There was a hole coming in Reggie's left shoe.

They entered the building. Reggie's reinforced steel-tipped heels rang out on the tiled floor.

They walked down a long corridor. On either side were rows of drawers in varnished wood, with brass handles. At intervals there were semi-circular recesses with urns in them.

'They call it the Garden of Remembrance, even though it's indoors,' said Elizabeth.

'The Corridor of Remembrance wouldn't sound right,' said Reggie.

At the end of the corridor, Elizabeth stopped.

'I didn't have any ashes,' she said. She took hold of one of

285

the brass handles, and pulled out the drawer. Inside was Reggie's briefcase, engraved with his initials, 'R.I.P' in gold.

She opened the briefcase and removed the contents. There were Reggie's gold cuff links, his red bedroom slippers, a certificate sent by the king to every schoolboy during the Second World War, a photograph of Reggie in the Ruttings-tagg College Small-Bore Rifle Team, a wedding photo, a photo of him as Brutus in the Sunshine Desserts production of *Julius Caesar*, and his old hairbrush, also engraved, in gold, 'R.I.P.'.

'He'd have appreciated that,' said Elizabeth.

They stared at the display in silence for a few moments. Then Elizabeth put everything back in the briefcase and slid the drawer back into position.

They set off down the corridor, arm in arm.

Elizabeth glanced at him out of the corner of her smiling, mischievous eyes.

'Why!' she said. 'I do believe you're crying.'

A Selected List of Humour Available from Mandarin

☐ 7493 0159 7	**The Complete Fawlty Towers**	John Cleese and Connie Booth	£4.99
☐ 7493 0178 3	**The Common Years**	Jilly Cooper	£3.99
☐ 417 05370 3	**Supermen and Superwomen**	Jilly Cooper	£2.95
☐ 7493 0252 6	**Turn Right at the Spotted Dog**	Jilly Cooper	£2.95
☐ 7493 0138 4	**The Secret Diary of Adrian Mole Aged 13¾**	Sue Townsend	£2.99
☐ 7493 0222 4	**The Growing Pains of Adrian Mole**	Sue Townsend	£2.99
☐ 7493 0020 5	**Pratt of the Argus**	David Nobbs	£3.99
☐ 7493 0097 3	**Second From Last in the Sack Race**	David Nobbs	£3.50